HUGO D INVESTIGATES:

Les Mauvais Garçons

BY

GN HETHERINGTON

Merci

I'm forever grateful to the wonderful group of people who come together and celebrate this tiny world I've created. It comforts me if it gives someone a small piece of happiness in a world gone crazy. Chris & Bill Bailey, Sandra Scott, Kathleen Pope, Joy Edwards, Jan & Renata, Jennifer Treib, Sharon Cox, Bobbie & Pete Jeal, Mandy Waite and Pam, Nicky and Julia. Your support gives me the nudge I need to keep going on days when I don't think I can or should! Thank you so very much for all your kind words and love for these boys and girls, I strive to do you all proud. Big hugs to June Russell and Jackie Waite who check in on me every day, which has been so needed this past year. I love you both and bless having met you. Special thanks to my French teacher, Bastien Geve, for his infinite patience, help with the manuscript and the very polite way he corrects me, *nooooooooooo*, with a sad face.

My inspirations as always keep my motivated. Sheena Easton, Julien Doré, Judge Judy (and the singing Rabbi) are my daily doses of company when I need it the most.

My husband Dan is really the best part of me and I will always consider him to be the greatest reward I'm never sure I deserved. Together we created an amazing life and as we head past our twenty-fifth (!) year together I celebrate and honour it with all I am. We've shared our lives (and our bed, much to his not-really annoyed pretence) with our furry babies, Charlie, Seth, Hugo and Noah and become the family I always dreamed of but never thought I'd find. This year has been tough, but we've got through it together.

Notes:

Montgenoux is, for the best part, a figment of my imagination, based loosely upon various regions of France. The story, the places and its characters are also a work of fiction.

For further information, exclusive content and to join the mailing list, head over to:

www.hugoduchampinvestigates.com

We are also on Facebook, Twitter and Instagram. Join us there!

The artwork on the cover, the website and social media accounts were created in conjunction with two incredible talents Maria Almeida and Deborah Dalcin and I'm indebted to them for bringing my characters to life.

For Charlie, Seth and Dawn. You may be gone but I think of you every day and miss you more than I can say. I hope you know it, and I hope you see it, but more than anything, I hope you're having such a good time, you don't miss me a damn bit. Je t'aime. Jusqu'à ce que nous nous revoyions.

Previously in the "Hugo Duchamp Investigates" series of books:

Hugo Duchamp, a Frenchman by birth, has spent much of his adult life living and working in London and has risen to the rank of Detective Superintendent in London's Metropolitan Police. He lives a solitary but content life. In 2015 in *Un Homme Qui Attend* (A Man Who Waits) Hugo finds himself ripped out of his organised life and supplanted back in the country of his birth when he is seconded to a small town called Montgenoux, a town reeling from the brutal murder of a young girl and a corrupt police force. Warned against getting involved, Hugo is soon embroiled in the investigation when a second girl is murdered and he finds himself in a race against time to catch a murderer that culminates in a fiery and deadly confrontation.

Months later, Hugo is thrown into another investigation, *Les Fantômes du Château* (The Ghosts of the Chateau) while still reeling from the aftermath of his previous investigation and trying to balance a new life in France and a blossoming romance. Following the murder of a maid working in a grand Château on the outskirts of Montgenoux, he finds himself pitted against two new adversaries and a family at war in an investigation that forces him to face his own mortality.

Battered and bruised, Hugo faces the prospect of a serial killer in Montgenoux in **Les Noms sur Les Tombs** (The Names on the Graves). A spate of apparent suicides share an unusual link, a mound of soil at the feet of the deceased and before long Hugo realises that there is someone in Montgenoux who is following a dangerous and baffling plan that threatens the lives and safety of those he has come to love.

The fourth instalment in the series **L'hombre de L'isle** (The Shadow from the Island) picks up after the shocking conclusion of Hugo's last investigation and the action switches to Ireland where Hugo races against time to solve the brutal murder of a priest in his most personal investigation yet, which will leave him questioning everything he thought he knew and believed in.

In **L'assassiner de Sebastian Dubois** (The Murder of Sebastian Dubois) Hugo's two worlds collide. His new life in Montgenoux is affected by an investigation from his past and he finds himself having to deal with a past he thought he had left behind and a pair of criminals who are determined to wreak their revenge on him. As he attends a crime scene at the newly opened Montgenoux prison, Hugo and Dr. Chapeau find themselves taken hostage and face a deadly race against time to escape their grasp of violent criminals with only one thing on their minds, Hugo's death.

The discovery of a thirty-year-old skeleton buried under the Beaupain vineyard in Montgenoux (**L'impondérable**) (The Imponderable) triggers a horrific series of events in the modern day resulting in the murder of a prominent citizen and a murder/suicide. It all seems like an open and shut case. Hugo faces a complex web of lies and crimes dating back to the eighties which have devastating effects upon Hugo and those he has come to love.

Fulfilling a promise, Hugo and his family journey to Moscow, Russia (**Le Cri de Coeur**) (The Cry of the Heart) but soon find themselves in mortal danger when Hugo is called upon to assist the local police following the discovery of a mysterious box and its grisly contents. After a body is discovered on the grounds of the Chinese Embassy, Hugo finds himself trapped inside with his family in danger on the outside. The clock is ticking and the deadly game has only just begun.

After a fire tears through Montgenoux, Hugo and his team must deal with the shocking aftermath of the death of an entire family (**La Famille Lacroix**) (The Lacroix Family) and the fallout as racial tension erupts through the town. When the prime suspect is murdered, Hugo must put aside his own grief to unravel one of his most complicated and heartbreaking investigations.

PART ONE

L'ENFANT PERDU
/ L'ENFANT A TROUVÉ

Paris, France
Décembre, 2001 / Décembre, 2010 / Décembre, 2019

The man with hair as white as snow-topped mountains scraped yellow-tinged nicotine fingers across a heavily pockmarked face. He pulled the hood of the red velvet robe over his face, leaving only a hooked Roman nose peeking out, a jot of dew hanging off the edge. He sucked it in, inhaling the crisp, damp air of the cellar and he smiled, glancing up, his eyes flickering in the swaying light provided by the solitary candle-lit candelabra which illuminated the room. The only sound emanated from the five men, standing on the lines of the pentagon, their breathing rapid, like children too excited to control themselves, their fingers twirling against the ties of their cassocks as if eager to rip open a present in front of them. One of them sucked in a hungry tongue, flapping against thick lips. He looked to the white-haired man, eyes imploring him. *Is it time? Can we begin? I'm hungry.* The white-haired man pushed a smile away from his face, aware it was not proper for him to show amusement or any emotion for that matter. There was a time and a place, and this was certainly neither of those. They were on hallowed ground, and respect and protocol must be upheld. *Respect the sanctity of those we represent.*

His head jerked upwards, tired, too-white eyes scanning the ceiling, searching for something, anything, which might indicate a change. He was not even sure what had caught his attention, if anything had at all, but he knew they had to be on high alert. There was too much at stake. There was too much to be lost. He shook his head, irritated at himself. They were forty-feet below ground, solid concrete wrapped the cellar, accessed only by a narrow, twisting stone stairway, cracked by the feet of hundreds of years' worth of light-footed zealots, each silently coming down to the sacred space for reasons so secret they were barely spoken of, and certainly never beyond *The Circle*, the group of men who had been entrusted with *The Secret*. He alone had the key, and it never left his person, tied around his neck with a simple piece of string. He had locked the door behind them, as he always did, and there was no reason to believe anyone even knew of the existence of the cellar, the entrance to it obscured by a bookcase. He knew his imagination was carrying him away; it was only natural. He could taste what was to come, like salt from the sea blown into his face, and his appetite, like his compatriots, was whetted. There was something about savouring the moment. It was part of the ritual after all, but knowing what was coming, knowing what the reward would be, was consuming. He wanted it. They all wanted it.

He turned, stepping into the pentagon. 'Frères,' he said to the four men around him. 'Bienvenue to this very special evening. I know how eager you are to begin,' he stopped, thin lips twisting into a smile, 'as am I, but I beg your indulgence because there are protocols to be followed. Transcribed by our forefathers and created to ensure our lineage continues.' He paused. 'There are, of course, those who seek to stop us, to see darkness where there is really only light, because through their own blinkered reality they project the darkness from their own souls onto us, what we do. The goodness we do, the greatness. Join me,' he said, outstretching his hands, the four men reaching across the pentagon and joining together, 'in our mantra.' He closed his eyes, clearing his throat.

le pouvoir de l'amour
le pouvoir de la création
coule à travers le lien sacré entre nous
nos doigts enlacés
notre sang combiné
nos âmes brûlantes du feu du Tout-Puissant
nous faisons ce que nous devons faire
on s'enflamme, on exhume
on boit
on se régale
ENSEMBLE,
NOUS PRIONS POUR CE QUI DOIT VENIR
AMEN

The white-haired man could not help smiling, filled with the pride of all the men who had come before him. He had begun his journey, barely a child himself, unsure of the path which was being laid down in front of him.

Unsure of the wisdom of the words spoken, the truth they told, indoctrinated as he had been by the stiff formality of his upbringing. His brothers had spoken to him, whispering into his ear. *There is a distinct path. There is a different story no-one had told you. Come with us and we will show you.* He had not wanted to, his soul seemed to scream in protest, but in that cellar, in the darkness, he had seen the light. He had seen the glory and all it had to offer. He had tasted the immortality. He smiled at his brothers. The men he had chosen to stand by him. To share in the glory. Finding them had been the hardest part. When one person left the pentagram, they had to be replaced, and it was not something to be taken lightly. The position was for a lifetime, and once in, only death would allow a person to leave. He had chosen wisely, fixated by a flick, a spark in the eye, telling him they shared a secret, a bond. The brotherhood had survived for Millennia because of the bond, the trust, and the careful choices made by the leader. The white-haired man folded his hands in front of him, his attention drawn to the whimpering in the middle of the pentagon - a sprawling mass of naked limbs, slowly awakening and the dawning realisation appearing. It was almost time. He smiled at his brothers and they all lowered their heads, eyes wide and bright as they watched. Beneath them, on the cold, stone ground, naked limbs sliding, two eyes snapped open, wide and terrified.

The white-haired man laughed, his voice light like a breeze on a summer's afternoon. 'Frères. It is time. Time to feast and honour those who came before us. This is the Annunciation!'

The five men dropped to their knees, their cassocks covering the naked young woman lying in the pentagram, her pointless, desperate screams echoing around the cellar. The white-haired man laughed, pressing his lips against the virgin skin. He sucked in scent through the hooked nose, his lips smacking together like a starving dog.

Cedric Degarmo sprinted along the alleyway, kicking cans out of the way, his feet slapping angrily against the wet cobbles. He pushed the air out of his lungs, sucking in damp replacement in order to keep going. The odour caught the back of his throat, and he fought the urge to retch. The smell he imagined was a mixture of sweat, vomit and sex, as pungent a combination as he had ever come across. He swallowed the bile back into his stomach. He did not want his first day as a rookie to be marred by forever being known as the young kid, fresh out of the national police college in Saint-Cyr-au-Mont-D'Or, the smell of carbolic soap still on his buzz-cut head, who threw up on his first chase. He narrowed ice-blue eyes, staring directly ahead, his ears focused intently on his surroundings as he tried to remember his training. *Isolate, separate.* Cedric knew he only had seconds to locate his prey before they would lose him in the night's mist. And there it was, only for the briefest of seconds, but it was enough for him to turn his head sharply and catch the slice of darkness moving across a shadow in the adjacent building.

'Lieutenant Intern Degarmo!' a woman's voice screamed from the darkness of the alleyway. Cedric did not stop. He could hear her running towards him, flat feet slapping unevenly against the ground. He cursed again at his damn misfortune for his first posting being under the tutelage of such an oddball. What was with the blue hair for starters? Like a weird Smurf with an enormous nose and green eyes, one of which seemed to be permanently veering in the opposite direction to the other. He had initially been pleased when told his first assignment was at Commissariat de Police du 7e arrondissement, situated as it was in a part of Paris swelling with tourist attractions such as the Eiffel Tower and the Louvre. He had imagined his days would be full of adventure. Instead, his first day he was ushered into a dimly lit hallway and told to wait. He had sat rigid for forty minutes, pretending he could not hear the argument being fought between his new Commander and Captain. A man and a woman whose boundaries did not seem to extend to keeping their private lives away from the Commissariat. After the row, which seemed centred around the stomach of Madame la Smurf, which he had assumed was because of her penchant for pastries, but was actually more to do with the child growing in it.

On his first day, Cedric had thought he would be ingratiated into a team with like-minded individuals, lean of body and focused of mind and to be told he would shadow a heavily pregnant Captain with blue hair was not how he imagined starting his career in the Police Nationale.

'Lieutenant Intern Degarmo!' came the scream again. Captain Charlotte "Coco" Brunhild skidded to a halt, pressing a hand against the wall of the narrow alley.

'Attend!' she exhaled, her other hand rubbing against her stomach. 'Mon Dieu, *attend!* He's only a goddamn fence, not Jack-the-fucking-Ripper!'

Cedric stared at her, blinking wildly, remembering all of his training whilst at the same time fighting every urge he had to ignore the oddball he had been assigned to. He stabbed his finger towards the building. *He's in there,* he mouthed. Coco turned her head, following the direction of his finger, her eyebrows creasing into a, *so what?* She gasped, watching helplessly as Cedric sprinted into the seemingly derelict building. 'Non!' she screamed, reaching down and pulling the radio hooked to her belt. 'Andre, send a unit to my location, the damn recruit has gone rogue on me,' she roared into the radio.

Andre, a seasoned dispatcher, cackled down the line. 'And what do you want me to do about it, *exactement?*' he asked, deadpan.

Coco sighed. 'Send someone to help,' she said pressing her stomach, 'I have the worst case of gas and can't run any further, not without leaving a mess behind me, at least.' She stopped, her eyes squinting with concern as she watched Cedric disappear inside the building. 'Cedric, just wait for back-up, you idiot!' She shook her head. The darkness of the night masked his retreating figure. She pulled herself erect and stumbled forward. 'Which part of *I'm heavy with child, so don't take off,* didn't the incompetent idiot understand?' she muttered to herself, smoothing down her woollen coat and staggering forward.

She stopped again and pressed her stomach, wincing. 'You can't be serious, you brat, you're ten weeks early. You're just like your damned brother, Julien wouldn't wait for me to be ready to deliver either.' She lifted her head. 'Cedric,' she wailed. 'For the love of Dieu, wait!'

Coco pulled herself together, compartmentalising her pain and focusing on the situation. What on earth were they doing? It had started out very simply. A telephone call from an informant regarding a young punk selling a fresh batch of ecstasy fresh from Amsterdam. She had picked herself up, taken her protege and headed over to the address, hopeful they would arrest the perp and she would be home by six o'clock, her feet up and a bowl of popcorn nestling on what remained of her stomach as she watched *The Mirror has Two Faces* for the umpteenth time. Instead, there she was, in a seedy back alley chasing after two kids, one whose training should have taught him better. And to top it all, her body was contracting in ways she was sure could only mean one thing, not the stitch from running she hoped it was.

'Cedric,' she wailed again, pressing a hand against the doorway and peering inside the building, her eyes straining to focus through the illuminating slices of moonlight. She stumbled inside, feeling the vibration of each step in agony. She focused her eyes until she could discern the direction of the retreating footsteps and stumbled in their direction.

'I've got the bastard!' Cedric cried.

Coco winced, moving as quickly as she could towards her intern, the indistinct echoes of scuffling feet and muffled grunts signalling to her a fight was in progress. She tried to recall what the young punk looked like and had a vague recollection of him being an emaciated dwarf with acne bigger than his biceps. Cedric Degarmo, on the other hand, was not the sort of man whose appearance could go ignored. As she stumbled forward, Coco chastised herself. She was *technically* in a relationship of sorts, and more importantly, she was probably *almost* old enough to be his mother, or aunt at least. So the fact he had cheekbones she could not believe were real, or blonde hair as lustrous as she had ever seen, or eyes as blue as Sinatra's, or… She stopped herself, a wry smile appearing on her face. Only *almost*, she thought again and ran in his direction.

Rounding the corner, the moonlight opened up an enormous derelict room and she spotted them in the centre, Lieutenant Intern Cedric Degarmo straddling the back of a young punk, grinning up at her, as proud as she remembered her first two children Barbra and Julien were when they first understood the use of the big yellow potty was not simply to throw their urine at her.

'I've got him, Captain Brunhild,' Cedric beamed, pride evident in his voice for his first arrest.

Coco nodded, steadying herself against the wall. She was about to respond when her attention was diverted to what appeared to be a makeshift shelter in the far corner of the room, a carefully constructed row of boxes and crates, presumably assembled by a homeless person for a home. Most of the windows in the building were blacked out, with only slithers of light appearing through the cracks, but there was enough light shining from the street to illuminate the entrance to the makeshift home. She narrowed her eyes, shaking her head gently, sure the adrenaline and the uproar in her uterus were causing her imagination to run wild. She continued to watch, her eyes focusing on the other eyes, locked in a game of chicken. She tried to extrapolate the position and was sure it was too high to be a rat, a dog perhaps, she wondered. Either way, she inched towards it, conscious of not alarming whatever it was in case it was dangerous. The closer she moved, the more the light cleared the way and she gasped as whatever had caught her attention scurried away. She frowned, there was something about the way it moved which troubled her, not like a dog at all, more like… more like her son Julian when he was playing with their dog on the floor. It made little sense to her. A child could not be there, should not be there.

'Captain Brunhild,' Cedric called, the confusion clear in his voice, a tinge of panic indicating his uncertainty what to do with his captive, 'where are you going?'

'Ssh,' Coco whispered, ignoring the pain in her stomach. 'Salut,' she whispered towards the mysterious set of eyes. 'Don't be afraid, I mean you no harm. I am a police officer, my name is Captain Brunhild, but you can call me Coco, all my friends call me Coco. Please don't be scared,' she added in the kind of tone only a well-practiced mother of troublesome toddlers could muster.

The silence was deafening, but she could hear the rapid movements of something pushing fearful bursts of air out of its lungs. Suddenly the scuffling indicated it was moving away and then it crashed against the edge, the makeshift boxes tumbling to the ground. Against her best instinct, Coco threw herself against the boxes, wrapping her hands around the tarpaulin. Instantly she could feel the body squirming beneath her and she knew exactly what it was. A child, more or less the same size as her ten-year-old. She pulled the cover off her arms, fighting around the bundle, and she saw him for the first time. Eyes wide and terrified, too young to really understand what was happening other than he was in terrible danger, a rancid teddy bear clutched to his chest as if his life depended on not letting it go. She relaxed her grip, but not enough to allow him to wriggle free because she knew if she did he would be gone long before she had a chance to stop him. His scent hit the back of her throat, and she had to fight the urge to retch. She knew only too well from experience how little boys would do practically anything to avoid the dreaded bath-time, but this was different. She stole a look at the child and her response was that of a mother of two, almost three, not a police Captain. The tears swelled in her eyes. Whatever this boy was doing in a derelict building, she suspected he had been without care for several days.

She touched his hand and he snapped it away. She touched it again, moving her fingers against his skin as lightly as a feather blowing across the surface. He did not move and she could sense his pulse vibrating beneath wafer-thin skin, fast and thready. She forced herself to look into his eyes, to hold his gaze and to transmit the signal she knew he so desperately needed. *You are safe. You can trust me.*

Coco dropped to the ground with a thud, her free hand rummaging in the pocket of her overcoat, tracing through the hole in the bottom she had never fixed because it gave her extra storage space. She smiled as her fingers folded around a set of playing cards. When her eldest child was having a tantrum, Coco recalled the only thing which would placate her was a game of snap. She pulled the cards out and handed them to the child. He stared at them, grubby face crinkling into a frown.

'You ever played snap, buddy?' Coco asked, her tone gentle and soft.

The boy turned his head in her direction, eyes as wide as the moon, flicking over her, appraising every contour of her face. She let him, knowing he needed to decide for himself whether she could be trusted. It took him a minute before he took the cards from her, pulling them close to his chest as if gripping a priceless artefact. Coco pulled her hands away and moved them together in a gentle slap. The boy jumped and she quickly repeated the procedure and then again, noting his sense of growing wonder.

'See, what you have to do is put the cards down one at a time, like so, see, this one is a roi,' she said placing it on the ground between them, 'this one a knave, and this one, ah!' she cried slapping the third card down, 'another knave, snap!'

The boy clapped his hands together. He dropped the teddy bear and immediately picked it up again. 'Snap!' he repeated, his voice croaking as if he had not spoken for some time.

'Captain Brunhild,' Cedric interrupted from across the room, 'I don't mean to interrupt your *tres* important interrogation over there, but I could do with a little help over here, y'know?'

Coco raised an eyebrow and smiled at the boy, tipping her head in Cedric's direction. 'Don't listen to Monsieur Grouchy-Pants over there. He's called Cedric, by the way, what's your name?'

The boy gave her an unsure look and scuttled away, back into his makeshift home. Coco watched him and as she contemplated crawling after him she was reminded again of the impending drama circumventing her cervix. She turned her head sharply towards Cedric who was still struggling in his attempt to restrain the punk.

'Instead of bitching, why don't you handcuff the perp to the radiator over there, and get over here. We have a lost child and,' she stared in horror at her stomach, 'another child about to make a very unexpected appearance,'

Cedric's eyes widened in horror, the realisation of what she was suggesting hitting him. 'I'll be right over, Captain,' he spluttered.

Coco looked again at the young boy, the terror clear on his face and she knew whatever he had been through, whatever he had experienced and led to him being alone in an abandoned building, had not been pleasant. She touched her stomach, hoping nothing similar would ever befall her own child. 'You'll be okay, kid,' she said towards the hidden child, hoping above all else it was true.

The sun sliced through the majestic spears of the Eiffel Tower. Beneath, a child played in the afternoon's light hue, throwing a rolled-up newspaper as a makeshift football, oblivious to the history of the post he used as a goal. A tourist lowered himself onto his haunches in an attempt to capture the excited toddler in his historical playing ground. He waved his hand, trying to catch the child's attention, but the child did not respond. The tourist followed the direction of his gaze. The child was shielding his eyes from the midday sun, looking towards the shadow from the Tower. The tourist scrunched his eyes, but they widened in horror when he realised what it was which had caught the child's attention. Tumbling towards the ground, as if in slow-motion was a person, his arms flailing from left to right, his mouth wide open, but there was no scream, no noise. As far as the tourist could tell, the person falling was smiling.

Captain Coco Brunhild stopped in front of the line of police tape and waited. Cedric Degarmo stepped past her, lifted the tape and stepped under, dropping it after him. Coco watched the junior Lieutenant with incredulity, her mouth pressing into a disgruntled tut. Cedric stopped, fixing her with a confused, *what?* Coco tipped her head towards the tape.

Cedric whistled. 'If I'd lifted it up for you, I would have gotten some withering look telling me how you're not an invalid and are perfectly capable of lifting a tape yourself, and don't deny it, you've been my boss for a long time. I know your moves and I know better than to fall into your mouth.'

Coco stepped under the tape, her ankle twisting as she navigated the pebbled pathway. She raised a hand to steady herself and Cedric lurched forward, catching her with his hand. She looked at him with surprise and then at his bicep, which was flexing and puzzled her. She supposed he was a handsome young man, with a sharp jaw and buzz-cut blonde hair and clear blue eyes. Definitely not her type, but he was, she supposed, not quite the ineffectual boy she still saw him as. He was a man, and after working with him for almost ten years, on his way to becoming a half-decent police officer.

'It may have escaped your attention,' she said huffily, extracting herself from his grip, 'but I have recently given birth.'

Cedric snorted. 'Believe me, I do know, the entire world knows! I even heard a rumour they were having news updates on CNN.' He shook his head. 'Nine months of mood swings, insane food cravings...' he grimaced, 'schnitzels with peanut butter? Varicose veins,' he paused and shuddered, '*haemorrhoids*. Believe me, Captain Brunhild, not only am I painfully aware you have recently given birth, I feel as if I have too, *again*.' His eyes flicked over her, 'and I still have nightmares about the last time you popped one out. My only solace is you're getting a bit long in the tooth for the procreating business so I may not have to go through it again.'

Coco suppressed a smile, remembering ten years earlier when on a seemingly routine bust, the child she was carrying decided to make his appearance almost two-months early, his first breath taken on the floor of an abandoned building into the arms of rookie cop Cedric, on his first week in the job. Coco had decided to name the child after him in an attempt to honour the man who brought him into the world, but all it had really done was to create an endless chain of gossip regarding the parentage. A fact which Cedric had, with too much gusto as far as Coco was concerned, gone to significant pains to protest he had never, *would* never, go there. She took a moment to assess her appearance. Sure, at almost forty she had a few miles on the clock, and she knew her blue-dyed hair prone to frizz was not to everyone's taste, or the hook of her nose, nor her dress sense, but she happened to believe her quirks were exactly what made her attractive. Who wanted to melt into a crowd when you could stand out in it?

'Captain Brunhild,' a deep voice called out from the shadows.

Coco turned around, a smile appearing on her face when she saw the handsome face of Dr. Shlomo Bernstein beaming in her direction. He was a handsome man, with thick wavy jet-black hair and a rugged complexion. He reminded Coco of someone she had once loved very much, a man long since out of her life, but only physically. She had made a choice, believing Paris was where her future lay and tried not to imagine how different her life might have been if she had stayed. She waved at Shlomo. They had both begun their careers at more or less the same time and had formed an instant connection, like two square pegs trying to fit into a round hole. Their Jewish ancestry aside, they had more in common as people who refused to conform for the sake of fitting in.

'I had no idea you were back in the fold,' the doctor said moving to her and wrapping her in a tight embrace.

Coco shrugged. 'Hi, Sonny. Yeah, well, the powers that be realised the Police Nationale really couldn't do without me after all,' she paused and tipped him a wink, 'oh and if they didn't give a woman returning from maternity leave her job back eventually, they'd face a lawsuit. But,' she smiled, 'I prefer to think it was my insane crime-solving ability which tipped the scales back in my favour.' She reached into her pocket and pulled out a pair of latex gloves, flicking them quickly onto her hands, her eyes squinting in the direction of the forensics tent. 'So, what have we got, Sonny?'

He signalled for her and Cedric to follow into the tent, pulling the flap open. Coco gasped when she saw the body.

'He's a child,' she cried, forcing herself to keep

staring at him. He reminded her of her second child, Julien, with more or less the same mop of blond hair swept high above his head. She had been at Julien for months to cut it, now she hoped he never would.

Dr. Bernstein shook his head. 'Not quite a child, Captain, but not far off it, I suppose. We're looking at late teens, no more I would imagine.'

Coco gave a tight smile. 'Honey, as far as I'm concerned these days, anybody under the age of twenty-five is a baby.' She shook her head, her eyes carefully moving across the body. 'But he really does look like,' she stopped, her voice breaking as she recalled that very morning when she wiped the jam from the cheeks of her own ten-year-old son. He had protested, but she could tell by the pressure of his cheek against her hand that he was not really so bothered. This child had blood on his cheeks and she had to fight every instinct she had not to spit on a tissue and wipe it away because it was not jam. *If only it could be jam.* She pushed the thought away, realising she was being paid to do a job, not be a mother, so she forced herself to keep staring at the young man, to really stare, to really SEE him. She guessed he was a little over 175 centimetres tall and bordering on being too thin, though it was the way most adolescent men appeared to her these days. He was dressed in tight blue jeans and a black-branded t-shirt, though both were ripped and torn, presumably by the fall, and they were covered in dirt and blood. His head lay turned to this side at an unnatural angle, a trail of blood spreading to his left like a scarf, an eye open in the blood's direction as if following its path. A snake of bruises spread around his neck like vines.

'Why are we even here?' Cedric asked with a tut. 'Some kid throws himself off the Eiffel Tower, it's sad I guess, but hardly worthy of the Crime Division.'

Coco turned her head sharply in his direction. 'And we're certain there has been no crime committed?'

Uncertain of her tone, Cedric glanced again at the young man's remains, appraising him with fresh eyes wondering whether they had missed something. The calls to the precinct had indicated it was nothing but a routine suicide. He studied the marks on the neck. Sure, he could see what the Captain was getting at, but just because he had bruises did not necessarily equate to foul play. He tapped his notepad. 'I have witness statements from half a dozen people who all pretty much say the same thing. The kid fell or jumped from the Tower.'

'Or was pushed,' Coco interrupted.

Cedric shrugged. 'Then why would he be laughing?'

Coco turned her head, laughing. 'Laughing? What on earth are you talking about?'

'At least two of the witnesses said he appeared to be smiling.'

Coco looked at the doctor for help. Sonny Bernstein shrugged. 'Don't ask me,' he said, 'I've long since stopped trying to understand human behaviour, but it's not too much of a stretch to imagine if a person is troubled enough to commit suicide, then seeing the end coming might be some kind of relief.'

'And what's your opinion, doc?' she asked. 'Suicide?'

Sonny glanced again at the young man. 'I couldn't say. I'll do the autopsy first thing tomorrow, we should know more then.'

'Did you find any ID?' she asked.

Sonny shook his head. 'Nope, all he's got in his pants are a packet of cigarettes and a condom.'

'Condom?' Coco asked sharply. 'Isn't that unusual?'

Cedric laughed. 'He's a kid. I'd be more surprised if he didn't have a condom.'

'Hmm,' Coco retorted, 'and no cell phone?'

Sonny shook his head.

'Now that is unusual,' she said. 'My eldest two would rather lose a limb than their damn phones.'

Cedric shrugged. 'Maybe it fell on his way down.'

Coco glanced around. 'Perhaps,' she agreed doubtfully, 'have uniforms do a wide search just in case.'

Cedric scratched his head. 'Really? All this for a jumper?'

Coco turned to him, fixing him with an icy stare. 'Suicide or not, there are likely people who care about him, are missing him. I'd rather the notification came from us rather than some John Doe bulletin on the ten o'clock news.'

'I'll run his prints and DNA, you never know, he might be in the system,' Sonny said.

Coco nodded and lifted her head towards the Eiffel Tower. 'Mon Dieu, I hate heights.' She gesticulated to Cedric. 'Let's go up and see if anyone saw anything. See you tomorrow, Sonny.'

Coco threw off her overcoat and flopped onto one of the chairs lining the wall of the morgue, a swoosh of angry air underneath her reminding her of the extra kilos she had gained. She looked to Cedric and judged by his smirk, he had seen it too. She hated the fact he ate nothing but junk food and yet never gained an ounce.

Dr. Bernstein finished washing his hands and began wiping them on a towel. 'How was the Tower?' he asked.

Coco visibly shuddered. 'Tall and windy,' she grumbled, 'and not a lot of use.'

'No witnesses?' Sonny asked.

'Not a single one,' Cedric replied.

'They're sending over CCTV footage today,' Coco said, 'so we should at least get an idea of who was coming in and out, but there are no cameras in the area we believe he jumped. What about you, anything from the fingerprints?'

'Nothing from Europol or Interpol. I've taken blood samples, and teeth impressions and they're running through the systems too but until we find something to match them with, there's not a lot I can tell you of his origins.'

'Damn,' she said, 'we're monitoring missing person reports, from Paris and beyond, but no matches so far. What about the autopsy?'

Sonny moved around the table and pulled back the sheet covering the young man. Coco took in a sharp intake of breath and Cedric stumbled backwards. There was something about seeing him there, naked and vulnerable, which rocked Coco almost more than she could bear. 'He was so young,' she repeated.

'But not so innocent,' Sonny muttered.

'What do you mean?' she asked sharply.

'Well, he was certainly very sexually active for a young man I believe to be no more than eighteen or nineteen.'

Cedric chuckled. 'Are you kidding? When I was that age I was getting more ass than I knew what to do with.'

Sonny looked at him coolly. 'I doubt your own ass had the same trouble, Lieutenant.'

Coco moved closer to the gurney. She could not take her eyes away from him. 'What do you mean, Sonny?'

Sonny moved next to her. 'Because of the stretching and scaring of the anal walls, I would say he was *extremely* sexually active. Of kids this age, I've only really seen this sort of thing before in rent boys.'

'Putain,' Coco muttered. 'Poor kid. Any of it recent?'

'There was spermicide present,' Sonny replied, 'so within the last twelve hours or so before his death, I would estimate, but no sperm or any other useable evidence. No hair or fibres and nothing under his nails.'

'A drugged-up prostitute gets fed up of his life and kills himself,' Cedric shrugged, 'wouldn't be the first, won't be the last.'

Sonny shook his head. 'We won't know for certain until we get the toxicology report back, but I found no track marks, no obvious sign of drug usage. His nose is clear, but that's not to say he wasn't high on other substances.'

Coco sighed. 'I almost hope the poor bastard was high, or what else would make him want to throw himself off the goddamn Eiffel Tower? What about the bruises on his neck?'

'They're just that, bruises. They didn't kill him, there were no fractured bones, the bruises could have come from a struggle right before the fall, or within a day or so before it. I just can't say with any degree of certainty.'

'Suicide,' Cedric said with a whine, 'next.'

Coco shot him another withering look but did not respond. She turned to face Sonny again. 'Can you send me the best cleaned-up picture of him you can, so I can at least try to get the poor kid identified. Somebody, somewhere, must be missing him.'

Sonny nodded. 'I hope so, but…,' he stopped, dark eyes clouding, 'let's hope this one is different. Bonne journée, Captain, Lieutenant.'

Coco turned her head, studying the young man again. Cold, blue eyes staring towards the ceiling. There was something she could not put her finger on. Something which was troubling her. The hairs on the back of her neck were tickling her. *There is something wrong here,* they were telling her. She shuddered, and this time not from the cold of the morgue.

PART TWO

LES MAUVAIS GARÇONS

Present Day

Hugo Duchamp sat with a thud, a crunching sound beneath him making him curse. He turned his head slowly as if trying to delay the inevitable. He stared sadly at the seat he had just planted himself in, knowing what he would see. 'Putain,' he groaned. 'Not again.'

Mare-Louise Shelan, Montgenoux Police Nationale receptionist appeared in the doorway to Hugo's office, red curls bouncing as she giggled. 'You didn't! Tell me you didn't break your glasses again, Captain? Oh, mon Dieu!' she cried, pressing her hand against her head in mock disbelief.

Hugo lifted the once-connected arm of his glasses, his mouth twisting into a grimace. He held it up, cheeks flushing red. Mare-Louise shook her head, reaching into her pocket and handing Hugo a package. He opened it, his eyes widening in surprise. 'A new pair of glasses?'

Mare-Louise nodded, gravely serious. 'I ordered three pairs and didn't tell you. I thought, incorrectly as it turns out, you would be more careful if you knew you were down to your last pair *again*.' She wagged her finger at him. 'But this really is the last pair, so unless you want to walk around Montgenoux feeling your way along the walls, or having me guide you, then be careful!'

Hugo dropped his head in shame, long blond locks of hair covering his shimmering emerald green eyes. He suppressed a smile, reminded again how unused he was to people looking out for him, actually caring for him. He had spent most of his adult life alone, living a sedentary life in London. It had been enough for him, or so he had thought. He lifted his head, his eyes locking on the set of photographs lining his desk. He had never been the sort of man to have personal photographs on his desk. Now he had four. Now he had a loved one. Now he had a son. Now he had friends. He was not sure why their likeness needed to live on his desk - his cluttered, messy, overflowing with work desk, other than he suspected they were there to remind him he was no longer alone.

He flicked on the new glasses. 'Merci, Mare-Louise,' he said, 'really, I don't know what I would do without you.'

Mare-Louise clicked her teeth. 'De rien. I'll order more, but s'il te plaît, go easy on the pair you have, at least until I manage to get you another!'

Hugo nodded and watched her disappear into the main office before turning his attention back to the piles of paperwork on his desk. It had been a busy summer in Montgenoux, swelled with tourists fresh from the Atlantic coast, looking for small-town charm. He knew towns such as Montgenoux often depended on tourists, but for him, as Captain of Police, the headaches often outweighed the financial value. There had been a spate of thefts and vandalism by a person who had so far managed to escape capture. In a way, Hugo had found himself relieved. Montgenoux had come together in a way he had not seen for a long time, fractured as it had become following the harrowing events earlier in the year when an entire family had been murdered, their killer setting the house on fire to destroy the evidence. A further murder had been committed, a young Syrian refugee had been sacrificed in an attempt to blame him for the crime. It had been particularly difficult for Hugo to bear, as the Syrian refugee was a friend, someone Hugo had felt he had been entrusted to care for. Hugo knew instinctively there had been nothing he could have really done to prevent the brutal murder of Ehab Menem, but it was still something he suspected would haunt him for the rest of his life. It certainly kept him awake at night. He was jolted into reality by the flickering light on his computer monitor, and he sighed. The only time the red light illuminated his office was when the Minister of Justice, Jean Lenoir, was calling. A conversation which usually involved Hugo being chastised for some imagined slight and ended in a not-so-veiled threat of losing his job. He clicked the *accept* button and leaned forward.

'Bonjour, Minister Lenoir,' he said warily.

Jean Lenoir's wide face filled the screen. Thin skin pulled over a muscular skull, piercing-blue eyes as cold as ice. 'Ah, Captain… Hugo, I mean… comment allez vous?'

Hugo sucked in his breath, the hairs on the back of his arm standing up. He was suddenly on high alert. Not just because Jean Lenoir was being uncharacteristically monosyllabic, but more because of what it might mean.

'Tres bien, merci,' he replied slowly, 'et vous?'

'Er, well, je suis…' Jean Lenoir trailed off, his head moving to the side. Away from the camera, Hugo could hear him hissing to someone in the background. *I've told you to tell the damn Prime Minister I'm not in the office.*

Hugo raised an eyebrow. What was it in Jean Lenoir's voice he did not recognise? If he did not know better, he might consider it to be fear.

'Forgive me, Hugo,' Jean Lenoir said as he reappeared on the computer screen, 'things are a little hectic today, as I'm sure you can imagine.'

Hugo frowned. 'Hectic? Pourquoi?'

Jean Lenoir threw back his head and laughed. 'Well, I suppose I should be thankful for small mercies the rag run by my imbecile of a nephew, hasn't caught up with the breaking Parisian news yet.'

Hugo felt his blood run cold. 'Has something happened in Paris?'

'A travesty, that is what has happened,' Jean spat, 'a monumental cock-up of global proportions.'

Hugo hid a smile. 'Excusez moi, Minister, but I'm afraid you will have to be more specific. I haven't read *Montgenoux Aujourd'hui,* nor heard anything.'

Mare-Louise appeared, gingerly placing a note in front of Hugo. *Captain Charlotte Brunhild from Paris is on hold, needs to speak with you.* Hugo cocked his head, his interest further piquing, wondering what could be happening in Paris and why everyone was suddenly seemingly interested in concerning him with it. He shrugged his shoulders towards Mare-Louise. *Take her number, I'll have to call her back,* he mouthed.

'Am I keeping you from something you consider to be more important, Captain?' Jean Lenoir interrupted, the sarcasm clear in his voice.

Hugo shook his head. 'Non, not at all, Minister. Now, tell me, what can I do for you?'

'How soon can you be in Paris?'

Hugo pushed back in surprise. He was not sure what he was expecting, but it was not that. 'What do you mean?'

Jean Lenoir clicked his teeth. 'Your time in England seems to have done little for your recollection of the beautiful French language, Captain.'

'Well, of course, I heard you, but I just didn't understand. Why would I come to Paris?' Hugo retorted.

'Because you owe me.'

'Because I owe you?' Hugo repeated, not sure he heard the Minister correctly, 'and what do I owe you, exactly?'

Jean Lenoir pursed his lips. 'Do you remember three years ago, a conversation between the two of us when you were in Ireland? A conversation concerning your petite ami, lost as he was in a maelstrom. You reached out to me, Jean Lenoir, Minister of Justice, and asked, non, *begged*, for my assistance. Have I refreshed your memory, Captain Duchamp?'

Hugo exhaled. He recalled only too well the time, and he had been trying to forget it ever since.

'Do you recall what you promised me at the time?' Jean continued. He waited for a response which was not forthcoming. 'You said you would owe me.'

'I was very grateful for your assistance, WE were very grateful for your help, though the fact remains, Ben was innocent of the crime he was accused of and just because the situation was *confusing*, it was my duty, OUR duty to ensure justice was served. Our conversations, such as they were, reflected that. We would have, should have done it for any French citizen facing similar problems.'

The Minister coughed. 'Our recollections are a little different, mon ami. I recall you begging me for my help. *Begging*,' he added, slowly emphasising the word.

'What is it, Jean Lenoir?' Hugo asked wearily. 'I agreed I would owe you. So what is this, you're calling in the so-called debt?'

Jean Lenoir did not answer immediately. The tick of the wall-clock echoed around Hugo's office.

Hugo continued. 'Instead of dredging up the past, perhaps we could just cut to the chase and you could tell me what it is that has you rattled enough to actually ask me for help because I know for certain, you can't be happy about having to do so.'

Jean Lenoir's eyes widened as if he was about to launch a rebuttal, but he still said nothing.

'There was a death two days ago,' Jean Lenoir spoke in hushed tones. 'A teenager fell from the Eiffel Tower.'

Hugo had a vague recollection of overhearing a

conversation regarding it but found he could remember no details. 'Well, that is certainly very sad,' he trailed off, not wishing to add *but* to the end of the sentence.

'I was on the Tower at the time of the accident having dinner with a… with a colleague.'

Hugo raised an eyebrow. 'Oh?' he questioned.

'Oh,' Jean repeated, 'and non, I saw nothing.'

'Excusez moi, Minister,' Hugo said, 'but I am having trouble seeing the significance, I mean, unless you knew the deceased.'

Jean Lenoir held Hugo's gaze but did not respond. 'Or did you?' Hugo asked.

'I don't believe so,' he answered cryptically. 'When the police could not identify the deceased, they issued a photograph to the press asking for help in identifying him. A few hours later, an anonymous photograph was sent to *Le Monde*, which they in turn published. A photograph which I am in, along with the deceased, taken at a private member's club of which I am a member. The press are speculating the dead man was also known to frequent the club.'

'Frequent?'

Jean Lenoir nodded. He lowered his voice. 'There is an indication he was a prostitute.'

Hugo coughed.

Jean raised a hand. 'Steady yourself, Captain. I do not, nor have I ever used such services offered by young men such as the one who died. Non, the club in question is merely a social club, of which I and a great deal of men and some women and others who identify in ways which remain a mystery to me. But we share a common thread. We are people in similar positions who need to be seen and who need to solicit the assistance of other like-minded individuals. We can hardly do so in full view of the great unwashed, non? Matters such of these by their very definition need the utmost discretion.'

Hugo nodded. 'I see. And were you aware there were prostitutes operating out of this club?'

'Aware?' Lenoir responded with amusement. 'It's a profession as old as time, Captain, you know that. The truth is I would be surprised if there weren't prostitutes, although I do confess some surprise at there being young male prostitutes,' he gave a sad sigh, 'but I suppose each to their own tastes.'

'And you were not acquainted with this young man, other than you are in a photograph with him?'

Lenoir shook his head. 'Non, at least, not as far as I recall.'

Hugo rubbed his chin. 'Then I'm still struggling to understand what the relevance is. You are a member of a club where this young man possibly worked, and you were having dinner near the scene of his apparent suicide. None of which is especially relevant, nor as far as I can see, would warrant a police investigation.'

'My *name* is relevant, Captain, my *rank* is relevant. As are the enemies I have made on my journey to where I am today. There is talk of my running for a higher position in the coming years, an especially public and prominent position. When a person is groomed for such, they come under a great deal of scrutiny, attract a great deal of attention, and a great deal of jealousy. People do not always want a person to succeed, and will use a scandal such as this to derail plans before they have time to gather steam.'

'But if you were there just to have dinner, then presumably you have an alibi and witnesses.'

The Minister sighed. 'At the time of the death, I had stepped out of the restaurant to smoke a cigar. I know, because I heard the commotion, though at the time I did not pay it much heed. Why would I?' He paused. 'However, I have just been informed, the board who are vetting me have appointed an Avocat as special counsel to investigate potential candidates, with particular emphasis on weeding out any scandals which would prove damaging and embarrassing further down the line.'

Hugo nodded again. 'I suppose I could see how this might be embarrassing for you, but really, no crime was committed and with what you have told me, your connection with the deceased was tenuous at best.'

Lenoir tutted. 'Unless you are a morally bankrupt Avocat, bearing unfounded grudges. Does that sound like someone familiar to you, Captain?'

Hugo frowned. As far as he was concerned, it sounded like a great many people who walked in such circles. 'Should it?' he asked.

'It should,' Lenoir spat, 'because the person who has been tasked with investigating me is your father.'

Your father. The words hammered at Hugo's skull. *Your father.* Two innocuous words which should mean nothing but opened up whole locked caverns in Hugo's brain. He knew little of his father's life. There had been no contact between them for decades and it was a part of Hugo's past he did not care to ponder.

'Pierre Duchamp has always been an asshole,' Lenoir hissed, 'but I don't need to tell you that, do I, Captain?'

'And this is why you're calling in the favour?' Hugo asked with incredulity. 'What do you think will happen? I'll come to Paris and get my father off your back?'

'Something like that,' Jean responded.

'Then you know nothing about me, and certainly nothing about my father. His lack of interest in me trails back through the decades,' Hugo breathed.

'You would at least be a distraction.'

Hugo shook his head. 'Not one which would benefit you.'

'I disagree. If it were seen you were supporting me, it would only help me and it might keep Pierre in check. Besides, your father is also a member of the club. What's to say he isn't involved somehow?' He paused. 'There is also another connection, a connection which further links your father to the club and one which I believe we could use to distract him from his vendetta.'

'Another connection?' Hugo asked. 'What?'

Jean Lenoir smiled. 'You might say he is related, by marriage at least, to one of the owners of the club.' He paused again as if for dramatic effect. 'Because of you.'

'Moi?' Hugo asked with surprise.

Lenoir nodded. 'Oui. One of the owners of the club is a man you are very familiar with. Sebastian Dubois.'

Sebastian Auguste Dubois. The name spiked irritation in Hugo. It shocked him to realise, however, that he felt no surprise. He knew he should give Sebastian the benefit of the doubt, but after a few years of experiencing first-hand Sebastian's character flaws, he found he could not. 'He's hardly a relative,' he offered weakly.

'Is he not your brother-in-law?' Jean shot back. 'I mean, is he, or is he not your husband's brother?'

Half-brother, Hugo thought but did not offer. 'Regardless, I still fail to see what my involvement could achieve. I'm sorry for you, Minister, truly I am, but it seems very clear to me, your involvement, if it could even be called such, is tenuous and anybody with half a brain should be able to see it. I understand the press may try to make something out of nothing, but unless I'm missing something, you should be in the clear. I don't know why my father is investigating you, or why it has you worried, but he can't make evidence appear out of thin air, nobody can.' He stopped. 'What does Sebastian have to say about all of this?' he asked, not really sure he wanted the answer.

Knowing Sebastian as he did, he felt sure the answer would neither be clear nor helpful.

'Well, that's just it, nobody knows because Dubois is missing.'

'Missing?' Hugo asked sharply, sitting straight in his chair.

'Oui.'

'Hmm,' Hugo contemplated, 'I suppose we shouldn't read too much into it. Sebastian is hardly the sort of man who sticks to any particular rules; he could have just gone off somewhere on a whim. He's done it before, and these days he has no money worries so can more or less do as he pleases.'

Jean Lenoir sniffed. 'I would have thought you of all people would know what he was capable of. I mean, didn't he once arrange for you to be murdered in order to save his own skin? Non, the fact he is suddenly on the run means only one thing as far as I'm concerned.'

He is up to his neck in it. Hugo found himself thinking along the same lines.

'Which is why you are coming to Paris, and bringing your husband with you,' Lenoir continued.

'You want me to bring Ben? Pourquoi?'

'Because I want him to find his brother, and for you to concentrate on dealing with your father,' the Minister replied.

While he thought he would like Ben to be with him, Hugo was still reluctant. He did not want to go to Paris and he could see no reason why he should.

'I've always thought you were a man of your word, Captain,' Jean said as if reading his thoughts, 'and at a time when you were desperate, I took you at that word.'

Hugo gave a quick nod. 'I understand, Minister, and I want to help, but as I keep saying, I hold no sway with my father, and as for Sebastian, well, the same goes. He's unpredictable, and he's irrational, and oui, if he is involved, the chances are he will lie low. As for Ben being his brother, it means nothing. They didn't even know about it until last year and it made no difference. There is no bond between them, and nor is there ever likely to be one.'

'I don't care about their *feelings*,' he said it as if it was a dirty word, 'I want Ben to find whatever rock his brother has crawled under. I want to know what Sebastian Dubois knows, and more importantly, I want him to give the police somewhere to look, somebody to focus on because I am sure he knows something or else he would have had no reason to run. I am very sure of that.'

'And how is Ben supposed to find him? We haven't heard from Sebastian in over a year. I wasn't even aware he was in the country, let alone Paris.'

'I don't know, and I care less,' the Minister swiped back, 'find the cockroach, do whatever you need to do. Make it be known he is needed to sign some papers, bribe him with money, I don't care, just get him back to Paris. I'm sure Dubois is the sort of man who is loyal to no-one but himself and his bank balance, so use that if you have to.'

Hugo found he could not argue with Jean Lenoir. 'And what do you propose I do with my father? Engage him in nostalgia? Reminisce over my entitled and joyous childhood?' Hugo asked sarcastically, angry at the stabs of hurt piercing him. 'You led me once to believe you knew my father, which means you must know he is not the sort of man prone to any such things.'

'I don't care what you do, just as long as you distract him. But more importantly, do your job. Stop him from shining attention on me by finding out what really happened that night on the Eiffel Tower.'

Hugo sighed. 'You want me to investigate out of my jurisdiction? You know it is not possible, the Police Nationale in Paris will not tolerate my interference. And to be honest, Minister Lenoir, under normal circumstances, nor would you. I can't begin to tell you how many times you have warned me, *threatened* me, not to tread where I shouldn't.'

Jean moved his head to the side, his eyes closing for a moment. 'The irony of the situation is not lost on me, Hugo, trust me. The truth is, a man in my position makes enemies. It is a necessary evil and one which I have never shied away from. However, those enemies are often waiting on the side-lines, eager to see those above them fall. The Commander in charge of the investigation is known to me, and he is one such man, as is your father.

Your father does not want me to progress because he covets the position I am being considered for. He, like the Commander, has been waiting for such an opportunity to derail me. I believe them to be less interested in the truth and more concerned with embarrassing and publicly humiliating me and ruining my career.'

'I'm very sorry, but...'

Jean shook his head. 'There is a third reason your input may be helpful. The Captain is also known to you, and as I understand it, the two of you have a good relationship. You are acquainted with Captain Charlotte Brunhild, are you not?'

Hugo smiled. He had met Charlotte, or Coco as she was known, only a few months earlier but despite that he had warmed to her, sensing them to be kindred spirits. 'We have met, oui, and while we got on, we have not had time to form any kind of relationship which might be helpful to you. Actually, I had no idea she was back on the police force, the last I knew she was working as an investigator for the OCBC.'

Jean Lenoir muttered something under his breath. 'Well, she is back in the Police Nationale, and the fact you are acquainted should assist you in your investigation. So you do see now, Captain, why I have called upon you?' He did not wait for a reply. 'Bien. I shall expect you to be in Paris by morning.' He stopped, his eyes darting from side to side, and when he spoke again it was in hushed tones. 'I'll text you a cell phone number, my *private* cell phone number. I believe it better for our future conversations to be discreet.' He reached forward, disconnecting the call and leaving Hugo's mind whirling.

'Hugo!' Coco Brunhild exclaimed. 'It's so good to hear your voice again. Désolé we keep missing each other's calls, my day goes from bad to worse.'

Hugo climbed out of the beaten-up Citroën, the gravel lining the Swiss cottage he shared with Ben and their adopted son, Baptiste, crunching under his feet. He smiled, there was genuine warmth in Coco's voice and it pleased him. He stopped, leaning against the car, igniting a cigarette. 'That's okay,' he replied, 'and I'm sorry it took me a while to get back to you. I'm guessing your original call concerned Sebastian Dubois, non?'

'Why, oui,' she answered in surprise, 'how did you know?'

Hugo smiled. 'The reason I couldn't speak to you at the time was because I was on a call with Jean Lenoir.'

'Ah,' she replied. 'I can only imagine how pleasant it was for you. Let me guess, Monsieur Paranoid thinks we're all out to get him, right?'

'Something like that,' Hugo replied. He paused. 'Does he have cause to be concerned?'

Coco did not reply immediately. 'Hang on,' she whispered. Hugo listened to what appeared to be her running along a corridor. 'Okay,' she said after a minute, 'I'm in the stationary cupboard now so we can talk privately.'

Hugo raised an eyebrow. 'Stationary cupboard?'

'Oui,' she replied, 'it's the only place in the damn

station you can have a private conversation,' she said before adding with a cackle, 'or sex.'

Hugo snorted. 'I know I shouldn't really be asking, but he wants me to come to Paris and help. I told him it was nothing to do with me, but…'

'He didn't give you a choice, huh? Figures, Jean Lenoir isn't the sort of man who takes no for an answer. Do you owe him something, is that it?'

'Well, sort of. Ben was in trouble a few years ago and Jean was one of the few people I could turn to for help.'

'And did he come through? Did he help Ben?'

'He did,' Hugo replied. He could hear her breathing down the line as she considered.

'And now he's calling in the marker.'

Hugo nodded. 'Oui, but as I said to him, it doesn't seem to me as if he has much to be concerned about, or perhaps I was wrong?'

Coco did not answer immediately. 'How much do you know?'

'Not very much, I'm afraid, other than a male prostitute fell off the Eiffel Tower.'

'He was a young man,' Coco snapped, her voice icy. 'Désolé,' she added quickly, 'I just mean he was so much more than what people might call him.'

Hugo frowned, unsure what she meant, but he waited for her to continue. She said nothing, so he spoke. 'I didn't mean to be disrespectful.'

'Oh, dear Hugo, of course, I know you weren't, you're not capable of it, as far as I'm concerned, a nice Jewish mother of four, he was just a child who died before his light had a chance to fully shine.'

'Jean mentioned he was concerned about the Commander in charge of the investigation, he mentioned something about bias.'

Coco snorted. 'Bias? More like outright hatred. Morty has been turned down four times for promotion, all because of Jean Lenoir.'

'Morty?' Hugo asked.

'Commander Mordecai Stanic,' she answered. 'And in the interest of full disclosure, I should also tell you Morty is my ex and the father of my two youngest. He hates me, and I don't much care for him either, but he was instrumental in getting me my job back. I choose to believe it was because I'm a good flic, rather than the fact he wanted to have to pay me less in child support. But anyway, he and Jean Lenoir go way back, way, way back and believe me, the love isn't lost, in fact, I'd go so far as to say I've never seen Morty happier than he has been since he discovered Jean on the hop.'

'Speaking of which,' Hugo said, 'is he? I mean, unless there's something I'm missing. What is it that has everyone so concerned?'

Coco cleared her throat. 'To be honest, not a great deal. I'm sure he's told you about the club.'

'He mentioned it,' Hugo answered.

'*énergique* is one of the hippest clubs in Paris,' Coco said, 'but vice knows it by another name, *les mauvais garçons*, because, frankly, the boys who go there, are pretty bad.'

Hugo could not help thinking that fact might explain Sebastian Dubois' involvement. Sebastian himself could well be described as the original bad boy. 'What do you mean?'

'Oh, you know the sort, rich, spoilt, over-privileged predominantly white men who think the whole damn world owes them a favour. The sort who doesn't give a damn about anyone other than equally rich white men and the favours they can do one another. They go to places such as *énergique* because they can "engage" in the sort of activities their normal buttoned-down lives don't allow and they can do so with little scrutiny or interference.'

Hugo scratched his head. He had known a similar club on the outskirts of Montgenoux and he shuddered at the thought of the terrible secrets it had held. 'Still, despite it all, I admit I'm having trouble imagining Jean Lenoir being mixed up in anything... untoward'

'You're probably right,' she answered, 'Jean is a pragmatist and a social climber, we all know that. He wants to be seen by the right people; he wants to be with the right people. I'm sure you know by now he has his sights set on a much higher position than Minister of Justice, but to get there he needs help, a lot of help.'

'And he can get it from frequenting this club?'

Coco laughed. 'Oh, come, come, Hugo.

Montgenoux may be sleepy in its way, but I know you worked in London, so you have to know these types of men. This type of power, thrives in places such as *énergique*. Jean may not be involved in any dubious activities, but that's not to say he doesn't know they're happening.'

'Are you suggesting he knows what happened to this young man?' Hugo asked.

'I don't know. He won't speak to me or anyone for that matter and he's giving us the run-around.' She paused. 'I still don't get why he's dragging you into this. I was only calling on the off-chance Ben may have heard from his brother.'

'Half-brother,' Hugo answered quickly, 'and to answer that question, non. Ben hasn't heard from Sebastian and isn't very likely to either. I telephoned Sebastian's mother before I left the station, and she hasn't heard from him either. They had a falling out some time ago, so I can't imagine she's lying.' He paused, reluctantly adding, 'all that being said, if Sebastian was in trouble, there is a chance he might reach out to me.'

'To you?' Coco asked, surprised. 'Pourquoi?'

Hugo did not answer immediately. His ties to Sebastian stretched back. He had tried to help him only because Hugo felt he owed Sebastian a debt for having once saved his life. He tried not to think of it too much because part of him was not sure Sebastian was not involved in the reason Hugo had needed saving in the first place. 'He has reached out to me in the past, for reasons which make little sense and which I won't bore you with,' Hugo answered. 'But tell me, do you have any reason to suspect Sebastian to be involved, other than his disappearance?'

'Non,' she replied. 'But again, like Jean Lenoir, until I actually get a chance to speak to them, I can't be sure of their involvement, or lack thereof. You sidestepped my question. What does Jean Lenoir want from you? Why does he want you to come to Paris?'

Hugo took a deep breath and then exhaled. 'I'm not entirely sure he even knows that, I'd even hazard a guess he's desperate and doesn't have too many people he can call on. I don't really know all the details, but it involves my father in some kind of investigation and by all accounts, there is no love lost between them.'

'Ah,' Coco said, 'I heard there was some kind of external investigation launched, but I didn't put the two together. So, Papa Duchamp, eh? I'm guessing your relationship isn't exactly rosy?'

Hugo snorted. 'You could say that, which is why it's ludicrous to think I could exert any authority over him.' He paused. 'I want you to know, if I do come to Paris, I don't intend on getting involved in the investigation, no matter what Jean Lenoir believes or requires of me.'

'Mordecai won't be happy,' Coco muttered.

'And I can't say I'd blame him. It's not the right thing to interfere in investigations out of our jurisdiction.'

'Oh, I don't care about chest-puffing nonsense,'

Coco retorted, 'and I don't believe you do either. Any cop who gives a damn about their job doesn't give two hoots about accepting help from others as long as the perp gets nailed, correct?'

'You have a point,' Hugo conceded, 'but as I said, if I come to Paris, I don't intend stepping on anyone's toes, especially yours and Jean Lenoir is just going to have to deal with that.'

'D'accord, listen, Hugo, I'll do what I can to help you, but if Mordecai suspects for a second you're trying to help Jean in any way, he'll kick you right out of the Commissariat. You'll call me when you get to Paris? We can have supper.'

Hugo nodded and looked towards his house. 'I will. Au revoir Coco, and trust me I have no intention of getting any more involved in any of this than I need to.'

Hugo stepped down from the train at Gare de Nord for the first time in several years, but he was immediately catapulted back to that day, his first back in France in over a decade. But now he realised he was no longer the same man. One reason he had been so reluctant to return to France, the country of his birth, was because of his fractured childhood. It had bothered him, moulded him, and still had a hold over him. But it had no longer. He had not truly believed it until that very moment when the scents and the sounds of the busy station bombarded his brain. He was not afraid. Not anymore. He could face Paris because although it had once been his home, the ghosts, whether they still walked or had moved on, were no longer there for him.

Benoit Beaupain stepped from the train, the sudden gust of wind from the station blowing the curls from his forehead, his clear eyes crinkling as he tried to get his bearings. Hugo reached around, holding out his hand to help his husband down the steps. A move so simple but Hugo realised one he would not have been able to make a few years earlier. Ben's lips spread into a wide, warm smile, blue eyes sparkling. 'I miss Paris,' he said, 'but I miss home more. I'm a moron with my paradoxical nonsense, non?'

Hugo smiled at the man he shared his life with. It was no understatement to say the first time he had met Benoit Beaupain he had been terrified of him. There was something about the angry, seemingly overly confident man-child which seemed at odds with the sadness in his hazel, golden eyes. A paradox indeed. Benoit Beaupain was not the man he pretended to be. He was better, and he was hiding, and Hugo recognised it because he was doing the same. They had learned to trust each other and to reveal their true selves.

Hugo ran his finger across Ben's hand before turning his attention to the hustle and bustle of the station. Paris was in his blood. He had been born there and spent his formative years basking in all the capital offered, but by the time he had left, he had hoped never to return. Now he was not so sure. The only thing he knew for certain was he did not want to see his father.

He and Ben had spent the previous evening weighing up their options. Whilst Jean Lenoir's request contained a veiled threat, there really was little he could do to force Hugo to help him. Ben's own initial reaction had been to allow Lenoir, Sebastian and Hugo's father to fight it out between them, because their lives, and the messes they made of them, had nothing to do with Hugo and Ben. However, as they had shared the evening together and discussed it, Ben had concluded it would be a good time for Hugo to close a door on his past. To deal with the omnipresent shadow of his father. *Face the devil and it will lose its power,* he had said, and he had been right. For too long Hugo had cowered in the shadows of men such as his father and Jean Lenoir. He had made a deal with

Jean Lenoir and he would honour it and then it would be spent. And as for his father? It was time to face him once and for all. Hugo and Ben had both awoken simultaneously with the same thought. *Let's do this.*

'I've booked us into this really cute boutique hotel,' Ben said, 'near the seventh arrondissement. It's not stuffy at all, and as we are on a budget these days, a breakfast buffet is included, so it's a win-win!'

Hugo raised an eyebrow. It still amazed him that Ben, a very wealthy man due to inheriting his share of his father's fortune, had chosen not taken a cent from it for himself, instead donated his share to various charities. With the bulk of his inheritance, he had finally decided to use it to build a hostel in Montgenoux specialising in helping troubled young adults, of all colours, of all sexualities. Every time Hugo thought of it, his heart swelled with pride. All Ben had ever said about it was he had all he needed in life, and there was no more he could ever want and it was time to give back. He grabbed Ben's hand, pointing at a newspaper kiosk in the centre of the station. It was decorated with a row of *Le Monde* newspapers.

Minister of Justice Jean Lenoir pictured with dead child BOY prostitute days before his murder.

Below the headline was a picture of a smiling Jean Lenoir next to a very young man and Sebastian Dubois.

'Mon Dieu,' Hugo said upon seeing the photograph for the first time. While there was no evidence of anything untoward, he realised the mere implication of impropriety was in itself dangerous for the career of a man such as Jean Lenoir. He wondered again how the photograph had ended up with the press. He picked up the newspaper, studying it carefully. He had seen a hundred like it before, taken at the sort of events he imagined this one had been. A staff photographer wandered around, snapping indiscriminately, putting strangers together, getting them to smile. Creating a sterile, impossible atmosphere. A party of strangers all smiling, their eyes sparkling as they transmitted the same lie. *We're here having the best time ever and we bet you're jealous you aren't important enough to be here.* Hugo suppressed a smile, wondering whether it was just his impression of a party which he had no interest in attending.

'No wonder Jean Lenoir is pissed,' Ben said with a faint smile. He raised his hands. 'Désolé, cheri, I know I shouldn't be so gleeful, but you gotta admit, there is a sort of karmic tone to all of this. I'm not saying Jean Lenoir deserves it, but he certainly had it coming. You can't piss off as many people as he has without expecting them to want a bit of retribution.' He shrugged. 'And I'm sorry, but I can't say I'll lose any sleep if Jean gets a little taste of his own medicine for once.'

Hugo did not answer. He did not need to.

* * *

'Ben!' Coco cried and pulled Ben into a tight embrace. 'It really has been ridiculously long, you beautiful child.' She playfully punched Hugo's arm. 'You didn't tell me you were bringing your fabulous husband with you.'

Hugo smiled. 'Oui. I keep forgetting you two knew each other in the past.'

'*Knew* each other? You don't know the half of it.' Coco winked, 'oh, the tales I could tell you...'

Hugo's eyes widened. Ben touched his arm. 'Don't listen to Coco, she's teasing you. Don't be mean, Coco. Hugo is very sensitive and will read into your jokes and it will keep him awake at night.' He turned to Hugo. 'When I was very young and first started working at Montgenoux Hospital, I was dating, if you could call it that, a Pompier who worked with Anton, who Coco was dating at the time. We went on a few double dates, nothing more.'

Coco smiled. 'Forgive me, Hugo, I am. Truth is, I was the bad influence back in the day, believe it or not.'

Hugo nodded, not finding it difficult to believe at all, although he chose not to dwell too much on Ben's past dating history. He took a moment to appraise Coco's ramshackle home. In a lot of ways, it reminded him of his own. Having a teenager living with him and Ben meant the house was never tidy and as far as Hugo could recall, Coco had four children. There were remnants and evidence of five inter-winding lives everywhere he looked. He liked it. He liked it a lot. Growing up, he knew better than to leave a book out of place and the sterile atmosphere had followed him into his adult life. He had lived a solitary, sterile life on his own in London and thought it was what he wanted. Until he had arrived in Montgenoux. Everything had changed when he arrived in Montgenoux.

As if reading his mind, she said. 'The two young ones are with their father tonight, and the two older,' she stopped, giving a sad look towards a staircase strewn with toys, 'they are upstairs, if they haven't climbed out of the window already. Barbra has a boyfriend, some local thug who she thinks is the greatest thing since sliced bread. I hate him of course. He's got a rap sheet as long as my arm, but all I can do is keep my fingers crossed she doesn't get knocked up at nineteen like I did. As for Julien, well, he imagines I haven't worked out he's in love with his best friend Matthieu yet, if he's even aware of it himself.'

Ben laughed. 'Poor Coco, you certainly have your hands full.'

'Oh, you have no idea,' she responded, sweeping into a crammed, overflowing kitchen, 'but what can you do? I drop broad hints about how I wish I had a gay child, so I'd never have to worry about decor or clothes again, but…'

Ben laughed again. 'Perhaps you're trying too hard.'

'Or he's just not into decor or fashion,' Hugo added, glancing at his own clothes. His own shopping habits usually involved in walking past a Gap store and buying whatever the mannequin in the window was wearing. 'There are some of us who have no real interest in either, you know.'

She stared at him. 'You think? I thought as long as my kids know I care enough not to care, then it would be enough, and certainly better than the alternative. I love my kids, whoever or whatever they want to love or be.'

Hugo and Ben exchanged a look, a thought passing between them, wishing they had their own "Coco" when they were growing up. Hugo reached across and touched her arm. A move so out of character for him, Ben's eyes widened. 'Believe me, when they look back, and they will look back, it will have been enough.'

Coco shrugged, flashing a shy smile. She turned her head around the messy, dish-strewn kitchen. 'I'd offer to cook, but well, if I did, you'd know why the local pizza parlour gives me a fifty per cent discount. Large stuffed crust?'

Hugo wiped his mouth with a napkin and took another sip of his beer. 'So, we saw the newspapers on the way from the station.'

'Ah, oui,' Coco replied. 'Although I do not understand where the photograph came from, certainly not me, and to be honest, it means nothing, but you know how these things can take on a life of their own. If the Minister wasn't being so difficult it wouldn't matter so much.'

'And the young man in the photograph, he is the deceased?'

'I believe so,' she answered. 'We issued a photograph to the press to help with his identification as is standard practice, and then four hours later, that photograph turns up. And the damn press won't tell us where it came from. Still no name for the poor child though. We have his prints, teeth, DNA but he hasn't shown up in any of the regular databases yet, but that's no surprise, we have a backlog as long as my arm. I hate not knowing his name, really I do, but I hate more the fact someone is playing games with us because if they had the other photograph, the chances are they must also know who he is.'

Hugo nodded his agreement. 'And the chances are, they might well know what happened.'

'And I hate that, really I do,' Coco replied.

'Do you this could be just about trying to implicate Jean Lenoir to derail whatever future plans he has?' Hugo asked.

Coco considered. 'It's certainly possible.' She moved away from the table and picked up her bag, extracting a thick folder. She handed it to Hugo. 'Here is what we have so far, I made you a copy. We spoke with the owner of *énergique*. Some complete Trump asshole type of man, and he did the standard *I know nothing, I saw nothing,* spiel. I didn't believe him, I don't believe him. But as I keep saying, if it wasn't for everyone wanting to believe Jean Lenoir is up to his neck in something shady, then this whole case would have been closed already.'

Hugo took the folder. He was surprised she was giving it to him. If the roles were reversed, he was not sure he would, or should, do the same.

Coco waved her hand. 'I know I can trust you, and to be honest, between us three, as far as anyone is concerned, even the Commander, there isn't much here to go on, or to indicate a crime has even been committed.'

'Then you're still considering this to be a suicide?' Ben asked.

She shrugged. 'Honestly, I don't see what else we can do.' She pointed at the folder in Hugo's hands. 'All the witness statements indicate all they saw, all they *really* saw, was a kid falling from the Eiffel Tower, but one of them, the Chinese kid, for example, describes it as looking like he was bungee jumping and having a whale of a time. Any defence Avocat will huff and puff about all of that, and at this stage, I can't even begin to imagine charging anyone with a crime, which is why I still don't understand why Jean Lenoir is so freaked.'

'Moi aussi,' Hugo replied, 'and I don't understand why he wanted my help with my father, or Ben's help with… Sebastian. I admit none of it makes much sense.'

'Unless he knows something we don't,' Ben added.

Hugo tapped his chin. 'Or perhaps he's just scared or feeling vulnerable. You know, Jean Lenoir doesn't strike me as the sort of man to have friends, people who care about him. That vulnerability may have translated to me, to us, helping him. The chance is he probably speaks to us more than anyone else in his life. His work probably is his life, and he is likely terrified of losing it.'

Ben tutted. 'He has people who could care about him if he only bothered himself,' he shook his head, 'dammit, you know how cute Bruno is and he's never once tried to see him, or ask how he is, or help in any way, for that matter.'

'Bruno?' Coco interrupted with a frown.

Hugo flashed Ben a look. 'Not our story to tell,' he answered Coco.

She looked at him. 'Is it relevant to my investigation?'

'I don't believe so,' he answered, 'truly I don't.'

She nodded. 'Bien, but if it was, I'd hope you'd remember sharing information works both ways.'

'Bien sûr,' he answered, 'but as far as I know, this is a personal issue which can have no bearing on your investigation.' He flicked open the file, his eyes scanning the autopsy report. 'I see the bruises on his neck were fresh so they could have come as a result of being pushed over the tower.'

Coco agreed. 'Or they could have happened earlier that day, or the day before, Dr. Bernstein couldn't be more specific.'

'And the sexual activity?'

'The day of his death, there was evidence of spermicide, but nothing more. No hair, no fibres, no links to anyone else.'

'And no CCTV?' Hugo asked.

'We have footage of the deceased entering the tower, alone, and wandering around the first level, also alone, but the area from which he fell, sadly there is no footage.'

Hugo considered. 'And Jean Lenoir?'

She shrugged. 'More or less the same. We have him on camera going into the tower and the restaurant, but when he steps outside for his telephone call or cigarette or whatever the hell he was doing, he is not on camera.'

'And do you know who he was with?'

'Non, not exactly,' Coco replied, 'as I said, we keep putting in requests to interview him and they keep getting ignored. Even Commander Stanic knows better than to crash our way into interrogating the Minister of Justice, and no Juge will force the issue. Which is why I was pleased Jean is at least talking to someone, i.e. you.'

'You said you don't know exactly who he was having dinner with, what do you mean?' Hugo asked.

'He entered and left the Tower alone, but the waitress seems to think he was having dinner with a young woman, a very young woman. But honestly, she didn't seem too sure and,' she chuckled, 'knowing Jean, it's hard to imagine anyone willingly chooses to eat with him.'

Hugo nodded. 'And as far as we can tell, there was no connection between Jean and the young man?'

'Apart from the club, and the innocuous photograph,' Coco replied, 'neither of which are enough for a Juge to drag him in for questioning.'

'But the photograph is odd,' Ben mused.

Hugo pursed his lips. 'It is, isn't it? I mean, there's nothing in it to suggest Jean knew the dead boy, but then someone must have put the connection together, must have known there was a photograph and that Jean was at the Eiffel Tower at the time of the apparent suicide.'

'Apparent?' Coco asked, raising an eyebrow.

Hugo shrugged. 'I understand there is no evidence of foul play, but something just feels wrong, almost as if there is a suggestion, just a suggestion of something untoward.'

'Untoward?' Ben asked, his brow creasing.

Hugo scratched his head. 'I don't know how to explain it, but there is something about it which is bothering me. The photograph, the scene of the death, the fact Jean was present at both and someone knew about it. If I didn't know better, it would almost seem as if Jean Lenoir is being deliberately targeted for some reason, or lured to the Eiffel Tower that night in order to implicate him, either way, something about it doesn't add up.' He paused. 'And I hate to say it, but I'm almost certain Jean isn't telling me the full story either.'

'What makes you think that?' Ben asked.

'Every conversation I've ever had with him,' Hugo replied with a snort.

Coco pulled her hair into a ponytail, flicking the blue tips over her shoulder. 'I think maybe you're reading too much into it. This could all be about someone with a grudge taking advantage of a situation, a tragic, horrible situation in which a young man took his own life,' Coco responded, 'and they're using it to embarrass the Minister. I mean, if some mysterious person was out to frame Jean Lenoir, then why this way? Because as far as we can tell, we're looking at a suicide, so apart from a bit of embarrassment, Jean is likely to walk away from this relatively unscathed. In fact, if someone was out to get him there would be better ways to do it, like framing him for an actual murder, non?'

'Perhaps,' Hugo conceded, still uncertain.

'Honestly, as far as I'm concerned, this is an open and shut case,' Coco said as she scanned his unconvinced face, 'you don't agree?'

Hugo did not answer for a moment. 'As far as I know, there is never such a thing as an open and shut case. I'll go and see Jean in the morning and ask him about the photograph. He claims not to know the young man, and I don't see why he would lie about it, but that doesn't mean he's telling us the full story and I'll make sure he understands if he wants my help then he will have to…' He did not finish his sentence, interrupted by a teenage boy bounding down the stairway, two steps at a time.

'Have you been in my room again?' the youngster hissed, a thin Adam's apple rising and falling in a croaky throat.

'As if!' Coco cried, her hand hitting her chest. 'Even

my crime scene guys wouldn't want to wade through all the rolled-up tissues littering your floor.'

The boy opened his mouth to respond but stopped upon seeing Hugo and Ben, faint-acned cheeks flushing. His eyes widened, and he looked down at his clothes. He was wearing tracks and a Lady Gaga t-shirt. He slunk against the wall, his mouth twisting into words which did not come.

'Pizza, Julien?' Coco asked him.

Julien nodded and did not answer, sliding into a chair next to Hugo. His eyes widened and they flicked lazily over Hugo, with obvious interest, like an animal weighing up its prey. Hugo glanced at his feet, feeling self-conscious, his cheeks flushing.

Coco moved next to her son, her nose crinkling. 'Julien, when was the last time you showered? You stink!'

Julien jumped to his feet, his nose crinkling. 'Non, you stink!' before stomping back up the stairs.

Coco smiled. 'Apologies for my son, despite his hormones developing, his motor skills don't seem to have caught up.'

Ben shook his head and laughed. 'Don't worry about it, everyone always ends up flirting with Hugo. It's only ever a matter of time and I am, sadly, used to it. I've tried talking to him about it, but it only seems to make the situation worse.'

Coco gave him a serious nod. 'I can see that, it must drive you mad.'

Ben shrugged. 'Not really, because I know whose bed he comes to each night, and at the end of the day, that's all that matters.'

Hugo cleared his throat, his cheeks flushing with embarrassment, and he rose to his feet. He tapped the folder against his chest. 'Merci for this, and for dinner. I'll read the file tonight and return it to you tomorrow.'

Coco nodded. 'As you wish, if you find anything I've missed let me know. I won't be offended, honestly, but I suspect you and Ben will be back on the train to Montgenoux by tomorrow.'

Hugo gave her a doubtful look. 'I hope so,' he said. 'I really hope so. I love Paris, but right now I don't want to be here for a moment longer than I have to.'

Jean Lenoir tossed the newspaper onto his desk with such force, a stack of files crashed onto the ground. He glared at Hugo, challenging him. 'Fucking garbage,' he cried, the anger raging in his throat. 'Known to frequent prostitutes? Prostitutes?' he spat. 'Prostitutes? I have never, *would* never...' He glared again at the photograph, his eyes crinkling in the way a person does when their vision is compromised but they are too vain to wear glasses.

Hugo raised his hand in an attempt to pacify the Minister. 'I understand your anger,' he replied softly, 'but really, you have to understand this is all puffing. There is no case, therefore there can be no investigation.' He paused before continuing. 'On the other hand, the photograph is cause for concern.'

Jean shot him an unsure look. 'What do you mean? What do you know?'

'You maintain you didn't know the young man?'

'I do *maintain* it, as you so eloquently put it.' Lenoir replied, snatching the photograph and raising it nearer his eyes. 'Are we even sure this is really the dead boy?'

Hugo nodded. 'You don't recognise him?'

Jean flung the photograph down. 'Non, why should I? I told you, I never met him.'

'Then what about the photograph?'

Jean pointed at it. 'The background decorations suggest the photograph was taken on Bastille Day. It was quite the party as I recall, and I suggest there are a dozen or more photographs of me posing with various people, most of which I am unlikely to have engaged in any sort of conversation with. These people do not move in any circle I am interested in.'

'But this is the one people are interested in,' Hugo replied, 'and of the three people in the photograph, one is dead and one is missing. Therefore, you have to admit, this photograph is certainly interesting.'

Jean laughed. 'And suspicious. Where are the rest of the dozens of photographs I probably posed for? Why is this the only one the press have? I take it you have spoken with the police regarding the investigation?'

Hugo did not answer.

'I knew it would benefit you having met Captain Brunhild. You are very similar, not like the idiot Commander. No doubt he is doing backflips at having such a photograph. No doubt your father is as well, in fact it wouldn't surprise me if he sent the damn picture to the press himself.'

Hugo wondered again what issues there could be between Jean and Pierre Duchamp. He considered what he should tell Jean about the investigation, because he certainly did not want to cause trouble for Coco, but the truth was, after reading the files, he had to agree with Coco's assessment. There was very little to go on or to suggest a crime had been committed. 'The press are doing what the press do,' Hugo said, 'making a story from nothing. As far as I can tell, there was no murder, just a suicide.' He paused. 'You have to know you have made enemies, Minister, and now you are trying to advance your career, it intensifies the scrutiny you are under. But if you have nothing to hide, then they can't make it up, can they?'

Jean looked at him with interest. 'If?'

Hugo smiled. 'If, oui. I wonder, will you tell me the truth? What are you really worried about? I don't believe for a second you have any involvement with teenage male prostitutes, nor would you push one to his death from the Eiffel Tower. I don't believe you'd get your own hands dirty in such a way,' he added with a wry smile.

Jean snorted. 'I'm touched by your faith in me.'

Hugo narrowed his eyes. 'But you are worried, and if you want my help you need to tell me why. If you don't want me to get on the next train back to Montgenoux, then you will have to tell me the truth. That's the deal.'

Jean lowered his head. A moment passed, and then another before he finally spoke. 'There was a girl.'

He spoke so softly, Hugo had to edge forward. 'A girl?' Hugo questioned. 'Do you mean a prostitute?'

Jean slammed his fist on the desk. 'Dammit, Hugo,' he growled, 'don't test me.'

Hugo raised his hand. 'Jean, this is not about judging you, I couldn't care less who you choose to spend your time with. Was she a prostitute?' he asked again, 'and is that why you are worried? Worried it will come out in the investigation?'

Jean sighed, narrow eyes glaring in Hugo's direction. 'There are no such things as prostitutes, not in the sense you mean, not in places such as *énergique*. Members pay a very hefty monthly membership to be part of the club, you see. And the membership comes with certain,' he paused before adding, '*perks.*'

Hugo raised an eyebrow but did not comment.

Jean continued. 'Don't judge me, Duchamp,' he hissed. 'Do you know how difficult it is for a man in my position to meet people? I mean, even if I actually had the time, there is the danger of those I do meet only being interested in my position and using me in one way or another, or to find a way to blackmail me. Establishments such as *énergique* have been operating since time immemorial for men such as me. A place to go, unwind and make contacts.'

Hugo nodded. 'And is this why you won't talk to the police?'

'It is nobody's business what happened between me and Delphine,' Jean sniffled huffily.

'Delphine?'

Jean nodded. 'Oui. Delphine Marchand.'

Hugo thought, perhaps for the first time, he saw a softening on Jean Lenoir's chemically enhanced too-smooth face. 'And you met her at the club?'

'Oui,' Jean replied. He turned his head, and when he spoke, Hugo could only describe it as being wistful. 'Believe me Hugo, I never went into *énergique* looking for anything other than a place to relax, and to make sure those who can aid me see my face, see that I am a team player. It is loathsome, but it is the way of power. I hated it at first, but then one day I saw her. I didn't mean to stare, but it was just she seemed so…' he trailed off as he searched for the words, 'out of place. Oui, that's it, like she didn't belong there. Shiny red hair in a little bob, freckles on a makeup-less face. It just made little sense to me why she was there, and despite myself, I talked to her. Most of the people you meet there are dreadful bores only out for themselves, or those who hang on your every word and say nothing in fear of offending you. But then there was Delphine, and for a young girl,' he stopped and shot Hugo an angry look, 'young *woman*, she had a lot to say, opinions worth listening to, not the vacant, pin-headed women who normally frequent the club and are only really interested in agreeing with everything you say, or perish the thought they might actually annoy you by having an opinion of their own. That was never the case with Delphine,' he added with a smile, 'she was certainly never shy about expressing her opinion.'

It was not lost on Hugo the person Jean Lenoir had just described was a younger version of Irene Chapeau, Montgenoux's pathologist and the mother of the child Jean Lenoir had never acknowledged as his own. And on top of that, if he did not know better, it almost sounded as if Jean Lenoir was talking about someone he loved. 'You're talking about her in the past,' he said.

With a shrug of his wide shoulders, Hugo could almost see the descent of the cool, efficient figure of the Minister of Justice. 'She was a woman I encountered, our paths crossed for the briefest of times and then went in opposite directions.'

Hugo nodded, sensing the tell-tale tone of hurt in Jean's voice. Had he imagined more in his relationship with the young ingénue? Had he discovered he was not the only man in whose arms she clung? 'And she was the one you were having dinner with that night on the Eiffel Tower?'

Jean gave him an uncertain look. 'Oui,' he answered finally.

Hugo took a moment to digest the information. 'And is it possible Delphine knew the young man who died?'

'I don't know,' Jean replied. 'It's possible, but we certainly didn't talk about that sort of thing, why would we?'

Hugo took a deep breath before speaking again. 'And did you have a sexual relationship with her?'

'Captain Duchamp!' Jean roared. 'That is none of your business.'

Hugo shook his head. 'It may not be, and believe me, I really don't want the answer, but if you want me to help, I have to understand what we're dealing with.'

The tall grandfather clock in the corner of the room clicked loudly into midday. Jean sighed. 'Oui,' he answered.

Hugo nodded. 'And no money exchanged hands?'

'I've told you, I don't pay for sex!' Jean hissed. 'Are you stupid?'

Hugo stood, slapping his hands onto the back of the chair. 'I certainly must be, dragging myself to Paris to help you and for what? To be insulted and lied to? You wanted my help, so I'm here, but unless we understand each other Jean, then I'm on the next train back to Montgenoux and you can carry out any damn threat you want but you'll be on your own.' He stopped, an uncomfortable silence descending on the room.

The Minister of Justice sighed. 'Désolé, Hugo,' he said. 'You must understand, none of this comes easily to me.'

Hugo nodded, wondering what it was he meant. He continued, realising the sooner he did, the sooner he could leave. 'So, am I correct in the assumption that these young men and woman were paid for by the club which in turn was paid for by its clientele subscription. There was never the exchange of physical money?'

'Oui, that is correct. Other than dinner or drink, of course.'

Hugo tapped his lips. 'Then that's good, surely, non?'

'What do you mean?' Jean asked.

'Only that no-one can make the claim you were using prostitutes, can they? All you really did was engage in a relationship with an employee of the club you frequented.'

Jean's lips twitched into a reluctant smile. 'Oui, that is ALL which could be claimed, or proved and anything else, well, anything else would be a case for legal action for slander. But none of that really matters, the mere suspicion of impropriety is enough to derail... to derail anything.'

Hugo tipped his head. 'Then I see no reason why you should not cooperate with the police, Jean. The fact you are not is only fanning the flames. Tell them what you have told me and leave it at that.'

Jean shook his head vehemently. 'I had my secretary provide them with a written statement. I did not see the young man, either at *énergique* nor at the Eiffel Tower. If we were there at the same time, then I am certainly unaware of it, and nor did we have any kind of conversation. There is nothing else to say. I won't be brought into anything which gives my enemies the ability to ask, or imply anything they wish.'

Hugo sighed again. 'But don't you see, the fact you are refusing to talk only amplifies the interest, the belief you have something to hide?'

Jean shrugged again. 'Let them. That is why you are here - deal with your father, while your husband deals with his brother. Give the investigation somewhere else to focus on. I cannot be seen to be implicated, but in the interests of justice, it must also be seen they have investigated me, but there was no scandal unearthed.'

Hugo pulled on his jacket. 'I only arrived last night and the only person I've spoken with is Captain Brunhild. I haven't approached my father, or even decided if I'm going to.'

Jean slammed his fist onto the table. 'Don't you understand, your father is gathering evidence against me? He will do anything to stop me. Putain, I thought you understood this.'

Hugo paused before continuing. 'Listen, I'll level with you, Jean. You asked me to come here with Ben to help, and part of me is actually flattered you did. But in all honesty, everything I am seeing, and everything I understand so far, shows there is nothing to investigate. So, let my father do his investigation, you will be vindicated and it can actually only help you for the public to know you have been thoroughly vetted for your next role.'

Jean patted the photograph. 'But something is off, you know it and I know it. For a start, where is Dubois? The fact no-one can find him is casting a shadow where there need be only light. People are creating scenarios in their heads, scenarios concerning me, and I want it to end. I am not used to being the object of hallway gossip. I don't like it and I want it to stop.' He stared squarely at Hugo. 'There are matters you don't know, CANNOT know, which are of grave importance to the Republic. Find Dubois and get him here, find out what he knows. Give your father something else to focus on, I cannot have him looking at me.'

Hugo tapped his chin. He could not deny Sebastian's disappearance was concerning him. 'To be honest, knowing Sebastian as I do, he may have just cleared out of town because he doesn't want to get involved. Remember, he is still on probation and now he has inherited some money, there isn't a chance he will let himself end up back in prison. Non, I'm sure he is lying on a beach somewhere waiting for this all to blow over.' He stopped, unsure of his own conviction. 'The police aren't aware of your relationship with Delphine, are they?'

Jean snorted. 'Not from me. I certainly haven't told them about her, for obvious reasons, nor am I intending to. If the police or your father want to talk to me then they will have to do it officially, *publicly*, to ensure there is no confusion as to my innocence. I have been clear on the issue and will not back down on it.'

Hugo nodded. He supposed if he was a man in the Minister's position, then perhaps he would be reticent about what he shared. 'And have you spoken with Delphine since? What does she say about all of this and what happened?' he asked, watching as Jean's eyes flicked towards his cell phone.

'Non,' Jean shook his head, 'her phone has been switched off, I believe,' he said in a way which Hugo understood meant he had been trying repeatedly. If it was true, it did not sit well with him that at least one other person was missing. He made a mental note to speak to

Coco about Delphine Marchand. There was something about it which troubled him. Two young people who seemingly worked as prostitutes at *énergique* were at the Eiffel Tower on the same night, and one of them fell to his death. Could it be a coincidence? He did not believe so. He moved towards the door.

'Where are you going?' Jean asked. 'To see your father and tell him to get the hell off my back?' he asked, the hopeful tone clear in his voice, like a child seeking reassurance.

Hugo turned away. 'Non, not yet. There are other more important things to do before resorting to that. First, I will go to *énergique*, I want to find out first-hand what they know about the young man and Delphine and why Sebastian is missing. I'll call you, Jean,' he added with as much reassurance as he could muster, certainly more than he felt.

Jean Lenoir, perhaps for the first time since they had met years earlier, gave Hugo a grateful, honest smile.

Ben lifted his head, his eyes flicking around the building with immense distaste. 'Isn't it amazing how clubs such as *énergique* seem exciting in an evening - full of promise for the adventure and promise of the night ahead, but during the day, seeing them through day eyes, they just seem so...' he paused, 'seedy.' He laughed. 'Dieu, I sound old.'

Hugo took a moment to appraise the nightclub himself. It was situated in an old Parisian tenement and apart from the neon sign, there was nothing else to indicate what the steep stairway down to the bowels of the building led to. He turned onto the road. There was only one way into the street and nowhere to hide. He imagined it was part of the appeal, affording the customers' privacy away from prying eyes. 'I think it probably has more to do with the amount of alcohol consumed,' he answered with a tight grin. 'And non, you're not old.' They moved down the stairs, and Hugo pressed the intercom.

'Yeah?' a gruff voice answered.

'Bonjour,' Hugo replied. 'My name is Captain Hugo Duchamp.'

'Police?' The tone of voice signalled the man speaking was not alarmed or concerned in any way.

'Oui,' Hugo replied, thinking he should add he was not acting officially but all he could think about was getting out of Paris as soon as possible.

The door buzzed open and Hugo and Ben stepped

inside the dimly lit foyer. It was how he imagined it would be, plush carpet and expansive sofas made of red leather and burgundy velvet. A pair of swing-doors pushed open and a man approached them. Hugo took a step back, there was something about the man's eyes which troubled him. They were as cold as an iceberg. The man stopped in front of him and Hugo guessed them to be about the same height, over six feet, but this man was much wider, with thick shoulders and expressive jowls. The man's hands rested on his stomach, scratching at an itch. Hugo found it difficult not to stare at the apparent fair coloured toupee the man was sporting which was at odds with the much darker hair on the side of his head.

'I am Captain Duchamp,' Hugo repeated, 'may I speak with the owner?'

The man licked his lips. 'You are,' he answered proudly before adding, 'one of them at least.'

'There are several?' Hugo questioned.

'We have investors,' the man replied, 'but I am the majority shareholder.' He held out a fleshy hand. Hugo took it. It was warm and wet. 'Je m'appelle, Michel Lomet.'

'Enchanté, Monsieur,' Hugo responded politely.

Michel sighed. 'Don't you flics talk to one another? I've answered your questions.' He shrugged his hefty shoulders. 'I know nothing.'

Hugo nodded. 'I understand, but if I could just trouble you for a few moments, I would be very grateful. You were acquainted with the young man who died, non?'

Lomet sighed again. 'As I said, the management cannot be held responsible for any *arrangements* made between my customers. And,' he paused, shooting Hugo a combative glare, 'you can't prove otherwise. But I'd like you to try otherwise and see how far you get, Captain.'

Hugo raised a hand. 'Bien sûr, Monsieur Lomet, but as you may know, we have been unable to discover the young man's identity and inform his next of kin, so any information you could provide us really would be greatly appreciated.'

He shrugged. 'But how? It's not as if I hold employment records for such transients.'

'A young man died, Monsieur,' Ben interrupted, 'and he's lying in a morgue all alone. If there is some way in which you can help reunite him with his family, then you should.'

Hugo raised a hand to try to pacify Ben. He turned back to Michel. 'Perhaps your co-owner may know more. Could we perhaps talk with him?'

Michel Lomet cackled. 'The fag? I doubt it, although he has a knack of sticking his nose in where it doesn't belong. I guarantee you he knows nothing either.'

'Do not use words such as those in my presence, Monsieur,' Ben growled, stepping from behind Hugo.

Michel's eyes flicked lazily between Ben and Hugo, his fleshy lips spreading into a smirk. 'Ah, bien sûr, désolé, no offence meant, I can assure you.'

Ben glared at him as if he was sure of no such thing.

Hugo cleared his throat. 'You are talking about Monsieur Dubois? Monsieur Sebastian Dubois?'

Michel nodded. 'Si. Came into some money and said he wanted to buy his way into a classy joint.' He spread his arms proudly, gesturing around the nightclub. 'And it doesn't get much classier than *énergique*. We have a very influential clientele, you know. But as for Dubois, he is not here at present.'

'Then where is he?' Ben asked.

Michel turned towards Ben, studying him as if he was vaguely familiar. 'Who are you, exactly, jeune homme? I didn't catch your name.'

'My name is Benoit Beaupain,' Ben answered, 'and I am here to see my brother, my *half*-brother, Sebastian Dubois,' he added as if speaking the words hurt him.

Michel raised an eyebrow. 'Really? The wine Beaupain's? Sebastian told me he'd crawled out of the vineyard a bastard, but a very rich one.' He cackled. 'How you must have hated having to share your fortune.'

Ben did not answer. 'I need to speak to my... to Sebastian. It's time-sensitive, and it concerns my late father's estate. It is in his best interests we speak as a matter of urgency.'

Hugo watched Michel intently as Ben spoke. They had agreed on the way over, one way it might be possible to smoke out Sebastian was if he knew there was money involved. He could tell Michel was wrestling with a thought and it appeared to Hugo if he did not know where

Sebastian was, there was perhaps a way he knew how to contact him.

'As I said,' Michel replied, 'I do not know where he is, but should he get in touch I will tell him his *brother* is looking for him.'

Ben tutted and threw his backpack onto a sofa. He reached inside and pulled out a notepad, scribbling onto it. He tore off a sheet and handed it to Michel. 'This is my cell number. Tell Sebastian unless he wants to lose out on a lot of money, and I mean a LOT of money then I need to hear from him within the next twenty-four hours.'

'As I…'

Ben interrupted. 'Just tell him there's a lot of money at stake, and he has twenty-four hours. And he knows me, so tell him if I don't hear from him by then, I'll make sure every damn cent goes to charity. He'll know I mean it, and I'm sure he'll be thrilled you were the one who sent him such joyous news.'

Lomet nodded his head slowly but said nothing, slowly placing the number in a lapel pocket. He turned back to Hugo. 'Is there anything else?'

Hugo shook his head. 'I also wanted to ask you about another employee, a young woman called Delphine Marchand.'

A wave of anger flared in Lomet's eyes. He shuffled on his feet. 'Who?'

Hugo studied Michel Lomet, watching him as a fleshy, pale tongue slid across dry lips. Hugo had seen the same expression more times than he could count and it was always for the same reason. A nerve had been touched, and Hugo did not understand why. 'Delphine Marchand,' he repeated, 'she is, as I understand it, also a *transient* worker here at your club.'

Lomet pressed air through a gap in his front teeth. 'And as I have already told you, I don't keep records.'

Hugo tucked his hair behind his ear, narrowing his eyes. 'Then how do they get paid? How do you pay their taxes? How are they recruited?'

Lomet cocked his head, a sly smile appearing. 'In the same way, Juges and Avocats get paid when they are called upon to produce little pieces of papers I believe you call Mandates.' He winked at Hugo. 'You do know what a Mandate is, don't you, Monsieur Policier?'

'Of course, I do,' Hugo retorted. 'Mais, what I am asking, surely, is not something we need to trouble the legal system with, is it?'

Lomet raised an eyebrow. 'In your opinion perhaps, but mine is different.'

Hugo nodded and turned away. 'Tres bien. I'll speak to my colleagues in the 7e arrondissement and have them arrange a Mandate for your personnel records,' he paused, 'and any other records they might consider pertinent in the investigation.'

'What are you talking about?' Lomet snapped, his voice rising sharply.

Hugo met his gaze, there was no mistaking the

tremble in his voice. 'We are dealing with a missing person, and an unexplained death, and therefore we must explore all avenues.'

Michel Lomet studied Hugo with interest like he was sizing him up. He smiled again. 'Then you must do what you must do,' he said.

Hugo met his gaze. 'I will…'

'Only,' Lomet interrupted, 'I wouldn't have too much hope of actually getting a Mandate.'

'Oh?' Hugo questioned, an eyebrow rising.

'My clientele is a very select group of men and women. Important people who do not tolerate invasion of privacy, and they will ensure the investigation goes no further. After all, why should it? All we are talking about is events which are of no concern to decent, respectable people.'

Before he could respond, Ben grabbed Hugo's arm. 'Let's get out of here, cheri. This place is making my skin crawl.'

Hugo nodded at Lomet. 'We'll be in touch, Monsieur Lomet.'

Lomet turned away, disappearing into the darkness of the club.

Ben led them into the street and stopped, pressing himself against the railing.

'What is it?' Hugo asked.

Ben pointed towards the club. 'That creep knows more about what happened than he's letting on.'

Hugo nodded. He was fairly certain of it as well. 'Perhaps, but I doubt he will tell us, and I suspect he might be right about the trouble we'll have in getting someone to issue a Mandate. There is something off about him, I agree, but I'm not sure it's enough to get us the help we need.'

Ben shook his head. 'Something off? A young kid doesn't throw himself off the Eiffel Tower for no reason, does he? And it seems as if no-one gives a damn.' He touched Hugo's arm. 'Désolé, cheri, I don't mean you, of course. I just hate the fact some poor kid is lying in a morgue with no-one looking out for him, wanting him back. Wanting to put him to rest. It's all any of us want at the end of the day, isn't it? Someone to care enough to bury us.'

'Of course, Ben,' Hugo replied. 'Remember, we're only seeing a part of the picture. I suspect there's a lot more to this than we know, but the fact is, it isn't my case and I really shouldn't get any more involved than I am.'

Ben pushed the curls from his forehead. 'But you heard Coco. She doesn't mind, and as you said, the local police aren't treating this as anything other than a suicide, so they're not going to waste time and resources on it, are they?' He pushed the curls away again with more force. 'I've never even met this kid, and I don't want him dumped in some damn Potter's Field somewhere. Or worse. Laughed at by some dumb-ass students in med school as he lies naked in front of them on a slab. Believe me, I've seen it happen before and it infuriates my every fucking nerve.'

Hugo touched Ben's hand, turning his head towards the sun. The Police Nationale was stretched enough as it was, and he could understand how cases had to be prioritised, but every instinct in him screamed. Ben was right. The chances were the young man had to have been loved by someone, hopefully, missed by someone. He sighed. 'I guess we're not going home today,' he said reluctantly.

Ben grinned. 'Are you serious? I mean, can you stay? Don't you have stuff to do in Montgenoux?'

'Definitely, always,' he answered, 'but Etienne, Markus and Marianne are there, so it's in good hands and they can always call on the Gendarmes if need be. What about you, aren't you expected back at the hospital?'

Ben shrugged. 'I'm due some time off, and besides, the reason I was so quiet on the train journey was because I was trying to decide.'

'Decide?'

He nodded. 'Yeah. You know I want to do something good with Papa's money, something honourable finally for the Beaupain name. Since I decided to open the youth hostel, it's all I can think about, but I can't figure out how to make it work, not if I stay working at the hospital at least. But being a nurse means so much to me, but having a place, a safe place for young kids, really, *really* seems like something I was meant to do. I've always wanted some good to come out of my whole mess of a childhood, and maybe, just maybe this is the way I can do it. I just need to try to figure out a way to do both and for it not to affect my life with you. Who knows, being away for a few days might clear my head, and if it helps find peace for this poor kid, then so much the better.'

Hugo lowered his head and kissed his husband. 'Then I guess we're staying.'

Commander Mordecai Stanic replaced the telephone receiver and pressed his body back into his chair, his mouth twisting into a mischievous smile. His hand slid the tie from around his neck. He pulled a notepad to him and scribbled, *Got him.* He pushed it away.

'Why are you looking so pleased with yourself?'

His eyes widened in surprise before his face tightened in irritation when he saw it was Coco Brunhild standing in his doorway. What was she even wearing? A black pantsuit dotted with small daisies, frizzy blue hair cascading over her shoulders. There were days, most days in fact, when he wondered what had ever possessed him to sleep with her, but he had, more than once, and it had resulted in two children. He was pleased despite it all; the children seemingly inheriting his looks, not hers. Having her back in the Commissariat was a mistake, he was sure, but it was the only choice he had. Nobody else wanted her and the child support was killing him. He scratched his cheek, his finger scraping across a five-inch scar, a reminder of his days in uniform when he had run into a drugged-up rapist. The scar had devastated him at the time, but in hindsight, the high profile arrest and injury had probably ended up being responsible for his fast-track promotion.

'What do you want, Captain?' he snapped.

'Who were you talking to?' Coco asked.

He glanced at the telephone and smiled again. He

had waited a long time to get revenge on Jean Lenoir but finally the pieces seemed to be falling into place and all because he had met a like-minded individual who appeared to hate the Minister of Justice as much as he did. He wondered what Jean Lenoir had done to piss off Pierre Duchamp, but he found whatever the reason, he was grateful he had. Duchamp had intimated, once they were free of Lenoir he would ensure Mordecai receive the promotion he deserved.

'Morty?'

'Dammit, Charlotte,' the Commander hissed, 'how many times have I told you, when we are at work, it is Commander, always Commander, comprende? And who I talk to in my office, behind a closed door, is none of your business.'

Coco shrugged her shoulders. 'Suit yourself,' she huffed. 'I just came in to say I was heading home.'

He looked at his watch. 'It's four o'clock,' he snipped.

She shrugged again. 'The babysitter just called claiming she's sick, again.' She stared at him, lip twisted. 'I could ask the *father* to help look after *his* kids, but I expect he'd say he was too busy making secret telephone calls…'

Mordecai was about to respond but thought better of it. He waved his hand dismissively, saying nothing.

Cedric appeared in the doorway. 'Captain,' he blurted, 'I just took a call from *Caron Auberge de Jeunesse*. It's a youth hostel downtown, and the owner said he recognised the photograph of the kid.'

Coco looked at him in surprise. 'The kid from the Tower? What the hell took him so long?'

Cedric shrugged. 'He said he doesn't have time to watch TV or read newspapers and he only saw it at all because he saw someone reading the newspaper on the metro.'

Mordecai flicked his fingers. 'Go, go,' he said quickly.

'But...' Coco began.

'I'll take care of the... I'll take care of it. Find out who the kid was and what he had to do with Jean Lenoir, that's your priority. Don't get bogged down in bullshit. Find me the link between this child-whore and Jean-fucking-Lenoir, d'accord?'

Coco stared at the Commander, realising there was no point in asking him again why he was so determined to make an issue out of the suicide because he had made it clear he would not discuss it with her. She nodded her assent.

Coco stubbed her cigarette out on the sidewalk and moved towards the taxi which was pulling up. She waved at Hugo and Ben as they climbed out.

'Who the f…' Cedric said.

Coco turned around. 'Captain Duchamp, may I present Lieutenant Cedric Degarmo. Cedric, this is Captain Duchamp from Montgenoux Police Nationale and his husband, Ben Beaupain.'

Hugo stepped forward and held out his hand. 'It's a pleasure to meet you, Lieutenant.' He frowned. 'Ah, I see, Cedric, you're the father of…'

A flash of irritation appeared on Cedric's face. Coco snorted. 'Oh, this Cedric isn't the father of my Cedric.'

Hugo scratched his jaw in confusion, struggling to think of something to say. Coco reached forward and touched his arm. 'Don't worry, it's very confusing. Nine years ago we were on a routine op and ended up chasing a perp. I guess I jiggled the baby loose and out he came, right there on the floor of a filthy warehouse. Of course, the Pompiers were stuck in a damn traffic jam, so it fell to the Lieutenant here to do the heavy lifting.' She patted Cedric on the back. 'In hindsight, it seemed fitting since he had just had his hand up my birth canal that I honour him by naming the bubba after him.'

Cedric's cheeks flushed. He cleared his throat. 'What the hell are Montgenoux Police doing in Paris?' he asked, quickly changing the subject.

Coco flashed him an amused smile. 'Captain Duchamp is running a dual investigation,' she answered.

Hugo shot her a look which clearly said, *I am?*

Cedric frowned. 'What do you mean, a dual investigation? Into a suicide? And why is this the first time I'm hearing about it?'

Coco pursed her lips. 'Because it is on a need to know basis.' She tapped the side of her nose. 'And the need to know is above your pay grade.' She paused. 'And mine, for that matter,' she added with emphasis, tapping her nose again.

Cedric gave Hugo a suspicious look and then pushed back his shoulders. He shook Hugo's hand. 'It's a pleasure to meet you, Captain, and your... and you Monsieur,' he added moving towards Ben and shaking his hand.

Hugo turned to Coco. 'Captain Brunhild, you said something about an identification when you called?'

She nodded. 'Oui. Somebody from the hostel called, I figured it best I call you rather than relay the information later.' She smiled. 'In the interest of full co-operation, of course. Have you spoken to Jean Lenoir?'

Hugo flashed an unsure look in Cedric's direction. 'As I said,' Coco interjected, 'Cedric has seen my vagina, so I'd say I can trust him with my secrets.'

'Will you stop saying that!' Cedric wailed. He waved his hand in an exasperated fashion. 'She told the frites stall owner the other day because for some reason he *really* needed to know.'

Ben laughed. 'Coco, you are terrible.'

Hugo smiled and then nodded. 'Oui, I spoke to Jean Lenoir.' He paused, wondering whether he should relay the conversation to Coco and Cedric. He knew Jean Lenoir would not want him to, would actively forbid him too, but the fact remained Hugo was acting unofficially and if he was to expect Coco's help he knew he had to reciprocate. And besides, if what the Minister had told him was the truth then he had nothing to fear. He cleared his throat and relayed the brief conversation he had with Jean Lenoir.

'Why didn't the creep tell us that?' Cedric grumbled.

'You know why,' Coco answered, 'and the truth is I can't say I blame him. He knows he wouldn't be treated impartially.' She looked squarely at Hugo. 'And do you still believe Lenoir is innocent?'

Hugo laughed. 'Now, that's a loaded question!' He considered. 'I can't say I believe he is completely innocent, non, but not in the sense he may have done something illegal, rather just he might know something, or is worried about something, which he chooses not to share. But as I keep saying, we keep coming back to the same fact. There is no murder and I'm not even sure we could even truly describe Delphine Marchand as missing.'

Coco shook her head. 'But something, *someone* drove the kid to throw himself off the Eiffel Tower and for the girl to hightail it out of there. And then there's Dubois.

Something is making people flee Paris like there is a zombie apocalypse.'

Hugo nodded. 'I agree, and I expect the reasons for it are something we may never truly discover. There are secrets buried in *énergique*, and they are probably what Jean is truly worried about, how they might affect his political aspirations. There is something he wasn't telling me, I'm almost certain of it. But the chances are the two may not even be connected. He's a complicated man, and he's privy to information which we can't, probably shouldn't know. We can't necessarily attribute his silence to be anything other than national security.'

Coco pursed her lips. 'I don't care about any of those bastards, I just want to find who this child belongs to.'

Hugo lowered his head. 'I agree.' He turned his head towards the hostel. It was a vast tenement building which was the length of a block, lined with thin windows covered in bars giving it the appearance of a prison. 'Shall we go in?' Hugo asked, not sure Caron Auberge de Jeunesse looked particularly safe or inviting.

Ben stepped onto the sidewalk, his attention diverted to a huddle of teenagers standing near the entrance to a park. 'I'll wait out here,' he said, 'and see if those kids might be more willing to talk to someone who isn't a flic.' He shrugged before adding with a dry a laugh. 'You never know, I may still have a bit of street cred.'

Hugo nodded, fighting the urge to add, *be careful.*

Instead, he fell into step behind Coco and Cedric as they made their way up the staircase to the hostel. He stopped in front of a wide metal sign above the doorway.

être perdu c'est être trouvé

To be lost is to be found. He noticed a bunch of daisies on the windowsill and smiled. Such a simple gesture against the sign and a sudden sense of warmth enveloped him. Amongst the dirty tiles, cigarette stubs on the ground, discarded wrappers, there was somebody here, somebody who seemed to care about those who walked through the door. It made him even sadder to consider they were there to find out about one resident who had been so dissatisfied with his life he had seemingly chosen to end it in such a violent way. He stared again at the daisies and exhaled when a single petal dropped to the ground because it filled him with a sadness he did not understand.

'His name was Marc Gassna, *possibly*.'

Coco scribbled down the name, her eyes widening with interest. 'Possibly?'

Dr. Victor Caron entwined his long fingers, stretching them in front of him. He gave a slow, exaggerated shrug. He was a slight man, dressed in what appeared to Hugo to be an expensive pinstriped suit. His hair was swept high and peppered with silver streaks which Hugo felt sure were not natural, but there was something about his face which Hugo thought made him appear kind. His eyes were grey, and wide, dulled with apparent sadness. Tight, tired lines creased his mouth and eyes. To Hugo, Victor Caron appeared to be a man who had seen a lot of the dark side of life.

Dr. Caron sighed. 'Unfortunately Captain Brunhild, many of our charges use fake names.'

'Charges?' Cedric interrupted, the tone of his voice cold, spiked with an unusual irritation.

Hugo watched as the doctor turned his head slowly towards the young detective and how he stared at Caron with something Hugo could not read - not pity, not anger, but something else. Distrust, perhaps?

'What kind of hostel is this, Dr. Caron?' Hugo asked, with interest.

Dr. Caron turned to him, interested eyes flicking over Hugo's face in a way which always made Hugo feel uncomfortable. He did not enjoy feeling as if he was being 'read' because he always assumed the reader would be disappointed. Dr. Caron smiled. 'It is a very good one.'

Hugo raised an eyebrow, there was something about the response which troubled him. He supposed the doctor was used to his work being frowned upon. People who looked after those on the fringes of society were often expected to do so with minimum assistance, but were expected to produce maximum results. He smiled at the doctor, hoping the smile would send the message Hugo was not the sort of man who judged. 'I'm sure it is, Dr. Caron' he offered weakly, not sure exactly why he had offended him.

Dr. Caron smiled at him. 'S'il vous plaît, my name is Victor and I find using my first name more beneficial than being called Dr. Caron. My customers here are often not capable of trust.'

'Capable?' Coco asked, surprised.

He nodded. 'We are not state-sponsored,' he replied, 'our social workers are trained but not officious. It is a new way of looking at the social problem of the disengaged, dislodged, disfranchised millennials. They come by many new names, but their problems are truly anything but new. Our children-future-adults need to walk the path to adulthood without a man, a woman, a doctor in clothes they could never afford, staring down their noses at them, telling them HOW to do it, just because they believe they know better because they have degrees and letters after their names. That is what this hostel is about, we dare to be different. A hostel by name, but a refuge by nature. We extend our hearts, and the children who enter know it. This is a safe place. Many of our guests are on the run. Running from abuse in one form or another, whether it be from a parent, a pimp, a partner, or sometimes even themselves. We are a sanctuary for the displaced.'

Hugo nodded, his attention drawn to a set of leaflets on the corner of Dr. Caron's desk. He did not have his glasses on, but he felt sure the words would read the same. He focused on a framed photograph behind Caron on a filing cabinet. It contained a group of men, one of which, a white-haired man with a hooked nose and pock-marked skin wearing a cassock. 'You work in conjunction with the Catholic Church?' Hugo asked.

Caron's eyes widened in a way which puzzled Hugo because they appeared to flash with guilt. Caron glanced over his shoulder and the photograph, his jaw tightening with irritation. He attempted a smile, but it appeared off-hand and fake. 'Monseigneur Augustine Demaral is a close, personal and very dear friend,' he offered by way of an answer.

Hugo nodded. 'And he is part of Caron Auberge de Jeunesse?'

Victor Caron linked his fingers together again, stretching them, the loud clicking of bones making Hugo wince. 'The Monseigneur has worked tirelessly for decades tending to his flock,' Caron replied. 'And continues to do so.'

Hugo cast a quick look at Coco. She shrugged. Hugo leaned forward, studying Caron's face, wondering what it was he was holding back. Caron sighed. 'The Monseigneur offers advice, nothing more.'

'You seem irritated, Dr. Caron,' Coco interrupted. 'Why is that?'

'Because,' Caron snapped back, 'I suspect you are trying to read something into nothing, as is so often the case.' He looked again at the picture. 'The righteous are always persecuted.'

Hugo frowned. 'I'm sorry, Dr. Caron, I don't understand what you mean.'

Caron sighed again. 'The Catholic Church has garnered a certain reputation, in part from the inclusion of bad seeds, but also in part by the dissemination of false information. In these days of technology and instant gratification the Church still wants to do good, but to be seen doing good is often mistrusted and misinterpreted.'

'For damn good reason, if you ask me,' Cedric muttered.

Caron shot the young Lieutenant a hateful look before continuing. 'To further the good work of the many good Catholics, it has become necessary to be creative.'

Hugo nodded. 'So, the Catholic Church is involved in Caron Auberge de Jeunesse but only in unofficial capacity?'

Caron dipped his head. 'Monseigneur Demaral is a man of vast experience who considers he was put on this earth merely to perform Dieu's bidding. The Vatican is sadly reticent to test public opinion and therefore Church-sponsored hostels are now a thing of the past. However, men such as the Monseigneur have not given up the work they began many decades ago which was spoilt by the actions of the odd man who was a wolf in sheep's clothing. They bowed to public pressure but did not give up their debt of duty and the promise they made to God.'

'What exactly does the Monseigneur do for you then?' Coco asked.

Caron leaned back in his chair. 'He provides spiritual guidance and assistance when needed, nothing more.'

'Assistance?' Hugo interjected.

'Oui, assistance.' He glanced at his watch. 'Is there anything else? I hate to hurry you, but I am a very busy man.'

'Tres bien, Dr. Caron, we'll try not to keep you much longer. About Marc Gassna, what can you tell us about him?' Coco asked.

The doctor paused, tapping a rhythm on the desk with his fingers. 'Not a lot, I'm afraid. Look, when I say we provide a sanctuary, a safe space for these young adults, that's exactly what I mean, safe from outside interference, including our own. We operate a no-question policy. Of course, I am a trained psychologist so I am here to assist should I be needed, but my role is largely administrative these days. We receive little public funding, so a great portion of my time is spent making contacts, trying to secure funding to keep us open.' He laughed. 'Which, believe me, is often incredibly dull having to spend my evenings wining and dining the upper-echelon of Parisian society.'

Hugo leaned forward in the chair and caught Coco's eye. She gave a quick nod to let him know the same thought had occurred to her.

'As it is, we get by on very little, with only a basic

skeleton staff. Along with me, there is only my assistant, three social workers who work part-time, a cleaner and a night shift supervisor and of course Justine,' Dr. Caron continued.

'Justine?' Coco asked.

He smiled. 'One of our great success stories. Several years ago she came to us after living on the streets for some time, prostituting herself and taking drugs. We worked with her, brought her around to our way of thinking, convincing her she was worth saving. After several months she emerged from her cocoon to become the adult she was always meant to be. It was only natural she should stay such is her investment in helping other young people like her. She greets each of them and gains their trust. They know they are safe here in no small part thanks to her. We pay her very little and she lives on the premises, but her devotion knows no bounds. We would simply be lost without her.'

'Is she likely to have known Marc Gassna?' Hugo asked.

He nodded. 'If anyone is likely to have, it is she. She will have booked him in and assisted him if she thought he needed it.'

'Is there anything you can tell us about Marc? Any thoughts you may have had concerning him?' Hugo asked.

'As I said, I only know what they allow me to know. When I saw the photograph on the front of the newspaper I recognised Marc instantly, although my first thought was surprise,' the doctor replied.

'Surprise?' Cedric interjected.

'Oui, surprise he took his own life. During my interactions with young Monsieur Gassna, I recall thinking despite it all, the young man was hopeful.'

'Hopeful?' Hugo questioned, 'and despite what?'

Dr. Caron shrugged. 'There is no telling the trauma inflicted on these young people and mostly they don't, *can't* talk about it. Each day is a test, and the best we can do for them is to let them know they are at least safe here.'

Hugo studied the doctor intently for signs of sincerity, or otherwise, but he was having trouble reading him. It was almost as if he was too practised, too polished and well versed, which Hugo supposed he had to be. He needed to be in order to make the hostel sustainable. It did not appear to Hugo he was lying. 'You said Marc Gassna was hopeful?'

The doctor nodded. 'I believe so, often here you see young people with the weight of the world on their shoulders, but I did not necessarily get that impression from him.'

'And did he have friends?' Coco asked. 'Or family?'

'Perhaps, although you'll need to speak to Justine if she was aware of any friends.' He reached forward and pulled a piece of paper from a folder and handed it to Coco. 'Here is his admission form.'

Hugo flicked on his glasses and peered over his shoulder. The paper was Marc Gassna's admission form, and other than his name and date of birth there was little else. 'Aren't they required to fill in a next of kin form?' Hugo asked.

'Requested and required are two very different things,' he answered. 'And oui, they are requested but they rarely want their next of kin to know where they are because it is them they are running from.'

'At least there's a date of birth,' Cedric said.

'If it's even real,' Coco replied, 'all the same, ring the Commissariat and have someone check birth records.'

Cedric stood up and took the paper, leaving the room.

'What about a young woman called Delphine Marchand?' Hugo asked. 'Is her name familiar to you?'

'What about her?' Victor responded quickly. Too quickly, Hugo thought.

'Did you know her? Has she stayed here, perhaps along with Marc?'

'I don't believe so, maybe,' he replied. 'Again, if anyone might know about Marc and his friends, then it will be Justine.'

Hugo nodded. 'Is there anything else you can tell us, doctor?' Hugo asked.

Dr. Victor Caron shook his head.

'Do you recall the last time you saw Marc?' Coco asked as she stood up.

He considered. 'I'd say earlier in the week, but I couldn't be certain, perhaps Justine can give you a more accurate idea.' He shook his head as he picked an errant hair from his blazer. 'Such a terrible tragedy, and a waste of a young life.'

Ben made his way across the pavement, pushing the curls off his forehead. He pulled his pack of cigarettes out of his pocket. 'Anyone got a light?' he asked the group of youths gathered outside the hostel, holding out the pack to share. The group stopped their conversations, turning and fixing him with intense, untrusting stares before scattering in opposite directions. He watched them wide-eyed, smiling to himself. 'Something I said?'

'They make it their business not to trust any oldies,' a breathy young woman's voice called out from the shadows.

Ben spun on his heels. 'Oldies?' he said with incredulity before shaking his head. 'Mon Dieu, I turned thirty this year, and you're right, when I was their age, I thought thirty was old too.' He shook his head again in disbelief, curls bouncing on his forehead, crystal eyes shining mischievously. 'Damn, I AM old.'

The woman laughed, stepping out of the shadows. 'You don't look so bad for such an old man,' she replied with a chuckle.

Ben smiled at her as she appeared in the sunlight. He guessed she was not much older than the others, but she appeared much different, dressed from head to foot in black, with matching hair and makeup. Her face was deathly pale, covered in white, gothic make-up. 'I suddenly feel very old,' he conceded.

'Are you a cop too?' she asked.

Ben shook his head. 'Non, but I am married to one of them.'

She raised an eyebrow. 'The weird looking one with blue hair?'

He smiled. 'Non, the cute one with blond hair and glasses.'

'Damn,' she muttered, 'the cute ones are always gay.' She stepped forward. 'Je m'appelle Justine Le Contre, I work at the hostel.'

'Ah,' Ben replied, 'did you know the boy who died?'

She nodded. 'Marc, yeah, sure. He was a cool kid. It's kinda fucked up he killed himself.'

Ben turned towards the hostel, wrestling with the thought of whether he should continue but he realised she might be more willing to talk to him than she would to Hugo, Coco and Cedric.

'It's a shame nobody has come forward,' Ben said cautiously, 'it would be awful if he lay in the morgue with no one claiming him, laying him to rest.'

Justine's eyes flashed in his direction telling him all he needed to know but she said nothing. He took a tentative step towards her. 'The police only want to do the right thing for Marc, Mademoiselle Le Contre.'

'And you think reuniting him with his parents is the right thing?' she snapped back.

'Isn't it?' Ben countered.

'Not of all us had the sort of parents worth reuniting with, Monsieur,' she said matter-of-factly.

Ben did not reply, because he could not help but agree. He exhaled. 'It's my own experience if you don't get the love you need from those who should give it freely, then you look elsewhere, in one way or another, in any way which makes sense to you. I'm not judging, believe me, I'm not, because I do understand. I just want to be sure that there isn't someone waiting for him, hoping he'll come back.'

Justine moved closer to him, her eyes flicking over him as if appraising him for sincerity. 'You were a runaway?' she softly asked.

He shook his head. 'Non, my journey was not as bad as many others, I'm very aware of that fact. I had love from one parent and it was enough to sustain me.' He paused, closing his eyes. 'I can't imagine what I would have done without my mother.' He opened them and stared at the hostel. 'But I guess I would have sought out somewhere like this.'

Justine followed his gaze. She opened her mouth and began to speak but stopped herself, instead dropping her jaw towards the ground. She kicked a can with her foot, stubbing her toe against the pavement. Ben watched her carefully but did not speak. She lifted her head and stared at the hostel, and Ben thought if it was even possible her paleness had intensified. 'Is there something wrong, Mademoiselle?'

She shook her head quickly. 'Non, of course not.'

Ben nodded, keen not to push her further. He

remained quiet, hoping she would speak.

'Why are you here?' she asked.

'I told you,' he answered, 'but if I'm honest, the truth is I don't know. It's a long story, but we're only really in Paris because Hugo, mon mari, was coerced into it. But since arriving, and the longer I'm here, the more I feel for some kid I never even met. Feel such heartache for someone killing himself in such a way.' He looked down the road as if realising something for the first time. 'I guess I feel guilty, guilty for the amazing life I have now, and guilty because my path could have been very different.' He shook his head. 'I don't expect you to understand because I don't really understand it myself, but if I can help this young man rest in peace, then I want to. I NEED to.' He turned back to her. 'You can trust me, and I realise those are just words you've probably heard a million times before, sometimes by people who don't mean it, but for what it's worth, I do.'

Justine dropped onto the sidewalk, her knees folding together. 'Do you have a cigarette?' she asked.

Ben nodded and pulled two out of his pocket and lit them. He handed one to her. 'I keep telling Hugo how bad a habit this is, but there's no denying how things sometimes look better through the smoke.'

She laughed. 'You're weird.'

Ben also laughed. 'I'll take that, I'd much rather be weird than the alternative.'

Justine sucked on the cigarette before spluttering a

plume of smoke into the air. She stubbed the cigarette out irritably. 'I came to this hostel because the alternative was far worse,' she said, 'and I stayed because I wanted to make sure there was always someone here, someone who didn't have an agenda.'

'An agenda?'

'Yeah. When you're an adult, you only do what you think is best for you. Sure, I know you're probably a good guy, but by helping others you're helping yourself to feel better or whatever. When I stayed at the hostel, I wanted to do it for the others who came after me, not for myself because there's nothing I need, nothing I want from anyone else. That's what hitting rock-bottom means, Monsieur, you just want to stop anyone else from getting there. But if they do, you want to help catch them and push them back up - no strings, no agenda.'

'And the people who run the hostel think otherwise?' Ben asked.

She shrugged. 'Everyone has agendas, budgets, that sort of crap and adults get caught up in the shit of life. The stench of sex, of drugs, of power, and once they get a taste of it, they'll do anything, to anyone, to keep it.'

Ben studied her carefully, wondering what it was she was getting at, but he did not want to push her.

She stared at him. 'And those sorts of people, powerful people, rich bastards, will do anything to keep what they have. *Anything.*'

Ben sat next to her, his eyes wide with concern.

'What happened to Marc, Justine?'

She played with a strand of her hair, pulling it to her mouth. 'I don't know. Do you think if I had known he was so close to the edge I wouldn't have done something? The truth is, I didn't see them much, but they seemed...' she searched for the word and then shrugged her shoulders, 'all right.'

'They?' Ben asked quickly.

She flashed him an irritated look before nodding. 'Oui. He was usually with a girl, sometimes others, but usually just him and a girl.'

'A girl,' Ben repeated, 'and this girl, have you seen her since Marc died?'

'Non,' Justine answered, 'I haven't seen either of them since the weekend, but that's not unusual. You have to understand, people only come here as a last resort - when they're broke, or beaten, or worn-down, or want to feel safe,' she paused before adding, '*safer*. I guessed Marc and Delphine were on the game, but it didn't matter, they always seemed to be together so I figured they were looking out for each other, that's why these kids usually travel in pairs. One takes care of business and the other keeps watch.'

Delphine. Ben's eyes widened when Justine spoke the name. It was surely too much of a coincidence for there to be two Delphine's. His brain was buzzing at the realisation Delphine was probably the same young woman eating dinner at the Eiffel Tower with Jean Lenoir at the time her friend was falling to his death. Which suggested to him, Marc was probably there to keep an eye on her. Or vice versa.

'And you're sure you haven't seen Delphine since...'

Justine nodded again. 'I'm sure. You don't think... you don't think something happened to her as well, do you?'

I hope not, Ben thought. 'I'm sure she's fine,' he answered, 'as you said, they didn't always come to the hostel. She may be working somewhere; she may not even know what happened,' he added weakly, not sure what to believe himself.

Justine stood up. 'My break's over, I'd better get back before I'm missed.'

Ben smiled at her. 'Merci for talking to me,' he reached into his bag and scribbled down his number. 'Here's my cell phone. Please call me if you think of anything, or if you need to talk or something, d'accord?'

She stared reluctantly at the piece of paper before taking it and walking away. She stopped by the door and turned back to him, her lips twisted in contemplation. Ben could tell she was thinking whether to trust him with something else. He met her eyes and did his best to relay his true intentions. 'You're not the first person to come looking for them this week, you know,' she said finally.

'Really?' he asked. 'Who else has been?'

She shrugged. 'I hadn't seen him before. He said his name was Axel. I guessed he was a friend, same sort of age, maybe a little younger, but he looked worried, very worried. I asked him to leave a number, and I'd call if saw Marc or Delphine, but he wouldn't. I didn't push it, because under the same circumstances I probably wouldn't have given out my number either to a stranger. I probably wouldn't have trusted me either.'

Ben nodded. 'If he comes back, would you call me? We can meet somewhere else, somewhere in the open.'

Justine tucked the paper in her pocket, nodded at him and ran into the hostel. The door slammed behind a row of fallen leaves, rising and falling, disturbed by the sudden gust of wind. Ben shivered.

Ben relayed his conversation with Justine Le Contre to Hugo and Coco.

'It can't be a coincidence that Marc's friend and Jean Lenoir's dinner companion were both called Delphine,' Hugo said, 'and that they were both on the Eiffel Tower at the same time.'

Coco turned to Hugo. 'Do you still believe Jean Lenoir knows nothing?'

Hugo considered. 'I don't know what to believe. I mean, as I said, I don't think he's telling me everything, but I'm still not sure we can read too much into it. The Minister is a very private man, and I don't believe he asked me to come to Paris to cover for him. Therefore, I have to believe it's because he is innocent and whatever it is he isn't telling us, it's because he either can't, or it's irrelevant.'

Coco pursed her lips. 'Maybe, I mean, it could be all one giant coincidence. Marc Gassna and his pal travel together when one of them has a, *ahem*, "date" to watch out for one another. But why then would Marc choose that moment to end it all? That's the part I don't get.'

'We still don't know for certain he did,' Ben replied, 'you've both got to know there are many ways to murder somebody and make it look like an accident.'

Coco glanced at her watch and tutted irritably.

'You have to be somewhere?' Hugo asked.

'I have to be twelve different places and no staff to

help, and as much as I hate to say it, this case is taking too long.' She reached into her bag, pulling out her cell phone. 'I hate doing this, but I can't pussyfoot around Jean Lenoir anymore.' She pressed a button. 'Mordecai? It's Coco. Can you call a Juge, or the Special Counsel, or whoever the hell can get us access to the Minister of Justice? Oui, something has come up. It's a little tentative, but we may have a link between the dead boy and the girl Jean was having dinner with, and as far as we can tell, she is missing too. D'accord, let me know.' She dropped the telephone back into her pocket. 'He sounded far too happy for my liking. I don't enjoy making Morty happy. I usually end up pregnant when I do.'

'Jean Lenoir will not be happy,' Hugo said, changing the subject.

'Tough,' Ben replied, 'and Coco's right. The fact Delphine is missing is more important than his pride. We need to know she's okay because the chances are she may not be, and I'll be so angry if he could have opened his mouth to save her.'

Coco grimaced. 'Don't say that, Ben.'

Cedric appeared from the shadows, tucking his cell phone into his pocket. He handed Coco a piece of a paper. 'The date of birth was real, here's the address. As far as I can tell it belongs to his parents. There's been no missing person report filed though.'

Coco squinted as she read it. 'Phew, I know the district. You can't buy a house there for less than five million euros.'

'At least,' Cedric replied, 'so if he's rich, what the fuck's the kid doing selling himself on the streets?'

Coco began walking towards her car. 'Since when was turning tricks a job only for the disenfranchised? Drain the swamp and you'll find quite a few trust fund kids who have been cast adrift.' She stopped, biting her lip and looking slyly at Ben. 'You coming with me to speak to the parents, Hugo?'

Hugo looked at her. 'Do you want me to?'

She nodded. 'I'd appreciate a second pair of eyes, especially when I ask them why they haven't reported their nineteen-year-old son missing after almost a week and when his photograph has been all over the news.' She turned to the Lieutenant. 'Cedric, head back to the Commissariat. I've asked Commander Stanic to get a Mandate for us to interview Minister Lenoir. When he gets it bring it right to me, and we'll go see old Jean, d'accord?'

Cedric nodded. 'Sure thing, Captain.'

Ben kissed Hugo's cheek. 'I'll see you back at the hotel, cheri. Bon chance.'

dix

Fleur Gassna placed a silver tray on the large ornate table which appeared so old and delicate, Hugo suspected it belonged in a museum. He and Coco had been shown into the large reception room and for a moment he had believed the Gassna home to actually be a museum. He sat perched on the edge of an uncomfortable chaise longue. It reminded him of his Grand-Mère's home, which he realised was probably only a few blocks away, most likely within walking distance. But it was a walk he could not, would not, make. He was not ready to face seeing the house in which he had spent most of his childhood and adolescence. A house filled with secrets and heartache, but with the distant memories of occasional laughter. A house so vast it covered an entire block.

He thought of the side alley which no one but he and the servants ever used. It was there, when he was barely fourteen. He vividly remembered being pushed into the shadows and felt the pressure of another person's lips on his own. Josef Doré. The name smashed against his skull, blown out of a locked, cobweb-covered box hidden deep within his consciousness. Josef, a school friend, had introduced him to something he had previously thought forbidden. A fruit so intoxicating Hugo believed he had tasted nothing so sweet. That day, in that moment, Hugo had known his life had changed direction, and he could never step back into the life his family had created for him. He pushed the thoughts away. He knew the time was

126

coming when he would have to face his past, but it would have to wait. He was not ready to see his father yet. He was not ready to face his past and risk it consuming him once again. It had taken him a long time, too long a time to crawl from that rabbit hole, and he did not want to risk looking over his shoulder.

He watched as Madame Gassna slowly lifted an antique café pot and poured two cups before handing them to Hugo and Coco. Her hand shook as she did so. It was thin and long, pale fingers barely able to hold the jewels which adorned them. She pivoted, engulfing Hugo in a stifling, sweet perfume as she moved swiftly to a chair opposite, smoothing down a Chanel suit as she lowered herself into it. The sunlight caught her face; it was tight and stretched, thin skin pulled across bone. It had left her hazel eyes wide and vulnerable, as if she was on the verge of a panic attack. She was a large woman, too large for the suit she wore and coiffured copper hair framed her face pulled into too tight curls. She folded her hands into her lap, sliding jewelled rings around her fingers. Judging by the size and sparkle of the jewels, Hugo imagined they should be fake but were probably not.

'My husband will be down shortly,' she said, her voice as deep as a man's baritone.

Hugo and Coco exchanged an anxious look, neither of them averse in the art of small talk. It comforted Hugo to note Coco appeared to feel as out of place as he did. 'You have a beautiful home, Madame Gassna,' he offered.

Fleur turned her head slowly as if looking at the room for the first time. 'I do,' she said in such a way it seemed neither an acknowledgment nor an agreement. Her finger trailed along the rim of the café pot. 'This was a gift from a dear friend of ours, Monseigneur Demaral, it came directly from a collection held by the Pope himself. It is quite rare and valuable. We should not use it really, but...' she trailed off as if she was not sure how to finish the thought.

Hugo grimaced, remembering his own café pot back in the Swiss cottage in Montgenoux. Its rim was chipped after it had been knocked over one day when Ben had reached over and surprised Hugo with a kiss. For that reason alone it was valuable to Hugo, and he was not sure what he would do with something so monetarily valuable. He imagined he certainly would not be using it. He dipped his head to show it impressed him.

The door to the room opened with a whoosh of cool air and the man Hugo presumed to be her husband, Corentin Gassna, entered. The stark contrast between the couple immediately struck Hugo. Corentin was as thin as his wife was large, but was dressed in similar fine clothes. His face was heavily lined but his eyes were bright and alert. He stopped in front of Hugo and Coco, throwing a cheque book onto the table.

'What has he done this time?' Corentin Gassna hissed. Unlike his wife, his voice was high and sharp. 'And how much is it going to cost me?'

'Excusez moi?' Coco asked, surprised.

'Marc. What has he done this time?' Corentin snarled.

Coco frowned. 'Monsieur Gassna. My name is Captain Charlotte Brunhild, and this is Captain Hugo Duchamp. Tell me, haven't you read the newspapers or watched television this week?'

Corentin Gassna gave her a quizzical stare. 'I rarely bother with such tripe. Pourquoi?'

Coco reached into her oversized bag and pulled out a newspaper. She unfolded it and placed it carefully on the table. Neither of the Gassna's moved, so she inched it forward. Hugo watched them both intently. Corentin's eyes flicked lazily to the newspaper, his pupils widening, but he said nothing. Fleur gasped, reaching forward and snatching the newspaper up. 'C'est mon enfant,' she cried. The sound, the guttural noise was instantly recognisable to Hugo. It was unique to the situation, and he had heard it too many times, seen the icy breath it produced too many times when a mother, a father, witnessed the face of the child they had borne but had just been told was now gone.

Coco leaned forward. 'Then it is Marc?'

Corentin snatched the newspaper from his wife. 'Are you telling me he was the one who threw himself from the damn Eiffel Tower?'

Hugo looked squarely at Fleur, her fingers entwined around a pearl necklace, clutching them as if they were a Rosary. 'Are you all right, Madame Gassna?' he asked softly.

She nodded but did not speak.

'We are very sorry for your loss,' Hugo said.

Coco cleared her throat. 'When was the last time you saw your son?'

The anxious look exchanged between the Gassna's showed they did not know.

'He came and went,' Corentin answered finally, 'and wouldn't listen to a damn thing we said, never has, not since the day he came.'

'Came?' Hugo interjected, leaning forward sharply.

Fleur nodded. 'Marc only came into our lives nine years ago. We had given up all hope of having a child of our own, and the authorities kept telling us we were too old.' Her voice cracked. 'And there he was, a little child, lost and alone, needing someone to look after him, and there we were, just waiting for someone to look after. It was as if our prayers, had we felt able to make them, had been answered.' She attempted to smile. 'He was the sweetest boy, even though he never spoke, not a single word, for over a year. I just knew he was watching, waiting to see if he could trust us, waiting to be sure we would not let him down, or worse. He had the biggest blue eyes, the whitest white hair I'd ever seen and so innocent. I found it unbelievable anyone could be cruel to him.'

Hugo thought she was talking with utter sincerity, but he could not decide what Corentin's stoic face was saying. He realised, however, just because the father was showing no emotion it did not necessarily mean he was feeling none. He knew how some adults conditioned little boys – instilling in them that showing no emotions was the remit of being a real man. Hugo had been raised that way and the only good thing he thought had come from it was his own distinct ability to completely ignore it.

Coco shook her head, blue hair falling over her face. She pushed it back. 'You adopted, Marc?'

Fleur nodded. 'Oui. We don't know where he came from. Nobody did. He was found you see, hiding out like a homeless person in some awful, rat infested slum and as I said, he didn't speak, not a word and nobody had reported him missing, so until they decided on a name the poor child was known as…'

'*L'enfant perdu,*' Coco interrupted.

Hugo and the Gassna's all turned to her in surprise.

'You are familiar with the case, Captain Brunhild?' Corentin asked.

'*L'enfant perdu,*' Coco repeated, muttering the words under her breath. Her head dropped, and she covered her face with her hands. After a moment she looked up, the colour drained from her face. 'I always thought calling him the lost child was stupid, but some social worker or psychologist thought it would be a good idea, a hook they called it, to sell to the press. Nobody likes someone being lost, they reckoned, and said it would get more attention.' She stood up and walked towards a marble fireplace, her eyes drawn to a silver-framed photograph in the centre.

She picked it up, a blond-haired, blue-eyed teenager stared back at her. She recognised the defiance, the veiled, not-so-subtle bored irritation because it was on every single photograph she had of her own teenagers. 'He finally got a name,' she whispered.

Hugo stood up and moved closer to her, placing a hand gently on her arm. 'Are you all right, Coco?'

She placed the photograph carefully back onto the fireplace and turned back to face the Gassna's. 'How did he end up with you?'

'My husband is on the board of the hospital where he was taken,' Fleur answered, shooting an anxious look towards Corentin. Hugo caught it and wondered what it meant.

Corentin coughed. 'After it became clear nobody was coming forward to claim him, we offered to foster him.'

'From the second Corentin brought Marc home, I'm not ashamed to say part of me hoped his real family never came for him,' Fleur said, 'it was my chance to finally be a mother.'

Then why did it all go wrong? Hugo thought and then chastised himself for it. He had seen enough in his life and career to know often with the best will in the world, sometimes parents and children just could not get on. Sometimes a person is so broken they cannot be fixed, no matter how hard they try.

'How did you know him, Captain Brunhild?'

Corentin asked again.

'I was the one who found him,' she answered. 'Dieu, he was the cutest of things, truly he was, and I'm ashamed to say after that night, I thought little of him. You see, the night we found him in the warehouse, I gave birth myself and well, with a new-born and two older children at home, my plate was full. I always meant to check what happened to him, but...' she trailed off, her head shaking as if she was too ashamed to finish the thought.

Fleur reached to her and touched her arm. 'You found him, that's all that matters. And as I said, despite it all, despite whatever path had led him to being where he was, he came around, and for many years we were happy.' She gave a sad smile. 'We were truly happy.'

'Then what went wrong?' Coco asked quickly before biting her lip, 'désolé, I didn't mean to sound judgemental. Believe me, I have four children of my own, so I know how difficult it can be.'

'It's all right,' Fleur replied hoarsely. 'The truth is, it's hard to pinpoint where it all went wrong. Somewhere around his sixteenth birthday, or what we imagined was his sixteenth birthday. We can't ever be sure of his real date of birth. When we finally adopted him he was given a date of birth, but no-one knows if it was real, least of all him. But it was sometime around his sixteenth birthday that he really changed. He was moody, staying out late, lying, stealing. It was such as shock because it was so out of character. There had been no signs you see, he was quiet, he was serious, always, but there was no malice to him, I'm sure of it.'

Corentin tutted. 'The truth is, we never knew his true character, Fleur, because we did not know where he came from, WHO he came from. It should have come as no surprise he was broken.'

'He was not broken!' Fleur hissed. 'He was just lost. He would have been found again. We would have found him or he would have found his way back to us, just like before, I'm sure of it.'

Hugo was studying Coco and thought she was going to cry. He placed a reassuring hand on her arm again and she looked up and gave a smile as if to say, *I'm okay*.

'When was the last time you saw Marc?' Hugo asked.

'Last weekend,' Fleur answered. 'Saturday afternoon. He said he was going to a party and would be back on Sunday.'

'He always said that,' Corentin grumbled, 'and he never meant it. It was a way to reassure you and make sure he left with cash from me. It was the same scene we had been playing for months. I only tolerated it for you, so you'd stop fretting for a day or two.'

Fleur gave him an imploring look. 'And what do you think we should have done? Lock him up again? You know that never worked. Marc could not be contained.' She turned her head towards Hugo and Coco. 'I always made sure he knew we were here, and that we loved him. I'm afraid it's all I could do for him. I hoped it would be enough, but…'

Coco's mouth twisted. 'That is all any of us can do for our children, Madame Gassna.' She exhaled, her hand pressed against her chest as if she had a pain. 'All any of us can do is to be there and hope they finally realise we are not the antichrist, and that they need us.'

Hugo closed his eyes and pushed away the thoughts invading his head. He knew he could put it off any longer, and he would have to face his own past. He decided to do it that evening before he had a chance to turn around and return to Montgenoux.

'Did he really throw himself off the Eiffel Tower?' Fleur asked.

'We believe so,' Hugo answered, 'but we know little of the circumstances, I'm afraid.'

Fleur shook her head in disbelief. 'I just don't understand why he would do such a thing.'

'Because he was broken,' Corentin repeated, 'he was always broken, an accident waiting to happen. Something like this was always going to happen, Fleur. Marc was never going to have a happy ending. I knew it. You just chose not to see it yourself.'

Nobody spoke as each of them wrestled with their own thoughts. Hugo had not heard of the case of the lost boy. 'And they never found where he came from?' he asked.

Coco shook her head. 'Non. There were no missing child reports to match him with, not in France nor when we extended the search worldwide. That's not to say he wasn't from some country far away where there was no documentation, or missing person reports, but as far as we could tell, he just appeared in Paris that day and nobody knew why.' She turned back to the Gassna's. 'And he never spoke of his life before you?'

Fleur shook his head. 'Non, and we tried in those early days. We had one psychologist after another talk to him, try to coax it out of him, but they said whatever was in there was so far buried it was probably best not retrieved.'

That does not mean he did not remember, Hugo thought to himself. *Or that he was not still running from it.*

'What can you tell us about his friends?' Coco asked.

'Friends?' Corentin snipped, 'bunch of deadbeats no doubt.'

'Do you recall seeing him with a girl, a redhead perhaps?' Hugo asked.

Fleur tilted her head in contemplation. 'Now you mention it, there was one day when I looked out of the window as he left and there was a girl waiting for him by the railings next to the park over the street. I remember thinking how pretty she was and hoping it was his girlfriend. He'd been so moody and withdrawn for a long time and when he saw her he smiled, the sort of smile you gave to someone you care about very deeply. It made me sad for us, but at the same time so pleased for him. And oui, I believe she had red hair, shiny red hair cut into a straight bob.'

'Is there anything else you can think of which might help us?' Coco asked.

Fleur shook her head. 'I don't believe so, I wish there was.'

'Could we see his room?' Coco asked. 'And then perhaps one of you could come with me to the morgue, I'm afraid I have to ask you to formally identify him.'

'I will do that,' Corentin blurted.

Fleur stood up. 'I'll show you to his room.'

The first thing which occurred to Hugo was how different Marc Gassna's bedroom was compared to Baptiste Beaupain's bedroom, the young man Hugo and Ben had adopted. Their own lost boy. On most days Baptiste's bedroom almost appeared as if a bomb had hit it, with clothes strewn all over the floor and plates and cups littering every available surface, growing their own penicillin. The comparison with Marc Gassna's bedroom was stark. It appeared almost clinically clean with no posters on the wall, no personal knick-knacks or any signs a teenager had lived there.

As if reading his thoughts, Coco said. 'Are you sure this is his room? Damn, if you could only see my kids' bedrooms.'

'We have a maid come in once a day,' Fleur replied. 'Corentin believes in keeping a tidy home,' she added matter-of-factly.

Hugo pulled open a drawer. It was empty. He tried another only to find a single, neatly folded t-shirt. A pair of jeans was all there was in a third.

'Didn't he have a computer?' Coco asked.

Fleur shrugged. 'Non, he had a cell phone, isn't that what young people use for everything these days?'

Coco moved towards the bed and lifted the mattress, peering underneath it. 'Clean as a whistle,' she grumbled. She glanced at Hugo. 'What do you think?'

'I don't think we're going to get any answers here,' he said simply. He lowered his voice to prevent Madame Gassna from hearing. 'My son's room tells a thousand different stories, and you just have to look at it to know so much about him.' He turned his head around the sparse room. 'This isn't a room a teenager lived in. He may have slept here, but he didn't *live* here.'

'I agree,' Coco said, stepping into the hallway where Fleur Gassna was anxiously waiting, as if she was afraid to enter the room. 'Merci for your time Madame Gassna, and again, please accept my sincerest condolences for your loss.'

'Oui, c'est Marc,' Corentin Gassna said in a flat tone, much as if he was discussing what he was having for dinner. He turned to Hugo and Coco. 'Did he suffer?'

Hugo faced Marc Gassna for the first time and sucked in a burst of dry, stale air. He had seen the photographs of the autopsy, but there was something about seeing Marc in the flesh for the first time, tidy and dressed, which made it even starker. More desperate and heartbreakingly sad. The young man was dressed in a smart black suit, not the normal attire for a teenager, and the clothes did not quite fit him, not just in size, but in the way they looked on his slight, young body. A body which would never grow to fit such clothes. He would not wear a suit to his wedding, nor to the funeral of a loved one. His suit was for his own funeral.

'Did he suffer?' Corentin Gassna asked again.

Coco's cheeks flushed, and she pulled her attention away from the young man, her eyes watering. She pushed a crinkled tissue over them. 'Non,' she answered, 'the doctors say in cases such as this, they…' she gulped, 'lose consciousness before…' she stopped, the sentence never finished.

Corentin nodded his head quickly, seemingly satisfied with the answer. 'Who do I speak to about making the arrangements?'

Coco pointed to a doorway on the other side of the room. Corentin nodded again to them both and shuffled from the room. Hugo watched him with an intense sadness, realising he had seen far too many people in similar circumstances. It had never gotten easier, it would never get easier, it *should* never get easier. He forced himself to look again at Marc Gassna. Suicide or murder, it did not matter, because something had driven the young man to throw himself from the Eiffel Tower and he wanted to know why.

'He looks like my Julien, doesn't he?' Coco asked, breaking the silence. 'It's not just me, is it?'

Hugo thought of the young man he had met in Coco's kitchen twenty-four hours earlier, shy and awkward, cheeks dashed with the warmth of living blood. As it should be. 'I suppose,' he replied, not knowing what to say. 'So, you really knew him?'

Coco did not answer, instead inching closer to Marc. His eyes were closed, and she reached forward, her head shaking as she brushed against the lids. 'He had the most beautiful eyes.' She slumped into a hard plastic chair, her bag falling at her feet and its contents spilling onto the ground. Hugo immediately dropped to his knees and began putting the assorted odd contents back where they came from. He closed the bag and gently placed it back onto her lap. 'He was a runaway, or so we thought, nobody knew for certain because he never spoke about it. Cedric and I were chasing a perp into an abandoned building and me being pregnant I had to stop. At first, I didn't realise it was a kid hiding in the dark; I thought it was an animal but then I saw those beautiful eyes. Beautiful but terrified, holding onto a teddy bear as if his life depended on it. I suppose to him, it probably did, his only constant in his little life. I'd gone into labour, so my mind was all over the place, but I tried to coax him out, and I did.' She shook her head. 'I'm so ashamed I forgot about him, but with a new baby, and two infants at home, it was just all too much and the truth was, Morty wasn't much use. But I meant to look for him, the young angel, but by the time I came back to work...' She stared at Hugo. 'You must think I'm a terrible person.'

Hugo shook his head. 'I don't. Look, none of us is perfect, but you did your job. You found the child and passed him on to the proper authorities, the people who are trained specialists who know how to look after lost children. You did the right thing, Coco, don't doubt that. The fact is, if we followed up on everyone we encountered in our lives, we wouldn't get a lot else done, would we?' He smiled at her. 'Think of it this way, if you hadn't of found him that night, god only knows what might have happened to him and because of you, he found his way to a new life. I don't know the Gassna's, but I get the impression they cared about him a great deal. Marc seems to have had a good life.'

'Then how did he end up throwing himself off the Eiffel Tower?' she cried.

Hugo bit his lip. 'I don't know, it could be many unrelated reasons. I don't pretend to know a lot about children, but it seems to me their emotions are like rollercoasters. They feel things deeply and in ways we as adults don't. Often it is too much to bear for them and the intensities of those emotions become too much for them. We don't know why Marc Gassna thought death was the only option, but we can try to find out.'

'But how?' she asked desperately. 'I'm up to my eyes in work, and as we keep coming back to, we don't exactly have a lot to go on.'

Hugo smiled. 'I've cracked cases with less, believe me, and I'm sure you have too. And you have help, namely me and Ben. We'll find out what happened to Marc Gassna, trust me.'

douze

Coco could see the anger nestling beneath the surface. Jean Lenoir was evidently struggling to keep his composure, and only barely managing. He pushed the Mandate across his desk with such force it flew towards Cedric, who caught it and placed it back on the desk. Coco suppressed a smile, vaguely amused to see her Lieutenant's usual cockiness had deserted him in the Minister's presence.

'Was this really necessary?'

Well, not if you'd bothered returning a single one of my telephone calls, you steroid-loving, limp-dicked asshole. 'Please accept my apologies, Minister Lenoir,' Coco replied with as much sweetness as she could muster. 'We tried to secure a meeting with you, but were unable to do so, therefore Commander Stanic thought it necessary.'

Jean muttered something incoherent under his breath. 'I am an extremely busy man, Captain Brunhild,' he said finally, 'far too busy to waste my time on such trifling insignificance.'

'A young man is dead, Minister Lenoir.'

'From suicide, Captain Brunhild.'

'A man you met, Minister Lenoir.'

'A hand I shook in a line of hundreds of hands.'

'A prostitute from a club of which you are a member.'

'*Alleged* prostitute.'

'Try telling his ass that.'

143

The exchange was quick, like rapid gunfire as they shot the words between one another.

Jean Lenoir sighed. 'Regarde, Captain Brunhild. I understand you might be under a certain amount of pressure from your... from a man who is so bitter from his own lack of success, he is prepared to risk his career and those of all around him by engaging in a vendetta so preposterous it will disintegrate the careers of anyone who engages in it. I strongly urge you to proceed with caution. I am entirely innocent, and I will remember those who have cast aspersions otherwise and they will pay. Believe me, they will pay.' He narrowed his eyes. 'And if you know anything of me, you know I am a man of my word. Enemies are not something I tolerate.'

Cedric coughed and shuffled uncomfortably in his seat, causing Jean Lenoir to smile. 'But it need not come to that, non? We are all adults, we are all professionals, non?'

'What can you tell me about a young prostitute using the name Delphine?' Coco asked quickly.

Jean's jaw flexed angrily. 'Nothing,' he hissed.

Coco shook her head. 'The reservation for dinner, *your* dinner, was made by a woman calling herself Delphine Marchand, a woman we have also identified as being a close friend of Marc Gassna, the young man who fell from the Eiffel Tower while you enjoyed your hors d'oeuvres.'

Jean did not answer.

Coco leaned forward in her chair. 'Regarde, Minister, I'm not interested in your social life, truly I'm not. Hell, I have enough trouble with my own, so I will level with you. This isn't going away. We both know it should, but until you talk, until you tell us what you know, or what you don't know, then Commander Stanic and the Special Counsel are going to keep circling because that's what they do. They can't stand you, and they want to see you go down. Me? I don't care either way, but I do care about the kid. I want him buried and at peace and to do that I want to be satisfied his death was accidental.' She tapped the desk. 'Listen, I get it. You're a busy man, you're an important man, you don't have time to go out, wine and dine, do the chatter, drop the lines, the things we need to do to get to the goal, you get me? Hell, I'm so over men that if I ever get the urge I might look at alternative ways of meeting them myself. Handsome, clean men whose only aim is to make sure that I, Charlotte Brunhild, is one hundred per cent completely satisfied. So, I get you, Minister. I get you and I promise you there is no judgement here, is there Cedric?' she added, poking the Lieutenant in the ribs.

Cedric lurched forward. 'Non, bien sûr,' he blurted, avoiding eye contact with Jean.

Jean narrowed his eyes angrily towards Coco. 'You're on very thin ice, Captain Brunhild.'

Coco shrugged her shoulders, flicking blue hair from them. 'I'm *always* on thin ice, Minister Lenoir, you of all people should know that. In fact, you once said it was one of the things which make me such an exceptional police officer.'

'I said no such thing, Captain Brunhild,' Jean huffed.

Coco smiled. 'Well, you may have had one or two champagne cocktails, but I thought you sounded sincere...' she paused. 'Écoute, Minister Lenoir. I didn't just say that to blow air up my own ass, I said it because I want you to know, to *understand*, my intentions are based purely on one thing which is to do my job, not railroad you, or make something out of nothing. I don't do politics. I'm a cop. I'm a good one who follows her heart, not her brain, which is why I'm damn lucky to have made it to Captain, but I won't get any further, I know that, so believe me when I tell you, I don't care what you did, as long as there was no crime. I have no interest in embarrassing you, but you know there are those who do and all I can say to you is this. Don't let them. Do not give them the satisfaction.'

'Captain Brunhild, I don't...' Jean Lenoir began. He stopped and shook his head before adding. 'I did nothing wrong.'

Coco nodded. 'I know you didn't. No offence, Jean, but you are as dull as the dishwater still floating in my clogged sink. You're ambitious, you're annoying and pig-headed, but there's one thing you're not, or so I thought.'

Jean stared at her with interest. 'And what is that, pray tell?'

'I don't believe you're stupid,' she replied, 'so quit acting it and giving Morty and Maître Duchamp the ammunition they need to annihilate you. I don't know what the problem either of them have with you is, and I don't care. I have no interest in getting embroiled in that mess, but you're being foolish if you think this is going away.'

Jean leaned back in his chair, his eyes trained firmly on Coco with such intensity she was having trouble holding it. But she did. 'You're wrong about one thing, Captain Brunhild,' he said finally, 'you will go far if I have anything to do with it. You and Captain Duchamp are the only two people in the country who aren't really afraid of me. I saw it the first time I met both of you. Of course, you're intimidated by my position, but I can see in the way you both always hold my gaze, that you are aware I could end your career but the fact is you don't care because you know, as long as you do your job well, then I won't interfere.' He smiled before adding, '*much.*'

'Bien, then talk to me. Tell me what is going on, for the love of Dieu,' Coco said.

He sighed. 'Well, the first thing you have to know is, Delphine's *situation* was irrelevant to me.' He raised his hand. 'Oh, don't look so sceptical,' he said, 'what I mean is, the reason *énergique* gets away with it, is that they do not use prostitutes in the old sense of the word. No money is exchanged, *ever*, merely their job is to entertain, and how they choose to *entertain* is entirely up to them, and they are paid handsomely for it,' he paused, before adding, '*I imagine.*'

'Bullshit,' Cedric muttered under his breath. He lifted his head quickly as if surprised by his own outburst, a flush spreading across his face.

Coco watched Jean carefully. She was not convinced by his explanation or entirely sure young people such as Delphine and Marc Gassna were as in control of their own lives as Jean Lenoir suggested.

Jean glared at him before turning back to Coco. 'You taught your apprentice well, Charlotte, although he does not yet appear to have mastered the muttering under his breath dissent you specialise in.'

Coco spread her hands in front of her and winked at Cedric. 'He is a work in progress, but I have hope.' She stopped, leaning forward in her chair, focusing her intention fully on Jean. 'You were having dinner on the Eiffel Tower on the night Marc Gassna died with Delphine, correct?'

Jean sighed before giving a quick nod of his head.

Coco smiled in appreciation. 'Why the Eiffel Tower?'

The Minister frowned. 'What do you mean?'

'I mean, why choose the Eiffel Tower for your date? It seems an odd choice, that's all. Was it your idea, or Delphine's?'

Jean considered. 'It was Delphine's. We usually dined at *énergique*, which suited me. I thought it odd, but she said she was tired of always being in a dark club, she wanted to go somewhere vibrant. She said she had never been on the Eiffel Tower, so…'

'So the Tower was her suggestion?' Cedric asked.

Jean nodded. 'Oui.'

'And did anything seem odd?' Cedric added.

'In what way?'

'Oh, I don't know, how did the girl seem? Was she anxious, nervous, frightened, maybe? Did it seem as if she was there to meet with someone?'

Jean sighed again. 'I don't know what you're implying Lieutenant Degarmo, but I can tell you as far as I recall it was a perfectly normal dinner.'

Cedric shrugged his shoulders. 'And yet her BFF was also on the Eiffel Tower and soon to take a nasty plunge from it. It can't be a coincidence.'

'I don't know what you want me to tell you. Other than the party at which they took the photograph, I don't think I've ever laid eyes on the dead boy before, and certainly not that night.' Jean said. He tapped his chin, apparently contemplating something. 'The only thing I can tell you is that we had a perfectly pleasant dinner. The conversation was light and unchallenging, which was normal between us.'

'And she never left the table?' Coco asked.

He shook his head. 'Non,' he said.

Coco noticed the slight hesitation. 'What is it?'

Jean tapped his fingers on the desk. 'As you know, I stepped outside at the *time* of the incident to smoke a cigar, when I returned to the table Delphine was not there. Some minutes later she came back, she said she had been to the bathroom…'

'But?'

He shrugged. 'I remember thinking at the time how her hair was mussed as if she had been outside.'

Coco and Cedric exchanged a look. 'And then you left?'

Jean nodded. 'After it became apparent there had been some incident, I thought it prudent to leave, and we did. I offered to have my driver drop her wherever she wished, but Delphine declined and said she had somewhere to be and would take the Metro. And non, I did not care to ask.'

Coco continued making notes. 'And you haven't heard from her since? Have you tried?'

Jean did not answer immediately, still tapping perfectly manicured nails on the desk. 'After I heard what had happened, I tried calling, but her cell phone goes directly to voice mail where it informs me the mailbox is full.'

'I'm going to need her cell number, Minister,' Coco responded.

Jean snorted. 'Captain Brunhild, do you think I don't have access to all the resources you do? And more importantly, I don't have to wait at the back of the queue.' He sighed. 'All I can tell you is, Delphine's cell phone has been switched off since that night and the last recorded position showed it as being in the vicinity of the Eiffel

Tower.' He reached into a drawer, pulled out a folder and handed it to Coco. 'This is everything I have. I also saved you the trouble of running a background check on her. The name she gave me, Delphine Marchand, is most probably a fake, there is no record matching that name.'

Coco tapped the folder. 'Merci beaucoup for this, Minister. I know it can't have been easy for you.'

Jean's jaw tightened. 'I'll tell you what's difficult, Captain Brunhild, and that is watching from the sidelines when those around you, those beneath you, scrabble at your feet in an attempt to tie your shoelaces together and watch you trip.' He smiled. 'I tie my own shoelaces and I will weather this storm and when I do, when I am standing even taller than those beneath me who have attempted to do me harm, I will crush them, make no mistake about it and unless you wish to become collateral damage, I'd suggest you would do well to remember that,' he turned his head towards Cedric, 'and that goes for you too, Lieutenant, and if you'd allow me to give you some advice it is this, remember the most obvious path for career advancement is not necessarily always the best one.' He stopped to answer his telephone as it began ringing. He snapped up the receiver. 'Oui? Oui. Ah, of course it is,' he passed the telephone towards Coco. 'Apparently, your cell phone is switched off and there is a Dr. Bernstein trying to get in urgent contact with you.'

Coco stood up and took the telephone. 'Salut, Sonny, what's up?' She stopped, her eyes flicking in

Cedric's direction. 'Okay, text Cedric the address and we'll be right over.'

Jean watched her with interest. 'Is everything all right, Captain Brunhild?'

Coco pursed her lips. 'I'm not sure. Cedric, we need to go right now. I'll call you later, Hugo.'

Hugo stared at his feet and lifted his shoe to a knee and used his elbow to rub the toe. He cursed when the smudge did not disappear and he was not sure it was not just his imagination, but it appeared to be getting bigger, spreading like a vine across his boots. He jumped at the ping of the elevator doors opening and he dropped his foot, stumbling out.

duchamp & prevost
avocat-affaires.

The sign hit Hugo like a blow to the chest, almost winding him. His eyes locked on the surname. *His* surname. But the letters seemed oddly out of place to him, as if his brain was having trouble arranging them into something he comprehended, like a language he had never seen before. He had stood outside the foyer for forty minutes, smoking cigarette after cigarette until his throat hurt, whilst fighting every instinct he had to turn around, find Ben and return to Montgenoux to the safety of the Swiss-style cottage they shared. To hear Baptiste's loud music, the gentle sound of the lapping pool water, the nearby happy cries of young Bruno Chapeau as he played with his mother. It was all a stark contrast to the clean lines of the law offices he now found himself in. He did not know what to do. He did not know what to say. He wished he had taken up Ben on his offer to accompany him, but for some reason, he did not want Ben to see him and his father together and he was not sure why. Embarrassment? Was he afraid he would show himself up? Get angry? Cry? Vomit? All Hugo knew for certain was, whatever his reaction, Ben would not care as long as he was by his side. But still, Hugo had decided to face his father alone. To look him in the eye and feel whatever emotion came to the surface and to do so, he knew he had to face him alone.

'Can I help you, Monsieur?'

Hugo spun on his heels to face a formidable looking receptionist staring at him with what appeared to be thinly veiled contempt. He looked down at his clothes, and while they may not have been high fashion, they were smart and comfortable. Tan chinos, a blue woollen peacoat, a red-checked shirt and brown leather boots. It was the sort of outfit he wore most days but suddenly, in these offices, they did not seem enough. He cleared his throat. 'I'd like to speak to Monsieur Duchamp, s'il vous plaît.' His voice did not sound like his own.

The receptionist stared at him over her the rim of her glasses, mild-irritation dripping from her. '*Maître* Duchamp is a very busy man I'm afraid. Do you have an appointment?'

Hugo shuffled on his feet, suddenly feeling very faint. 'Non, pardon, I just thought...' he stammered before lowering his head, blond locks falling over his face. It felt comforting to him to have the warmth of his hair and the scent of Ben's custard-apple shampoo. 'My name is Captain Hugo Duchamp,' the words stumbled out.

'Pardon?' she asked.

Hugo exhaled and lifted his head, tucking his hair behind his ears. 'My name is Captain Hugo Duchamp of Montgenoux Police Nationale,' he said with vigour, 'and oui, I would like to speak to *Maître* Duchamp.'

The receptionist opened her mouth to respond, before her lips tightened, her eyebrow arching into an interested peak. Her eyes flicked over Hugo with interest before she stood up. 'Follow me,' she gestured with her hand, leading Hugo along a long hallway. She knocked on an unmarked door. It was only a few seconds, but seemed much longer to Hugo until the silence was broken by a deep voice. 'Entrer.'

The receptionist pushed open the door and walked in, Hugo a few steps behind. 'Maître Duchamp, I have a Captain Duchamp from the Police Nationale who would like to speak with you.' Hugo noted she said it with a faint hint of amusement before stepping back and with the flick of her arm, guiding Hugo fully into the office. She left, closing the door behind her. Hugo stepped forward, his eyes flicking around the office, focusing on the books, the ornaments, anything but the person behind the desk. His eyes locked on a row of photographs, half-wondering but already knowing there would be none of him. He forced himself to look at his father for the first time in what must have been over fifteen years.

Pierre Duchamp smiled. The sort of smile which caused his dark eyes to crinkle and was neither kind nor malicious, rather practised. He pushed himself back in his chair. His hair was as dark as Hugo's was light, thick and black, greying at the temples, swept over a high, lined forehead.

Don't frown that way, Hugo, or else you'll end up with a creased forehead like your papa.

Hugo stepped forward again, noticing the photograph of Madeline Duchamp was between him and his father, just as she had been in life. The formidable mother and grandmother bridging the generations with her own force and strength of will.

'You introduced yourself by your rank,' Pierre Duchamp said. His voice caused Hugo to start. He remembered it, but it seemed alien to him now, like an actor's voice from a movie Hugo had long since forgotten. 'And not as my son,' he added, the admonishment was subtle, but it was there.

Hugo closed his eyes for a second before he spoke, saying a silent prayer to whoever was listening that when he spoke his voice would be even and firm, just as was Pierre's. 'I had assumed they wouldn't know of me,' he said.

Pierre's left eyebrow raised, a slight smile twisting on the mouth Hugo had always been terrified of. 'Well, of course, people know I have a son. Why wouldn't they? It's hardly a secret. Any fool with a computer simply has to

Google the name and become privy to all of your *exploits*. Therefore, of course, I admit to you.'

Hugo did not know how to respond, or even if he wanted to. He shuffled on his feet, glancing down at them. He bit his lip upon noticing the scuffs on his shoes. He looked up, startled to find his father standing in close proximity to him. He stepped back.

'Shouldn't we hug?' Pierre said, the trace of something bordering on sarcasm evident.

Hugo tried his best to hold his gaze. 'Should we?'

Pierre moved closer, placing his hands around Hugo's shoulders. Hugo stumbled back, his whole body tensing. He lifted his arms and stiffly patted Pierre's back.

Pierre laughed. 'You're as stiff as an ironing board child.'

Hugo stumbled yet further back, blood flushing his alabaster cheeks. He turned his head, eyes locking on something else, anything else.

'Has something happened?' Pierre asked quickly.

'What do you mean?' Hugo snapped.

'I mean, why are you here now all of a sudden? You have been in Montgenoux for three years and this is the first I am seeing of you. I assume there must be a reason for it and for your first trip to Paris since your arrival from London.'

Hugo tutted. 'Yet, you seem to know a lot about my life, odd seeing as this is the first time we have spoken in years.'

'I believe they also have telephones, even in a backwater such as Montgenoux, and a postal service, although if they don't, it might explain why I received no invitation to your wedding.'

Hugo sighed. This was not what he had come for. The recriminations between father and son could span a decade and the truth was neither of them would win, and probably neither of them cared enough to try.

Pierre moved closer to Hugo. Hugo stepped back but came into contact with a wall and could move no further. In a second his father was toe to toe with him, standing a good five inches smaller than him and larger in girth than Hugo remembered him. Pierre tilted his head and was studying Hugo with such a burning intensity it made him extremely uncomfortable.

'We have the same shaped face,' Pierre said. 'Isn't that odd? I've never noticed it before, like two pieces of identical bones with skin pulled over them.' He shook his head. 'The eyes are not mine, nor is the nose and certainly not the lips, nor the overlong hair. The feminine comes from your mother, and mon Dieu, you are as pretty as she was.'

Hugo gulped. He did not want to hear his father talking of his mother. He did not even want to think of his mother at that moment. The other side of his abandonment. They were both just pieces on the chessboard of Hugo's life. A chessboard which had been abandoned and was now covered in dust and cobwebs.

'Is that why you hate me? Because I remind you of her?'

'Ta mére?' Pierre asked in surprise. 'Why would I hate either of you? Your mother was, *is*, a very beautiful and charming woman. Fun. Often fun, when used to describe a person it is bordering on being sarcastic, but in Daisy's case it just happens to be true and part of her unique charm. The problem was she was not capable of, and had no interest in assimilating to the life expected here in Paris, so she had to go. It was not her fault, really, merely the way she was born and raised. She knew no better.'

Had to go. The words struck Hugo because it was exactly how he felt. He had never matched up to the image of the Duchamp name, and therefore he had to go.

'Why are you here, Hugo?' Pierre repeated. There was a weariness to his voice, and it occurred to Hugo for the first time perhaps his father was as uncomfortable with the meeting as him.

'Jean Lenoir contacted me,' Hugo said.

Pierre guffawed. 'That's what this is about? Mon Dieu, Jean must be desperate if *you* are his best asset!'

Hugo was not sure which way to take the comment, but he had to admit it was more or less what he thought. 'I've only been here for a day or so but even before I got here I knew Jean was not guilty of any crime. We're not friends, but I know him well enough to know he wouldn't get involved in anything shady. He's far too ambitious for that.' He paused. 'Which can only mean some people are afraid his political aspirations may actually come to fruition and are therefore latching on to a tragedy as leverage to stop him.'

Pierre looked at his son in a way which Hugo could only describe as impressed. 'I have been appointed Special Counsel, oui,' he said, 'but regardless of my personal thoughts concerning Jean, of which I have numerous, my only concern is for the Republic and the fact in which I believe Jean to be wholly unsuitable for the position he covets. He will not, as long as I have breath in my body, become Prime Minister.'

Hugo took in a sharp intake of breath. So that was it. He had suspected the stakes were high.

'You are involved in the investigation?' Pierre asked.

Hugo shrugged. 'Non, merely observing.'

Pierre laughed again. 'You are a Duchamp, Hugo. We don't "merely observe" anything. In this world, there are two types of people. Those who appear to have the power and those who really have the power. Jean is neither, he will always be a useless plebeian.'

Hugo nodded, wondering what it was his father might have against the Minister, before realising there could be many reasons.

'But I am grateful to Jean for one thing,' Pierre said, 'for bringing you to Paris finally. Is Benoit with you?'

Hugo frowned. It felt strange to hear his father speak his husband's name. He gave a curt nod.

'Bien,' Pierre nodded. 'Dinner ce soir the three of us? Have you spoken to your mother?'

Hugo frowned. 'Non, have you?'

Pierre nodded. 'Oui, bien sûr. She came back to Paris for a show last year. We had a few very charming dinners. It is amazing how time and distance can make one forget differences. She is very proud of you and all of the fine work you have been doing in London and Montgenoux. We both are.'

Hugo steadied himself against the wall, his mind whirling with a thousand different thoughts, but it was the taste of anger on his lips which presented itself first. He did not know what to say, or rather, he did not want to say what his thoughts were telling him to say. He wanted to scream; he wanted to rage, but more than anything he wanted to cry. Both of his parents were in Paris and neither of them saw fit, nor held any apparent desire to see him. The thought staggered him. Was he so horrible even a parent would find him unlovable? As he was about to speak, his cell phone began ringing and he found himself overwhelmed with relief for the distraction. He pulled it out of his pocket. 'Oui?'

'Hugo,' Coco Brunhild blurted, 'sorry to bother you, but I thought you'd want to be here. I'm at Champs de Mars at 5 Avenue Anatole, just down from the Eiffel Tower near the river. You'll find it easily enough, just follow the police cars and the tape.'

Hugo was suddenly on high alert. He recognised the

urgency in the Captain's voice because it was something he had used himself many times. Something had happened. Something important which Coco believed had a bearing on the investigation. 'What is it?' he asked.

Coco sighed. 'An hour ago a tourist spotted something in the Seine which she thought was a body. Turns out it was. And there's something about it, something which makes me think there is… a connection with our suicide. Can you come?'

Hugo stared at his father. 'Absolutely. I'm not doing anything important.'

Dr. Shlomo Bernstein watched the River Seine lapping against the slipway and splashing onto his feet. It was tranquil, and it felt calm, but it was not lost on him he had only moments earlier pulled out the remains of a young man whose end had been anything but calm. He turned to face him. His body bloated and purple, hair matted against a gapingly open skull. Shlomo had carefully removed the black tarpaulin which had covered him, discarding the bricks which had been tied to him to weigh him down and his heart had ached when he first saw the wide-open bloated eyes which no longer saw but told a story of their own. He felt he could see the horror in those eyes. The horror the young man must have felt knowing his end was coming.

'Sonny,' Coco Brunhild called out from the dock.

The doctor turned, watching as Coco and Cedric stepped into the taped off area and trudged their way towards him, hands stuffed into pockets and grim, tight expressions on their faces. Coco stopped, pushing a lock of hair from her face and using her other hand to shield the sun from her eyes. Shlomo recognised the look on her face. Playing the tough Captain, making her way in a man's world with a sheer force of will and a determination most men could only hope to achieve. But there were moments, flashes of light which emanated from her eyes at crime scenes where he could see her struggles, the humanity she had to bury to function in a man's world.

'Jesus fucking Christ,' Coco grumbled, pulling on evidence boots with one hand, all the time her eyes locked on the dead body. 'It's another fucking kid,' she hissed.

'Male Caucasian, the same sort of age as our recent suicide,' Sonny murmured in agreement.

Coco stopped next to him, touching his arm lightly. 'You said there were similarities?'

He nodded. 'I'll examine him properly at the morgue and give you a better idea of whether he was sexually active, but there was this.' He reached onto the fold-out evidence table and passed her a sealed plastic bag.

'A condom wrapper?' Cedric asked, peering over Coco's shoulder.

'The same brand of condom,' Coco replied.

'So?' Cedric asked. 'I'm pretty sure if you check my bedside drawer you'd find one of them too.'

'And then there's also this,' Sonny continued passing another evidence bag to Coco. She held it up to study the contents. A gold business card with a red lining and only one word printed on it. *énergique.*

'That damn place again,' she sighed. She stared at Sonny. 'What happened to him?'

Sonny dropped to his haunches next to the body. 'He has been in the water for a while so he's quite badly degraded. It might take me a little while to examine him properly, but here's what I can tell you for sure right now. His death was blunt force trauma to the skull, probably hit with some kind of heavy implement. Heavy enough to take half of it away.' He pointed to the tarpaulin. 'He was wrapped in this, and if you look here, and here, and here, what do you see?'

Coco peered down. 'Scratch marks?'

Sonny lifted the dead man's hand. 'I found scrapings under his fingernails which match the tarpaulin.'

'Merde,' Coco groaned. 'He wasn't dead when he went into the Seine, was he?'

Sonny shook his head. 'I don't believe so, although judging by the wound to his head, even if he had received immediate help, it would still likely to have proved fatal.'

'But still, he wasn't dead when the bastard threw him in.'

Cedric lowered his body, his head moving quickly as he studied the remains. 'He's been in the water for a long time.'

Sonny raised an eyebrow. 'You have a medical degree I wasn't aware of Lieutenant Degarmo?'

Cedric's cheeks flushed. 'Non, it's just…'

Sonny stood up and patted him on the back. 'Only messing with you there, buddy. But you're right. He has been in the water a while and he was weighed down. It looks as if the ropes which were used to tie him were gnawed at by fish and it dislodged him from his resting place. Good job it did, or he may never have floated to the surface.'

'How long are we talking, doc?' Coco asked.

Sonny considered his answer. 'Perhaps a week

judging by the state of the body, probably not much longer than that, I'd say.'

Coco looked at him in surprise. 'A week?'

He nodded. 'Oui. Pourquoi?'

She stared at the young man, a frown creasing her brow. 'Then he was probably murdered before our other boy jumped.'

Cedric whistled. 'Which could explain a lot. Two lovebirds fight, one kills the other and is filled with guilt and remorse and then throws himself off the nearest tall building.' He thumbed behind him where the Eiffel Tower cast an afternoon shadow over the dock where they stood.

'Let's not jump to conclusions, Lieutenant,' Coco admonished. She turned around, her jaw tipped in contemplation, staring at the Tower. 'But you are right about one thing. Too much of a coincidence for my liking.'

'Captain Brunhild,' Hugo called from across the way.

'Hugo,' she smiled, gesticulating, 'come over.' She smiled, watching Hugo pulling on a pair of forensic boots. She noted he was already wearing gloves. 'You carry them with you?'

Hugo gave an embarrassed smile. 'I do,' he laughed, 'you never know when you will need them.'

'Preach,' she agreed.

Hugo stopped just short of the remains, his head shaking slowly. 'They look very similar,' he said.

'Just what we were saying,' Coco replied. 'Hugo, can

I present you to Dr. Shlomo Bernstein? Doc, this is Captain Hugo Duchamp, a colleague.'

Sonny stepped forward and held out his hand. 'Enchanté, Captain. Call me Sonny though, everyone does.'

'Nice to meet you,' Hugo said shaking his hand. He stepped around the body, lowering himself. 'He's been dead a while, hasn't he?'

Sonny joined him. 'Oui, a week, little more.'

Hugo did not answer, his attention locked firmly on the young man's eyes.

'What are you looking at?' Sonny asked.

Hugo lifted himself up, pressing his hand into the crook of his back. 'Désolé, nothing really. I was looking at his eyes. I always look at the eyes first at a crime scene. I know it makes little sense, I mean it's usually obvious they're dead, but I still look as if they will give me some answers and make my job easier.' He shrugged. 'They can't of course. They don't, but I always look. I always hope they'll tell me at the very least, their suffering was brief.' He gave the doctor a sad smile. 'I know it sounds strange, but it is what it is.'

Sonny cocked his head, studying Hugo with interest. 'Not at all, Captain Duchamp. As far as I'm concerned, it makes perfect sense, and my job is to listen to people who can no longer talk. I can't say I'm always successful, but we keep trying, non?'

Hugo smiled. 'It's the least we can do.'

'You think they care?' Coco asked, staring numbly at the body. 'Look at him. He's gone. He doesn't give a fuck about what happens now.'

Hugo took a deep breath. 'I'm not sure I agree with you, Captain...' he raised his hand, 'please don't misunderstand, I'm not professing to know, or understand about what... comes next, but we have to try to believe there is something, or else...' he left the sentence unfinished.

'It's what, pointless?' Coco posed.

Hugo shrugged. 'We tell ourselves what we need to, to enable us to do our jobs. Some people believe in the afterlife, some people are convinced we will meet our deceased loved ones again, others...'

'Sit on the fence?'

Hugo smiled. 'I believe life can be awful but death need not be,' he answered. 'I can't say I believe in the afterlife but I do believe in one way or another, we meet again. I think it's the last gift our brain gives us when it knows time is running out. Like static on a television screen, we can't make out what's there but perhaps when the time comes our consciousness gives us the gift of seeing our past, the faces, the smells, everything we missed and lost. Then the light and the static become clear and we become part of it. I don't know what happens when we die, but I believe we are reunited, whether that's for a second or for eternity, I can't say and I'm not sure it matters.' He stared at the corpse, pushing the sadness he felt away. 'I hope our boy found what he needed when he closed his eyes. That's all.' He turned around, his cheeks flushing as he realised everyone was watching him. He lowered his head, hair falling over his face.

'Quite the philosopher, aren't we, Captain Duchamp?' Cedric asked with a smirk.

Coco stepped in between them. 'You should try it sometimes, Cedric. Anyway, let's go, we have a lot to do.'

'We do?' Cedric asked. 'Such as?'

'Well, while we wait for Sonny to get ready for the autopsy, I say we pay a visit to *énergique*. Two dead men in less than a week and the only connection we know for certain begins there, and I want to know why.' She turned to Hugo. 'Coming?'

Hugo nodded.

quinze

Hugo climbed out of Coco's car and stretched. Coco followed him and slammed the door behind her. 'You said you'd been here already?' she asked. 'What were your impressions?'

Hugo considered his answer. 'It's the kind of place which always makes me feel uncomfortable,' he said, 'but that's not to say it means there's anything wrong. I've never been the sort of person who fits in a place like this.'

Cedric passed in front of him. 'It's not so bad, really.'

Coco stopped dead in her tracks. 'You've been inside *énergique*?' she asked, a bite clear in her voice.

Cedric gave her an uncertain look. 'Yeah. Once. Twice maybe, I can't really remember. When you were on maternity leave Commander Stanic took the whole department here to celebrate cracking the Debussy case.'

Coco and Hugo exchanged a look. Coco said. 'But why here? Why not the piss-hole next to the Commissariat where you all usually crawl into?'

Cedric shrugged. 'Dunno. He said it was a special occasion and because it was such a big bust, the top brass were pushing the boat out and treating us.'

Coco glanced at *énergique's* nondescript exterior, an unconvinced look on her face. 'He never mentioned it to me. But then again, why would he?' She turned to Hugo. 'Do you think it's odd?'

He shook his head. 'I don't believe so, we already

170

know a lot of important people come here. It makes sense the police would as well.'

She tapped the side of her nose. 'I don't like the smell of this whole sorry business, because something stinks, really stinks and I've got a bad feeling about it, a really bad feeling.'

Hugo decided his initial impression of Michel Lomet had been fairly accurate. There was something about one of the owners of *énergique* which bothered him and he was not sure why. It was not as if Hugo had not come across a handful of men such as Monsieur Lomet in his career. Men jacked up on success and power. High on the secrets they were privy to, basking in the spotlight of the lights shining around them, inhaling the scent of women and men who would not normally be in their orbit. Men such as Michel were so sure of their position and those who would protect them, it left them with an arrogance so strong it permeated the air. However, Hugo could not decide whether Michel Lomet was just fiercely guarding the secrets he was in charge of, which had nothing to do with the investigation, or was hiding something pertinent. Protecting the guilty. His act, whatever it was, was good and Hugo could see why Sebastian Dubois had ended up there. Sebastian had finally got his wish. Wealth and power.

Michel pushed the photograph of the second dead young man across the table. 'I've never seen him before,' he said with a nonchalant shrug of his shoulders, 'and really, this is all bordering on harassment. I have had the press camped out on my doorstep for days now in an attempt to get at my clients and all because of a non-story which has nothing to do with *énergique*.'

'The death of two young men is hardly a non-story, Monsieur Lomet,' Coco replied coolly.

Hugo dragged his attention away from the wisps of hair on the top of Lomet's head, which were rising and falling each time a breeze moved across the cavernous main room of the club. 'How do you explain the card we found on the dead man?' Hugo asked, already knowing the answer.

Lomet snorted. 'Do you know how many business cards we hand out, Captain? Because I certainly don't. Thousands, hundreds of thousands. The young man could have gotten it anywhere, from anyone. He could have picked it up on the street. How on earth am I to know?'

'Could he have gotten it from Delphine Marchand, perhaps?' Hugo asked.

A glint of anger flashed across Michel Lomet's eyes. And then it was gone. The mask slipping back into place. 'Who?' he said, tongue sliding across dry, fleshy lips.

'Delphine Marchand,' Hugo repeated. 'The woman we talked about the last time I was here. The woman you claimed not to know. We have now been informed by a witness he met her here at your club and that she was,' he paused, 'employed to spend time with him both here and outside.'

Lomet threw back his head and laughed. 'Minister Lenoir of all people should understand the importance of discretion.'

Hugo leaned forward in his chair. 'I never said the witness was Minister Lenoir.'

Lomet shrugged but did not respond.

'What about Mademoiselle Marchand, Monsieur Lomet?' Coco pressed.

Lomet pushed himself backing his chair causing it to groan under the pressure of his bulk. The suit he wore, while of good quality, was badly stained. He turned his head slowly, fixing a pair of watery eyes on Cedric. 'Have you asked your young sidekick if he knows this mysterious young woman?'

Cedric shuffled uncomfortably in his chair. Lomet snorted again. 'Oh, don't squirm, jeune homme, Papa Lomet is only joking with you.'

There was something about the way he spoke the words *Papa Lomet* which made the hairs on the back of Hugo's arm stand on end and reminded him of another man, a man whose name Hugo only spoke in his nightmares. A man so sadistic and evil, his crimes were barely comprehensible. Hugo was not sure the sort of man Michel Lomet was, or that he was evil anyway, but he did not like the man, and he certainly did not trust him.

Lomet turned his attention back to Hugo and Coco. 'I assumed it was our revered Minister of Justice behind this little intrusion and the fact is, I can't say with any certainty if the young woman in question worked here or not. And my gentle teasing of the young Lieutenant was just a reminder that on any given night *énergique* is filled to the rafters with extremely important men, many of which I am sure are known to you - colleagues, bosses, men from the highest echelon of Parisian society.'

'Nobody is above the law, Monsieur Lomet,' Coco said.

He threw back his head and guffawed, fleshy jowls wobbling against his chest. 'Come along, Captain Brunhild, you can't really be so naïve, can you? Laws are not made for men such as these, you know it as well as I do. They make the laws and more importantly their downfalls would have a catastrophic effect and therefore they will not, *cannot* be allowed to fall.'

Hugo interrupted. 'I disagree.'

'Then you're a naïve fool,' Lomet replied. 'What did you think coming here would accomplish? That I would hold up my hands and say, *mais oui, I run a disorderly establishment with hookers and drugs, and oh, that is just the tip of the iceberg as to what really goes on.'* He sniggered. 'The three of you would be handing out parking tickets in the back of beyond before you took a breath. And that's if you're lucky because believe me, these people are capable of much worse and I know because I've seen first-hand what they can do. The fact remains, so what if a couple of rent boys wind up dead? They came from nowhere and that's where they go back too, and nobody is any the wiser or gives a damn.'

'I give a damn,' Hugo hissed through gritted teeth.

'And so do I,' Coco added.

Lomet extended his hands. 'Then at least you will keep each other company. Look, I'll make it easy for you and save us all some time because frankly, I won't say another word. If you refuse my advice, then be it on your own heads.' He reached into a drawer and pulled out a card, throwing it to Hugo.

Hugo flicked on his glasses.

Alexander Esnault
06-23-12-46-54

'Who is Alexander Esnault?' he asked.

Lomet smiled. 'The man who can, if he so chooses, answer your questions.'

'So chooses?' Coco asked with a frown.

Lomet nodded. 'Oui. But don't thank me. If you call that number, if you speak with this man, I fear you will be opening a trapdoor to a bottomless pit and if you go inside, if you stare at the monster, the door will slam behind you and lock you inside.'

Coco scribbled furtively into her notepad. Lomet watched her curiously. She looked up. 'Désolé, I was just writing that down. My oldest kid, Barbra, is always failing literature. Her teachers say she has no imagination, so hearing you speak so eloquently I thought I'd give it to her to use for her next assignment.'

Lomet looked amused. 'You are mocking me, Captain.'

Coco moved her fingers an inch apart. 'Un peu. Thanks for the warning, but I don't scare easily. Who is this man, and what does he have to do with our dead kids?'

Lomet shrugged. 'Maybe everything, maybe nothing.' He sighed. 'Let us say, for the sake of argument, that an establishment such as *énergique* needs to bring together different parties with *different* interests. In order to facilitate this *discreetly,* it is necessary to engage the help of third-parties.'

Coco snatched the card from Hugo. 'Goddammit, this guy is your pimp, isn't he?'

Lomet smiled. 'My *facilitator*, you might say.'

She studied the card. 'And this is where you get your boys and girls?'

Lomet nodded but did not answer.

Coco gave him a sceptical look. 'And that's all you have to tell us, right?'

He nodded again and stood, extending his hand towards the door. 'And that is the last time you will get through those doors without a Mandate. My times of extending courtesy have elapsed and if you don't like that, I suggest you take it up with either Minister Lenoir or Commander Stanic and tell them both I look forward to seeing them again at *énergique* very soon. I'm sure they can remind you of how allegations of harassment look on personnel files.'

Coco looked between Hugo and Cedric. 'Let's get out of here. I need some fresh air.'

'Are you sure you don't mind me observing?' Hugo asked Dr. Bernstein.

Sonny smiled as he stepped into his scrubs. 'Not at all. We're all on the same side, non?'

Hugo nodded and moved to the observation area next to Coco. The door to the autopsy suite swung open and Cedric entered waving a piece of paper in the air, an excited look on his face. He pointed to the remains of the young man on the gurney. 'Say bonjour to jeune homme Jack Boucher.'

Coco's eyes widened. 'He has a record?'

'Oui,' Cedric replied, handing her the paper. 'Fingerprints are in the system, a couple of drug and prostitution busts since he turned eighteen last year. He also has a sealed juvenile record.'

'Well, see what you can do about getting it unsealed,' she replied.

He nodded. 'Commander Stanic is on it.'

She looked at him in surprise. 'Not like Morty to get his hands dirty.' She shook her head and muttered. 'He really wants Jean Lenoir to go down, doesn't he?' She lifted her head. 'Eighteen years old, you say?'

'Yeah, poor kid,' Cedric said. 'I've called the Commissariat in the eighth arrondissement and they're emailing me over the arrest files.'

'Bien,' Coco replied pensively. 'I want to see the basis of his arrest and who he was arrested with. What's the bet it was something to do with *énergique*? Dammit, it all keeps coming back to that shit-hole in one way or another, doesn't it?' She turned to Hugo. 'Any luck tracking down Sebastian Dubois yet?'

He shook his head. 'Non, but we suspect Michel Lomet may have had an idea where Sebastian is so Ben laid a few crumbs, told Lomet he needed to speak to Sebastian urgently and that it involved a great deal of money. If I know Sebastian at all and he is in touch with Lomet, I believe he'll call Ben soon and when he does, I'll let you know.' He paused. 'In fact, I could ask my tech guy in Montgenoux, Etienne Martine, to put a trace on Ben's cell phone so we can track wherever Sebastian calls from.'

'Are you sure? Wouldn't Ben mind?'

Hugo frowned. 'Why would he? Ben has nothing to hide and as far as I'm concerned, if *énergique* and Sebastian are tied up in the murder of a young man, I'd like to know why. I know Sebastian, and I'd like to say I don't believe he's capable of such things, but in all honesty, I can't. If he gets in touch, we should know where he is and more importantly, why he went away and what he knows.'

Coco smiled. 'Bien and remind me not to get on the wrong side of you anytime soon.'

'I'm not one to bear grudges,' Hugo replied, 'but when someone agrees to trade my life for their own, I tend to be unable to see the best in them again.'

Sonny raised an eyebrow and cleared his throat. 'D'accord, shall we begin?' He moved around the gurney, removing the cover and exposing the now naked remains. Hugo took a sharp intake of breath. At only eighteen years old, Jack Boucher looked small and fragile in death. Hugo's eyes locked on a small heart tattoo on his right bicep, and he felt his own heart tightening. He hoped Jack Boucher had felt some love in his tragic, cut-short life. He suspected he had certainly not felt it enough.

'We have a well-nourished Caucasian male in his late teens,' Sonny began ambling around the gurney, his eyes moving in the same way Hugo saw Montgenoux's Dr. Irene Chapeau. Careful and considered, not wanting to miss a single detail, and he could see Dr. Shlomo Bernstein was no different. He was not prone to melancholy, but he hoped when his own time came, there would be someone like these doctors watching out for him.

Sonny tucked his mop of black curly hair back into the cap he wore and he lowered his head to examine the skull. He flicked his eyes between the skull and the bank of x-rays hanging on the wall. 'As I originally thought, this could have likely proven fatal anyway, even if he had gotten help right when it happened. But he was alive when he was tied up and thrown in the river, and I can't say for certain, but if you ask me, there was a 50/50 chance he could have been saved.'

Coco shook her head in dismay, her eyes narrowing angrily as she studied the remains of Jack Boucher's face. 'Whoever did this was in a deadly rage, huh? I mean, to go to such extremes to make sure he was dead. They must have really hated him or wanted to be damn sure he was definitely dead.'

Sonny shrugged. 'You could say that. I've seen a lot of cases like this and there's never one easy answer. Love, rage, they're very similar in the heat of the moment.'

Hugo spoke. 'Destroying the face in such a way is sometimes a personal attack, or to hide evidence.'

'Or mask the identity,' Cedric added.

Coco sighed. 'So, basically, there could be several reasons some nut job caved in this poor kid's skull.'

Sonny gave her a grim smile. 'Tres bien, I'll begin.'

Forty minutes passed in silence as the police officers watched with bated breath as Dr. Bernstein completed the autopsy. Hugo found himself unable to take his eyes away, and as hard as it was, they kept locking on the tattoo. It reminded him of the heart-shaped birthmark Ben had on his hip and seeing it made Hugo sad in ways he could hardly bear.

'There's not a great deal else I can tell you,' Sonny said finally. 'We must wait for the blood and toxicology samples which may give us more. They certainly should further pinpoint the time of death, but I believe he has been in the water for a week. Not much longer.'

'Which would almost certainly mean he was dead before Marc Gassna,' Coco said.

Sonny nodded. 'Oui, that is my belief. And the examination of his lungs, which contain water, confirm he was alive when he was bound and thrown in the Seine. We know he either came to in the water or was already conscious, because of the scrapings on the covering.'

Cedric shook his head. 'That's an awful way to go.'

Nobody spoke. A minute passed.

'We're looking at an almost identical young man to Marc Gassna,' Sonny continued. 'I imagine them both to have been sex workers. Due to the length of time jeune Monsieur Boucher was in the river, I'm afraid there isn't any physical evidence. I can't even tell you if he had sex immediately prior to death. As you can see on the torso, there is severe bloating and evidence of the body beginning to be broken down. If it hadn't broken free, we would have much less to work with, or even be able to identify him.'

Coco frowned. 'But what do we have to work with, exactly? A murder similar to the suicide?' She shook her head. 'Even Morty cannot deny the possibility Marc Gassna killed Boucher and then committed suicide.' She shrugged. 'Well, at least I suppose it means Jean Lenoir is in the clear.'

'Does it?' Cedric asked. 'He could still have killed both though, couldn't he?'

She shook her head. 'Non, I never really believed he was involved, and with this new discovery, I don't think we will even get near him again. If he gets an Avocat onto us, it will be hard to prove this is anything but a big vendetta against the future, whatever it is, he's trying to be.'

Hugo looked again at Jack Boucher. 'And I have to agree, I don't believe Jean Lenoir is capable of this kind of frenzied attack. Nor would he get someone to do it on his behalf, for that matter. He's protective of his career, I get that, but having somebody murdered, non, I don't buy it.'

'And the Procurer will want this all tied up neatly and discreetly,' Coco added. 'Which is good news for Jean, non?'

'But not for Jack Boucher or Marc Gassna,' Hugo concluded.

Cedric stood and turned to Hugo, studying his face intently. 'What is it, Captain Duchamp? You don't look happy.'

'I'm not,' Hugo replied, standing and stretching his back. 'While I agree this could all be tied up and dealt with, there's something about it I'm just not buying.'

Coco shrugged. 'But what can we do? You heard Sonny, there is no physical evidence. I have my team checking CCTV in the area but we don't know exactly when he went in the Seine, and there are no cameras on the boulevard so unless there's a smoking gun…'

'Case closed,' Cedric added.

Case closed, Hugo replied with a shudder, not sure he believed it.

The first thing which struck Hugo about the home of Jack Boucher's parents was how different it was to Marc Gassna's. He lifted his head towards the block of nondescript and decaying apartments and strained to read the address Coco was holding. *Twelfth floor.* He sighed, already sure the lifts would be out of order. 'Damn you,' he muttered to himself, shaking his head, irritated at himself for forgetting the real reason he was there and how little an out-of-order lift really mattered.

'What's wrong, Captain Duchamp?' Cedric asked.

Hugo gave the young Lieutenant a tight-lipped smile. 'Nothing really, I was just reminding myself to quit with first-world problems. And s'il vous plaît, it's Hugo, especially when I'm here in such an unofficial capacity.'

'There's no such thing as unofficial in our jobs,' Coco interjected. She glanced up at the tower. 'And what's the bet the damn lift doesn't work?'

Hugo smiled, and they continued across the concrete jungle.

Coco held up her ID card. A middle-aged man frowned, reaching down and pulling a broken pair of glasses from the lip of a stained white t-shirt. He flicked them on a thin, pinched face, and his pupils dilated instantly, firing with fear.

'My name is Captain Brunhild, and these are my colleagues Captain Duchamp and Lieutenant Degarmo,'

Coco said. 'May I ask who you are?'

'Pourquoi?' the man asked, suspicion clear in a light, hoarse voice.

Hugo noticed the man's head jerk backwards towards an open door at the back of the dimly lit hallway.

'Are you the father of Jack Boucher?' Coco continued.

He sighed. 'What's the brat done this time?'

'May we come in?' Coco asked softly.

The man considered and with a reluctant shrug of a shoulder indicated for them to pass him. 'The second door on the left,' he muttered.

Hugo fell in line behind Coco and Cedric as they made their way into the house. The man moved past them quickly and started to pull the first doorway closed. Hugo turned his head quickly to see what it was the man seemed to be desperate to hide. He could only see in the room for a second but it was long enough to see a stack of boxes, one of which seemed to be for a large television, the sort Hugo had never been brave enough to have in his own home because he was worried he would never be able to understand how to work it. He longed for the days when it was possible just to turn a television on and it would be ready to go. The door slammed shut, pushing a blast of musty air into the hallway.

'Through there,' the man said, guiding them into a cramped living room. A woman with tight black curls and a long, pointed face looked up sharply, dropping a pair of knitting needles into her lap. 'It's the police, Ana,' he said. The woman gave a quick, resigned nod and folded the knitting into a neat pile and placed it onto a side table next to her. Her calmness unnerved Hugo. It was as if she had played this scenario over and over, and she was in no hurry to hear the bad news the police were about to share. It hurt Hugo to see her naivety, for he felt sure this would not be the scenario she was expecting, but it would be one she would wish for the rest of her life.

'My name is Randolph Boucher, and this is my wife Ana,' he said. 'And oui, we are Jack's parents.'

'Is he safe?' Ana Boucher asked. 'He's been gone longer than usual, if there is such a thing. He usually calls, just to let me know he's safe, that he's okay, but it has been a while.' She lowered her voice. 'Is he in trouble?'

Hugo and Coco exchanged glances. Hugo drifted towards a row of photographs on a bureau. A smiling young man greeted him, young and vibrant, and much more alive than the last time Hugo had seen him.

Coco cleared her throat. 'I'm very sorry to have to tell you this, Madame et Monsieur Boucher, but we have reason to believe your son, Jack, has died.'

The shriek was instant, but to Hugo's surprise, it came from Randolph Boucher, and was gut-wrenching. Ana Boucher, jumped up from her seat and threw her arms around her husband, pulling his head to her chest as he began sobbing. She guided him towards the sofa. She pulled out a blanket and wrapped it around him.

'What happened to our boy?' Randolph asked, the veins throbbing in his neck.

'We don't know for certain,' Coco answered, 'but I must tell you at this stage we are treating it as suspicious.'

'Suspicious?' Ana snapped. 'You mean he was murdered?'

'There are indications his death was not natural,' she answered. She met their anxious faces. Their eyes were locked onto her, searching for answers she could not give. 'I also have to ask you to formally identify him,' she added as if the words pained her to speak.

Randolph shook his head vehemently. 'I can't, I just can't, not mon petit garçon,' he sobbed.

Ana stood with determination. She moved across the room and picked up a plain wooden cross from a hook on the wall. She kissed it before turning to face the police. 'I'll do it,' she said with determination. She handed the cross to her husband. 'Call Monseigneur Demaral, he'll know what to do. There are arrangements to be made.'

Randolph lifted his head slowly and took the cross from her, quickly dropping it to the ground as if was a red-hot poker. He nodded.

'I'm ready.' Ana said bluntly.

Coco nodded. 'Tres bien.' She placed a hand on Ana's arm and moved her towards the door. Hugo followed, his eyes flicking around the room. There was something about it which troubled him. The brand new television, the seemingly expensive stereo equipment seemed out of place in an otherwise modest home. He watched Randolph Boucher as he cradled his head in his hands and began weeping, the unmistakable sound of a broken heart echoing around the room.

Ana Boucher turned her back on her son as Dr. Bernstein replaced the white sheet and stepped backwards discreetly. She moved towards the window at the centre of the room, the afternoon sun cut through the stained glasses windows, sending slithers of red, green and yellow around the room. She lifted her hand to touch a yellow rose, her fingers recoiling suddenly. 'This room is exquisite,' she said.

Hugo looked around the room and agreed. Rooms such as these were often clinical, or prone to enforced cheerfulness as if brightness might lighten the darkness within, which invariably it could not. The stained glass window and the single yellow rose were stark and powerful and he liked the message they gave.

'Madame Boucher,' Coco said, guiding the woman towards a row of chairs lining the wall. 'Can you confirm the deceased is your son, Jack Boucher?'

She nodded. 'Oui. He is my son.' She stared at the now-covered body. 'Can you believe he was once so small? Tiny. The smallest baby I think I've ever seen, but oh my, I should have known even then, because when he first opened his mouth the scream was as loud a sound as I'd ever heard!' She gave a sad laugh. 'But he was such a good boy.' She looked anxiously between the three policemen. 'I expect you must think what on earth kind of mother I must be? I don't blame you. But you must believe one thing. I loved my son, we both loved our son, and we did our best by him. They love us until they hate us, until they love us again. We did our best,' she repeated.

Hugo noticed Coco's eyes were reddening. 'Of course, you did, Madame Boucher. We are destined to follow our own paths in this life and the best we can do it to make sure those around us, those in our lives, know they are loved. The choices, the decisions they make, must be their own. We can't make decisions for them, as much as we might like to.'

'But we were his parents…'

He shook his head. 'Parents aren't perfect, nobody is. You said Jack telephoned you regularly, which means he cared about you, and I'm sure he loved you. Anything else, his life decisions were his own.' He gave her a sad smile. 'We're all guilty of being stubborn, and our mistakes have to be our own. We might watch them being made from the side-lines but we are resigned to offering a shoulder when life goes wrong. It is often the best we can do.'

Ana lowered her head. 'He began selling himself when he was fourteen years old. Selling himself? Can you even imagine what goes through a person's mind to actually *choose* to do that? I spent so much time telling him to keep his nose clean, to keep away from all the drug dealers on the estate. It never even occurred to me he'd end up messed up in something so…' She did not finish her sentence. 'Is that how he died? Something to do with… what he did…'

'We are investigating the circumstances of Jack's

death,' Cedric replied, 'but it's early days.'

She nodded. 'I suppose it doesn't matter, isn't it how these stories always end? You live that sort of life and it always catches up with you one way or another. But still, I should have done more. I should have helped him to find another way to live.' She raised her hand. 'I don't need platitudes, I know my place and I'll have to spend the rest of my life going over what I could have done, should have done differently.'

Coco coughed. 'What can you tell us about Jack? His friends, where he lived when he wasn't at home, that sort of thing?'

Ana shook her head. 'I can tell you nothing, really. He hasn't lived at home with us for a long time. Once we discovered what he was *doing*, well, it was no longer possible for him to stay. We gave him a choice, and he made his decision. But as he left, I made sure he understood he would always have a home with us if he wanted it and that he would always be loved. But he said it was too late, and that there was no going back.'

No going back. Hugo wondered what young Jack Boucher could have meant by those words.

'What about his friends?' Coco asked again.

Ana shrugged. 'I didn't know them, he certainly never brought any to meet us.' She paused. 'Although there was one time, oh, it must have been several months ago. He came home to get something from his room, and I looked over the balcony and a young girl was waiting for him. The prettiest little thing, short red hair. He seemed happy with her. I hoped he was happy with her, at least.'

Hugo looked sharply at Coco, a flash of awareness passing between them. It could not be a coincidence. Was Delphine Marchand a link between the two young dead men? It certainly made finding her an even bigger priority. She may be a witness, or more worryingly her own life could be in danger.

'I wish I could tell you more,' Ana added sadly, 'but I know nothing else.' She stared at Coco. 'Will you get who is responsible? Will you promise me you'll make them pay for what they did to my child?'

Coco nodded, knowing she should not. 'I promise.'

Hugo flopped onto the bed and closed his eyes. The scents and the sounds of the bustling Parisian street beneath him drifted lazily into the room, the thin curtain rising and falling. Ben lay in silence next to him, curled in a foetal position. He reached across and touched Hugo's cheek, his own scarred finger resting on the strawberry-shaped scar on Hugo's cheek. They were wounds they had both obtained during the preceding few years and they both took some kind of comfort in them, taking them as a reminder of how close they had both come to losing their lives.

'Tough day?' Ben asked.

Hugo opened his eyes, rolling over and lighting a cigarette. He stood and cranked open the window, leaning over the sill and sucking in a lungful of air. 'I forgot how noisy Paris is,' he said.

'You miss it?'

Hugo considered. 'I never thought I would. I mean, when I left I really didn't look back. But now, perhaps with hindsight, and now I'm grown and have no ties here, it actually feels nice to be back. And the sound doesn't scare me. In fact, I love it.'

Ben stood and took the cigarette from Hugo, taking a long drag. 'We could always live here. I always wanted to, you know. I dreamt I'd run away from Montgenoux into the arms… into the arms of… *someone*.'

Hugo shrugged. 'Sure we could, it's nice not to be

193

G N Hetherington

scared of it anymore, that's for certain. I don't see the ghosts I thought I would.'

'Do you want to talk about seeing your father?'

Hugo shook his head. 'Not really, and not because I'm bothered by it, rather, because I'm *not* bothered by it. Non, let's deal with what we have to deal with here and then get home. We can talk about it then. D'accord?'

Ben leaned in and kissed his husband, pulling Hugo's full lips to his own, teasing them with his tongue. 'You always taste so good,' he breathed into Hugo's mouth.

'Et tu,' Hugo replied.

Ben pulled away, straightening himself. 'The walls are so thin,' he grumbled, 'and after spending all afternoon in here, I know more about the couple next door than I really need to,' he said with a shudder. 'Straight folks are weird,' he added with a chuckle.

Hugo pulled a sad face. 'Désolé, cheri. How about I make it up to you and we go out for the evening, just the two of us?'

Ben moved back and kissed him again. 'I don't care what we do, as long as we're together but unfortunately we need to wait in for a call,' he added, his mouth twisting into a grimace.

Hugo gave him a quizzical look. 'We do?'

Ben handed him his cell phone. 'I got a text earlier.' Hugo flicked on his glasses.

Ben, I'll call you tonight at 7 pm Paris time, Sebastian.

194

'I guess money really does talk,' Ben said.

Hugo glanced at his watch. Fifteen minutes until the call was due. 'It gives me just about enough time to ring Etienne and ask him to trace the call.'

'Obviously, I did nothing wrong, cheri,' Sebastian Dubois said.

Ben threw the cell phone onto the bed as if he was barely even to look at the FaceTime call. Hugo picked it up and moved to the table in front of the window, propping the cell phone against the window.

'Then why did you run?' Hugo asked.

Sebastian ran his hand through his unruly mane of red curls. Hugo scanned the scenery behind him. Wherever he was, it was a similar time zone to Paris. The sun was setting behind him, and Hugo could hear the distinctive sounds of seagulls and lapping water.

'I didn't run, I *haven't* run,' Sebastian snapped back defensively. 'I merely decided to have a vacation.'

'Bullshit,' Ben muttered in the background.

Sebastian chuckled. 'I see my brother is still enamoured with me. How about you, Hugo, are you still enamoured with me?'

Hugo raised his hand to pacify Ben. 'Aren't you ever going to get tired of being a prick, Sebastian? You take some perverse pleasure in trying to get under people's skin for no good reason other than sheer devilment. And here we are again, Ben and I roped into whatever mess you have gotten yourself embroiled in and I'm sick of it. Just tell us what is going on at the club you own so we can go back to Montgenoux, and you can go back to leading whatever kind of debauched life you choose. What is going on in *énergique?*'

'I don't know what you mean,' Sebastian answered defensively.

'The hell you don't,' Hugo shot back. He knew enough about Sebastian to know he was a terrible liar when pressured. 'Two young men are dead, and as far as we know more could be in danger,' he continued. 'What can you tell me about a man named Alexander Esnault?'

Sebastian's eyes widened. 'I have no idea who you are talking about.'

His tone told Hugo all he needed to know. Sebastian knew exactly who Alexander Esnault was and what he did. 'Listen, Sebastian, the Paris police are looking for him. It's only a matter of time before they find him and we interview him. If there's anything you need to tell us, then now is the time. Get your side of the story out first.'

Sebastian slammed his fists onto the table in front of him. 'I don't know what the hell you think I know, or what the hell is going on, but I've done nothing wrong.'

'Ha, that would be a first,' Ben muttered.

Hugo continued, deciding to try a different way to get through to Ben's half-brother. 'Sebastian, we're not saying you are directly involved, perhaps you just got scared. You are still on probation after all, but honestly, running is not the answer. If you have nothing to hide, then you can't be sent back to prison for a crime you didn't commit.'

'How do you know?' Sebastian asked desperately. 'If there is an investigation and if it's discovered *énergique* is involved in... things it shouldn't be, then I could find my pretty ass back in the slammer again before I know it. And after last time, well, you know why I don't want to go down that road again. Even a cat has to run out of lives, eventually.'

Hugo paused, realising Sebastian could be correct. If he was aware of illegal activities in a business he part-owned, it could well mean his probation would be revoked. 'Sebastian, you said to me once a long time ago you trusted me, is that still true?'

Sebastian swallowed. 'Of course, it's true. You and I saved each other Hugo, and we will be forever linked because of it.'

Behind them, Ben tutted. Hugo continued. 'Bien. Then trust that I will do my best to help you, whatever the mess you have gotten yourself into. If it's just a case of your business partner, Monsieur Lomet, operating illegal activities then I would imagine a good Avocat could argue your case quite successfully, and these days you can afford a good Avocat, right?'

'The cops aren't going to listen to me, a convicted felon, are they? They will try to pin whatever they can on me, unless...'

'Unless?' Hugo asked.

'Unless you're saying you're going to protect me,' Sebastian retorted.

Hugo shook his head. 'I'm not going to "protect" you Sebastian, but neither am I going to do anything to make life difficult for you, unless I have to. As long as you have done nothing illegal, then you have my word I will do what I can for you.'

'Your word?' Sebastian asked cautiously.

Hugo ignored Ben's intense gaze. 'My word. But you are on your own, Sebastian, and unless you talk to me, right here, right now, then I will withdraw that offer and you will be at the mercy of the Parisian police who, as you said, are not necessarily going to be interested in looking behind the past of a convicted criminal, especially when one of his crimes was conspiracy to murder a police officer.' He paused to let his words resonate. 'Tell me what you know right now, or I will turn over your location, because by now my associate Etienne Martine will have traced this call, in fact,' he pulled his own cell phone out of his pocket, 'ah,' he said triumphantly, '*dear Hugo, I have traced the call on Ben's cell phone and can confirm Sebastian Dubois is in the Hotel Regina, Biarritz under the name S. Duchamp.*' Hugo put down the phone. 'You could have come up with a more original name.' He stared into the camera. 'So, what is it going to be? Do I pass this on to the police and Ben and I can go back to Montgenoux and never look back? Because believe me, there's nothing we want to do more.'

Sebastian sighed. 'You have to understand, what goes on at *énergique* started long before I ever got there,' he began wearily. 'Alexander Esnault has been supplying Lomet with...' he paused, 'whatever he needs, for a long time.'

'Prostitutes?' Hugo asked.

Sebastian shrugged. 'Oui, and whatever else the club might need. Listen, you gotta promise me if you speak to Alexander you'll be careful. He might look gorgeous and act like a pussycat, but it's all a lie, a front. He's one of the nastiest, most dangerous men I've met and as we all know, I've rubbed noses with some of the worst. He scares me, and I don't scare easily.'

Hugo looked at Sebastian in surprise and indicated for him to continue.

'If a prostitute died, you shouldn't look much further than Alexander, not that you'll ever pin anything on him. As far as I know, he's never even been arrested, probably because most of his clients are rich, influential men who couldn't afford to have him open his mouth.' Sebastian continued. 'I can't stress it strongly enough to you, Hugo, to watch what you're doing with this man. I didn't leave Paris because I was scared of the police. I'm more scared of Alexander and what he could do to me if I speak out. He's had his hooks in *énergique* long before I got there, and he pretty much unofficially runs the place.'

Hugo took this in. 'Did anything happen in the last

few weeks leading up to the deaths?'

Sebastian shook his head. 'Non, nothing special.'

Hugo watched him carefully, not sure he was telling the truth. He pressed on. 'And what made you leave so suddenly?'

Sebastian bit his lip. Hugo could see he was wrestling with himself, considering how much he should tell. Finally, he sighed before clearing his throat. 'Alexander came into the club to see me and Michel and told us some kid had thrown himself off the Eiffel Tower. He said there would be a lot of questions so we had to get our house in order and make sure under no circumstances we acknowledged who the kids were, or what they were up to.'

'Kids?' Hugo interrupted, leaning forward, suddenly alert. 'He definitely said, kids, as in plural?'

'Yeah, kids, pourquoi?' Sebastian asked.

Hugo took in this new information because it indicated Alexander Esnault knew about the murder of Jack Boucher and the alleged suicide of Marc Gassna. 'What else did he say?'

Sebastian shrugged. 'Only to keep our mouths shut, if we knew what was good for us. He looked straight at me and reminded me of my past and what he could do to me if I didn't keep my mouth shut.' He shuddered. 'I don't know whether he meant I'd wind up back in jail, or something else, either way, I just went home, grabbed a bag and before I knew it I was on a train. I didn't even think about it, I panicked I guess. I didn't want the police to find me, I didn't want anyone to find me. And here I am. Scared shitless and throwing myself at your feet again.' He snorted. 'We keep coming back to the same scenario, don't we? Will you by my saviour again, Hugo?'

Hugo did not answer, his mind turning over different thoughts. 'Why are you so worried about Alexander Esnault?'

Sebastian turned his head away. 'What do you mean?'

'You know exactly what I mean, Sebastian,' Hugo shot back. 'What do you know?'

'The question you should be asking,' Ben interrupted, 'is what does Alexander Esnault know about Sebastian?'

'Ah, brother dearest, you hold me in such high esteem,' Sebastian quipped.

'Quit calling me that,' Ben grumbled, 'and quit the bullshit and tell Hugo what he needs to know. What does the pimp have on you?'

Sebastian lapsed into silence.

'Sebastian…' Hugo said.

Sebastian sighed. 'He may, or may not, have recordings.'

'Recordings?' Hugo and Ben exchanged a look.

Sebastian nodded. 'One week Michel had to go out of the country, so he left me in charge. Which meant…' he paused, 'dealing with suppliers, one of which was

Alexander and what I didn't know, what Michel, the bastard, omitted telling me, was that Alexander doesn't trust anybody, and he makes sure that whoever he deals with he has enough dirt on to make sure they don't turn on him.' He pursed his lips. 'I can't remember exactly what I said, but I'm sure it was enough to land me in a whole heap of trouble.'

'But if he used it, then surely it would implicate him too,' Hugo reasoned.

Sebastian stared. 'Don't you get it, yet. It's not about that with Alexander Esnault, it's about control with him, making sure everyone bows at his feet, is terrified of him. And I mean it when I say, I'm terrified of going back to prison, but I'm more afraid of what he could do to me.'

'Is he really so bad?' Hugo asked.

'Oui,' Sebastian replied, 'in fact, I can't believe Michel gave you his name.'

'I imagine the discovery of the second body probably convinced him,' Hugo said, 'especially since it's more clearly a case of murder.'

Sebastian's eyes widened. 'Second body?' He turned his head. 'Yeah, sounds like Michel, he may be scared shitless of Alexander, but he's not stupid, he has his own protection too. He will not want to take the rap for something Alexander did.'

Ben said. 'So what are you going to do, keep running?'

Sebastian smiled. 'I'm a chicken and I'm not

ashamed to admit it,' he said, 'you know that, brother.'

'Two young men have died, Sebastian,' Hugo interjected, 'and as far as we know, there could be more in trouble, their lives could be in danger. Don't you think you should try to help them?'

Sebastian's eyes flickered with anger. 'Don't try to make me feel guilty. I knew those kids, I spent a lot of time with them. Hell you might say I identified with them, we came from similar backgrounds after all. I hate that something terrible happened to them.'

'But not enough to stop profiting from someone else having to sell themselves instead of having to do it yourself. Don't bullshit us, Sebastian, with all this "I could relate to them" nonsense because you made money from them and now they're dead,' Ben hissed. 'If you'd cared about them after what happened to you, then any normal person would have learnt their lesson.'

'I have learnt, brother dearest,' Sebastian retorted, 'and that's why I made sure these kids were properly looked after, not sucking someone off in a back alley. Don't you see that? The kids we used ended up in places like the Ritz and got good money for doing it. The alternative, the one offered by Alexander, was very different I can assure you. These kids were happy to work at *énergique,* because it gave them a life, a safer, better life, than the alternative.'

'You would say that,' Ben snapped back, 'but they still ended up dead, didn't they?'

'And I keep saying, it had nothing to do with me. Who was the other kid?'

'His name was Jack Boucher,' Hugo answered.

Sebastian's eyes misted. 'Poor kid. Hell, Marc was a messed up kid, but so was Jack. They all are in one way or another. Most of us who sell ourselves don't do it because we like sex. We do it because it seems as if it's the best, the *only* option we have. I considered it to be my duty to make sure these kids, if that is what they chose to do, were at least safe. The fact Marc killed himself is heartbreakingly sad, but it was probably inevitable.'

'What do you mean?' Hugo asked.

'He never told me his story, he didn't need to. There isn't much originality in the storyboards of these kids' lives. Something happened, or rather someone happened to destroy him when they should have been protecting him. As you both know, I've been down that particular road myself so I know the signs, which meant I knew not to push him because the truth is, we all have the same sort of stories. I'm sure Marc was no different, except he wasn't able to get past it and that's why he killed himself.'

'And what about Jack Boucher?' Hugo asked. 'He was clearly murdered.'

'Damn,' Sebastian hissed, his mouth twisting angrily. 'Damn that bastard Alexander to hell.' He stared straight down the camera. 'I know nothing about it, I swear to you, Hugo.'

Hugo nodded, not sure how much value he put in

Sebastian's word. 'How many prostitutes worked out of *énergique*?' he asked.

Sebastian shrugged. 'It depends. On a day-to-day basis, maybe two or three. Some of our clients like to have the same escorts, some like to try a little something new, sometimes we have, ahem, special interest parties, so honestly, it varies. But yeah, you might say kids like Marc and Jack were regulars.'

'What about Delphine Marchand?'

'Dieu, she's not dead, is she?' Sebastian cried.

Hugo replied. 'I don't know, but she is certainly missing.'

'What the hell is going on? What is Alexander up to? Cleaning house, perhaps?' Sebastian asked with a groan. 'Yeah, I know Delphine, a pretty little redhead with freckles like mine, actually, she reminded me of your friend, Irene. It was funny seeing the walking steroid factory Jean Lenoir crawling all over her. I thought he's just like the rest of us after all, led by his prick.' He scratched his head. 'There was a gang of them who all hung around together, Marc, Jack, Delphine and a couple of other kids whose name I can't remember. They were cute though - two gay kids in the throes of that all-consuming first love, which was a bit at odds with their chosen career, I can tell you!' He turned his head to see Ben in the corner of the room. 'Actually, they reminded me a little of you two, all withering looks and the whole will-they won't-they vibe going on. Quite stomach-churning, but there you go.'

'Why do you hate me so much?' Ben asked suddenly.

Sebastian's eyes widened. 'Why do you think, brother? Because you had the life I should have had, and you have the man who should be mine. I hate you because you have my life.'

'Oh, mon Dieu!' Hugo cried. 'Will you quit this childish rubbish, Sebastian? We are all too old for it and there are more important things going on. Can I tell the police you will return to Paris?'

Sebastian shook his head forcefully. 'Absolutely not, as I said, if Alexander Esnault is on the warpath I want to be as far away as possible. I'm certainly not going to risk my life, or ending up back in prison for something which has nothing to do with me.'

'But what about the people who have died and the others whose lives could be in danger?' Hugo asked.

'Not my problem. I'm selfish, but that's the way it is. I haven't gotten this far on my own steam to stop now. Nobody helped me when I was in the gutter, and I'll be damned if anybody will drag me back into it. It took everything I had to get where I am today and no bastard is going to take it away from me.'

'Leave it, Hugo,' Ben growled, 'waste no more time on this asshole.'

Hugo nodded. 'I will pass on your location to Captain Brunhild, Sebastian.'

He shrugged. 'I'll be checked out by the time you've finished your call, and I'll be off somewhere fabulous. That's the great thing about finally having money, it opens so many doors and I can disappear for years if I have to.'

Hugo sighed. 'The police will catch up with you, Sebastian, or someone else will, and you won't have my help or my protection. You will be on your own.'

Sebastian winked at the camera. 'I always have been, but at least I'm good looking AND rich now, so on that note, I'll wish you both au revoir. We'll see each other again, I'm certain of it. Je t'aime.' He reached forward and disconnected the call, leaving Hugo staring at the black screen.

Ben touched Hugo's shoulder. 'Do you think he told you everything he knew?'

Hugo turned his head. 'I doubt it very much, but as always, we'll never really know what Sebastian Dubois truly knows until it's too late. But I know one thing for certain. He is scared. Dead scared.'

Hugo watched the Paris streets whizz past him as Lieutenant Cedric Degarmo deftly manoeuvred the car around traffic jams with an ease which caused Hugo to shudder. He imagined his own beloved, banged-up Citroën would not last a day in the French capital. They were driving in silence. Hugo, Coco, and Cedric. Police officers sharing common thoughts. It was not the sort of uncomfortable silence of strangers where one party felt inclined to break it with talk of the weather or something equally mundane. As they had begun the journey, Hugo had filled them in on his conversation with Sebastian and the Parisians had listened with interest but little comment.

'Is it really worth dragging the Dubois creep back to Paris?' Cedric asked finally.

Hugo turned his head. He had been watching a carefree young couple riding along on push bikes. They seemed as if they had not a care in the world, but he had wondered if it was true. Was not everyone just wearing a mask of one kind or another? 'Even if you did,' he replied to Cedric, 'I can't see it would justify the expense and hassle it would undoubtedly cause you. I know Sebastian and what that tells me is whatever he might know, he's never going to share unless there's something in it for him.'

'And do you think he knows more than he's letting on?' Coco asked.

Hugo nodded. 'Oh, almost certainly, but it must be

measured against the possibility it is more to do with fear of self-incrimination rather than any viable information which could assist you in your investigation. And as I said, I get the sense he's dead scared. I would recommend holding off on him for now. I have Etienne Martine keeping track of him and we already know,' he glanced at his watch, 'that at this precise moment he is sitting on a plane, business class, on his way to Ibiza.'

Coco raised an eyebrow. 'Ibiza, you say? I always fancied myself on a dance floor in some exotic locale, maybe I should go get him myself.'

Hugo smiled at her. 'Perhaps.'

They were silent again, and it was broken only by the screeching of car brakes and Cedric angrily hissing, 'Putain!' He slammed his fist against the dashboard. 'Move out of the way, fucking loser!'

Coco smiled at Hugo's concerned face. 'A little different to streets in Montgenoux, huh?'

Hugo smiled. 'Oh, you'd be surprised. We actually have blind drivers in Montgenoux.'

Coco gave a serious nod. 'That doesn't surprise me in the slightest.' She turned back to face the windscreen. 'It was interesting though what Dubois had to say about Alexander Esnault because he was right about one thing. Esnault has no record, not even a sniff, which for a pimp and drug pusher means only one thing as far as I'm concerned.'

'He has help,' Hugo sighed. 'There seems to be a lot

of that going on, doesn't there?'

'I reached out to some of my informers,' Cedric said, 'and they pretty much confirmed Esnault has protection. They all know better than to sell in the seventh arrondissement or to mess with him.'

Coco pulled a grimace. 'I cannot wait to meet this charming man,' she said.

Hugo was not sure what he imagined the home of an alleged sex and drug trafficker would look like, but it was not the relatively normal-looking apartment block Cedric pulled up in front of. The building was much the same as most of the apartment blocks in the French capital. Tall, thin windows stretching to the sky, the shadow of the Eiffel Tower throwing a half-darkness on them. Hugo was again reminded of his childhood and how each morning he would awake, throw off his blankets and rush to his balcony, craning his neck over the railings to reassure himself the Tower had not disappeared overnight. He had known it was a foolish thought, but in the darkness of night when sleep evaded him and the creaks of a sleeping house haunted him he imagined the Tower, like everything else in his life, was going to leave him.

Coco climbed out of the car. 'I know this building, it's new. I actually looked at an apartment here once, out of my price range, but for this guy, it seems a little... modest, non?'

Hugo shrugged. 'Perhaps he's just trying to keep a

low profile, rather than shine a light on how he really pays his bills.'

Coco scanned the names next to the foyer door. 'Ah, there he is,' she pressed the buzzer.

'Si,' the reply came barely a second later.

'Salut, my name is Captain Charlotte Brunhild, I wonder, am I speaking with Monsieur Alexander Esnault?'

'You certainly are, entrer chérie,' he replied, 'and take the lift to the top floor. I'll make café.'

Hugo appraised Alexander Esnault carefully as he wrangled with one of the fanciest café machines Hugo had ever seen and he was sure that like Esnault, he would have difficulty using it. He took the chance to take in Esnault's home. It appeared to be what Hugo would describe as a typical bachelor pad, filled with all the latest tech and large leather sofas. Dead centre in the room was a huge Warhol-style painting of Esnault's face, a handsome smile filling the room.

Esnault's appearance was more that of a fashion model than of a criminal kingpin, Hugo thought - tall and lithe with blond hair scraped into a tight knot on the top of his head. When he turned around, he greeted his guests with the warmest of smiles and twinkling jet-black eyes which flicked over Hugo, Cedric and Coco with a mixture of amusement and burning interest. Hugo thought he could see no maliciousness in it, rather a man used to giving his full, undivided attention to the person speaking to him. Whatever, whoever, Alexander Esnault was, he was certainly a man who would be difficult to read, which Hugo knew from experience meant he was likely very dangerous.

'The famous Captain Duchamp, I've heard a lot about you,' Alexander said to Hugo. His voice was deep with the faint hint of an accent Hugo could not discern.

'Famous?' Hugo asked in surprise, wondering how on earth a man such as Esnault could possibly know who he was.

Alexander indicated for them to move to the leather sofas which stretched the full length of the wall. Hugo sat and immediately fell back, his legs flailing underneath him. Alexander chuckled. 'Oh, I should have warned you. The sofa moves, moulding itself to your shape. They're a bit of a drag to get used to, but once you do, there is something magical about them. Especially when you have company,' he added, with a twinkle.

Hugo struggled to find a more dignified position to sit in. 'Famous?' he asked again.

'Oui,' Alexander said, sitting opposite the detectives with much more grace. 'Your father speaks highly of you, as does the Minister of Justice. They're both dear friends of mine, so accordingly I feel as if I know you as if we are friends ourselves. Good friends are such a rare commodity, don't you think? In a world gone mad, I take great comfort in having such friends who care for me, watch out for me. You know what I mean?'

Hugo caught the expression on Coco's face as they simultaneously realised Esnault was warning them off.

Alexander turned his head. 'And you, of course, Captain Brunhild, the Commissariat de Police du 7e arrondissement's finest. I keep telling Morty he was a fool to let you slip through his fingers.'

Coco's jaw flexed angrily, but she did not speak.

'And you, Cedric,' Alexander said to Cedric, 'I believe I have seen you before but we've not had the pleasure yet, but I'm sure that will all change over the coming years as you rise up the ranks as Morty assures me you will.' He paused, sipping his café. His lip twitched, dark eyes thinking with interest, reminding Hugo of a cat toying with its prey, knowing full well it would pounce and destroy it at any moment. 'Écoute, we're all busy people and we don't want to waste each other's time, oui?' He flashed a perfectly even, white smile. 'I'm sure you have come to my door with all manner of preconceived ideas regarding who I am and what I do and I don't blame you for it. However, if you leave with the same opinion, then that will be something which disappoints me, and I am not the sort of man who likes to be disappointed.'

'What is it you do exactly, Monsieur Esnault?' Coco asked.

He smiled. 'I shall only respond if you all call me Alexander. I am not a formal man. My job, my vocation, you might say, is to become rich in a way not dependent on money,' he laughed seeing their confused faces, 'oh, don't misunderstand me. I am rich, filthy rich you might say, but I did not start that way, non, my life story began very differently, in a slum. Fortunately, I barely remember it. I was rescued and taken into an orphanage and the religious zealots taught me all I needed to know about making it through life.'

'And what did they teach you?' Hugo asked.

'To take every hard knock like a man, to learn from it, and to make sure it only happens once,' Alexander answered. 'When I made my first million I came to one conclusion which has served me well ever since.' He narrowed his eyes. 'Nothing makes you richer, or more powerful than listening to the desires of those around you and fulfilling those desires.'

'A pimp is a pimp, however you dress it up,' Coco muttered under her breath.

'Au contraire, Captain,' Alexander snapped back, but there was no malice in his tone, just the same amused lilt. 'A pimp, as you know, takes a cut from people selling themselves on the street. It's seedy, and it's unnecessary and frankly dangerous for all those involved. As I said, I was not born into a life of wealth and privilege so when I got the chance to be around those who were, I made sure to watch, and hell I even took notes and you know what I discovered? The great secret, the secret nobody wants to share because it would tip the delicate balance of the hierarchy. Do you know what that difference is, the one between us and them, the haves and the have-nots?'

'There isn't one,' Hugo answered.

Alexander clapped his hands like an excited child. 'Exactly, Hugo, exactement! We all have the same base desires and carnal needs,' he stopped, tipping his head and winking, 'well, not exactly the same, some people are just freaky. Anyway, it became apparent to me whoever provided and fulfilled these desires would be a very important person. A tres, tres, *tres* important person. I wanted to be that person. I wanted to be the sort of person important people trusted, went to for help to fulfil the desires they were afraid to ask for.'

'Oh, Jesus Christ, just get to the point!' Coco cried. She stopped as if embarrassed by her outburst.

Alexander grinned. 'You're right, you're not here to arrest me, so there is no reason to be sheepish.'

Coco's eyes widened. 'I'll arrest anyone who commits a crime, Monsieur Esnault, regardless of who they are or who they know. If your "friends" told you anything about me, they should have told you that. I don't scare easily,' she smiled at Hugo. 'None of us does, so make idle threats as much as you like, Captain Duchamp and I aren't afraid of hard work. So, if we have to we'll spend the rest of our lives doing the crappiest jobs we have to and we'll do it with a smile because we'll know we did the right thing, and we didn't go down without a fight.'

He winked again. 'Oh, my friends did indeed tell me all about you both,' he paused, 'but I'm sure you don't need reminding that sometimes there is more than one way to destroy a person and if you do it right, you don't even need to touch them. Aim for their heart because that's where the real pain lies.'

Hugo pulled his body erect. 'I warn you, Monsieur, I...'

Esnault raised his hand. 'I talk in mere conjecture, of course. Let me go back to my original point. I have committed no crimes, and good luck proving otherwise. I merely provide a link between those buying and selling and it is done in a way which is fair and harmonious. If you are asking, do I sell sex? I shall say non, I do not. I sell nothing but companionship between those wanting it and those willing to provide it. Of course, nothing in life is free, so there must always be an exchange of wealth. After all, we all require to be paid for our time, non? Just as you are being paid to sit here and drink my café.'

Hugo suppressed a sigh. 'What other services do you provide, Monsieur Esnault?'

Alexander fixed Hugo with an intense stare from the darkest eyes Hugo thought he had ever seen. Alexander's pale lips spread into a smile. Hugo recalled how Sebastian had described him, and he could see now exactly what he meant. Alexander Esnault was a handsome, charming man, with a warm smile and a pleasant demeanour. His dark eyes sparkled with kindness. But Hugo had been around long enough, encountered enough people to know one thing for certain. Despite any rational evidence, Alexander Esnault terrified him.

Alexander chuckled. 'I am a businessman and what good businessman does not assess what their clientele want, truly want, and then provide it to them.' He leaned forward in his chair. 'We're all adults here, non, mes amis? And we all know you will leave here and make a neat little report for your superiors stating you interviewed me as a witness, found me to be helpful but ultimately having no substantive information to assist in your investigation.' He clapped his hands together. 'And there we have it, case closed, and we can all go about our daily lives again with no one being hurt.'

Hugo started. 'Two young men are dead, Monsieur Esnault, at least one of them murdered and other young people are missing. This is serious and we are not going away, no matter who or what you think you know.'

Alexander nodded. 'I like your gumption, Hugo, truly I do. I admire you for it even, however, I do believe you are making more of this than there need be. There is no need for an investigation. Nothing happened which was not supposed to happen.'

Coco shot him an incredulous look. 'What are you even talking about? Two children are dead, possibly more are in danger and you, my dear, are one of the few common denominators. So, tell us what you know and quit the pre-rehearsed bullshit. You can threaten us in your ever-so-vague fashion from here until next week, but it means Buckley's to me.' She tried to stand but struggled with the sofa. Cedric shot Hugo an anxious look and between the two of them helped her into a standing position. She pulled her woollen coat straight. 'But, Monsieur, I'll tell you what does matter to me. Those kids. And if anything happens to another one of them and I find it involves you, or you could have prevented it, then I'll be back and if it's the last thing I do, I'll make sure you pay. Now, are we on the same page?'

Alexander cocked his head in apparent amusement. 'Do you know where these children were before I found them?' he asked. 'Sucking off tourists for five euros in a seedy back alley, and that's if they were lucky. They might get a room for a night in some flea-ridden hotel where if they made it through the night with only a black-eye or a cracked rib or two then it was a pretty successful night. I give these young people control. Dignity. Power.'

'And all for a healthy cut off the top,' Coco snorted.

He shrugged. 'We all have to make a living, and thanks to me and my contact, my protection, they live a much safer, happier life. I'm sure I need not remind you of the life lived by transients. With my help, these people operate nothing but a bartering system. Rich, powerful men can indulge their fantasies without fear of recrimination or blackmail. It is a win-win for all involved and one in which nobody gets hurt, unless they want to,' he added with a wink.

'Try telling that to the two young men lying in the freezers in Dr. Bernstein's morgue,' Hugo bristled.

'As sad as it is,' Alexander retorted, 'what happened

has nothing to do with me. You have to understand, there is a certain amount of jealousy attached to their line of work, if, for example, one person attracts the attention of a rich patron, it can lead to a great deal of bitterness and resentment, and how it manifests itself can often be very serious. I have no doubt that is what occurred in this instance. Petty jealousy erupting into a deadly encounter followed by bitter recriminations. Tres, tres tragic. As far as I know, any of us know in fact, all we are dealing with here is the splintering of a friendship, torn apart by jealousy. One child murders another and then is so overcome with guilt and remorse they cannot bear to carry on. Le fin.'

Coco turned her head between Hugo and Cedric, her eyes rolling as she did. 'Let's get out of here,' she muttered to them.

Hugo pushed himself off the uncomfortable sofa. 'Merci for your time, Monsieur Esnault.' He followed Coco and Cedric towards the door. He stopped and turned back. 'Make no mistake, Monsieur, we're not done here. We will find out what happened and if we have to lift up a whole lot of rocks to look under, then we will. If you have nothing to hide, and you want this investigation to be over, then I suggest you bear that in mind and do what you can to help us. Au revoir.'

Alexander Esnault smoothed his hair. 'Mais oui, Captain Duchamp. My regards to your lovely husband, Ben, and to your charming son Baptiste. And to you,

Captain Brunhild, tuck your four children up safely tonight.'

Hugo and Coco glanced at each other, barely able to hide the shudder they each felt.

'Is this Ben?'

'Oui,' Ben answered, shaking the sleep from his head. He pulled himself up, throwing his legs over the side of the bed. Hugo turned over in his sleep, the sheet sliding over his body. Ben reached over and pulled it back.

'This is Justine, Justine Le Contre, from the hostel, do you remember me?'

'Bien sûr,' Ben answered quickly, suddenly alert.

Silence. All Ben could make out was her slow breathing and the sounds of traffic behind her. He thought he could hear hushed, anxious voices near her. He also believed he recognised the anxious way she was breathing. She was worried, and he imagined deciding whether she could trust him. He held his breath. If he was going to proceed with opening his own hostel, he knew he had to find a way to be trusted by people who generally held no stock in assurances. She had called, so it appeared she had at least decided to give him the benefit of the doubt.

'Can we meet?' she spoke finally.

'Absolument,' he answered.

The line became muffled as if Justine was covering it with her hand. It sounded to Ben as if she was talking to someone in the background. 'Okay, but it'll have to be somewhere public,' she said.

'I don't really know Paris,' Ben answered, 'but I'll meet you wherever you want.'

'D'accord,' she replied quickly, 'I'll text you an

address, but come alone, and no police. They'll be watching and if there are any police, or anyone other than you, then they'll go and you'll never hear from them again. Do you understand?'

Ben stared at Hugo as he slept, making a snap decision. He nodded. 'Je comprends.'

Ben climbed out of the taxi and flicked on his sunglasses. The sun was spreading a yellow beam across the morning sky, throwing a warm glow over the Parisian morning. He had left the hotel without waking Hugo, feeling bad at having only left a note, but he had known Hugo would not have wanted him to go alone and Ben knew he would not have needed much encouragement for his husband to accompany him. He stepped into the park; it was early, barely eight o'clock, but it was already busy with dog walkers, people hurrying to and fro and to the east of the park in front of a large sculpture, a group of elderly people were engaged in tai chi. Ben moved slowly across the raised concrete play area, heading towards a row of seats. Justine had told him to sit on the furthest bench from the road, and he could see why. It was situated near the entrance to a densely wooded area where he imagined someone could watch without being seen and disappear into the undergrowth should they need to. He sat, filled with a mixture of fear and anxiety. He suddenly realised how out of place he felt and wondered what on earth he thought he was doing.

'Monsieur?'

He looked up, recognising the heaviness of Justine's voice. He narrowed his eyes, squinting into the still misty darkness of the woodland. Slowly she emerged, dressed from head to foot in black with a hoodie pulled tight covering most of her face. She stopped near the entrance, wary eyes flicking around the park. After a moment, she extended her arm behind and gesticulated with her hand. Ben watched as three people, two young men and a young woman, stepped out of the dark protection of the undergrowth. The youngsters, barely adults he guessed, watched him with eyes wide, like animals wary of being attacked. He noticed the three of them were holding hands so tightly it was as if their lives depended on it. Ben recognised Delphine Marchand from her description, shiny red hair cut into a bob and a face full of freckles. He could see why people had called her a young Irene Chapeau. He missed his best friend and wished he was at his house with her, their feet dangling into the swimming pool and talking about something, anything or even nothing, because it did not matter so long as they were together. The life he was seeing in Paris scared him more than he thought it should. He had always considered himself to be an adventurous man, but now, faced with adventure, he realised how far from the truth his belief was.

Justine led the three young adults towards him. Ben stood and held out a hand. They all looked at it as if they were unsure why he was offering it and what they were meant to do with it. He took it back, self-consciously stuffing it into the pocket of his jeans. 'Salut,' he breathed, 'my name is Ben Beaupain.'

'We know, we Googled you,' one of the young men said, stepping forward. He was smaller than Ben, with long black hair tucked behind an ear. He pressed his glasses onto his nose, green eyes appraising Ben with an intense, burning suspicion.

Ben nodded, wondering what on earth they may have discovered about him.

The second youth, a taller, athletic blond with piercing blue eyes, grinned. 'We figured you'd be trustworthy because of the amount of trouble you've gotten into,' he chuckled with a deep, confident voice.

Ben tried to shrug nonchalantly. 'I'm not sure about that,' he replied with a sheepish grin, 'but you can trust me.'

Delphine Marchand stepped in front of the other two. 'I'll be the judge of whether or not you can be trusted,' she snapped, her voice cold and lacking any of the warmth of Irene's. He supposed he could not imagine the life they had led, nor how difficult it might have become for them to trust anyone. Still, they had reached out. He moved across the path. They stepped back, the darker youth moving behind the blond youth. Ben raised his hand. 'Désolé,' he said stopping. 'I won't come any further.'

The dark-haired youth's head jutted out from behind his friend. 'Did you really rescue the street kid from the prison in Ireland?'

Ben's jaw tightened. 'It wasn't really a prison, not in name at least, but oui, me and my husband helped Baptiste.'

'And then you adopted him?' the youth shot back.

Ben nodded. 'It's complicated, but oui, we adopted Baptiste last year.'

The three youths exchanged looks which Ben did not comprehend. It was almost as if the three of them had created their own private language.

'Easy thing to do when you're rich,' Delphine shot at him.

Ben shrugged. 'Perhaps, except I'm not rich. I'm sure if Google got it right it should have told you any money I inherited from my father's estate I have given away in one form or another. In fact, I'm using most of it to open a youth hostel in my hometown.'

Delphine glared at him defiantly, jutting a hip forward in a way which also reminded Ben of Irene. 'Why? Got a taste for young flesh?'

Ben chuckled away his irritation. 'Hey, I was born in 1989, which hardly makes me ancient, my own flesh isn't so far off young either, you know. Besides, I'm married, very happily married.'

The blond youth gave Delphine a playful punch on the arm. 'That's you told, Delph,' he laughed. He smiled at

Ben. 'My name is Axel. Axel…'

'No surnames!' Delphine shrieked.

'Why not?' Axel countered.

'Because Google works both ways,' she snapped back, 'do you want people finding out your real name? Or where you came from?'

Axel shrugged. He nudged a shoulder playfully against the dark-haired youth. 'And this is mon mec, Jérémie.'

Ben smiled as Jérémie's cheeks reddened.

Justine Le Contre stepped in front of them. 'They came to me at the hostel because they need help. They need money, and I don't have any to give them.'

Ben frowned. 'Money?'

Axel nodded. 'Yeah, we need to get out of Paris, and fast.'

'Pourquoi?' Ben asked.

Jérémie stepped out from behind Axel. 'Have you seen them? Have you seen Marc and Jack?' His long, black hair fell across his face but he did not move it. Ben could see he was struggling to keep his emotions in check.

'Non,' Ben said in a whisper. 'But Hugo, mon mari, has.'

Jérémie nodded. 'Did they suffer?' He closed his eyes as if he was trying to shield himself from the answer. Ben wondered what his relationship was with them. Whatever it was, it appeared to have been a close one.

'Of course, they fucking suffered,' Delphine hissed.

'Marc fell off the fucking Eiffel Tower and Jack...' she stopped, her voice cracking.

Ben studied the three of them intently, realising he should try to remember everything they said so he could report back to Hugo and Coco. He nudged away the thought in the back of his mind that he should probably have told them where he was going. He faced Delphine. 'Weren't you on the Tower when it happened?'

Delphine cocked her head defiantly, her mouth tightening into an angry snarl. 'What have you heard?' she snapped, moving closer to Ben. He stepped back, stumbling against a kerb.

'Chill, Delph,' Axel said, 'we need help, you said that yourself, and we don't exactly have many people we can go to, do we?'

'I want to help,' Ben added reassuringly, 'and so would my husband. I promise you, you can trust Hugo.'

Delphine shook her head angrily. 'No police. They're all the same, they come into the club and expect something for nothing.'

'That might be true of some people, but not Hugo, I can assure you,' Ben retorted. 'I get you need money and you're scared, but what are you going to do? Run away? You have to know running away won't solve anything and you can't run forever. You have to trust someone and by coming here you've taken the first step, but I can only do so much. Hugo can do more, he can protect you. I'm not saying some cops aren't dangerous, but Hugo isn't one of them, and he knows others who can help, who can be trusted.'

Delphine stabbed her finger towards Justine. 'I told you this was a waste of time. All he wants to do is to hand us over to the police.' She glared at Ben. 'Don't you get it, that's how we got into trouble in the first place, by trusting people we ended up in this mess and I promise you, we won't make the same mistake again. Two of us died, they won't get a chance to get rid of any more of us.'

Ben did not reply as he considered how he was going to win their trust. They had taken the first step, primarily because they knew they needed to get away and to do so they needed money. It was like walking on eggshells and he was wary of putting the wrong words together. 'Tell me what you want then.'

The three of them exchanged an anxious look. 'As Axel said, we need to get out of Paris and fast,' Delphine replied, 'we have a target on our backs and they will not stop until they get to us and stop us before we can talk.'

Ben frowned. 'Then talk. Écoute, I get you don't trust authority, if I was in your position I guess I'd be the same, but use that distrust. Talk to Hugo or Captain Brunhild. They're both great people and they will do whatever they can to help you.' He stopped, clenching his hands together and pressing them against his heart. 'I know you have no reason to trust me, but I promise you, I swear on everything I am, Hugo Duchamp is the best person I have ever met. He will literally walk through fire for you, strangers or not, rather than put you in danger. He's done it before and it nearly cost him his life and despite that, and despite how much I wish otherwise, I know he would do it again, for a stranger, without thinking twice about it. It's one of the things I love most about him,' he stopped smiling, 'and one of the things I could happily wring his neck over. I don't know what you three and your friends have lived through, and I know you have no reason to believe me, and the privileged life I've led, but I beg you, trust me, trust Hugo and trust Captain Brunhild. We will do whatever it takes to protect you.'

Jérémie touched Axel's shoulder, rubbing it gently with his hand. 'He's right, Axel. What are we going to do, run forever? I don't know about you, but I don't want to spend the rest of my life looking over my shoulder.' He reached over, stroking Axel's cheek. 'Remember how we said we would see the sea? To feel sand between our toes? We've never been out of Paris. We've never seen the ocean. I want to see the ocean. I want to see the ocean with you and I want to smile, and I want to dance and sing and run and hold your hand and shout to the world. *Hey, fuck you if you hate me, but this is my mec and I love him. Him. Him. Him.* I don't want to spend the whole time thinking our past will catch up with us at any moment. I don't want to wake up every morning and wonder whether today will be the day I lose you. Our life needs to be better. We deserve that Axel, don't we?'

Axel turned his head slowly towards Jérémie before

grinning. He said nothing, instead reaching over and ruffling Jérémie's hair. His lips pursed into a kiss. He cut off, his eyes widening in horror.

'You fucking bastard!'

Ben spun around, his eyes narrowing in confusion. It was Delphine who had spoken, her words angry darts spat into the air. He followed her gaze. She was standing stock still, staring at the opposite side of the clearing. A man was staring back at her with an expression on his face Ben could only describe as being challenging, sarcastic almost. Like the cat that got the cream. Delphine grabbed Axel's and Jérémie's arms, pulling them away. 'I told you it was a fucking set up. I told you we couldn't trust anyone.' She glared at Ben. 'I knew it was too good to be true, you bastard. You'll pay for this!'

Ben threw his arms into the air. 'I don't understand what's going on here, I've done nothing wrong.' He looked again at the man who had attracted Delphine's interest. He had not moved, standing legs slightly apart, hands resting on his hips. Ben was sure he had not seen him before but guessed they were of a similar age. The man was shorter and slighter than Ben, with fair hair scraped into a bun on the top of his head and the blackest, most piercing eyes Ben thought he had ever seen. 'Who is that man?' he asked. There was something about the man which was familiar to him and it took a moment for him to place him. He was almost certain he had seen the man outside the hotel he and Hugo were staying in. He remembered because he had thought at the time the piercing eyes were staring straight at him.

Justine Le Contre pushed her arms through the air. 'Get out of here,' she hissed at Jérémie, Axel and Delphine. 'Get out and run, and don't look back. I'll do whatever I can to buy you time, he won't get past me, not when I've got a breath still in my body.'

Ben watched helplessly as the three disappeared into the darkness of the trees. 'Who is that man?' he asked again, panic clear in his voice.

Justine gave him the angriest of glares. 'He is le Diable, and you brought him here. Whatever happens to those kids is on your head now, you bastard.'

Ben lowered his head as if it was too difficult for him to lift it. He kicked his feet at the pebbles beneath him, a cloud of dust covering them. He could hear the sounds of the surrounding park, children playing, people laughing, but he did not lift his head. He did not want to see. He did not want to hear.

'Ben...' a voice called out, followed by rapidly approaching feet. Ben did not need to look to know who it was, and the evidence of concern and worry in the light, manly voice.

'Ben,' Hugo said, rubbing his hand across Ben's back. 'Ça va?'

Ben did not answer.

'Ça va?' Hugo asked again, his voice rising.

Ben lifted his head. His eyes were red as if he had been, or was on the verge of crying. He spotted Coco and Cedric a few steps behind and shook his head angrily. 'Great, everyone is here to witness my humiliation.'

'Humiliation?' Hugo asked with a confused frown.

Ben shrugged his right shoulder, pushing Hugo's hand away. Hugo's face crinkled in confusion. 'Ben,' he whispered.

Ben jumped to his feet and moved away, pushing his hands into his pockets. 'Merde, where are my fucking cigarettes?'

Hugo pulled out his own pack, moving quickly to Ben and handing it to him. Ben snatched them and lit one, exhaling smoke so quickly it made him cough. He sucked on the cigarette hungrily while avoiding eye contact with Hugo. Hugo exchanged a puzzled, anxious look with Coco and Cedric.

Hugo approached his husband cautiously. 'What happened, cheri?'

'I fucked up, as usual, that's what happened. Jesus Christ, I'm glad my father is dead or else I'd have to deal with his *I-told-you-you're-a-complete-failure* stare,' Ben snapped back throwing the cigarette to the ground. He cursed and pulled out another and lit it. 'And my stupidity and arrogance may have just placed three kids in terrible danger.'

Coco stepped towards the clearing, keen eyes processing the scene. 'What do you mean, Ben?'

He moved away, stopping in front of the trees marking the entrance to the park where he had witnessed the young people disappearing into. He shook his head. 'I thought it would be better, *easier* if I spoke to them. Justine Le Contre said they were scared of the authorities so I thought I'd play the big man and race on down here and do my whole, *I'm a cool kid like you guys, and you can trust me, and hey, mon mec is a flic and he's a cool guy too, and you can trust him,*' he shook his head more angrily this time, 'what a fucking arrogant, delusional idiot I am to think I could A) do anything useful to help them or B) stop them from getting into more trouble?' He turned to Hugo. 'Back in Montgenoux I used to think I was a big fish in a small pond, but two days in Paris and I realise I'm just a small, pathetic fish no matter where I am and my stupidity could have just landed those kids in a whole heap of shit.'

Hugo approached him and gingerly touched Ben's arm. 'You're going to have to explain to us what happened. But I know one thing for certain, you are none of those things. You are the best person I know, THE best person,' he repeated the words, emphasising each syllable. 'And I don't know what happened here exactly, or why you called hysterically and told us to get over here, but I know you.' He smiled. 'And I love you, and you know you need a moment to convince yourself you are exaggerating so that's what we will do. We're going to stand here and mediate. We will enjoy this beautiful Parisian morning and take in the air as we should do on such a beautiful morning.'

Ben pulled himself back, gawping at Hugo. 'What on earth are you talking about, Hugo?' He turned to Coco and Cedric. 'What on earth is he talking about?'

Coco shrugged. 'Beats the shit out of me.'

Hugo grinned. 'I got your attention, didn't I?'

Ben gave him a reluctant smile. 'Justine called to tell me that Delphine Marchand and her friends were willing to talk to me, but only me.'

Hugo nodded, turning his head and gesturing around the park. 'You came to meet with them in an open space, which was very wise.' He paused. 'Oui, you should have told me, I understand why you didn't, but...' he did not finish the sentence because he knew he did not need to.

Ben shook his head angrily, sucking on the cigarette as if his life depended on it. 'Non, I fucked up, and I fucked up bad. And the truth is, they didn't even tell me anything, other than they're scared, dead scared, and that they need to get out of Paris fast and they need money. They didn't tell me why, or who was after them. There wasn't time because stupid bastard I am, I led him right to them.'

'Him?' Coco asked, her voice sharp as she moved towards him. 'Who?'

Ben tried to meet her gaze, but the burning intensity unnerved him and he instead turned in the direction of the clearing. 'The man. Justine Le Contre called him the devil, and I could see what she meant. He didn't look bad, there was just something about him, something wrong, something off. I don't know how to explain it other than that.'

Hugo raised an eyebrow in Coco's direction. 'You said you led him to them. What did you mean by that?'

Ben stepped further into the darkness of the clearing, taking in a sharp intake of breath at the sudden change of temperature as he moved away from the sunlight. 'When Justine pointed him out, standing over there, it only took me a moment to recognise him, although we never spoke - I recognised him from this morning. When I came out of the hotel, he was standing

on the other side of the street, staring straight at me -
straight through me is what it actually felt like. At first, I
thought he might know me, but there was no recognition
on his face. He was smiling, but it was just cold.' He
shuddered. 'To my shame, I thought nothing of it and I
should have, damn it. I should have because he must have
been watching me and he must have followed me right
here. I led the devil straight to those poor, terrified kids.'

Hugo frowned and scratched his head. 'I'm sure it
must just be a coincidence. Somebody who looked similar.
I mean, who even knows you in Paris and would follow
you?'

'They knew exactly who he was, and he knew who
they were because he took off right after them, so don't
fucking patronise me,' Ben snapped. He raised his hand.
'Désolé, I'm just a little fried. I know you're just trying to
make me feel better.'

Hugo moved into the clearing and touched Ben's
hand. 'It's okay, cheri, truly it is. If you say it was the same
man, then of course I believe you. What can you tell us
about him?'

Ben pursed his lips, tilting his head and closing his
eyes as he concentrated on retrieving the memory. 'And I
realise it sounds a little crazy, I understand why Justine
called him the devil. There was just something about him,
his eyes weren't cold, they were just... just, oh merde, I
can't explain it. There was just something *wrong* about
him.'

'What did he look like?' Coco asked.

Ben shrugged. 'White. About my height, thin but in a worked-out sort of way, you know? The blackest eyes I think I've ever seen, and blond hair, scraped back into one of those buns everyone seems to have these days.'

'What did you say?' Coco asked, her voice wary as she moved quickly towards him.

Ben's eyes flicked between Hugo and Coco. 'A topknot bun, he had a topknot. Hey, I'm not judging, just not everyone can get away with having one.'

'Putain,' Coco muttered under breath.

'What is it?' Ben asked, alarmed.

'He led him straight to them,' Cedric grumbled.

'What does he mean?' Ben asked Hugo, his eyes wide with panic.

'We don't know that,' Hugo said to Cedric. 'Why would he even be watching our hotel? And if he was going to, surely he's got people to do that sort of thing for him. I don't imagine he's the kind of man who gets his own hands dirty.'

Coco shook her head slowly, biting down on her lip. 'It can't be a coincidence. We just talked to him, and we made it pretty clear we would keep investigating and you heard what he said. He even mentioned Ben by name. It makes sense if it was true when he said he didn't know where the missing kids were that he might keep an eye on us in case we found them first.'

'Will someone tell me what the hell is going on?'

Ben roared.

Hugo rubbed his arm reassuringly. 'I'm sure it's nothing, it's just the man you described sounds like somebody we interviewed.'

'Somebody very dangerous,' Coco muttered.

'What?' Ben cried. He stared imploringly at Hugo. 'What does she mean?'

Hugo lowered his head. 'We know nothing, Ben,' he answered softly. 'The man is a witness and possibly involved in some crimes. His name is Alexander Esnault.'

'Alexander Esnault?' Ben cried, shrilly. 'The guy Sebastian was talking about? The one he's terrified of?' He covered his mouth in obvious shock. 'Putain.'

'And you led him right to the very kids who were probably running from him,' Coco snapped.

'Captain Brunhild,' Hugo interrupted sharply. 'That's not very helpful, particularly considering we don't know a damn thing. And how was Ben supposed to know someone might follow him? As I was going to say before, how would Alexander Esnault even know who Ben was and that he was worth following?'

Coco shrugged. 'He could have had your cell phones bugged.'

Hugo gave a look of disbelief. 'I think you're getting a little carried away. We don't even know how Esnault is involved, or if he is at all. As far as we know he's nothing more than a petty pimp and/or drug dealer, and I'm not sure his reach would extend to bugging telephones.'

'We don't know how far this goes,' Cedric interjected, 'or who Esnault is being paid to protect, but we know there are some pretty big names mixed up in all of this and they have power, and access to technology even we probably don't have. Esnault more or less confirmed these guys will do anything, *anything* to protect themselves.'

Hugo turned around. 'If that's all true, and it was Alexander Esnault who followed Ben, then he has to know Ben would tell us and we'd figure out it was him, which means whatever he is up to, he isn't likely to hurt the kids.'

'Isn't likely?' Ben cried.

'Désolé,' Hugo replied, 'bad choice of words, what I mean is, the chances are he just wanted to get to them before we did to warn them to keep their mouths shut. From what I saw of Alexander Esnault he seemed to me to be the sort of man for whom self-preservation is most important. He knows if we keep digging we're likely to find out the extent of his business which probably has nothing to do with the murder, and that's why he wanted to get to them first.'

Ben, Coco and Cedric all gave him a doubtful look. He shrugged. 'I don't know, and nor do any of you.'

'Still, Ben shouldn't have...' Coco began.

'Captain Brunhild,' Hugo snapped, the bite evident in his voice. 'I don't want to fall out with you, but Ben did nothing wrong and you know it. The fact is, when those missing kids got in touch with Justine Le Contre, they reached out to Ben. They trusted him, not you, not the police. We know they're alive because of Ben and the chances are they got away and because Alexander followed them, we now know for certain they have information which worries him.' He stepped back into the park and flicked on his glasses, straining his eyes as he viewed the streets which lined it. He pointed. 'Regarde, there, there and there. There are CCTV cameras, which means they are almost certain to have picked him up, which gives you something to throw at him, non?'

Coco looked at the cameras and then turned to Cedric. 'I want the footage and then we will go pay a visit to Monsieur Esnault and find out exactly what the hell he's been up to.' She turned to Ben. 'Désolé, Ben, I didn't mean to…'

Ben held up his hands. 'It doesn't matter. Just find those kids so I can damn well apologise to them, d'accord?'

Coco nodded and stepped away.

'I've heard a lot about you, Captain Duchamp,' Commander Stanic said, pressing a cold, hard hand into Hugo's. Hugo fought the urge to drag his hand away, offering the Commander a tight smile. He was not sure what he had been expecting from the Commander of the 7e arrondissement and the father of two of Coco's children but he was surprised by the tall, muscular man with olive Mediterranean skin. He was also older than he expected, probably fifty or so, making him a good decade older than Coco. Hugo could not imagine they had anything in common, or rather, he supposed, that might have been the point.

'Enchanté, Commander Stanic,' Hugo replied, 'and I'm especially grateful to you for extending the hand of professional courtesy to me.'

The Commander pushed himself back in his chair, fingers absent mindedly scratching at a long scar on his right cheek. It appeared to Hugo he was being appraised with a mixture of puzzled confusion as if the Commander could not decide whether Hugo was being facetious. 'You're not on duty, Captain, officially at least, so no need to be so formal.'

Hugo glanced at the nameplate on the desk and nodded. 'Merci, Mordecai, and my name is Hugo.'

The Commander laughed. 'Dieu, only my mother calls me Mordecai.' He indicated for Hugo to sit on the vacant seat next to Coco, who was picking at her fingernails. 'Or people I owe money to,' he added, shooting a haughty look in Coco's direction. 'Everyone else calls me Morty.'

Coco opened her mouth to respond but instead blew a loud raspberry. Morty's cheeks reddened. 'So, tell me where you're at,' he said sullenly.

Coco cleared her throat and brought him up to date with the investigation. He listened intently, jotting occasionally on a notepad. When she had finished he spoke. 'You have every right to be concerned about Alexander Esnault.'

Hugo leaned forward in his chair. 'He mentioned he knew you.'

The Commander appeared visibly angry. 'I'd hardly say he knew me, or that I know him. I've seen him at the club and it's always been damn obvious he has the ear of some pretty powerful people. That became increasingly obvious all the times his name has come up in an investigation and each time, one way or another he's wriggled away like some damn worm on a fishing line.'

'What sort of investigations? Serious stuff?' Coco asked.

'Oui,' he replied, 'when you were... away there was a series of drug-related murders. Pushers from different areas were "made an example of" you might say, and the word on the street was Esnault didn't just give the order for the hits. He carried them out himself. He not only enjoys getting his hands dirty, he's not afraid of doing it because he believes, or he knows, he is untouchable. I need not tell you, either of you, how dangerous it can be when criminals lack any kind of empathy.'

'I thought so,' Coco exhaled.

'And we're talking pretty brutal stuff too,' Morty continued, 'check the files, they're all still open because they are,' he stopped, making air quotes with his fingers, 'unsolved.' He snorted. 'And one of the few times in my career my boss hasn't come down on me about having open cases on the books. In fact, when it comes to Alexander Esnault it seems it is actively encouraged to look the other way.'

'What made you sure Esnault was responsible for these crimes?' Hugo asked.

Morty patted his stomach. 'Gut. And he pretty much admitted it to me during the investigations, but,' he shrugged, 'as I said, friends in high places and all that. I wasn't actually warned off investigating Esnault, but the implication was clear. *Move on.*' He stopped and doodled something on the notepad. 'I've met a few sociopaths in my career and there's no doubt in my mind he's right up there, but...' he trailed off, leaving the silence hanging in the air.

'I hate to say it,' Coco said, shooting the Commander with a sly look, 'and it's pretty much a first, but I have to agree with Mordecai.'

Hugo sighed. 'I agree, but we come back to the point. Why follow Ben? Is he really the kind of man with resources enough to put traces on calls? Or was it just a fluke? And why do it in the first place? Unless…'

'Unless?' Coco asked.

Hugo rubbed his jaw. 'Maybe we're looking at this wrong. Perhaps he was following Ben for some other reason.'

'A warning,' Coco said simply.

Hugo nodded. 'I got the impression Alexander Esnault is a bully. A man used to getting his own way, and he's dangerous because he's not afraid of getting his own hands dirty because he knows he has protectors.'

'You think your husband's life could be in danger?' the Commander asked.

Hugo and Coco exchanged an anxious look. 'It could have been meant as a warning, a sort of, look how close I can get, remember, he mentioned your children too, Coco.'

Coco and Morty shared an anxious look. 'He did what?' Morty hissed through gritted teeth.

Coco raised her hand. 'He was puffing, he knew all about us because no doubt that moron Michel Lomet tipped him off we were going to see him. As Hugo said, Alexandre Esnault is the kind of man who likes to be in control. It wouldn't have taken him long to make a few telephone calls to find out some information on us both. Just his way of showing off. I'm not worried.'

Hugo watched her closely, not entirely believing her assertion because it was not one he entirely shared himself.

He continued. 'The fact Ben was meeting with Justine Le Contre and the others could have been just an unlucky coincidence,' he sighed, 'either way, Alexander Esnault is a dangerous man, and we need to know more about him.'

'We need to talk to him again,' Coco added. 'I need to know why he followed Ben, and why he went after those kids. And more importantly what happened afterwards.'

Morty shook his head. 'Even if we have CCTV footage, you know as well as I do it means nothing. He'll just claim it was a coincidence, and he will never admit going after those kids or having any involvement in their disappearance. Hell, he won't even last ten minutes in custody even if we could get him that far.'

'They could be in real danger, Morty,' Coco shook her head. 'And as much as I think he's probably an arrogant prick who just likes to show off, I don't like him knowing about our kids or Ben, just in case he feels cornered. We all know what damage psychos can do when they feel cornered.'

Morty picked up the telephone. His face muscles flexing. 'I'll arrange for a patrol to monitor Ben's hotel and your house, and I'll get my mother to go over and stay with the kids.'

Coco chuckled. She looked at Hugo. 'Alexander Esnault might think he's scared of no one, but he's not met Mama Stanic and believe me, she'd give him a run for his money.' She stopped, the seriousness appearing on her face again. 'As for Ben, I'm sure he won't like it, but perhaps you could ask him to keep a low profile from now on and certainly no more unexpected trips out.'

Hugo nodded. 'There's no need. He's waiting for me outside, and under the circumstances, I don't intend on leaving him alone again while we're still in Paris.' He stood. 'But the truth is, I don't enjoy feeling like we are sitting targets, and I hate the fact Esnault is so convinced he's untouchable. And right now, I want to understand exactly what kind of protection Esnault has.'

'And how are you going to do that?' Coco asked.

'The Minister of Justice asked me to come to Paris to look into this situation,' Hugo replied, 'and if he wants me to stay, he will have to help us as well and that means finding a way to call Alexander Esnault off because if Esnault is protected, we're going to need someone on our side with as much power.' He pulled out his cell phone and input a number. 'Bonjour. Je m'appelle Captain Hugo Duchamp. puis-je parler à Monsieur Le Minister? Ah, oui? Merci beaucoup au revoir.' He hung up and placed the telephone back in his pocket. 'Apparently, the Minister is unavailable because he is out of the office at a birthday celebration at… guess where?'

Coco jumped up, pulling her cardigan from the back of the chair. 'Our favourite den of inequity, perhaps?'

Hugo nodded. He glanced at his watch. It was almost seven pm. He pursed his lips. 'I suppose it might be a good chance to see *énergique* when it's full of clients and what sort of clients they might be.'

Morty pointed to the two of them. 'D'accord but you can't go dressed like that. They'll not let either of you through the doors looking the way you do, so get changed before you go.'

Coco looked down at her dress, fingers picking at a food stain on the lapel of her shirt. 'Oh, I don't know, this was clean on yesterday.'

'And so was the baby sick,' Morty grumbled. He paused, giving them the once over. 'And take Cedric just in case anything happens.'

Coco raised an eyebrow. 'Are you saying Captain Duchamp and I aren't capable of looking after ourselves?'

Morty laughed. 'I wouldn't dare, but I'd feel better if you have some extra muscle with you. You two might be able to talk your way out of trouble with your sparkling wit and knowledge but just in case you need someone who can give a good thump, I'd be happier if Cedric was on your tail.'

Coco gave him a doubtful look. She smiled at Hugo. 'Let's go, Hugo. You and your lovely husband can escort me. I'd quite like to see how the other half live and spend their evenings, wouldn't you?'

I can't imagine anything worse, Hugo thought, giving her a weary smile.

Hugo stepped out of the cab and reached behind, feeling for the reassuring hand of Ben. Their fingers touched and wrapped around each other. He smiled, narrowing his eyes ahead of him. At night, *énergique* was exactly as he had imagined it would be. Pulsating music vibrated onto the street, and flashing neon lights cast moving flashes onto the pavement. Fake laughter and indecipherable chatter fought with the relentless beat of music he had no desire to listen to. He watched as a man and a woman exited. The man's hand was wrapped around the woman's waist, his fingers tapping against her breasts, his tongue darting in and around her ear. He whispered something to her and whatever it was, it caused her to playfully slap his arm. It seemed to Hugo like a pre-rehearsed dance, the silent formation of a contract. They moved across the sidewalk towards the open door of a limousine. Hugo bit his cheek, wondering what it was about him which was missing. It hurt him he was missing the ability to take part in such dances. They seemed fake to him, and he had no desire to become something he was not. He was looking into a world he did not understand and every part of him told him he did not want to. He did not belong in places such as *énergique* and he never would and it had taken him a long time to realise he did not need to. He was fine as he was.

'You two scrubbed up well,' Coco said, stepping out of the taxi.

Hugo tipped his head towards Ben. 'Thank Ben. We went shopping and if it were up to me, I,' he glanced down at the crisp linen suit he was wearing, 'wouldn't have bought this.'

Coco nodded, smoothing her dress, an emerald green velvet gown and tugged at it as if a desperate attempt to pull out the crinkles. 'I swear I don't know what I do to dresses to make them look so bad. Honestly, it didn't look this terrible on the mannequin.'

Hugo smiled. 'You look lovely,' he said.

'A million bucks,' Ben agreed.

Cedric climbed out of the cab, tugging irritably at the bow tie he was wearing. 'As long as I live I'll never understand why a person has gotta get dressed up like a penguin just so they can get into a glorified knocking shop.'

Coco gave him a quizzical look. 'This isn't your first rodeo, Lieutenant. I wanted you here tonight, not for muscle but so you could show us the ropes. I want to see the real *énergique*, not the whitewash they will be more interested in showing us.'

'I don't know why you think I could...' Cedric began.

Coco raised her hand and headed into the lights of the club. 'Come on, sweeties! Let's show these old, probably mainly white, rich folks how to really party.'

Hugo stopped abruptly in the foyer, causing Ben to

crash into him. 'What's wrong?' Ben said in surprise at their abrupt stop. Hugo did not reply, his eyes fixed firmly in front of him. 'Who are you staring at?' Ben asked, trying to see what had caught Hugo's attention.

Hugo stepped to the side, focusing on a narrow hallway leading into what he presumed was the main area of the club because of the laughter, excited chatter and clinking glasses. 'It doesn't matter, it's nothing,' he answered, 'let's just get this over with,' he added with a bite to his tone.

Ben exchanged a puzzled look with Coco and they stepped behind Hugo as he led them towards the entrance. Ben stared at the men who had seemingly caught Hugo's attention. He recognised neither of them and as far as he could make out, one man was older, perhaps in his sixties and the other much younger. There was something about the older man which he recognised, something about the shape of the dark hair swept over a wide forehead. He turned his head sharply; the realisation hitting him like a sledgehammer. Could it be? He did not have a chance to ask Hugo, who by now was five strides ahead, so he ran to catch up to him, slipping his arm through Hugo's. He nuzzled against his neck, the familiar scent of soap and Chanel hitting his senses in a way nothing else ever had. Hugo pushed open the door and a gust of air and noise enveloped them. Hugo stopped, his eyes darting from left to right. He muttered something and continued heading towards the bar where a row of champagne flutes lined the marble top. Hugo lifted one of them, drained its contents and then took another. Within seconds he took a third. Ben appeared by his side, rubbing Hugo's back gently.

Coco and Cedric appeared moments later. Coco glanced at the champagne with suspicion. 'Are these free?' she asked the barman.

The barman gave her a pitying look and nodded. 'Bien sûr,' he said as if it was obvious and a stupid question to ask.

Coco tipped her head, her mouth twisting into an impressed smile. 'In which case, we're going to need more, MUCH more.' She turned to Hugo. 'What's up, Hugo? You look like you've seen a ghost.'

Hugo turned to her. 'Not a ghost,' he replied, 'but it might as well be.' He took another drink and turned, pressing his body against the bar. He lifted his head. At over six feet tall he could see above the crowd of people and he found at that moment he hated them and all they represented. Gay, carefree laughter had always felt alien to him, and the tangible feeling of never fitting in, never being part of anything was as stark and painful to him than it ever had been. 'Where the fuck is Jean Lenoir?' he hissed through gritted teeth. 'I don't want to be here for a second longer than I have to.' He looked at Ben. 'In fact, once we've seen him, how about you and I get the fuck out of here? Tonight. Back to Montgenoux, away from this... *this*.' He stopped and took another drink, gulping it desperately.

Ben pulled back his head, staring sharply at Hugo as if he did not recognise him. 'Oh, merde. Was that man in the hallway your father?' he whispered.

Hugo turned his head and slowly nodded. He raised his hand before Ben could say anything else. 'Let's just find Jean Lenoir so we can get out of here, okay?'

Ben nodded. He pointed towards an exit in the far corner of the room. 'Regarde, there is a balcony, let's go and have a smoke and take a breath, d'accord?'

Hugo pursed his lips in contemplation and reluctantly followed Ben, Coco and Cedric close behind. As they stepped onto the balcony, Hugo sucked in the cool night air as if his life depended on it. He felt on the verge of a panic attack and it angered him in a way he did not understand. He was reminded of the time only a few short years earlier when he had returned to France for the first time in over a decade and he had been paralysed with a sense of overwhelming fear and panic, terrified of turning corners and seeing a face he recognised. He was angry because he believed he had spent the following years emerging from the cloud of uncertainty and loneliness which had tainted his childhood, but he had receded back to the young Hugo, terrified of disappointing his father but knowing there was no way to avoid it. Instead, he had turned away, skulking like a child rather than the thirty-eight-year-old man he was. He took the cigarette from Ben and sucked hungrily on it, giving his husband a smile he knew was everything but sincere.

'Are you all right?' Ben asked, the concern clear in his voice.

Hugo nodded. 'Sure. A bit embarrassed, I don't know why I did that. I mean I should have introduced you, but…'

Ben rubbed Hugo's arm. 'Non, you shouldn't. I have no interest in meeting either of your parents, honestly I don't. The fact is, I don't trust myself around them. Sorry if that's shit of me, but it is what it is and I am who I am.' He squeezed Hugo's arm. 'Tu es mon homme, mon mec et j'adore.' He paused. 'And I'm sorry but I'd rip the head off anybody who hurts you, and I don't care if it is your parents, because they of all people owed you more, still OWE you more.'

Hugo kissed the top of Ben's head. He inhaled the cigarette. 'Let's just find Jean Lenoir so we can get out of here,' he said in a whisper.

Coco drained her glass and handed it to Cedric. 'Lieutenant, bring more of this free alcohol, if I had to go the trouble of paying a babysitter and buying a new pair of stockings, and wearing underwear which is in danger of cutting off my circulation, then I might as well make the most of it.' She turned to Hugo. 'Did I ever tell you about my father?' she asked.

He shook his head.

Coco took a drag on his cigarette. 'By most standards, he's a good old traditional Jew. Goes to Synagogue, keeps a kosher house, follows the Talmud laws, except…' she paused, her tongue darting across her lips, 'for the last twenty years he's been schlepping his secretary, a certain Mademoiselle Marstein. All tits, blonde ringlets, and blood-red lipstick. Everyone knows, Mama, the Rabbi, but they all turn a blind eye because he's "such a good man."' She gave a short laugh laced with irony. 'I tell you this to remind you, to be a father is not necessarily a stepping stone to being a good person. When I was eighteen, I fell pregnant "out of wedlock" as they call it. He threw me out of his house saying I had made my own bed, and now I had to lie in it without his or my mother's help because of the shame I had brought upon the family. I love and loathe my father in equal measures but I see him for what he is, a weak man plagued with his own insecurities, and I choose not to let him have any influence over my life and how I live it. It's incredibly freeing. I roll up for dinner occasionally and smile at him through gritted teeth and rose-tinted eyes and then I go about my own business sticking two fingers up to the hypocrite.'

Hugo nodded. 'You're right, of course. It's just I much prefer an ocean or at least a few hundred miles between me and my father. I…' he stopped, turning his head sharply. Some raised voices had caught his attention, and he cocked his head, trying to determine which direction it was coming from. It was difficult to distinguish between the idle chatter of the patrons and the voices he recognised.

'That's Jean Lenoir, isn't it?' Ben asked. He looked

around. 'But where is it coming from?' He moved across the balcony and peered over. He stopped, a breath of air pushing out of his lungs. He hesitated, stumbling on his feet. 'Let's go inside,' he said turning around.

Hugo frowned. 'Well, is it Jean Lenoir or not? That's why we're here, after all, to see him…' He halted, his left eye twitching as he cocked his head to the left as if trying to focus on something in particular.

You're an asshole, always have been, always will be.

Hugo recognised the voice of Jean Lenoir but could not see him, and he wondered what had been done to annoy the Minister of Justice this time.

Takes one to know one, Jean, you social-climbing Neanderthal.

The reply hammered against Hugo's skull. The voice of his childhood. The voice of disapproval and mild contempt, part boredom and part irritation.

'Come on, let's go,' Ben said, tugging at Hugo's sleeve. Hugo did not move. Ben looked helplessly at Coco.

'Let's go have dinner somewhere, Hugo,' Coco said, 'my treat. We don't really need to see Jean Lenoir tonight.'

Still, Hugo did not move. His left foot began tapping anxiously against the ground. His right hand shook as he took the cigarette to his mouth. 'Shh,' was all he said as he inched forward. He stopped in front of the balcony and inched his head forward to look beneath. He could see the back of his father's head, his arms gesticulating angrily towards Jean Lenoir. Neither man looked up. Hugo knew he should leave, but he was again locked to the spot he found himself in.

'*And don't think I don't know why you dragged Hugo all the way to Paris,' Pierre Duchamp continued.*

'*And why would that be?' Jean Lenoir replied, sarcasm clear in his voice.*

'*To embarrass me.'*

'*Embarrass you? What are you talking about, Pierre? Is this all really about me getting the job you thought was yours?'*

'*The job was mine!' Pierre hissed. 'I should have been Minister of Justice. They promised it to me and believe me, I had to kiss enough pinkies to get it, and then you came along with your secrets and suddenly I'm out in the cold.' He laughed. 'But they say what goes around comes around. You became Minister when you didn't deserve it, walking over the battered body of your predecessor and now the same will happen to you. And when I walk over you, Jean, I will make every step count. You mark my words.'*

'*You are insane, Pierre. Delusional and insane,' Jean Lenoir snorted. 'And your petty vendetta will do nothing, achieve nothing.'*

Pierre stepped away, his feet slapping angrily against the pebbled walkway. '*And the sad thing is, you thought bringing Hugo to Paris would do what, embarrass me? Stop me? If that's the case, Jean, I'm here to tell you, you are wrong, dead wrong, and the only person my half-breed of a son will embarrass is you.'*

'*How would Hugo embarrass me?' Jean replied. 'He's a fine, honest police officer.'*

'*He's weak and mild, as dull as the stripes on your suit, Jean,' Pierre retorted. 'And he's been that way all of his life, born a long gangly mess of girly limbs. It was quite the shock to me when I first saw him in the hospital, I can tell you. The fact is, he should have been a girl, at least then his sex would have been useful, instead he's ridden the shirttails of the Duchamp name and capitalised on quotas of diversity. Hell, if he had to I'm sure he'd decide next week he was a transvestite or transexual or whatever the hell the buzzword is at the moment. The only thing my son is good at is using his mouth to pleasure other perverts and his ass to entice them. And that is the man you think will embarrass me and stop me from ruining you?' Pierre chuckled. 'The only thing you have done Jean Lenoir is made my job of finishing you off once and for all even easier.'*

'It's true,' Jean interjected, 'when his name came up as a possible replacement, someone to fix the hell of a mess in Montgenoux, I took it as a sign. I thought it would embarrass you, the gay, effeminate son who was sure to fail in a town already in self-destruct mode. Oui, I thought it would be the end of you, one way or another, and you'd crawl back under the rock you came from.' Jean sighed. 'And then something very unexpected happened. He turned it around, solved the crime and restored order in a way I never imagined possible. And he's done the same with every other crime which has come his way since.'

Pierre Duchamp muttered incomprehensibly.

Jean continued. 'And the fact is he is one of the finest, most honourable police officers I have ever met, and believe me, I don't say that lightly. And the fact he has no interest in pursuing furthering his career, which he could do if he wanted to, means he will most likely spend the rest of his life doing something you and I will never do. Making an honest to God difference. Saving real lives on a day-to-

day basis, while we sit in our nice, expensive offices complaining about our expense account dinners and trips.'

'My son,' Pierre interrupted, 'could have had that life. It was his birthright.'

Jean snorted. 'And instead, he ran in the opposite direction, determined to do the complete opposite to you. I mean, have you even bothered to see your son in action? How he deals with people at the lowest points in their lives? How he helps them?'

'Philanthropy is overrated,' Pierre sniped, 'and it's boring and doesn't pay the bills.'

'You really are a piece of work.'

'Oh, come on, Jean! We're cut from the same cloth - you and I. Hell, under the same circumstances I would have used Hugo too, it was a good call trying to get him to distract me, but you should have known it wouldn't derail me. His presence won't stop me from doing the one thing which means more than anything to me in the world right now.'

'And that is?' Jean asked.

'Getting rid of you. I may have missed out on becoming Minister of Justice but I've set my sights even higher now and when I ruin you, and I WILL ruin you, Jean Lenoir, be under no illusions about that. And when I'm finished with you, your drug-taking, your use of prostitutes and Dieu knows what else I can throw at you will all ensure that the only job you'll be able to find is training overweight idiots in gyms.'

'Bring it on, Pierre,' Jean retorted, his voice loud and confident. 'I'm more than up for the challenge. You won't harm me; you can't harm me. The best you have on me is the fact I slept with a *young woman, a legally adult young woman, who may or may not be a prostitute. You'll never prove either way, and there was certainly no money exchanged hands, so be careful of the lies you spread. But you are wrong, your son is the ace up my sleeve. He will solve this murder and every lie you've told about me, every half-truth you've spread will echo around the corridors of Parisian power, believe me, because I'll make sure of it. And your little dream, your foolish dream, will be dust. And as for Hugo. Well, as long as I am in office, I will make sure he gets the chance to keep doing what he's doing. I'm sorry he had a father like you. I can't do anything about that, but what I can do is make sure he has a friend like me to ensure idiots like you can't harm him. So, do your worst, Pierre because I guarantee you, I know how to fight dirty too and despite what you think of him, so does your son. He can take care of himself when he has to. Au revoir.'*

Hugo turned to Ben. 'Can we go now?' he asked, his voice weak and thready. He moved towards the exit.

Coco looked at Ben. 'Do you want to slap Pierre Duchamp as much as I do?' she whispered.

Ben headed towards Hugo. 'Oh, you have no idea what I would do to him if I met him right now, but you would probably have to arrest me. Let's get Hugo out of here before I do something I'll NOT regret.'

Coco flopped heavily onto a chair and indicated for Hugo to take the seat opposite her. He did, lowering himself slowly and crossing his legs. He took a moment to take in his surroundings. The main office at Commissariat de Police du 7e arrondissement was a hive of activity and bore little similarity to his own office in Montgenoux. In comparison, it felt cold and clinical, and he found himself yearning for the warmth of Mare-Louise Shelan, who ran the Montgenoux Police Nationale with military precision. He missed Etienne Martine, the world-class forensic expert who had also become a true and trusted friend. Hugo realised he even missed his two young Lieutenants - Marianne Laurent and Markus Garrel and their constant bickering. For the first time in his life, Hugo realised what he was feeling was homesickness. He loved Paris. He almost felt it in his bones, but it was not home to him now, and he realised nor could it be as long as his father was there.

'I thought we'd go through the lost boy files,' Coco said, breaking his concentration.

'Pardon?' Hugo asked with a frown.

'The lost boy files,' she repeated slowly, genuine concern etched on her face as she studied him. 'Are you okay, Hugo?' She paused, tapping crooked and broken fingernails of varying colours on her desk. 'I mean unless you want to talk about what just happened at the club?'

Hugo studied her face and all he saw was kindness and genuine concern. He gave her a lopsided grin. 'Mon Dieu, non!' he exclaimed.

'Thank goodness for that! I'm no good at polite social chit-chat either,' she retorted. She returned a smile. 'For what it's worth, your father is an asshole.'

Hugo threw back his head and guffawed. 'That felt good,' he said afterwards, 'and yeah, he is.'

'But as for Jean Lenoir,' she added, 'who knew there was a heart beating beneath those intense pectoral muscles?'

Hugo nodded. The Minister had surprised him as well, staunchly defending him in such a way, and it was indeed out of character and very much a surprise. On the contrary, Jean Lenoir had shown little evidence of having any kind of respect for Hugo over the few years they had worked together. 'You said you wanted to look again at your files concerning the so-called lost boy, pourquoi?' he asked Coco, changing the difficult subject.

'Well,' Coco replied, 'while some might call it thorough and efficient police work, I actually call it clutching at straws and hoping to pull something out of the air.'

Hugo rubbed his jaw. 'And what are you hoping to find?'

She stared at the slim folder in front of her and held it up. Two sheets of paper fell from it and wafted down. 'It's not much to show for a young kid found on the streets, is it?'

Hugo nodded. 'You did what you could, Captain. If you hadn't discovered him, something terrible could have happened. I know it feels as if we should always check up on those who cross our paths, but in our jobs, we both know it's just not possible. What are you hoping to find?'

'A clue,' she answered, 'something which might point us in the right direction as to how this poor kid ended up the way he did.'

Hugo reached across the desk and touched her hand. 'Coco, you may never get the answers you're looking for and you can second guess what happened back then from here to next week. But you'll never truly know what you could or couldn't have done which might have made any difference.'

She slammed her hand against the desk. 'I have to do something, I can't close this case like I did last time. Move on and forget all about the cutest kid like he didn't exist, like he didn't matter a damn, non, I can't do it. I let him down last time; I can't let him down again.'

Hugo picked up the discarded pieces of paper. 'Then let's do what we do best. We may not get the chance to follow up on our cases, but there's one thing we can do now.'

'What's that?'

'Follow the paperwork. That's one thing we can rely on in France. There is always a lot of paperwork.'

Coco glanced around her ramshackle office and

nodded. 'You can say that again. And what do you think the paperwork will tell us?'

Hugo shrugged. 'I'm not sure, but hopefully, it will give us a place to start. A way to figure out the lost boy's journey from the day he met you, to the day he died. Who knows, it might give us a clue to how he ended up the way he did, or even where his friends might go.'

Coco gave him a sceptical look. 'You're putting an awful lot of pressure on a scrap of paper, aren't you?'

Hugo smiled. 'Maybe, but it's worth a try, right? And besides, what have we got to lose? You have a babysitter and I doubt I'll get much sleep tonight, so we should try to put our time to good use, non?'

She nodded. 'You're right, of course. Let's see if we can discover what happened to that beautiful boy.' She bowed her head, eyes quickly scanning the sheet of paper in a way Hugo understood. It was the way a seasoned investigator performed their duties because they knew that while every second counted, nothing could be missed. Lives depended on it.

After he had finished reading, Hugo stood and stretched, pressing his hand into the crook of his back. 'There's not much there, but what there is, is interesting, non?'

Coco raised an eyebrow and held up the folder. 'Did we read the same document? As far as I can tell there isn't anything of substance.' She shook her head. 'Which makes it all the more depressing. After I found him, Marc Gassna spent three months in a private wing at a hospital before being fostered. There is nothing else.'

Hugo smiled. 'I didn't spot it right away either,' he said picking up the paper again. He walked around the desk and placed it in front of Coco, pointing to a section near the bottom. 'Read that.'

Coco's eyes crinkled as she attempted to read the photocopied paper. 'It's so small and bad quality, I can't...' she stopped, eyes widening. 'Son of a bitch. It says *Physician in charge, Dr. Victor Caron.*'

Hugo nodded. 'Exactement. Presumably, the same Dr. Victor Caron who now runs the Caron Auberge de Jeunesse.'

Coco pulled her head back, tapping her chin in contemplation. 'But what does it mean? Or does it even mean anything? I mean, he's a doctor. Paris isn't that big really when it comes to doctors who might specialise in dealing with troubled children. It's probably not much of a coincidence really, is it?'

Hugo shrugged. 'Maybe not, but we know now he was acquainted with Marc Gassna at different points in his life and the doctor never mentioned it.'

'Hmm,' Coco replied doubtfully, 'but then again, there's no reason to suggest he even recognised Marc. Remember, it wasn't his real name, and there's no indication Dr. Caron would have known the child he looked after ten years ago was Marc Gassna. The truth is kids change and you don't even notice. Last night I looked at photos of Julien when he was ten and compared them with how he looks now and I'm telling you, if I didn't know better, I'd guess my cute as a button ten-year-old had been kidnapped and replaced with a pimply, angry alien teenager I've got now.' She met Hugo's gaze and then smiled. 'But you do have a point, it is certainly interesting.' She shrugged again. 'But what's the bet even if we ask him, he'll say he didn't recognise the poor kid.'

'Which we can't disprove,' Hugo agreed. 'Still…'

'Still…' Coco added. 'You're right. There's something about it which stinks.' She crinkled her nose. 'Or am I reading too much into this because I want to. I want to find a nice neat solution to tie this all up and let myself off the hook?'

Hugo did not answer. He moved across the office, tracing his finger along a dusty bookcase shelf as he considered. 'I agree, we are perhaps reading too much into it, but there is something else. It may be nothing but I believe there is a third connection.'

'A third?' Coco asked in surprise.

He nodded. 'Oui. When we met with Dr. Caron, he suggested much of his time was spent wining and dining potential investors.'

Coco threw her hands in the air. 'Oh, Dieu, I forgot all about that. He didn't mention *énergique* by name, exactly, but it wouldn't be too hard to find out if he is a member and if he wants the big-wigs to help him out and fund his hostel, then *énergique* is the sort of place he might go.' She frowned.

The door to her office burst open, followed by a red-faced Cedric who had obviously been running. 'He's on his way up,' he said breathlessly.

'Who?' Coco asked.

'The Minister,' he replied.

Hugo and Coco exchanged a puzzled look. 'I don't think I want to see him,' Hugo said.

Coco glanced over his shoulder. Jean Lenoir was striding across the Commissariat, moving officers out of his way like a bowling ball. 'Looks like you don't have a choice,' she said, 'the steroid junkie is about to... Minister Lenoir, delightful to see you,' she said jumping to her feet, 'and how handsome you look in your tuxedo.'

'I... well...' Jean Lenoir stammered. He looked at Hugo in the corner of the room and nodded, a flush spreading to his cheeks. 'Captain,' he said curtly.

'Minister,' Hugo replied, unable to make eye contact with him.

'What can we do for you at this late hour, Minister?' Coco interrupted, the faint lilt of amusement clear in her voice.

The Minister cleared his throat; he shot an anxious look in Hugo's direction but continued to face Coco. 'It was brought to my attention you were at *énergique* tonight,' he began, 'and I wanted to ensure there was no misunderstanding.'

'Misunderstanding?' Coco questioned.

He nodded. 'Oui. I realise, under the circumstances, my being at *énergique* tonight might be misconstrued.'

'Your social life is none of my concern, Minister,' Coco said with a shrug.

Jean raised his hand. 'I was there under duress, I can assure you. It was the birthday party of the son of a... er... colleague and my presence was expected.' He finally turned to Hugo. 'Why were you there?'

Hugo turned his head and met the Minister's eyes. He smiled and at that moment, they both understood what had happened. Jean Lenoir sucked in a breath.

'We were there to talk to you about Alexander Esnault,' Hugo said.

'Who?' The Minister asked quickly. Too quickly.

Hugo raised an eyebrow and repeated the name.

'I have no idea who this man is.'

Coco tutted. 'Minister Lenoir, assume we know how to do our jobs, and then consider your answer again, search that memory of yours. I'm sure you meet a great many people on a daily basis, but Monsieur Esnault is not one you are likely to forget.'

Jean continued to hold Hugo's gaze. Finally, he sighed. 'Oui, I am *aware* of Monsieur Esnault,' he said warily. 'Whatever you are thinking, please let me disabuse you of it. I have no connection with that man and am sure I have never even had a conversation of substance with him, and anyone who says otherwise is a liar.'

'Are you aware of who he is? What he does?' Hugo

asked.

The Minister's nostrils flared. 'I'm not an imbecile, Hugo.'

Hugo nodded. 'I never said you were, which is why I find it so difficult to understand how you could be so... so...'

'So?' Jean asked.

'Foolish,' Hugo concluded.

'Foolish?' Jean repeated, the surprise evident in his voice.

Hugo moved towards him. 'Oui. If you know what kind of man he is, the sort of crimes he is involved in, then I'm at a loss how you can be involved.'

Jean sighed. 'I never took you as being naïve, Captain. There are men like Alexander Esnault all around us, men who get their hands dirty so others don't have to. I don't condone it and nor should you, but there is very little which can be done about it. And besides, we need men such as this.'

Coco's eyes widened. 'Need? I don't believe I'm hearing that from you of all people, Minister Lenoir.'

He smirked. 'Why not? I'm a realist. I don't like Esnault or his type, and if it was up to me, he would rot in a jail somewhere, but it is not, because, as I'm sure you are aware by now, he has committed no *provable* crime.'

'But he is dangerous,' Hugo snapped.

'Of course, he is, but his friends are more dangerous.'

Hugo slammed his fist on the desk. 'You know, I'm getting sick to death of this bullshit. I've spent my entire career refusing to be intimidated by people in power, and I haven't come this far to start now and there's nothing they can do to me to change my mind.'

Jean Lenoir sighed. 'Now who is being naïve? What are you imagining could happen to you, lose your job? Discredited? Believe me, if that was all you had to worry about then I might agree with you.' He flopped onto a chair and began picking fluff off his tuxedo jacket. 'Have you heard of the journalist Sandra Omar?'

Coco shook her head. 'The name rings a bell,' Hugo answered, 'but I'm not sure why.'

'She won the Pulitzer Prize four years ago for her work reporting on a paedophile ring following a genocide in Syria. They trafficked children from the country, and she made it her mission to try to discover what happened to them.'

Hugo nodded, vaguely aware of the story.

'She is currently sitting in a Thai jail,' Jean continued, 'after authorities found heroin with a street value of over a hundred thousand dollars in her belongings. She'll spend the rest of her life in jail, if she's lucky because the alternative is worse.'

Hugo's face tightened. 'Are you suggesting they framed her?'

Jean Lenoir shrugged. 'I'm not suggesting anything, other than at the time of her arrest she was working on a follow-up article concerning how a billionaire French industrialist was involved in the trafficking and how some of the children from Syria had ended up in Thailand where they were being forced to work in the sex trade. Several of them turned up dead, brutally murdered.'

Coco tapped her fingers on the desk. 'And why are you telling us this?'

He shrugged again. 'I merely use it as an example. There are suggestions the reporter got too close and pissed off the wrong person with far-reaching consequences. My point is Hugo, no-one is untouchable, despite what we might think. And there is always fallout and danger. I tell you this for your own good, and I would advise you to listen to me carefully. I don't expect you to like me; I don't need you to. But I want you to know I am truthful, and I love our country with all I am. That is why I act the way I do. It is for our Republic. It may appear I turn a blind eye, but that does not mean I'm doing nothing.'

Hugo glared at him. 'Merci, but I still don't understand, the Jean Lenoir, Minister of Justice I know would be the last person to warn anybody off, particularly over a criminal such as Alexander Esnault, no matter how influential his friends might be. I don't buy it. Is this all because you want to become Prime Minister and you're afraid of rocking the boat?'

Jean folded his hands in his lap. He smiled. 'You don't know me half as well as you think you do if you believe that, Captain Duchamp. My ambition is nothing compared to my integrity.' He met Hugo's gaze. 'In hindsight, it was a mistake to ask you to come to Paris.'

Hugo's eyes widened. 'It was?'

The Minister nodded. 'It was not my intention for you to be placed in danger,' he turned to Coco, 'nor for either of you or your families to be placed in danger.'

'Then we are in danger?' Coco asked.

Jean paused. 'As you know by now, Alexander Esnault is a very unique man. A man who believes he operates outside of the law and is therefore untouchable.'

'Believes?' Hugo interrupted.

'Oui,' Jean answered before lapsing into silence.

Coco frowned. 'Is that it?' she asked. 'Is that all you have to say?'

'Son of a bitch,' Hugo groaned, slapping his forehead. 'I should have known.'

Jean Lenoir fixed him with a look of steel. He stood and crossed the office, closing the door and pulling down a pair of broken, dusty blinds. He coughed, wafting a cloud of dust away from his face. He looked at his now dirty fingers with distaste, wiping them on a handkerchief he pulled from his lapel. He spun around, staring directly at Hugo.

'Should have known what?' Coco asked Hugo, confusion clear in her voice.

'It's all a damn set up,' Hugo said flopping into a plastic chair. It buckled beneath his weight and he had to steady himself on a filing cabinet. He watched Jean Lenoir as he retook his seat. 'Isn't it, Jean?'

Jean Lenoir sighed as he carefully folded the handkerchief and placed it back into his lapel pocket. He still did not speak, his mouth twisted into a defiant purse.

'Jean Lenoir,' Hugo said, raising his voice, 'either you level with us right now, or...'

'Or?' Jean asked with amusement.

Hugo shrugged. 'I don't know, but I'll think of something which I guarantee you won't like.'

Jean threw back his head and laughed. 'Oh, very well,' He stopped, his eyes narrowing into angry pinpricks. 'Although I must remind you both of the importance of discretion and what I am about to tell you must not, CANNOT leave this room.'

Coco waved her hands. 'Hey, discretion is practically my middle name, don't you know,' she said with utter sincerity.

Hugo smiled. 'As is mine.'

Jean Lenoir shook his head. 'I don't know why I tolerate you two, really I don't.' He paused. 'Understand, there are certain matters which I cannot speak of, not necessarily because I don't wish to, but because they are issues of national security.'

Hugo nodded. 'What exactly is going on? And please explain to me why you have been lying to me this whole time.'

Jean smoothed a crease in his trousers. 'I have not been lying to you, *per se*, Hugo. Rather, I have been selective with what you have been told, and the reason for that is complicated, but please be assured it was for your own good and in your own best interests.'

Hugo gave him a doubtful look. 'You'll understand if I don't believe a word of what you're saying, Jean.'

The Minister shrugged as if he could care less.

'You said Alexander Esnault was untouchable,' Coco said, 'is that what this is about? You're conducting some kind of clandestine investigation?'

'And this whole business about there being a vendetta against you, was what? Lies?' Hugo asked.

Jean turned his head towards him. 'Non, of course not,' he snapped back, 'the vendetta is real, my so-called paranoia is not.'

Hugo ran his fingers through his hair. 'Then you will have to explain it to us, and we need the truth Jean, or you are on your own.'

Jean smiled. 'That's hardly a threat, Hugo. Men in my position are usually on their own. But I will tell as much as I can without compromising national security.'

Coco leaned forward in her chair, reaching into her drawer and pulling out a packet of crisps. She opened them and began crunching loudly, her eyes trained on him as if she was watching an exciting television programme.

'Late last year I was approached by...' Jean paused, '*someone* who suggested it might be time for me to consider my future position in the Republic. It was, of course, something I had already considered. However, I'm canny enough to know positions such as the ones I covet, are, mostly, subject to the support of a few very select men who rarely recruit outside of their own circle.'

'But something changed?' Hugo asked.

Jean nodded. 'These men, while tolerant of certain behaviour, indulgent you might say, baulk when that behaviour becomes dangerous and has the potential to topple the delicate house of cards they live under. They informed me how a particular senior politician had become involved in the seedy underbelly of Parisian society.'

Coco snorted. 'Show me a politician who isn't.'

Jean smiled. 'Perhaps, but it was apparent he had gotten involved very deeply, very deeply indeed. Drugs, prostitutes were only the beginning, and under normal circumstances that could be tolerated. But as time went by he became more and more involved, more and more hooked and dependant and that was when Alexander Esnault began turning the screws.'

'Turning the screws?' Hugo asked

.   'Oui. I suppose it was an attempt to legitimise his operation, but he was given permission to bid on government contracts and won, not necessarily because he was the best candidate because he most certainly was not, but because of who and what he knew.'

'What sort of contracts?' Coco interjected.

'It began with cleaning contracts in government buildings and progressed to catering events. All of which enabled Alexander Esnault to get his foot in the door. It only became apparent the extent of his holdings when it was brought to the attention of the President that there was a Europe-wide Interpol investigation into Esnault and his business holdings because they were believed to be a front for several rogue Middle-East organisations and laundering money for them.'

'Mon Dieu,' Hugo whispered.

'Exactement,' Jean agreed. 'Imagine the scandal if it was discovered the French government was involved in such schemes, and all because some hyped-up politician could not show decorum?'

'So, what did you have to do with all of this?' Hugo asked.

'It was suggested,' Jean replied, 'I would be the front runner to be his replacement should I show the tenacity and leadership skills in making the whole situation disappear before it blew up in all of our faces.'

Hugo frowned. 'And how were you supposed to do that?'

Jean laughed. 'Nobody said the path to power was easy. To begin with, I decided it was necessary to understand the extent of Alexander Esnault's reach, how far he had infiltrated, and to whom he had compromised. This meant I had to trust no one, talk to no one, and there was only one way to do that.'

Hugo sighed. 'To become one of them.'

Jean nodded. 'You really couldn't have believed me

to be the sort of person who spent his nights in a tacky discotheque, non?'

Hugo smiled. 'It did seem out of character, I must admit.' He shrugged. 'But I figured everyone gets lonely sometimes.'

'And you considered me the sort of man who would use prostitutes?' he added with a tut.

'Speaking of Delphine Marchand,' Coco questioned, 'what does she have to do with all of this?'

Hugo answered, staring at Jean Lenoir. 'I'm guessing you were using her for information, oui?'

'It didn't take me long to understand what was happening at *énergique* and that there was corruption at the highest level,' his eyes narrowed and he lowered his voice, 'not only from the political arena, but also the judiciary and the police.'

Coco turned her head towards Commander Stanic's office. She bit her lip, incomprehensibly muttering.

Jean rubbed his eyes. Hugo noticed how drained he looked and if he was not mistaken, he appeared sad. 'It all began innocently enough, I can assure you,' Jean continued, 'and Delphine approached me.' He paused. 'As I told you yesterday, I found her disarming, and... and different.' He stared directly at Hugo. 'I expect you'll read too much into it, but, it was nice to be with someone where there are no complications.'

'I'd hardly call hooking up with a prostitute complication-free,' Coco muttered.

Jean shot her a hateful look before continuing. 'I'm not proud of it. She reminded me of…' he shook his head, 'anyway after we became close, she began sharing with me. I didn't push it at first. I did not want to scare her off, but I wanted to understand how Alexander Esnault's operation ran from the inside, and Delphine was instrumental in helping me to understand.'

'Did she know what you were trying to do?' Hugo asked.

Jean shook his head. 'Not at first. But after a time it became apparent that she too was looking for her own way out. Alexander Esnault, in reality, is no different to a back-alley pimp. Oh, he can dress it up in a hundred different ways - about how fortunate those who work for him are, how looked after they are, but the truth is much harsher and darker than that. Rich men pay for extras and they expect them to be given freely and without reservation. I met Delphine one evening, and she was visibly distressed. One of her friends had been brutally raped by a number of men at a party. He could not go to the police because he was being paid for sex, and it would be near to impossible to prove what had taken place was against his will, but what he experienced was so severe, it was a final straw for Delphine. She said they had to get away from Esnault and *énergique* before one of them died.'

The word hung heavy in the room.

Hugo and Coco shared an anxious look. 'Who was raped?' Hugo asked.

Jean shrugged. 'Delphine did not tell me, *would* not tell me. She was fiercely protective and angry. Angry with such ferocity, it was as powerful as I've ever seen.'

Hugo sighed. 'It might explain why Marc Gassna killed himself.'

'Or Jack Boucher was murdered, to stop him from talking,' Coco added.

Jean shrugged. 'Anyway, I decided to use her anger, so I told her my real reason for being at *énergique* and like a shot, she said she would do whatever she could to help me bring down the rotten bastards.'

'And did she?' Coco asked.

Jean sighed. 'She didn't get a chance. We'd barely had a chance to talk about it, to formulate a plan. We'd agreed she would wear a recording device. It was important to gather as much evidence as possible, not just against Alexander Esnault but for those he came into contact with.'

'But she hadn't gone so far as to actually use the recording device?' Hugo interrupted.

Jean lowered his head. 'She had begun wearing a wire only that week,' he answered in a whisper. 'Alors, oui.'

'And you don't have the recordings?' Hugo asked.

He shook his head.

Hugo pursed his lips in contemplation. He tapped his chin. 'Then I wonder where the recordings are, or even if there are any, and if there are, what do they reveal...' he began before trailing off.

'It certainly opens up possibilities,' Coco took over, 'or maybe it doesn't,' she added with a confused frown.

'What does my father have to do with all of this?' Hugo asked. 'Is he implicated in the corruption?'

Jean did not answer immediately. 'As I told you, our rivalry goes back to my arrival in Paris and securing the Ministerial office - an office your father believed by rights was his. As for his culpability in the corruption, all I can tell you is that the Special Counsel investigation was implemented by the Minister who I am investigating. A sort of pre-emptive discrediting of my findings, you might say and one in which, it pains me to say, I lent credence to by my actions. The point remains, however, regardless of my shortcomings, your father is either directly implicated in the corruption or willingly covering it up for his friends.' He turned directly to face Hugo. 'And I want you to know, either way, I intend to ensure he faces the full consequences for his actions. Do you have a problem with that, Captain?'

Hugo met his gaze. 'I wouldn't expect anything less, Minister.'

Coco sighed. 'This is all very interesting, I'm sure, but how exactly does it help our investigation?'

Hugo moved across the room. 'We need some leverage on Alexander Esnault, Jean.'

The Minister shook his head. 'I've told you, and as much as I wish it otherwise, until I have concrete proof there's nothing I can do. He is protected. There is no leverage.'

Hugo smiled. 'In these five years I have gotten to know you, Jean, I would have never imagined you to be scared.'

Jean's eyebrow arched. 'Scared? What are you talking about?'

'Scared of the influence of people more powerful than you,' Hugo answered. 'That isn't the Jean Lenoir, all powerful Minister of Justice I thought I knew or was slightly terrified of.'

Jean fixed Hugo with an angry stare. '*Slightly*?' he retorted.

Hugo smiled. 'My point is, regardless of the bigger picture, or whatever end game there is at play, Alexander Esnault is, as far as we know, a pimp, a drug-dealer and potentially mixed up in murder, blackmail, and who knows what else. We know three young people are on the run, and we know he's in pursuit of them. If he hasn't caught up to them, then I'm sure it's only a matter of time until he does. Add to the mix the not-so-veiled threats to mine and Captain Brunhild's family, then the fact is, he should be under arrest.'

Jean tutted. 'On what grounds? With what evidence? Come, come, Captain, you know better than this. You cannot arrest a man such as Alexander Esnault unless you have enough concrete evidence to make it stick, and that includes witnesses who can testify. We have none of that.

If we were foolish enough to arrest him, he'd be out within hours.'

Hugo nodded. 'I'm aware of all of that and under normal circumstances, I would agree with you. But these aren't normal circumstances and therefore we shouldn't act as we normally would.'

'What are you proposing, Hugo?' Coco asked.

'Just that we are playing against time. We don't know why those young men died, or who is responsible, but we do know three other young people are on the run, afraid for their lives and the only common link we have is Alexander Esnault and *énergique*. I don't know about you, Captain, but I don't enjoy playing catch up with crooks who believe they're immune.'

'But I have to, and I hate saying this, agree with Minister Lenoir, if we brought in Esnault we'd not get anything to stick,' Coco answered, 'and you can just bet he's got some hotshot Avocat who'll make us look like fools. Listen, I'm not afraid of getting hauled over the coals and if I thought we had anything on him, he'd be here already. Do you think we can prove he did anything?'

'Probably not,' Hugo responded, 'but if we make a big enough fuss about it, maybe involve the press, it sends a clear signal. Esnault is under investigation. It might just be enough to get him to back off and give those protecting him a chance to reflect and consider their own positions. More importantly, it would shine a big old spotlight on Alexander and his operation, and might prevent him from any further action and give us a chance to find those missing kids before he does. They might even reach out if they know Esnault is in trouble.'

Jean Lenoir and Coco considered his words.

'You may have a point,' Jean said finally. He looked towards the office. 'And the Commissariat is on a main street in the seventh arrondissement, there are press sniffing around all the time. If they were to witness Esnault's very public arrest, it would certainly draw attention to him and those who protect him might not be so willing to do so if they risk exposure.'

'But isn't that the whole point, Esnault has dirt on all these so-called powerful men?' Coco asked.

Jean nodded. 'I'm sure he does,' he replied, 'but blackmail only really works as a threat. If Alexander Esnault is news himself, he's not likely to want to expose anyone else, because to do so, he risks further incriminating himself.' He smiled at Hugo. 'It may just work, with enough of a fanfare. It might buy you time to find Delphine and the others, and it may prevent Esnault from making any more of his veiled threats. But I don't think he's the sort of man to be held down for too long. You need to move, and you need to move quickly.'

Coco looked at her watch. 'I'm beat, let's do it first thing in the morning. I'll make sure there are plenty of press around and we'll make sure to say nothing about the VIP we're bringing in. That's sure to convince them there's something to dig for, I...'

The door to her office burst open, bouncing against the wall. Everyone looked up, greeted by Cedric's anxious face.

'Haven't you heard of knocking, Lieutenant?' Coco scolded.

'Captain Brunhild, there has been another death,' he answered breathlessly.

'What?' Coco gasped.

He nodded. 'The 6e arrondissement reported a suspected suicide. Someone jumped from an apartment block. When they interviewed witnesses, they cast doubt on the suicide theory. Several of them reported seeing the deceased struggling with someone.'

Coco frowned. 'And what does this have to do with us?'

'The person who died is called Ana Boucher,' he waited a moment before adding. 'Jack Boucher's mother.'

Coco gave Hugo an anxious glance. 'You might want to let Ben know you won't be back any time soon. I'll make sure there's a patrol watching the hotel and my house because it looks like it's going to be a long night.' She turned to Jean Lenoir. 'Do what you have to do, but I want an arrest mandate for Alexander Esnault on my desk by morning. If he is involved in this, then I want him off the streets once and for all and I don't care how we do it.'

Jean Lenoir nodded. 'Keep me updated, Captains.'

vingt-six

For the second time in a matter of days, Hugo lifted his head towards the spiralling apartment block, it appeared almost as tall as nearby neighbour the Eiffel Tower, whilst sharing none of its glamour or sophistication. Despite it being after midnight, the surrounding area was alive with activity, and not just related to the police presence. He imagined this particular banlieue, situated as it was in the heart of Paris, separated from the grandeur and glamour of everything the capital had to offer by a twenty-foot heavily graffitied brick wall, was not somewhere tourists would or should venture. The lights of the tower moved across the wall lazily, flicking light over it, casting shadows on the men and women on the opposite side, neither acknowledging nor aware of each other.

'I grew up on a banlieue just like this,' Cedric said appearing by Hugo's side. 'Not here, in Marseille, and man, it made this estate look like Disney World. Bit out of your comfort zone, huh, Hugo?'

Hugo nodded, feeling no need to deny it. 'It's true. I actually grew up not too far away from the other side of that wall, but it might as well have been a thousand miles away.'

'Lucky you,' Cedric replied.

Hugo shrugged. 'Oh, I don't know. There is no guarantee of happiness on either side of that wall. Darkness walks everywhere.'

Cedric gave him a sceptical look. 'Still, a bit of money makes things a little easier to bear, non? The only reason I didn't end up running drugs for the local boss was I was more afraid of my Grand-Mère than I was him.'

Hugo looked at him in surprise. 'You were raised by your grandmother?'

Cedric nodded. 'Yeah, turns out my parents preferred needles in their arm than feeding their four kids. You?'

'You could say I was raised by my grandmother too.' He smiled at Cedric. 'See, we're not so different after all, are we, no matter where or who we came from.'

'Your father is a twat,' Cedric said

Hugo smiled at his choice of slang because it reminded him of his time working for the Met Police in London. 'He certainly is, Lieutenant, he certainly is.' He turned towards the apartment block. Coco had moved ahead of them and was struggling her way into a forensic suit. 'We'd better try to figure out what happened here.'

Cedric sighed before adding. 'It's hardly new. Somebody died because they realised it was a better option than living.'

Dr. Sonny Bernstein slotted a head torch into place and stepped under the police tape, Hugo, Coco and Cedric a step behind him. Ana Boucher lay in front of them, only partially covered by a tarp and enough for Hugo to see her body was lying in an unnatural angle, a foot bent back the wrong way, an arm twisted the wrong way around her head. Eyes wide and open, staring into the night sky as if stargazing. A trickle of blood ran from her open mouth, twisted into a malevolent smile. He felt a crushing sadness at the loss of another broken soul whose last moments on earth had been horrific and heartbreaking. In his four decades, Hugo had never managed to make peace with the way in which man's ability to destroy and hurt seemed to know no bounds.

'I fucking hate life sometimes,' Coco announced as if reading Hugo's mind. 'Who am I kidding? I hate life most of the time for what it throws at people. Pauvre femme.'

Hugo moved across, his eyes narrowing as he met Ana Boucher's. He had looked into them barely twenty-four hours earlier and he had seen nothing but pain and despair. Now he saw death, and he realised that perhaps the two were inexplicably linked. A parent learning of their child's death sees their own death as a way to combat the grief. *It should have been me.* That was what he had seen in Ana Boucher's eyes. *It should have been me.* He turned to Cedric. 'You said there were indications this was not a suicide?'

Cedric shrugged his shoulders. 'Fuck knows. A couple of junkies,' he said, tipping his shoulder towards the crowd gathered adjacent to the forensic tent, 'said they saw her all the way up there,' he pointed towards the top of the apartment block, 'struggling with some nondescript dude all dressed in black, or he was black, or Muslim, or perhaps another person of differing skin-hue,' he added, reading from his notepad, 'and said-person pushed her off. It's all very, *maybe*, or *perhaps*, or *could-have-been*, which all amount to a whole lot of nothing as far as I'm concerned. Her kid died, and she chose to end it. You don't have to be a genius to see it for what it is.'

Hugo stared again at the apartment block and shuddered. The night was getting colder and the beginning of a light drizzle was dampening his face. He turned to the Eiffel Tower and could see the sun illuminating the summit. It would be over them in an hour or so and another day would begin, and lives would carry on. He felt helpless because he knew then that whatever had occurred, whatever had begun, had started long before his arrival. He was far behind. They all were. The only thing he was sure about was whatever had led to the death of Ana Boucher and her son was because of circumstances, chains of events which had begun much earlier. People were dying to cover something up and to protect someone, he was sure of it. The only thing he knew for certain was time was ebbing away from them and there was a very real possibility whatever had been started had not yet been finished. All of which meant they had to find the missing teenagers, not just because their lives were in danger, but because for whatever reason, he was sure they held a key to unlocking a mystery he did not yet understand. The trouble was, he did not understand how to achieve it. Whatever trust they had that enabled them to reach out for help had been broken and Hugo felt sure they would not risk it again, which meant Hugo and the others had to find another way to them.

He turned around, his eyes moving across the Parisian skyline. He knew only too well how easy it was for a teenager to disappear in Paris when they did not want to be found because he had done it himself more times than he cared to remember. And the streets were dangerous enough without running from persons who meant you harm.

'Are you all right, Hugo?' Sonny Bernstein asked.

Hugo smiled at the doctor, nodding. 'The darkness of night always amplifies my fears,' he answered.

'Your fears?'

'Oui,' he replied, 'I can't stop thinking about the three kids on the run when it's dark like tonight. They're probably terrified, and it can only be worse during the dark hours.'

'We have alerts out for them,' Coco added, 'but there's not a lot more we can do. We don't even know their full names and until we drag Alexander Esnault's sorry ass into the station in a few hours, chances are we will not get very much further.' She touched Hugo's arm. 'Try not to worry.' She turned to the doctor. 'What we do we have, Sonny?'

'A tragedy,' Dr. Shlomo Bernstein answered glumly.

'Cedric, what are the witnesses saying?' Coco asked.

'Only that Madame Boucher appeared to struggle with someone shortly before she fell, but as I was just telling Hugo, I'm not sure how accurate that is, I mean,' he pointed towards the apartment building, 'I have perfect eyesight and I'm as sober as a Juge, sadly, but I'm not sure I'd be able to tell what happened if I saw it myself.'

'And what about her husband?' Coco interjected. 'Have we found Monsieur Boucher?'

Cedric shook his head. 'Non, the first officers on the scene searched the apartment, and there was no sign of him.'

Coco pursed her lips. 'So, he's either on the run or in danger himself.'

'Or in a bar somewhere,' Hugo added, 'he had terrible news today after all.'

'I want an urgent call out for him either way,' Coco said to Cedric.

'It's done, Captain. Patrols are combing all the local watering holes; if he's around we'll find him,' Cedric answered.

'Is there anything you can tell us from the body?' Hugo asked Dr. Bernstein.

Sonny lowered himself and fully pulled back the covering, revealing the battered remains of Ana Boucher. 'A tragedy,' he repeated.

Coco raised an eyebrow. 'An accident sort of tragedy or a murder sort of tragedy?'

The doctor did not answer immediately, taking his

time as practised eyes appraised the remains. He stood, straining his eyes between where the body now lay and where it had come from. 'You'll need to get the forensic guys to confirm it, but I feel fairly confident in telling you from the injuries to the body and the position in which she landed, then it is unlikely she got there by jumping.'

'How you can be so sure, doc?' Cedric asked.

'Well, she is lying on her back, for a start,' Sonny replied, 'and that is extremely unlikely to have happened if she jumped.'

'Couldn't she have just spun around or something as she fell?' Cedric countered.

'Anything is possible, I suppose,' Sonny continued, 'but I believe it unlikely, and there is also this,' he reached down and lifted Ana Boucher's left hand, twisting it gently to expose the fingernails.

Hugo leaned forward, flicking on his glasses. 'Two broken nails and… what is that debris, skin?'

'I've taken scrapings and will examine it back at the morgue, but oui, I'd say so.'

'Then we have the DNA of whoever she struggled with?'

'Peut-être,' Sonny replied.

Hugo turned his head towards the apartment block, his lips pursed. 'Or of course, she wasn't pushed and someone tried to stop her from jumping and in the struggle was hurt. Under the circumstances, a suicide isn't too much of a stretch to believe.'

'If it was a struggle, then where is he?' Coco asked.

Hugo shrugged. 'They might not have wanted to get involved. People often don't, especially in places like this.'

Coco followed his gaze. 'What the hell is going on, Hugo? Something stinks, and I'm not just talking about Cedric's cologne.'

'Hey,' Cedric grumbled.

Coco raised her hand. 'Oh, don't pout, get up there and check the area. Check for scuff marks from shoes, get the tech guys to print the entire balcony and the apartment. I want to know exactly who was up there.'

'That could take all night.'

Coco smiled. 'Then you'd better get started. We've got to pick up Alexander Esnault first thing, and I don't want to be late.'

Cedric nodded and made his way towards the apartments. Dr. Bernstein stepped in front of the tape. 'I guess this means you don't want me to put the autopsy off until daylight?'

Coco flashed him a grateful, uneven smile. 'I'd be honoured if you didn't, you are up after all. It seems a bit pointless going to bed now just to get up again in a few hours, non?'

His face twisted into a resigned scowl. 'D'accord, give me an hour to get organised and meet me at the morgue.'

'Génial, which gives us just enough time to sniff around the Boucher home. There was something off about it. Coming, Hugo?'

Hugo nodded. He too had considered there was something unusual about the home of Jack Boucher's parents and welcomed a chance to view it again.

Hugo and Coco stepped into the darkness of the hallway. Hugo flicked on the light, a hard light causing him to squint. The long hallway was badly in need of painting, with long slips of torn wallpaper along the length of the wall. They moved into the apartment.

Coco crinkled her nose. 'What is that smell?'

Hugo took a moment, sucking stale air through his nose. 'Bleach?' he offered.

Coco nodded. 'Yeah, I think it is. Strange, non?'

Hugo shrugged. 'It's not so unusual, people use bleach all the time,' he replied. He stared down at the floor, lowering himself onto his haunches and pressed his fingers into the carpet. It was wet. He lifted his fingers, his nose crinkling. 'The bleach is in the carpet and there's a lot of it,' he said.

'Damn,' Coco replied. 'I'd better get the forensic squad up here. Watch where you're stepping.'

Hugo nodded as they inched along the hallway. He stopped in front of a door and pushed it open, stepping inside the Boucher's bedroom. 'Now, this is what caught my eye the last time we were here. All the empty boxes. Not too unusual in itself, but it seemed to me Monsieur Boucher was very keen for us not to see them. Now, it could be for several reasons, possibly because they're stolen. It doesn't appear as if the Boucher's have a lot of money, but either way, I'd like to know why he didn't want us to know.'

Coco sighed, running her finger along a Formica dressing table, moving a fine layer of dust as she did. The bedroom was decorated sparsely. She stopped at a stack of letters. Coco picked them up, casually flicking through them.

'We should get a Mandate, non?' Hugo said.

She shook her head. 'I don't need a Mandate to tell me what most of these are, because I have a similar stack of my own back home. They are final demands for payment.'

'Final demands?' Hugo asked.

'Yeah, gas, electric, water, the usual. When it comes to choosing between putting food on the table and keeping warm, a hungry stomach usually wins.'

Hugo lowered himself to study the empty boxes. 'Sixty inch 3D televisions can't be cheap,' he said.

'More than I can afford, that's for sure. My TV is so wide and heavy I need a wheelbarrow to move it from one room to another,' Coco replied, 'and you're right, I don't get the impression the Boucher's could afford it either.'

Hugo stood up and moved across the cramped bedroom, his eyes flicking around the walls. There were no pictures on the dirty-white walls, only a large wooden cross above the bed. Hugo stepped in front of it, tapping his chin as he stared at it.

'What is it?' Coco asked.

Hugo did not reply immediately. 'I knew there was something I couldn't quite put my finger on. At first, I thought it was all the empty boxes.' He looked at them again. 'And I'm still not convinced they aren't important, so we really should try to find out where they came from and how they could afford them if they couldn't pay their bills. But there is something else.' He pointed at the cross. 'I know I keep saying it may be nothing and I'm perhaps reading too much into it, but all of my time as a police officer I've learned to underestimate nothing, no matter how small or inconsequential things might appear.'

Coco frowned as she stared at the cross. 'A wooden cross? There doesn't seem to be anything special about it, the same as thousands of other households across France have, I would imagine.'

Hugo nodded. 'Probably. But it might also give us a link between the people we have met in the last few days. Do you remember what Ana Boucher said to her husband right before we left for the morgue to identify her son?'

Coco tapped her head in contemplation. 'Something about making arrangements for the burial, non?'

Hugo nodded. 'Oui. She told her husband to telephone somebody called Monseigneur Demaral.'

'Yeah, something like that,' Coco agreed. 'Ooh, wait…' she trailed off. 'Why does that name ring a bell?'

'Because we've heard it before,' Hugo replied. 'More

than once, in fact. Remember?'

Coco moved across the room, dropping onto a ramshackle wooden chair. It groaned underneath her. 'Everyone's a critic it seems,' she grumbled. 'It's the middle of the night, Hugo, so you're going to have to bear with me. I know I've heard the name, but I'm having trouble placing it...'

Hugo moved across the room, pulling a dirty curtain away from a window, trails of condensation snaking down the glass. He peered into the darkness of the night and could just about make out Dr. Bernstein arranging the removal of Ana Boucher's remains. His heart squeezed against his chest, knowing the pain she must have felt in her final hours and he hoped, as he always did in situations such as these, that he would be able to find some kind of justice for her, and if her spirit still survived somewhere, it would get the peace it needed. He turned to face Coco.

'Ana Boucher said Monseigneur Demaral was their "dear friend" and that wasn't the first time we'd heard him called that. Dr. Caron also described him the same way.'

'Oh, yeah,' Coco replied, 'he said something about the Monseigneur operating as some kind of unofficial advisor at *Caron Auberge de Jeunesse,* right?'

'Oui,' Hugo replied, 'and it doesn't end there. Fleur Gassna, Marc Gassna's mother, also called the Monseigneur a good friend.'

Coco frowned, scratching her head. 'Wait, what are you suggesting?'

Hugo shrugged. 'I'm not suggesting anything, really. Just pointing out something which seems a little odd. And there's something else. When we talked with Alexander Esnault, he also said he had spent his youth in a Catholic home. He didn't mention Monseigneur Demaral, so there may be no connection, but I got the impression from what Dr. Caron said that Monseigneur Demaral had been involved in a Catholic children's home which I got the impression was closed down because of some kind of scandal. There may be no link of course and my imagination may be getting carried away, but the fact that at least three, possibly four, of the people we've spoken to regarding the deaths of Marc Gassna and Jack Boucher have some sort of connection with a man known as Monseigneur Demaral is interesting, don't you think?'

Coco considered. 'Well...' she said, unconvinced as if she believed it was stretching.

'I'm not sure any of them would know each other in normal life. The Gassna's and the Boucher's both indicated they did not know their son's friends and Dr. Caron suggested he did not know the real names of the young men who died, so I can't imagine he would know their parents either.'

Coco stood and moved next to the window, watching with Hugo as Ana Boucher's body was loaded into a van. She shook her head. 'And if you're right about Alexander Esnault, well...' she tutted. 'Hugo, I don't want to get involved with the Catholic Church. Careers die on smaller crosses than that,' she smiled shyly, 'if you pardon the expression.'

He shrugged. 'It can't harm, can it? It may be nothing, but at the very least, it's probably worth having a conversation with this Monseigneur Demaral, non?'

She turned back. 'Yeah, but this case is already a can of fucking worms, bringing in the Church, man, that's a whole new level of crazy we could do without. Young, underage prostitutes, children's homes, abuse. I don't think you have any idea the kind of shit storm we could cause by getting involved in poking that kind of hornet's nest.'

Hugo looked at Ana Boucher's bed, the small imprint of a head still on the pillow. 'I don't think we have a choice, Coco.'

She nodded. 'All right, let's get to the morgue and then grab a couple of hours sleep before we tackle Alexander Esnault and the damn priest. Did I tell you how much I hate this damn case?'

Hugo stood stock-still as if he was a statue. He was wearing a pair of thin tennis shoes and the tiled floor of the morgue was sending a cold snap up his body. He shivered and pulled off his glasses. He did not need to read the two signs on the doors. It was desperately sad to see the names of a mother and son next to each other in such a way, but at least they were together again, he supposed. Dr. Bernstein opened one of the doors, sliding the gurney out and guiding it onto a table in the centre of the room. He zipped open the bag, revealing Ana Boucher. Hugo and Coco watched in silence. The doctor nodded at them, as he pulled on a mask and picked up a scalpel.

'Lieutenant Degarmo, we've finished in the apartment,' a young woman called out from the doorway.

Cedric turned around, flashing a smile at the young woman. He recognised her from the Commissariat. As far as he could tell she was some kind of forensic expert on loan from Sweden, or Denmark, or some other place he had no idea about other than it was seemingly always dark and cold. She had always intrigued him. Tall and whip-thin with a mop of dyed platinum hair atop an otherwise shaved head. She was unique and unlike any other woman he had ever met, certainly nothing like the prissy Parisian woman who always seemed to turn their nose up at him. He decided to play it cool. 'And I'm sure you did an outstanding job,' he murmured.

The young woman raised a pierced eyebrow, casting shade in his direction. 'Well, it is my job,' she replied, boredom clear in her clipped, heavily accented voice. She stepped onto the landing, gesturing behind her. 'And this is what I found,' she said, flashing a torch into the dark hallway leading into the Boucher home. Cedric moved quickly to her side, peering inside. His eyes followed the glow of the torch which was illuminating the carpet, a massive violet stain glaring at him. 'What the hell is that?' he asked.

'Blood,' she answered, 'and a lot of it.'

Cedric frowned. 'I saw Madame Boucher and according to the doc, her injuries were consistent with a fall, not an attack. And this looks like too much blood to me.'

The forensic tech shrugged her slight shoulders, flicking the torch into the walkway. She focused on a series of black smudges leading away from the apartment. 'It is a lot of blood. I'll send the sample to Dr. Bernstein and he can compare the two, but it's obvious somebody attempted to clean it up, badly as it happens, but they did throw some bleach down which might make it difficult.' She added with a frown, pointing to the wall. 'They missed those bits however, no bleach which means we have a good chance of comparing the two sets of blood.'

'Anything else?' Cedric asked.

'These,' she pointed to the smudges, 'appear to be

scuff marks from shoes, as if someone was dragged away from the apartment, which would fit, non?'

Cedric frowned again, shaking his head. He pointed in the opposite direction. 'But Madame Boucher went over the building over there, not the other way.'

The tech shone the torch along the walkway, shining on the snaky smudges which trailed all the way to the end of the walkway. 'I don't know what to tell you, but the marks go all the way to the end.'

Cedric sighed. 'Let's go,' he said leading the tech away from the apartment, stepping carefully along the way.

'That looks like blood, there, there and there,' the tech said, placing markers next to the drops. They reached the end of the walkway, stopping by a large chute.

'What the hell is that?' Cedric asked.

The tech pulled back the lever, revealing a large rubbish drop. She shone the torch inside, revealing what appeared a large blood mass. 'More blood, and it looks fresh,' she said.

'What the hell is it…' Cedric groaned.

'Garbage disposal. All of these buildings have them, an easy way to get rid of your rubbish and to try to stop residents from just throwing stuff over the side…' the tech paused before adding with a knowing smile, 'and if you ask me, it looks big enough for a body.'

'Goddamnit,' Cedric sighed.

She flashed him a smile. 'I have a forensic suit which should just about fit your abnormally large limbs,' she said, flicking pale eyes over him.

'Are you kidding me?' Cedric countered, glancing down at himself as if suddenly self-conscious. 'I'm not crawling into some fucking rubbish tip,' he replied glaring towards the open drawer

The tech pointed at the blood. 'The blood is fresh and the chances are whoever went in could still be alive, so unless you want Commander Stanic to read you the riot act, I'd jump to it if I were you.'

Cedric looked back towards the apartment as if weighing up his options. He sighed. 'Give me the damn suit then,' he groaned, 'tonight just keeps getting better and better, doesn't it?'

The forensic technician pulled open the door, instantly recoiling as the stench of rotten waste engulfed her. She covered her mouth, stifling a retch. 'I don't think these get emptied as often as they should,' she said through gritted teeth.

'Fucking great,' Cedric groaned.

She smiled at him. 'Well, look at it this way, at least we can be sure any evidence will still be in there, right?'

Cedric glared at her and moved towards the large stainless steel bins and hoisted himself up, using his legs to push himself up. 'Shine the torch up here,' he said, 'I can't see a thing.'

The technician pulled a box from the side and stood on it, lifting her arm, throwing light on the top of the bins.

'Jesus Christ!' Cedric cried as a panicked rat ran across the top of the bins, a mouldy piece of meat sticking out the side of its mouth. 'There's nothing in here,' he blurted.

The technician raised an eyebrow. 'You know you will have to get in to be sure, right? You French men are so prissy, terrified of getting your nails dirty, or your hair mussed.'

He glared at her. 'Isn't this your job, not mine?'

She snorted. 'You really want me, a girl, to crawl around all that muck, while you stand by and watch?'

Cedric flung his body over the top, landing in the rubbish with a squelch. 'Bloody typical, all women's lib and until it comes to not wanting to get your hand's dirty, gets on my...' he stopped, pressing his eyes against the side of the bin.

'What is it?' she asked, straining as she stood on her toes to shine more light on the top. Cedric did not answer. She peered over the top to see he was bent over, pulling boxes and bags away, frantically throwing them over his shoulder. The technician focused the torch on the area and gasped as slowly her eyes realised what he had found. A man, his face bloody and swollen. She gasped. 'Is he alive?' she asked, aware judging by his face, the chances were he was not.

Cedric still did not speak. She could make out he was now holding the man's wrist aloft.

'There's a pulse,' Cedric cried, 'not much of a one,

but he's still alive, for now at least. Get help, now!'

'There's nothing really to tell, I'm afraid,' Dr. Bernstein addressed Hugo and Coco forty-five minutes later. 'I'll send the blood samples to the lab and we should get the results in a day or two, but I don't see any red flags.'

'Nothing?' Coco asked wearily.

He shook his head. 'Other than I stand by my initial assessment she either fell or was pushed, rather than she deliberately jumped. I've taken the skin samples from under her nails and we'll run them through our databases and hope something comes back.' His eyes flicked over Ana Boucher's remains. 'Other than that, she was in perfectly ordinary health, her stomach contents show she had barely any digested food in her, but I suppose after her day, eating was probably the last thing on her mind.'

Coco pulled the collar of her woollen coat tight around her body and moved to the head of the gurney. She shook her head. 'What a fucking stupid waste of a life,' she turned towards the storage drawer containing Jack Boucher, 'a pair of fucking lives.'

He gave her a helpless look. 'Désolé, Captain, I wish I could give you more.'

'It's not your fault, Sonny, we could do with catching a break though.' She faced Hugo. 'This is getting on my nerves now. What are we missing? Because dammit, I know we're missing something.'

Hugo stared at the remains of Ana Boucher. 'I hope after we've spoken with Alexander Esnault again, and Monseigneur Demaral we may start to understand.'

She gave him a sceptical look. 'I like your optimism, Hugo; I only wish I could share it.' She stopped as her cell phone began ringing. 'Cedric, what's up?' she answered. 'What? Are you serious? What hospital are they taking him to? Okay. Hugo and I will meet you there.' She disconnected the call. 'Cedric found Randolph Boucher.'

Hugo nodded. 'I'm guessing he's hurt?'

'Oui, badly too by the sounds of it. The paramedics at the scene couldn't say whether he would make it or not.' She turned to Dr. Bernstein. 'Let me know if you find anything else or hear from forensics, Sonny.'

He nodded. 'Bien sûr. Where did Cedric find Monsieur Boucher?'

'That's the damnedest thing,' she replied, 'Cedric told me he found him dumped in a garbage chute at the apartment building.'

Hugo frowned. 'A garbage chute? That's strange.'

'Strange?' Sonny asked.

'Oui. I mean, whatever happened last night, why would someone throw Ana Boucher off the side of the building and then dump her husband in the garbage? Those are two very different things and it makes little sense.'

Neither Coco nor Sonny replied.

'Well, if Randolph Boucher comes around, we'll be

sure to ask him that very question.'

Alexander Esnault fluffed the violet handkerchief in the lapel pocket of his Gucci suit and then patted his head, making sure his hair was smooth. Dissatisfied with a stray hair, he tucked it back into the top-knot and then smoothed it down again. Coco watched him with interest, pulling at the blue tips of her own hair. Alexander watched her with a burning interest.

'The blue dye isn't the problem with your hair, cherie,' he said, 'it's the frizziness. A good conditioner and an iron is all it needs.'

Coco regarded him in surprise. 'An *iron*?'

Alexander ignored her, instead turning to Hugo. 'And you have very beautiful hair for a man, too much of it perhaps, but I sense you use it as a shield to keep prying eyes away, non? I like my hair long too, but I tie it away as I like to actively encourage people to watch me,' he added with a smile.

Hugo self-consciously tucked his fringe behind his ear and stifled a yawn. He had slept badly after retiring to his hotel after they had been refused entry to see Randolph Boucher as the doctors worked to save his life. He was eager to get through with the interview so they could return to the hospital.

'As interesting as these fashion tips are,' Coco drawled, 'I've had two hours sleep, and I'm about at my limit of coffee tolerance and believe me, you don't want to see what happens when I reach that limit, so can we get on

306

with it?'

Alexander gave a nonchalant shrug. 'This early morning tryst was your idea, not mine, Captain. I was still enjoying a perfectly pleasant night with some *friends* when I was so rudely dragged out of bed.' He looked aghast. 'And with a Mandate of all things, I mean, I would have come if you had only asked. There was no need to get so formal was there?' His face pinched angrily. 'And whoever arranged for the photographers to herald my arrival was a nice touch. A stupid touch, a *dangerous* touch, but well played, nonetheless.'

Coco shrugged. 'Nothing to do with me. The press like to hang around police stations in Paris because they never know who is gonna turn up.'

Alexander folded his fingers together. 'Strange that they seemed to know me, I mean, I'm hardly a somebody. Stranger too they seemed to know my arrival was not entirely voluntary.'

Coco shrugged again.

Alexander smiled. 'Still, if you had nothing to hide, you don't need to fear the consequences, do you?' He stared at her. 'You could have just asked me though. I would have met with you willingly.'

'Under the circumstances,' Coco replied, 'we thought it best we make this more formal, so we all know exactly where we stand and there are no misunderstandings. Am I right in thinking you have waived your right to have your Avocat present with you?'

'Well,' Alexander answered while staring directly at Hugo, 'as you said, under the circumstances, it is probably best there are no misunderstandings which is why I have asked my Avocat to join us.' He looked at his watch. 'And he should probably be here by now. If I were you, Captain Brunhild, I'd head down to reception and check he isn't cooling his heels. He is not the kind of man who likes to be kept waiting, and as he charges by the minute, nor will I be when I see his bill!' he added with a chuckle. 'Seriously though, chop-chop.' He clapped his hands together, winking at Coco.

Hugo fought the urge to say something. There was something about Alexander Esnault's face, despite its smooth innocence, seemed to trigger the desire to reach forward and slap the smugness from it. Instead, he pushed himself back in his chair, taking a moment to study him when Alexander did not realise he was being watched. He hoped to have a moment to see it for real, not when Alexander was putting on a performance, for Hugo was sure of one thing - everything Alexander Esnault did was thought out and reasoned. He was like a painting, stoic and framed, but dependent on how it was viewed. Different angles showed different shadows. As Coco left the room, Alexander's head jerked back towards Hugo, eyes widening in surprise when he realised he was being appraised. A sly smile appeared on his face, a tongue flicking lazily over his lip. 'We are alone, at last,' he said lazily in a drawl which reminded Hugo of somebody who originated from the American Deep South.

Hugo pushed away the urge again, narrowing his eyes. He knew he was not good at showing his emotions, they were often misread, but he tried his best because he wanted Alexander Esnault to understand Hugo knew who he was, who he *really* was.

Alexander moved his head to the side, a strand of blond hair falling across his face. He did not move it. 'You interest me,' he said. 'I don't think I've ever met anyone like you before. I had thought the stories about you to be exaggerated, your honesty to be a myth. You see, I believe every man to have a price.'

'I do not,' Hugo replied.

Alexander shook his head. 'You do, everybody does. And it is my job to evaluate just what it is, what it takes to get a person to do exactly what I want them to do. You'd be surprised at how easy it is.'

Hugo sighed. 'What you actually are is a bully. Monsieur Esnault, nothing more; nothing less. You threaten and bribe to get what you want. And I expect if you come across an honest man, a man you can't control or manipulate, you won't let that stop you and you'll stoop to any level to make them do your bidding.' He paused, his emerald green eyes hardening. 'Such as following their loved ones, just to let them know you can, for example.'

Alexander smiled. 'You don't have a very good opinion of me, Hugo, which is very sad, and might I say, very incorrect. I so wanted to impress you, and it hurts me to be so misunderstood by you of all people.'

Hugo was surprised. 'It does?'

Alexander nodded. 'Very much so. You're judging the book by its cover and not bothering to read it. I am not who or what you think I am,' he added solemnly. 'I am so much more,' he added with a flirty wink.

Before Hugo could respond the door to the office opened again, and Coco entered. She glanced at Hugo, mouthing, 'désolé.'

Alexander clapped his hands again. 'Ah, here's my Avocat now,' he said cheerfully.

Hugo turned his head slowly. There was something about Esnault's tone which he did not like. It was triumphant almost. Hugo closed his eyes, sucking the stale air from Coco's office into his lungs. Pierre Duchamp was standing in the doorway, dressed in a suit which probably cost more than Hugo's annual salary. 'Oh, of course, it is,' Hugo muttered through gritted teeth. Coco moved quickly to her desk, flopping onto a chair, biting down hard on her lip. Hugo flashed her a reassuring look. *I've got this.*

He pointed towards an empty chair next to Alexander Esnault. 'Take a seat, Maître Duchamp,' he said in the most even tone he could manage. He wanted to scream, but he knew he would not. He would not give his father the satisfaction of knowing he had gotten under his skin.

Pierre Duchamp stood with angry determination, coughing a response. He glanced down at the plastic chair with a large cut through the centre of it and pulling a handkerchief from his jacket wiped across the surface. He lowered himself gingerly. 'I see you failed to exercise my client's rights, Captain Brunhild,' he said sharply, 'I realise you've been away from the Police Nationale for a while, but this is too much. My client is…'

Alexander raised his hand. 'Chill, Pierre. We're just here for a friendly chat, that's all, nothing more.'

'If you have nothing to hide, Monsieur Esnault, then why do you need your Avocat?' Hugo interjected.

Pierre glared at Hugo but seemed unable to meet his gaze, instead turning back to face Coco. 'Am I correct in understanding you are also allowing police officers from other jurisdictions to interview my client?'

Coco sighed. 'Hey, as your client himself just said, this is not an interview, it is just a chat between friends, non?'

Alexander bowed his head in agreement.

Coco indicated for Hugo to continue.

'Monsieur Esnault, I'd like to ask you where were you yesterday morning between approximately 9:45 am and 11:30 am?' Hugo asked.

'That sounds like an interrogation,' Pierre Duchamp said, 'and a question which my client has no obligation to answer.' He faced Hugo. 'What is this all about, Hugo? I'm at a loss to understand how this is of any of your concern. You have no place in Paris.' He paused before adding. 'You never have.'

Hugo's jaw flexed, and he swallowed, desperate to moisten his dry throat. When he spoke again he did not want to sound weak, or angry, or sad, or any emotion Pierre Duchamp could misinterpret as he saw fit. He would not give him the satisfaction of creating his own false narrative. He knew he had to speak now, or else Coco would take over the conversation. 'I may be out of my jurisdiction,' Hugo began hesitantly, 'but I am working in conjunction with Captain Brunhild and with the express permission of the Minister of Justice. Now, shall we cut the nonsense and actually get down to business so we can all stop wasting each other's time? I don't know about either of you, but I have places to be and people I'd much rather be with.'

Pierre Duchamp pulled back his head, staring at Hugo in surprise. He shrugged. 'You invited us here, you have the floor.'

Hugo nodded and repeated his question to Alexander Esnault.

Esnault smiled at him. 'I was in Paris, as I always am. This city is my home, I belong here. It is in my blood.'

'I see,' Hugo replied, 'and where exactly was your blood yesterday morning? Was it, perhaps, on Rue de Marceau, outside Hotel á Bertrain?'

Alexander tapped his chin but did not reply. He shrugged his shoulders as if casting off an insect. 'I expect,' he said finally with a smile, 'you already know the answer to that question.'

Hugo watched the young man carefully as he tried to understand who he was, *what* he was. He had encountered many men like him before; he was sure of that. What was he? Hugo could not be sure, men such as Alexander Esnault often came with many different names - sociopaths, psychopaths. The only thing Hugo knew for sure was there was something about him which required careful scrutiny and understanding. As it stood, Hugo could not yet determine whether Alexander was a joker or a monster. Or both.

Hugo sighed. 'Monsieur Esnault, s'il vous plaît.'

'What are you, in your childish way, implying, Hugo?' Pierre Duchamp asked.

Hugo replied. 'Your client knows exactly what I am referring to.'

Coco coughed and leaned forward, tapping a DVD case on the corner of her desk. She said nothing as she leaned back, pulling the DVD towards her.

'After our conversation, I decided I would like to speak to you further, to continue our conversation,' Alexander said, his eyes locked on the DVD, 'and so I came to your hotel.'

'And how did you know which hotel I was staying in?' Hugo asked.

Alexander ignored him and continued. 'And when I arrived, I thought better of it, and decided not to bother you.'

Hugo raised an eyebrow. 'And what about Ben?

Why did you follow my husband?'

Alexander shook his head. 'I don't know what you're talking about. I've never even met your husband, so I would certainly have no reason to follow him.'

Coco dropped the DVD case onto the floor and gingerly picked it up, mouthing, *oops*, as she did.

Hugo pointed at the DVD. 'Please do me a favour Monsieur Esnault and try to remember that the Police Nationale actually know what they are doing. There are CCTV cameras all over Paris watching our every move, whether or not we like it. It's just a fact of life, although at times such as these, they can be very helpful.'

'And a gross invasion of privacy,' Pierre Duchamp muttered under his breath.

'That's not something for us to debate here,' Hugo retorted, 'merely to accept it as a fact of life.' He stared at Alexander again. 'What I don't understand, and what I want you to clarify is, was it just an accident you followed Ben, or did you go to the hotel for some other reason?'

'Hugo, I really don't know what you are talking about,' Alexander replied. 'I told you, I came to see you, nothing more, nothing less.'

Hugo tutted loudly. 'Stop wasting our time. We know you followed Ben to the park because he saw you, and we saw you, thanks to the CCTV cameras, so I ask you again. Why did you follow Ben? What was the plan?'

Alexander sighed, stealing a sly look towards Pierre.

Pierre shrugged his shoulders and Hugo recognised the bored expression on his face because it was the same one he had spent most of his childhood trying to avoid. It had only taken him a short amount of time to realise the look was not boredom; it was a warning. Danger was approaching. He shuddered, casting the shackles of his childhood free. He would not allow Pierre to exert that kind of power over him anymore.

'My question,' Hugo continued, 'and I'll keep asking it until you give me an answer, is, what was your plan? I was aware of your not-so-veiled threat towards Captain Brunhild and me regarding our families. Was that was this was about? To follow Ben to show me you mean business and I should not keep asking questions?'

Alexander laughed. 'You put far too much stock into my words, Hugo. I truly mean little of what I say and the rest is huffing.' He paused. 'Very well, I'll level with you because, as your father will attest, I have actually committed no crimes. You see, for some time I have had *Caron Auberge de Jeunesse* under surveillance.'

'Pourquoi? Coco asked.

'Somebody stole something from me,' he answered.

'Stole something?' Hugo asked in surprise. 'What?'

Alexander shrugged his shoulders, stealing a sly glance towards Pierre. 'It doesn't matter, suffice to say though, it was something I require back.'

Hugo tapped his jaw. 'And this item? Who stole it? Marc Gassna, perhaps? Or Jack Boucher? Or Delphine

Marchand, or her other friends?'

Alexander shrugged again. 'It could have been any of them, or all of them. They are like a pack of wolves, truly they are. And just as vicious,' he added.

Hugo and Coco exchanged a confused look.

'And this item, you were waiting for them to show up at the youth hostel?'

'Oui,' Alexander replied. 'After…' he coughed, '*everything* that has happened, people are lying low, as I'm sure you can understand. But it makes the search for the stolen item no less important or time-sensitive.'

Hugo wondered what on earth it might be Alexander Esnault had lost and the lengths he would go to retrieve it. 'But how did that translate into you following Ben?'

'He was seen and overheard talking with the tramp who works at the hostel, the implication being if the wolves surfaced, there was a chance they might reach out for help.' He stopped, a sly smile on his face. 'It was divine providence I followed him that morning because really I had no idea where he was going and who he was going to meet. It was *quite* the surprise. But he looked excited, so I imagined he wasn't going on a simple shopping trip.'

Hugo nodded. 'And you saw him with the people you're interested in and when they saw you, they ran. Why are they so frightened of you, Monsieur Esnault? What happened when you followed them?'

'They got away,' Alexander spat distastefully. 'They

were quick, and they'd obviously scoped out the area before agreeing to meet there. They disappeared into the bowels of the park, and I'm ashamed to say I lost my bearings. They were gone before I even came close to catching up with them.'

'And you expect us to believe that?' Coco asked.

Alexander pointed at the DVDs. 'If you don't have it on there, then I suggest you broaden your search. Ten minutes later I finally found my way out of the park, at the opposite side I think, and I finally managed to get a signal on my cell phone. My driver picked me up shortly afterwards and drove me home. Alone. I'm not doing your job for you, Captain Brunhild. I'm sure if you check the CCTV from the other side of the park, you'll see what I'm telling you is the truth. And I was alone when I got in my car. There were no bodies placed in my trunk, nor, I imagine, corpses found in the park. I'm sure I would have heard so if that were the case.'

Silence. Pierre Duchamp cleared his throat and rose to his feet. 'Well, this is all very interesting I am sure, but I think we are done here. I am also sure you will agree, my client has been more than cooperative.'

Hugo raised his hand. 'We have a few more questions before you go.' He smiled politely. 'I promise we won't take too much of your time, Monsieur Esnault, and we would be very grateful for your cooperation. After all, two young people are dead and three others are missing. I'm sure you'd agree it is in all of our best interests to do what we can to put an end to this, whatever this is, as soon as possible.'

Alexander gestured for Pierre to sit again. Pierre flopped huffily onto the chair. 'You have two minutes,' he grumbled. 'I'm due in court and I can't, *won't* be late just to indulge you and your fantasies.'

Hugo stood and crossed the room. It was small and only took him a second and he felt foolish, chastising himself for a big gesture which had amounted to nothing. He did not move, his back to the room, the voices in his head reminding him of the demons he had fought against all of his life.

You are wet and weak, and you will amount to nothing.
You are an embarrassment to the Duchamp family name. Thank Dieu, Papa is dead and didn't live to see the child left to carry on the family name.
You are everything I am not, and that is unbearable.

Pierre Duchamp coughed. 'We are behind you, Hugo,' he said with amusement causing Coco to tut loudly. 'Although I'm sure you could do with brushing up on the police manuals you are staring at.'

Hugo turned around, sucking as much air into his lungs as he could. 'Monsieur Esnault, what happened to Marc Gassna and Jack Boucher? And s'il vous plaît, I want the truth.'

Alexander smiled. 'The truth has many different

facets as you should know. If you're asking me a specific question such as, did I murder them, then the answer is a resounding non.'

'Then did you have them murdered?' Hugo asked.

'My client has now answered your questions, and unless you have any evidence implicating him, then he has nothing else to say,' Pierre Duchamp interrupted, 'and you're even more foolish than I give you credit for if you imagine he's going to even respond to that particular question.'

Hugo continued. He scratched his head. 'Why were you surveilling *Caron Auberge de Jeunesse*?'

Alexander gave him a surprised look. 'What do you mean?'

'I mean, why that particular youth hostel?' Hugo replied. 'How did you know the missing young people would go there? I've checked, it's certainly not the only hostel in Paris, and it's out of the way, so I have to wonder why you would even know to look there in the first place.'

Alexander turned to Pierre, who gave him a slight shrug of his left shoulder. 'Because in another time, another life, I used to stay there myself. So when I see kids who might need a bed for the night, I point them in that direction.'

Hugo watched him with interest, realising he had not expected that answer from him. 'You used to stay at that hostel?'

Alexander nodded, picking at his expensive jacket.

'Oui, my life did not always appear this way,' he answered. 'When I told you I looked after the young people who I came into contact with, I meant it and it was because I recognised myself in them. I know all too well of the pitfalls and the dangers that can befall them. *Caron Auberge de Jeunesse* is a place where they can be safe for a night or two should they need it.'

Hugo found it difficult to reconcile the two Alexander Esnault's. Was he a ruthless, dangerous pimp, and drug dealer or a caring elder whose mission was to help the disadvantaged? Or could he be both? He studied the younger man's face and for one of the first times in his career, Hugo found it was difficult to read him. Esnault's face betrayed no secrets. Whatever or whoever Alexander Esnault was, he was a man so practised in wearing a mask he had become an expert at it.

Pierre Duchamp lifted his arm, glancing at the Rolex he wore on his wrist. He sighed. 'As I said, I'm due in court,' he muttered. He turned away from Hugo. 'We are done here, Captain Brunhild. I suggest if you wish to speak to my client again you contact me directly, although I can assure you there had better be a good reason for wasting our time. ' He nudged Esnault. 'Alexander, let's go.'

Alexander rose to his feet, all the time his gaze fixed firmly on Hugo. 'If you find those kids, be sure to send them my best and let them know I am always here for them, whatever they need, whatever they have done. Will you do that for me, Hugo?'

'Before you go, one last question,' Hugo replied. 'Are you acquainted with Monseigneur Augustine Demaral?'

Alexander stumbled against his chair, the legs scraping across the floor as he pushed it backwards. 'Who?' he replied quickly as if forcing the word out in a desperate breath.

Hugo watched the younger man carefully. He had turned his head, his bottom lip pushing against the top one nervously.

Pierre stepped in front of Hugo. 'Half of Paris must know the Monseigneur. He is a benevolent man whose good deeds are insurmountable. What possible interest could you have in him?'

Hugo looked at Coco and she twisted her mouth in consideration as if she was also surprised by Pierre acknowledging he knew the Monseigneur. But there was something else which caught Hugo's attention, and something which he was not sure he understood. Alexander's face was pale and anxious, his head dropped. He was fidgeting anxiously with the hair on the top of his head. Hugo turned back to Pierre. 'No reason. I was just wondering if Monsieur Esnault knew him, that's all. Aren't you interested in why I'm asking? '

'Alexander, let's go,' Pierre ignored Hugo, moving towards the door, ushering Alexander to follow him.

Alexander seemed to pull himself together and

stood, drifting towards Pierre. He stopped in front of Hugo. Whatever had just happened to him had passed, and he had regained his composure and his expression was playful, almost antagonistic once again. 'My best to your husband, Hugo. Love and life are so fleeting, aren't they? I hope the two of you cherish each moment you have together.'

Hugo exhaled, watching helplessly as Pierre and Alexander left the room. He closed the door after them and pushed the air out of his body as if he could not breathe.

'Well, what did you make of that?' Coco asked.

Hugo did not answer immediately. He was still staring at the door, his face a mask of contemplation. 'I think the only time we had a genuine reaction from either of them was when I mentioned Monseigneur Demaral,' he answered. 'I would even go so far as to say Alexander looked panicked, scared even.' He shook his head. 'Now, what on earth could a priest have done to inspire fear in someone such as Alexander Esnault?'

'Monseigneur Augustine Demaral,' Hugo read aloud from the computer screen, 'was born shortly after the end of World War II in a tiny village in Northern France. Nazi's had murdered his father after it was discovered he had been hiding fleeing Jews in the family barn. From an early age, young Augustine felt the call of God like a gentle whisper in his ear and he knew there was no other choice. His calling was his destiny and his destiny has been fulfilled and the spiritual light from Heaven shines through him.'

Coco yawned. 'Creepers, who writes this garbage? I mean seriously, all we're missing here is hearing how he rescues sick kittens and hand rears them back to life.'

Hugo smiled. 'He could be a good man,' he offered.

Coco gave him a doubtful look. 'Listen, all I'm saying is, I'm sure there are lots of decent, non-hypocritical religious folks, but I have yet to meet one. You can't be telling me you buy into their sanctimonious double standards, do you?'

Hugo considered for a moment. His own relationship with religion was a complicated one. His Grand-Mère, Madeline Duchamp, had been a devout Catholic, and had raised Hugo with the belief he would be too, but he had realised at an early age it was not a path for him, whether or not he wanted it to be. As an adult, he had come to realise that religion, in its most innocent and wholesome form could be a force for good. However,

323

when beliefs and rigidity combined, it was one of the most dangerous forces in the world. 'I used to love going to Synagogue,' he answered.

She raised an eyebrow. 'Well, I wasn't expecting that. You did?'

He nodded. 'Oui. When I was younger, I was involved with someone Jewish, and our Saturday mornings together were usually spent at a Reform Synagogue. I can't say I was converted, but I enjoyed it. The words and the spirit touched me, and yeah, I actually felt accepted. I can't say that about too many places in my life. If the relationship had lasted, who knows?'

'Bully for you,' she replied, 'my experience of Synagogue usually involved sitting in the women-only section watching my mother scratching at her cheap nylon wig, only speaking when she was spoken to.'

Hugo studied her. 'Somehow, I can't see you that way.'

Coco pulled at her hair, flicking the dyed blue tips over her shoulder. 'How do you think this started? Papa said it killed Rabbi Solomon, which I thought was a little excessive, but...' she gasped as the door to her office was thrown open with such force it bounced off the wall. 'Jesus, Cedric,' she shouted at the young Lieutenant, 'how difficult is it to knock and gently open the door? One of these days you'll give me a damn heart attack.'

'Désolé, Captain,' Cedric said. 'I've got something you need to see,' he added, handing her a manila folder.

Coco took the folder from him, 'you look pleased with yourself, Lieutenant,' she said, flicking it open, squinting to read the small print, 'and usually when a man looks so pleased with himself I find out six weeks later I'm pregnant and I wonder how the hell I missed it.'

Hugo covered his mouth, suppressing a chuckle. 'What is it, Lieutenant,' he asked, 'what did you find?'

'A can of worms, that's what I found,' Cedric replied.

Hugo moved behind Coco's desk and flicked on his glasses, bending down to read the paper she was holding. She squinted at the small print before handing it to Hugo. 'Here, you have the glasses, you read it.'

Hugo moved the paper nearer his face, flicking on his glasses, scanning the paper quickly but with deep concentration. 'It's the juvenile police records of Marc Gassna and Jack Boucher.'

'About time,' she grumbled. 'Anything noteworthy?'

Hugo continued scanning the paper. 'There are several arrests, basically what we might have expected, prostitution, theft, public intoxication and...' he trailed off, 'now that is interesting,' he added after a moment.

'Quoi?' Coco asked.

Hugo placed the paper on the desk. 'Four years ago they were both arrested for an assault on a certain Monseigneur Augustine Demaral.'

'They were?' Coco replied sharply. She turned back to Cedric. 'What happened?'

Cedric glanced at his feet, slowly shrugging his shoulders. 'Maybe you should ask the Commander about it,' he mumbled in response.

Coco's eyebrow raised. 'Morty? What does he have to do with this?'

Cedric did not look up. 'As I said, you'll have to ask him,' was all he said before turning and leaving.

Commander Mordecai Stanic flung the folder onto his desk, scattering dust into the air. He picked up a mug and slugged the contents, grimacing as he did. 'Whoever makes the damn café in this station ought to be shot.'

'Well?' Coco interrupted impatiently.

'Well, what?' Mordecai retorted.

Coco tapped the paper angrily. 'The damn juvenile detention records.' She stopped, her eyes scanning his face as if she recognised something, something she did not like. 'You know exactly what I'm talking about, don't you?'

The Commander lowered his head, scratching at his desk with a broken fingernail. 'It's not relevant.'

'It's not relevant?' Coco screeched. 'It's not f-u-c-k-i-n-g relevant?' she repeated loudly.

Mordecai lifted his hand. 'Keep your voice down Captain, and don't speak to me in that tone of voice, I'm warning you.'

Coco stepped back. 'You're warning me?' She frowned. 'What the hell is going on, Morty?'

He slammed his fists onto the desk with such force

Hugo jumped. 'How many more times do I have to order you to give me my proper title.'

'Oh, don't tempt me,' Coco retorted.

'Commander Stanic,' Hugo interrupted, keen to attempt to defuse the potentially volatile situation. 'We'd planned on speaking with Monseigneur Demaral, therefore any information you might have could be very useful.'

The Commander turned to face Hugo, his mouth twisting angrily. Hugo recognised the look in his eyes. Anger, but the anger was tempered with fear, like a child being caught with their hand in a cookie jar. It worried Hugo, although he was not sure why.

'You can forget about talking with the Monseigneur,' the Commander muttered under his breath.

Coco cocked her head. 'Say what now?'

He looked at her but pivoted back to Hugo. 'The Monseigneur is currently away from Paris.'

'And where the hell is he?' Coco said, stepping in front of Hugo. She raised her hand. 'Désolé, I mean, where on earth is the priest?'

'He is on retreat.'

'Retreat?' Coco asked in surprise. 'What is that supposed to mean?'

Mordecai leaned back in his chair. 'It's a perfectly normal thing for a member of the Church to do. He is in Rome, I believe, on retreat.'

Coco cast a sideways look at Hugo, who shrugged his shoulders. 'And when is the Monseigneur back from his "retreat"?' Coco asked, emphasising the quotation marks with her fingers.

'You don't have to say it like it's a dirty word, Captain,' Mordecai said. 'He is a very fine man, and his good works are well known throughout Paris and the rest of the world. Sadly he isn't a young man and has been in ill-health, which is why he is in Rome on retreat.'

Coco opened her mouth to reply but closed it again in exasperation. Hugo touched her arm gently before speaking. 'What can you tell us about the assault?' he asked the Commander.

Mordecai leaned back, his head lolling behind him, and he closed his eyes. 'It was a long time ago, and it amounted to very little,' he answered.

'Four years isn't so long and frankly, I'll be the judge of whether or not it's important to my investigation,' Coco snapped. 'What the hell is going on, Mort... I mean, *Commander*? This isn't like you.'

Mordecai sighed. He turned to face Coco, dark eyes narrowing angrily. 'This is exactly like me, Captain Brunhild, doing my job as I should be and as you should be. This bears no relevance on your investigation, so move on.'

Coco and Hugo exchanged incredulous looks. Coco shook her head. 'I'm doing my job,' she sniped, 'or at least trying to, and I can't believe you of all people are deliberately withholding information from me.'

The Commander sighed once again. 'Monseigneur

Demaral wasn't even in Paris during either of the deaths, so there is no way it could involve him, and therefore of any relevance to the investigation.'

'But something which happened in the past could,' Hugo interjected. 'Regarde, Commander Stanic, neither Captain Brunhild nor I am interested in dragging up a past when it is irrelevant, but we have to be in possession of all the necessary facts. Imagine if the Minister of Justice were to discover leads weren't followed up, he'd have all of our jobs.'

The Commander glared at Hugo. 'This has nothing to do with that fool.'

Hugo shook his head. 'It is everything to do with Minister Lenoir, not just because it's his job, and one he takes very seriously, but because this whole business has been made personal for him. If we don't investigate then he will and I think we all know he will be much less sensitive than we would, non?'

He tutted loudly. 'You can say that again, knowing Jean Lenoir, he'll make it his personal mission to bring down the Catholic Church just so he can see his face on newspaper headlines and he wouldn't give a damn about how many decent lives he destroys in the process.'

Coco moved towards him. 'Morty, s'il vous plaît, talk to us. You know you can trust us. If there's nothing to see then we won't make a big deal of it, but we need to know, you have to understand that. I learned everything I know from you, and this, whatever this is, isn't you.'

Mordecai turned his head slowly towards her. He sighed for a third time, pushing the air out of his lungs as if he could bear it there no longer. 'The Church and the State should always be kept apart because when they are not, the problems created tend to consume whoever is around them, like a tornado.'

Coco laughed. 'Okay, Monsieur-Drama-Queen, I hear you, but really, what is this about?'

The Commander stood up and walked across his office. He closed the door and began pulling down the blinds, a dust cloud causing him to splutter. He turned back into the office, pushing himself through the narrow gap occupied by Coco.

'Until four years ago, Monseigneur Demaral was in charge of a youth home for troubled and abandoned children,' he said taking his seat again.

'You make it sound like it was a pound for stray mutts,' Coco muttered.

The Commander ignored her and continued. 'In a lot of ways it was. Kids nobody wanted, kids so badly damaged nobody knew what to do with, or cared for that matter. Everyone loves a sad puppy story and they'll bend over backwards to help, but when you get a kid, so traumatised by abuse they are broken, then society looks the other way, whether from guilt or because they just don't want to see a child with the devil in their eyes. Kids like that end up in institutions and very quickly become dangerous adults. The Church tried to prevent that.' He made the sign of a cross across his chest. Hugo watched carefully. There was something about the way he did it which seemed awkward and he was not sure why, almost as if it was not something he was used to doing.

'Oh, save me the sanctimonious Catholic Church rhetoric you've been feeding me as long as we've known each other. Your mother hated me because I had the audacity to be born a Jewess, not for any other reason she bothered to discover. If she'd hated me because she didn't like my politics or my damn blue hair I could have stomached it. But to hate me because my ancestors kneeled a different way was just... just... stupid.'

'Ma mére is a saint...' Mordecai whispered. There was a bite to his tone as if he was passing a warning.

Coco's eyebrow arched in a sarcastic triangle, and she bit down on her bottom lip.

'What about this children's home?' Hugo asked.

'For many years it was successful,' the Commander answered, 'but as time went on and support was withdrawn, funds depleted, it became run down and neglected. There was talk of problems, neglect, abuse, the usual nonsense.'

'The usual non-sen-se?' Coco spat out as if the words were more than she could bear.

Mordecai ignored her, addressing Hugo instead. 'For decades there has been a multitude of cases against the Church and with each payout come another dozen more.'

'Often with very good cause,' Hugo replied. He

raised his hand. 'Bien sûr, I understand there will always be people taking advantage of those kinds of situations, but it can't distract us from the very real harm which has been done. These problems at the hostel are you saying they were entirely unfounded?'

The Commander stared at Hugo. His dark eyes were cold and challenging and it was all Hugo could do to stop himself from looking away. 'The truth is,' Mordecai answered with obvious reluctance, 'I don't really know.'

'You don't really know?' Coco interrupted irritably.

Mordecai nodded. 'Before you get all high and mighty with me, Captain Brunhild, I suggest you, for once, actually take a breath and use the two ears God gave you to listen to what I am saying.' He paused and turned back to Hugo. 'Four years ago I was alerted to an incident at the hostel. The Monseigneur had been assaulted, beaten viciously and left for dead and the building had been set alight. A patrol caught the two boys, Marc Gassna and Jack Boucher, fleeing the scene, their fists bloody. They freely admitted to the assault and arson, saying it was the only way to stop the abuse.'

'What kind of abuse are we talking about?' Hugo asked.

'They claimed there was a system of sexual and physical violence by the men who ran the hostel, including the Monseigneur. The boys were arrested and brought here to the 7e arrondissement while the Monseigneur was taken to hospital. They put the fire out, but not before significant damage left it a shell of a building. It was later demolished. As for the Monseigneur, he sustained major, life-changing injuries, and it was decided it was in his best interest to retire from his position in the church.'

Hugo looked at Coco, exchanging a thought. *Or did he make a deal? Retire and disappear into a nice, cosy retirement.*

'But we've seen the records. They released the kids without charge, how come if the Monseigneur's injuries were as bad as you say?' Coco posed.

The Commander shrugged. 'He declined to press charges, said it was all a big misunderstanding.'

Hugo and Coco both waited for him to elaborate. He did not. 'A big misunderstanding?' Coco spat.

He nodded. 'He said he caught them *together*, in unholy activities and they were embarrassed and lashed out. I tell you he is a good Christian man who believed the children had already been through enough in their lives after suffering horrendous abuse, and he was certainly not going to add to it. Therefore, without his cooperation, there was no reason to hold them or no reasonable chance for a prosecution. They were released into the custody of social services, and that was the end of it. Case closed.'

Hugo folded his hands in his lap but did not speak.

'Case closed,' Coco repeated.

'Now, I'm sure you'll understand why this has nothing whatsoever to do with your investigation, so move on,' the Commander said. 'Am I making myself clear, Captain Brunhild? *Move on.*' He added the words, the unmistakable lilt of a warning threaded through them.

Coco moved towards the door, gesturing to Hugo. 'Oh, you've made yourself perfectly clear, *Commander Stanic*. Hugo, let's go.'

Hugo stared at the battered body of Randolph Boucher and considered whatever had happened to him and his wife had not been pleasant. Yesterday had been brutal to them. The beeps of the life-support machine hurt his ears, hurt the migraine which was threatening. He pressed his temples, hoping to rid himself of it.

'I finally found the doctor,' Coco said entering the hospital room, 'and he says it could go either way.'

Hugo nodded. 'Monsieur Boucher hasn't regained consciousness?'

'They don't believe so, certainly not since he got here, and as far as I can tell, they don't expect him to anytime soon. He's in what they call an induced coma, something about it being a way for his body to try to heal itself,' Coco replied. 'But according to the scans, they don't hold up too much hope.'

'I see,' Hugo said.

'And they checked under his nails, no blood or skin, so whoever fought with Madame Ana Boucher, it apparently wasn't her husband,' Coco added.

Hugo stared again at Randolph Boucher. His eyes were already swollen and bruising. 'He took a hell of a beating.'

Coco scratched her head. 'And then dumped in a garbage chute while his wife gets thrown off a building. Whoever is behind this is a sadistic son of a bitch.' She dropped her bag and pulled out a folder and began flicking through it, dropping crime scene photographs onto the bed.

Hugo stepped beside her, flicking on his glasses. 'I'm still having trouble trying to understand what happened in the Boucher apartment,' he said. 'And why we have two very different crimes, it's almost as if...'

'There were two different perps,' Coco concluded.

Hugo tapped his chin. 'Well, it would explain why the crimes and the disposal of the bodies were so different, but there need not have been two perps.'

Coco shook her head. 'I can't see it. I just can't visualise a scenario, can you?'

Hugo considered for a moment and lifted the crime scene photographs and began placing them on the window ledge. 'We can see from the first photograph there is no evidence of any kind of struggle in the living room, and nor here, in either bedroom, or the bathroom, or the kitchen. Only in the hallway.' He paused. 'And there is a lot of it and if you look at the blood splatter pattern, it's more highly concentrated by the front door, leading into the house, not out of it.'

Coco moved closer, squinting at the photographs. 'You're right,' she replied, impressed.

'Which would suggest the attack came from the inside, not the outside,' Hugo added.

Coco frowned. 'And?'

Hugo gave a quick shrug of his shoulders. 'Well, I know we're only assuming the blood belongs to Randolph

Boucher until it's confirmed by forensics, but it seems likely, in which case, it would seem odd the attack came from inside the house.'

'Unless the attacker was Ana Boucher,' Hugo interjected. Coco frowned again. 'You believe the demure Madame Boucher lashed out at her husband, dragged his body to the waste chute, and then calmly threw herself off the building?'

They lapsed into a pensive silence. 'It's a stretch,' Hugo said finally, 'and it doesn't explain the witness who claims they saw Madame Boucher struggling with someone before she fell.' He lowered his head to study the photographs once again. 'Unless it happened this way. Madame Boucher was home alone, the murderer came to visit, and she let them in, either because she knew them or she was intimidated into allowing it, or perhaps just trusted them. They could be there offering condolences so she had no reason to suspect anything untoward, for example.'

'Untoward?' Coco questioned doubtfully. 'But why would anyone want to murder Madame Boucher?'

Hugo shrugged again. 'Maybe she knew something, or the murderer thought she might know something. We don't know what the story is here. They could believe the Boucher's could have information which might implicate the killer, no matter how small or inconsequential it might be, or whether they're even aware of it.' He began pacing, warming up to his formulating ideas. 'For all we know this may have meant to appear as a murder-suicide, or even a suicide pact because the truth is, after the Boucher's had just lost their son, we may not have looked too closely at it.'

'I get that,' Coco conceded, 'but if that was the case, then how the hell did it go so badly wrong?'

Hugo considered. 'Well, let's say Madame Boucher was attacked, and the intention was to make it appear as if a mother, grieving at the loss of her only child, took her own life. Afterwards, the murderer returned to the apartment to make sure there is no trace of him there and…'

'Monsieur Boucher arrived home unexpectedly…' Coco concluded.

'It fits,' Hugo posed. 'And the killer had to take extreme action because Monsieur Boucher knew immediately something was up, perhaps he saw something or heard something. We can't really know, but either way, he knew this person should not be in his house. So, they struggled and Monsieur Boucher was incapacitated, hence all the blood,' he turned towards the hospital bed where Randolph Boucher lay fighting for his life, 'and there's every reason to suspect the murderer believed Monsieur Boucher was dead, or at least dying so he had to move quickly to dispose of the body. However, by then Madame Boucher has been discovered and there were people around who had no doubt alerted the police. Therefore, the murderer had to improvise to get rid of the body. He could have left it in the house, but perhaps he wanted a chance to get away, a chance for this to still look like what he had originally intended.'

'But they must have realised we would have gone looking for Randolph Boucher and his body would have been discovered, eventually?' Coco reasoned.

'Or would it?' Hugo questioned. 'It's happened before where bodies have disappeared and it's assumed they went into landfill because once they do it's often impossible to retrieve them. It was a calculated risk, and it might have worked. If Cedric had not discovered Monsieur Boucher, we might have assumed he was on the run after murdering his wife. That was, after all, our first thought, non?'

Coco stared at him. 'This is a mess. A complicated, ridiculous mess.'

Hugo nodded. 'I know and I wish we could get a handle on all of this, Coco, before it gets any more out of hand and anyone else gets hurt.'

Coco sank onto a plastic chair, her body crumbling like a rag doll. She lifted her head slowly, pursing her lips. 'Did you buy what Morty had to say?'

Hugo looked at her as if he was unsure what or how to respond.

'Don't spare my feelings, Hugo,' she answered, 'just because I slept with him doesn't mean I like him. He was bullshitting one way or another, I'm sure of that. I just can't decide why, or whether it matters.'

Hugo pursed his lips. 'That's more or less what I

was thinking. He could be holding back information for many reasons which we can't know and those reasons may have nothing to do with this case. I suppose what I'm really wondering is, do you trust him?'

Coco turned her head. 'I do, I mean I *think* I do, but that wasn't like the Morty I know, not really. He's rigid; I get that, he likes to follow the rules, but he's not scared off easily. I mean, you've seen how he is with Jean Lenoir. He hates him with a passion and will do anything he can to bring him down. So, either there is no connection between this mysterious Monseigneur Augustine Demaral and what happened to Marc Gassna and Jack Boucher, or there is and Morty doesn't want us to find out what it is.'

Hugo frowned. 'But can you think of a reason why he might do that? Money? Bribery? Blackmail?'

Coco closed her eyes and lapsed into a heavy silence. 'Well, if he's being paid off, I'm certainly not seeing any of it,' she answered finally, 'and honestly, I just can't see it. I really can't, and I don't think I'm the sort of woman who looks at things through rose-tinted glasses but dammit, not Morty. He's a Catholic, a failed Catholic perhaps, but a Catholic nonetheless. He told his mother it was an "accident" we had sex and I ended up pregnant, like he tripped up and fell into me and accidentally ejaculated into me or something.' She paused, winking at Hugo before adding, '*twice*.'

Hugo chuckled.

'Of course, the old witch believed her prince of a

son,' Coco continued. 'Perhaps that is what this is all about, some misplaced loyalty to his mother. Maybe she is friends with the Monseigneur, I wouldn't put it past her, the only people she cares a damn about wear sackcloths. And if anything would make Morty turn a blind eye, his mother might just be it.' She stopped. 'As you know we have two kids together, one son, and he dotes on Cedric, I know he does. He's always been good with Julien, even though he's not his and has never made him feel left out when he came over. So I have to be honest and say I can't imagine any scenario, in any world, where the Mordecai Stanic I know would willingly cover-up child abuse. Unless he's a damn good actor or I'm not half as smart as I think I am at judging people.'

Hugo nodded. 'Then maybe he was right. Maybe we are looking in the wrong place and the connection with Monseigneur Demaral has nothing to do with what has happened.'

Coco's eyes locked on Hugo's. 'Do you believe that?'

He paused before shaking his head. 'Sadly, there's something we're not seeing. It may be nothing, but if you're asking me whether as a policeman I'm convinced, then I would have to say, I don't think I am.'

She stood up. 'Nor am I. So, let's find out what the fuck is going on and why we're being lied to.'

'How?' Hugo asked. 'Where do we even begin?'

Coco's face contorted into a miserable expression.

'Well, we start with the only person who truly knows Morty and might know when he's lying and why.'

'Mama Stanic,' Coco breezed, leaning forward and bending her body. Hugo watched her and suppressed a smile. He had never seen Coco being demure, or rather, attempting to be demure. She seemed like a child wearing ill-fitting heels with freshly dotted rouge on her cheeks. The air was thick with a sickly lavender perfume which Mama Stanic seemed to have bathed in. Hugo held his breath, trying to give his body a chance to adjust to the stuffiness of the room and the old lady's scent.

Mama Stanic dodged Coco, pulling her head to the left before Coco's lips connected with her face. Fleshy lips wobbled against an over-painted cheek. 'Charlotte, what are you doing here?' she asked in a way which showed no warmth. 'Is there something wrong with my Mordecai?' she added, obvious panic appearing in her voice.

Coco touched the elderly woman's shoulder. 'Non, Mama Stanic, Morty is fine,' she answered, touching the elderly woman's shoulder in a way which was obviously difficult for the both of them.

'*Mordecai*,' Mama Stanic corrected. Her eyes locked on Hugo who was standing behind Coco on the doorstep, blond hair covering his face as he stared at his feet. 'Who is he?'

Coco stepped back, gesturing towards Hugo. 'Ah, this is a colleague, Captain Duchamp. We were in the area and I thought it would be nice to introduce him to my... to you.'

Mama Stanic pulled her head backwards, the look clear on her face informing them she was not buying it. Her eyes, tired and blue, flicked between Hugo and Coco with irritation, finally giving way to curiosity. She reluctantly stepped backwards, gesturing for them to enter. 'It would have been nice to have had notice. It is not polite to drop around uninvited, at least that was how I was raised, but ah, times have changed.'

Coco smiled at Hugo and tipped her head, indicating he should go into the house. 'Buckle up, it's going to be a bumpy ride,' she muttered under her breath as he passed.

'I would give you one of my good cups,' Mama Stanic addressed Coco, passing her a mug with a chip on the lip and a crack down the side, 'but the last time I did you broke a porcelain cup which had managed to survive two World Wars but not your,' she glared at Coco's hands, 'unnaturally large fingers.'

Coco self-consciously placed her hands behind her back.

'Now, are you going to tell me why you are really here?' Mama Stanic asked, 'because we both know you'd rather be anywhere other than my parlour, Charlotte.'

'Oh, now Mama Stanic, that's not...' Coco began. She stopped and shook her head. 'I can't even lie about it. You're right, I WOULD rather be anywhere else but here.'

Mama Stanic threw back her head and laughed, her heavy bosoms bouncing against her chest. She crossed the kitchen and reached into a cupboard, extracting a bottle and three shot glasses. 'That's more like it, Charlotte, a bit of spunk. I always knew it was there but wondered why you bothered to hide it. It's almost midday, so you'll both join me for an apéritif.' She poured them and handed them to Coco and Hugo, who took them reluctantly.

'Merci,' Hugo said, wincing as the clear-coloured alcohol stung the back of his throat.

Mama Stanic chuckled again and refilled the glasses. 'What are you after, Charlotte? And the truth please, I'm an old woman and haven't time to waste on your nonsense.'

Coco pulled out a kitchen chair and sat down, drinking her second shot. 'Wow, this stuff has a kick,' she acknowledged.

Mama Stanic looked proud. 'It's the secret to my good health and long life, you should be so lucky,' she added, not managing to sound exactly sincere.

Coco took another drink, looking wistfully at the bottle. 'So, that's who I have to blame.'

'Careful, Charlotte, I may be small but I have a mean right hook. Ask Mordecai, he bore witness to it more times than he should when he was a boy, or,' she paused, 'when he made dubious choices as an adult.' Mama Stanic stopped, fixing Coco with a challenging look. 'What do you want with me exactly, Charlotte? I know you're not foolish enough to dare to ask me to speak to my son on your behalf.'

Coco met her gaze with as much dignity as she could. 'I want to know about Monseigneur Augustine Demaral and why Morty is hell-bent on protecting him.'

Mama Stanic gasped, her hand pressing against her lips. With her free hand, she made the sign of the cross, her lips twisting into a rapid-fire prayer. 'The Monseigneur is a Saint,' she whispered when she had finished. 'And Mordecai knows it. Do you know, when my Mordecai was a child he got into a fight at the children's home?' She stopped, her fingers wrapping around the small cross tied around her neck. 'I used to help out, so Mordecai would often play with the other boys and one day he got into a fight. It was nothing serious, the usual boy nonsense, fighting over football or something, but Mordecai fell to the ground and gashed his cheek open on a jagged rock. The Monseigneur picked him up and carried him to the hospital himself, covered in Mordecai's blood. And he was carrying on, oh how he was carrying on! Screaming like a banshee by all accounts, but the Monseigneur just held him tighter and made sure he was safe and looked after. The doctors said if he had not of gotten to the hospital as quickly as he did, the scar would have been much worse. That is the sort of man the Monseigneur is, thinking only of the little ones and asking for nothing in return. He is a Saint,' she repeated.

Coco suppressed a yawn. 'So I keep hearing, but really, what's the scoop?'

Mama Stanic glared at her. 'There is no "scoop" and

I won't tolerate any of *that* kind of talk again.'

'Talk?' Hugo interjected quickly, catching her emphasis.

She gasped again, recovering her mouth as if she had spoken out of turn. 'Rien, there is nothing to tell you.'

Coco reached across the table. 'Mama Stanic, there are two young men dead, probably murdered and there are other children in danger. We need help and for some reason, everyone is looking the other way. You have grandchildren now, think of them.'

'You don't play fair, Charlotte,' Mama Stanic grumbled. She moved across the kitchen and poured herself another drink, wincing as the alcohol hit the back of her throat. 'They were all just rumours, silly rumours by charlatans who were only interested in making money. They mistakenly believe the coffers of the Catholic Church to be never-ending.'

Hugo nodded. 'What happened?'

She turned her head slowly. 'There was a boy. That's all it took. One boy from a poor community and before we knew what was happening there was another, and another and another.' She shook her head with irritation. 'All saying the most horrible, disgusting untruths about Monseigneur Demaral, a man so pious he has no darkness in his heart.'

'What did these boys claim?' Hugo asked. 'Sexual abuse?'

Mama Stanic pursed her lips, nodding quickly. 'Lies.

347

Filthy, dirty, disgusting lies.'

From her seat, Coco blew a raspberry. Mama Stanic stabbed her finger towards her. 'And there it is, people who ought to know better always seeing the bad in everyone, with no proof, and be damned of the consequences.'

Coco's eyebrow raised. 'You could hardly call several kids coming forward as being no evidence.' She stared at Hugo. 'But I don't remember hearing about this, or reading any reports, which means the investigation never actually got very far.'

'And nor should it have,' Mama Stanic interjected, 'the shadow cast on the Monseigneur was so bad, so traumatic he vowed after the fire he would not personally get involved with children again. I can't tell you how much of a tragedy it was that innocent children were deprived of the kindness and Godliness of such a great man.'

'About this fire,' Hugo said, 'what can you tell us about it?'

She shrugged her shoulders. 'Very little. The Monseigneur caught two of the scoundrels up to no good. They damn well nearly killed him when he tried to stop them, beat his face to a pulp, it was awful. I know because I visited him in the hospital. He could not open his eyes to see or his mouth to speak for weeks. His legs were so crushed by them hitting him with steel pipes he could not walk properly for a long time.' She pursed her lips angrily. 'The little... they should have spent the rest of their miserable lives in prison paying for what they did. They beat him half to death and then lit the match and left him to burn. I am a God-fearing woman and I believe in forgiveness, but those children should have paid for what they did.'

'Speaking of which,' Coco mumbled, 'why didn't they go to prison? The attack sounds like attempted murder to me…' she trailed off, waiting for Mama Stanic to finish the thought. She did not. 'Why didn't they?' Coco finished.

Mama Stanic looked between Coco and Hugo, her face a mask of concern. 'What is this about, really about? And why are you here instead of talking to Mordecai? My Mordecai did nothing wrong,' she added with a defiant twist of her mouth before lowering her voice, 'only what a good Catholic should do.'

Coco flashed Hugo a look of concern. 'What did he do, Mama Stanic?' Coco asked.

'Only what he should have done, the right thing,' she answered. 'The Monseigneur did not want to be responsible for the destruction of their lives, no matter what they had done to him, that is the sort of selfless, honourable man he is. He did not want them to go to prison.'

Hugo nodded. 'But the police officers who attended the scene had already arrested them,' he said. He looked at Coco. *And Commander Mordecai Stanic made the charges go away.*

'The Monseigneur begged Mordecai, implored him to help, to save these ungodly children in the name of Dieu. And he did what he had to do.'

'Which was what, exactly?' Coco snapped.

Mama Stanic shrugged her shoulders again. 'His job. He is a powerful man, my Mordecai, and he knows the difference between right and wrong. He did what he had to do,' she repeated.

But he could not have done it alone, Hugo thought.

Coco rose to her feet. 'Merci for the hospitality, Mama Stanic. Let's not make it so long next time.'

Mama Stanic gave her a suspicious look. 'My Mordecai isn't in any trouble, is he?'

Coco forced a smile. 'Non, of course not, I'm sure everything is as it appears to be.' She flicked her fingers towards Hugo. 'Captain Duchamp, shall we?'

Delphine Marchand pulled her body through the crawl space, wincing as a barbed wire pulled at her already shredded stockings. She felt the blood trickle down her thigh and it felt oddly reassuring to her, as if a reminder she was still alive, she could still feel. There were times she wished she did not feel, did not remember. She wanted nothing more than an off switch. For a moment she allowed herself to see his face again. His smile. The eyes with the warmth of a puppy dog and the wisdom of a Buddhist monk, all wrapped up in a gorgeous, slightly awkward, body of a teenager. But he was gone and Delphine felt as responsible for it as the person who had led him to his destruction. If she had not dragged him with her to... if only she had... Her life was full of one regret after another, each pushing her on a path of despair which terrified her. She could not, she would not fall into the rabbit hole which had consumed the only person she had ever truly loved.

She pulled herself up, eyes scanning the deserted beach, her only company the seagulls eagerly scouring the sand for leftover food from the tourists. Their sad cries told her there were slim pickings, and she was pleased. She had chosen Sceaux because she remembered being there when she was a child and how in late summer, the tourists rarely ventured away from Paris. They had left Paris in a mad panic, needing to flee but not wishing to draw attention to themselves, and Sceaux was the only place she could think of. A place to rest and catch their breath while watching who may be behind them. She stooped down, tired eyes focusing on the lumpy tarpaulin under the boardwalk, satisfying herself that at first glance it appeared to be nothing conspicuous. She allowed herself to breathe, pulling as much of the fresh, cool salty morning air as she could. She was cold and had slept fitfully but for a moment she felt rejuvenated, ready for a new day. Prepared for a fight. Instinctively she tapped her chest, finger coiling around her bra until she found what she was seeking. A small USB device, sewn into the lace. It was all she had, and she would die to protect it. But she did not want to die before she found a way to use the information contained on the USB. She did not want to die until she made sure those responsible paid for what they had done.

'Dee…' a voice called out, dragging her back. She turned her head sharply as the tarpaulin was thrown back and Jérémie Berger sat up, one hand pushing through unkempt black hair, the other searching for his glasses. He flicked his glasses on, squinting to find her. His eyes widened with genuine happiness, and he waved excitedly in her direction. She attempted a genuine smile, watching as Jérémie pulled his limbs apart from the still sleeping body of Axel Soudre. Their skin had been pressed against each other for so long it stuck. Jérémie crawled to his feet and followed the trail Delphine had left. He moved quickly and was next to her in seconds. He jumped to his feet, pulling his lean body into a stretch.

'I slept well, did you sleep well?' he asked with the wonder of an excited child.

Delphine bit the inside of her cheek, fighting the urge to verbally slap him down, admonish him for his childish rhetoric. She forced herself to remember it was different for Jérémie and Axel. They were lovers, connected in ways she did not understand, buoyed on by each other's strength and the force of power of being loved, *really* loved by someone. It amazed her still because their own journeys had not been dissimilar to her own and in many ways they had lost even more than her, sacrificed even more than her. But their resilience shone like a star in the night sky, and it both amazed her and made her angrier than she dared admit. She hated the fact she wished they were as terrified and angry as she was, although she did everything she could to make sure they were not.

'You're smiling,' Jérémie said, 'what's with that?'

Delphine pulled his head towards her and kissed it. She tickled his chin in the same way she had done for years, despite knowing it should have stopped a long time ago. But she did it because it reminded her of a time when the world was different, hard and difficult but full of a hope she now believed was for other people. His skin was shiny and smooth, with only the hint of coarse hair beginning to push through. The smell of sand and stale sweat was more pleasant than it should be because to her it reminded her they were alive. They were free. 'I'm not always a sour bitch, y'know?' she replied. 'We do have fun sometimes.' She stopped, her face twisting angrily. '*Did* have fun.'

Jérémie pulled away, wrapping his arm around her shoulders. 'I know you're older than me, but you don't have to protect me forever. I can protect you now too. WE can protect YOU.'

She nodded. 'Je sais.'

Jérémie moved away from her, stepping gingerly over the stoned beach. He was wearing espadrilles which were worn and threadbare, but he walked purposefully into the water which was lapping gently against the shore. He turned his head to the East. 'Do you think some tourist pissed into the Seine in Paris and I'm standing in it now?'

Delphine snorted. 'You are the weirdest kid.'

'But I love him.'

Delphine and Jérémie turned their heads. Axel had risen and was standing nearby, dressed only in his boxer shorts and with the expectant smile of a lover he beckoned Jérémie towards him. Delphine exhaled wearily. 'You two are disgusting.'

Jérémie moved back to the shore, tongue darting across his lips, his eyes widening, the shine of desire evident. Delphine tutted. 'Perverts.' She looked at her watch. 'Okay, I'm going to check around,' she shook her head, 'do what you have to do but be ready to leave in half an hour, d'accord? We can't stick around.'

Jérémie answered distractedly, walking towards his

lover, their eyes locked together in silent desperation. 'Yeah, see ya, Delph,' he called without looking at her.

Hugo stepped onto the balcony, pulling out a cigarette and lighting it. It was barely seven o'clock and already the streets below the hotel were alive and vibrant. It was true what they said. Paris rarely slept, and it made him feel a pang of nostalgia, something which he thought he had lost. He was glad he was reclaiming his love for the town of his birth, and he knew it was in no small part due to sharing it with Ben and the new friends he was making.

'You're smiling,' Ben said, stepping out of the bedroom and immediately nuzzling Hugo's neck. 'I hate waking up and feeling for you in the bed only to find you're not there. For those few seconds, I imagine you were just a dream and I have to stop myself from balling.'

Hugo kissed his head. 'Not a dream, cheri.' His cell phone began ringing. 'It's Etienne,' he said answering it. 'Etienne, hey, how are you?'

'Bien, Hugo,' Etienne Martine replied. He was the forensic expert who worked with Hugo and he had become one of Hugo's closest friends. 'Montgenoux misses you. We all miss you, Mare-Louise is walking around with a face like thunder, convinced Paris will get her claws into you. Truth be told, we're all a little worried about it.'

Hugo smiled. 'Then you can all rest. All we can think about is coming home and if we had our way, we'd be on our way back right now.'

'That's what I like to hear,' Etienne replied, 'so I'd

better do whatever I can to help finish your work there, non?'

'That would be nice. Have you found something which could help?'

'I'm not sure,' Etienne answered. 'I've been scouring all the CCTV I could access trying to track the path of those three missing kids, and it's not as easy as it sounds. Thousands of cameras and only the descriptions Ben gave me to go off…'

Hugo smiled because he knew Etienne, and if anyone could work technological miracles, it was him.

Etienne continued. 'As you know, that creep Alexander Esnault left one side of the park and he was alone. I traced his journey back to his apartment and he got out of the car alone and his driver left, parked the car and went to a café. I didn't find any sign he caught up with the kids at all.'

'That's good news at least,' Hugo said, 'and Captain Brunhild had some officers search the park and there were no bodies so we have to believe the three kids made it out alive.'

'Oh, they certainly did,' Etienne replied, 'forty minutes after Alexander Esnault came out of the park they did too, out of the same exit.'

Hugo frowned. 'Forty minutes later? Then where were they?'

'Dunno, perhaps they found somewhere to hide,' Etienne said, 'after all, they chose the meeting point so they probably scoped it out in advance and already had found somewhere to hide in case they needed to.'

'And you're sure it was them?'

'Well, going by Ben's description, oui. I believe it was them, or else there were three very similar looking youths exiting the park looking as if they were terrified.'

Hugo nodded. 'And where did they go?'

'There's a Metro station about a block away, they made their way there.'

'Damn,' Hugo cried in exasperation, knowing once they had gone into the Metro system it would be virtually impossible to figure out where they were heading or when they exited.

Etienne said nothing for a moment.

'Etienne?' Hugo asked, daring not to hope for too much.

'I'm not being dramatic,' Etienne said, 'but it took me all night, analysing footage from each station on the line, either way, plus connections to different lines, but forty minutes ago I found them.'

'Oh, Etienne, I'm so grateful,' Hugo said, 'and I realise it's not your job to find these kids, but...'

'It is my job,' Etienne replied, 'just cos they're not in Montgenoux doesn't mean I shouldn't help find them if I can. Anyway, I used face-scanning technology so I could scan all the station exits. The three of them left the Metro and took the Paris RER line B where an hour later they alighted the train at a place called Sceaux.'

'Sceaux?' Hugo asked. The name rang a vague bell with him, but he could not remember why.

'Yeah, Sceaux. It's about eight miles away from central Paris, just before the commune of Antony. It's a small coastal town.'

'Ah, oui,' Hugo added, 'I've been there once. My Grand-Mère said it was the sort of place where old, dull people went to die. I actually thought it was rather nice. And they're still there?'

'I'm not sure,' Etienne replied. 'I've only just found them, and they headed in the direction of the beach but I couldn't find them after that because there aren't many cameras.'

Hugo glanced at his watch. 'And when did you last see them?'

'Yesterday afternoon. I'm monitoring the station to see if they go back, but not so far.'

Hugo pursed his lips. 'So, less than twenty-four hours.' He shook his head. 'The chances are they've moved on somewhere.'

'Or they're lying low,' Etienne reasoned. 'I'm not blowing my own trumpet necessarily but whoever is after these kids isn't likely to have access to my kind of software. So, these kids probably, *hopefully*, think they're safe to lie low for a while, that's what I'd do if I was running.'

Neither of them spoke for a minute. 'They don't trust the police,' Hugo said finally, 'they don't trust anybody.'

'But they can trust you,' Etienne reasoned, 'you just have to make them believe it. And they will. Just talk to them. Tell them you want to help and they'll believe you, trust me, they'll see your goodness. Either way, you have to try.'

Hugo snorted. 'I'm not sure about that, but you are right, I have to try. Merci again, Etienne. I don't know what we'd do without you.'

'No worries, Hugo. Let me know if I can do anything else, salut.'

Hugo placed his cell phone back in his pocket.

'Etienne found them?' Ben asked anxiously.

Hugo nodded. 'I believe so, at least where they were yesterday. How about coming with me on a trip to see if we can catch up with them?'

Ben gave him a doubtful look. 'I think I'm the last person they'd want to see.'

Hugo touched his arm. 'What happened wasn't your fault and they'll see that. Besides, I need you. I need your help.' He smiled. 'I don't know if you're aware of this about me, but interacting with three teenagers isn't something which comes naturally to me, and we need these kids to be safe. But just as important, I have a feeling they hold the key to this whole mess, and we need them if we will ever stand a chance of understanding what happened to their friends.'

Ben smiled. 'Then let's go get them.'

Coco lifted her bag, the contents spilling onto the shiny tiled floor of the morgue. Cedric moved to help and then stopped, his eyes widening when he saw the displaced items. 'You're on your own,' he muttered, moving back across the room and flopping onto a chair.

Hugo appeared next to her and began assembling the items, gingerly placing them back into the bag.

'Désolé,' Coco said. She pursed her lips, studying Hugo's face. 'I get why you want to go after those kids, but...'

Hugo raised his hand. 'I know it could be dangerous, and I know they could follow us. I'm aware of all of those things, but doing nothing is...' he paused, 'not really an option. And honestly, as good as Etienne is, there is every chance someone else has been doing the exact same thing and is also on their way to Sceaux. Ben and I are booked on the next train, and we'll be careful. I've done this sort of thing before, and I know what I'm doing.'

Coco gave him a doubtful look. 'It's not you I'm worried about. I still think I should come with you, or at the very least have the local police do a search.'

Hugo shook his head determinedly. 'Non, absolutely not. If they're watching, which I'm sure they will be, it might scare them off and could even expose them to more danger. They've reached out to Ben already, and I have to believe they'll know he didn't deliberately lead Alexander Esnault to them. They are the key to this whole affair, I'm sure of it.'

'When is your train?' Coco asked

Hugo glanced at his watch. 'In an hour.'

She nodded. 'Merci for asking me if it was okay for you to go. I know you didn't need to so I appreciate it,' she said with a smile.

Dr. Bernstein walked into the room, his hands full of folders, which he placed on his desk. 'Bon matin, amis,' he said, 'how are we all?' he asked, which was met with assorted grunts. He smiled. 'That good, eh? Well, I have some news of varying interest.'

Coco pulled out an electric cigarette and sucked on it, the red tip glowing. 'About bloody time, what is it?'

Sonny raised an eyebrow in her direction. 'Wrong side of the bed this morning, Coco, or the wrong bed perhaps?'

Coco snorted. 'Chance would be a fine thing, Sonny. What have you got? I'm ratty and hungover and I fucking hate electronic cigarettes. So, whatever you have to tell us, make it good, s'il te plaît.'

Sonny flashed her an amused look. 'D'accord, Mademoiselle Grumpy Pants. Well, the fingernail scrapings I took from Madame Ana Boucher came back and they did not belong to her husband.'

'They are in the DNA database?' Coco gasped.

'Non, they are not,' Sonny replied.

'Dammit, Sonny,' Coco grumbled, 'then what good are they to me?'

'Well, if you'd let me finish,' Sonny continued flopping into his chair, 'I'll let you know what the DNA does tell us.'

'Désolé,' Coco repeated, 'I didn't sleep well, and it seems to have reduced me to being a total bitch this morning.'

'Pourquoi?' Sonny asked, 'I mean, I'd hardly describe you as being Mademoiselle sweetness and light, but this, you're not usually so... sour.'

She sighed. 'I was thinking about Morty, and not in a good way. Something about this is bothering me, and I can't work out what it is, or even why it's bothering me.'

'Have you tried talking to him? I mean honestly, one on one away from the Commissariat?'

'Ha, although he knocked me up twice we don't have the sort of relationship, professional or otherwise where we can open up to each other. But I know him enough to know there's something wrong, something which stinks about this whole business.' She sighed before adding sweetly, 'anyway, enough of my problems. Please tell me what you found, Dr. Bernstein.'

He cleared his throat. 'As I said, the DNA wasn't in any of our existing databases, but it raised a flag because of similarities with another sample I recently submitted.' He paused as if for dramatic effect.

'Et?' Coco snapped in exasperation.

Sonny stood and handed her a piece of paper. 'While there is no recorded match for the DNA, it shows familial similarities with the DNA sample of Marc Gassna.'

'Familial?' Cedric asked.

'Oui,' Sonny replied. 'Most likely father, brother, perhaps an uncle. A male member of the same family line.'

Coco pursed her lips in contemplation. She turned to Cedric. 'Have you finished going through the CCTV footage around the estate where the Boucher's lived?'

Cedric nodded. 'Oui, what there is of it at least. Most of the cameras don't work and haven't for some time. The authorities don't bother fixing them because they know they'll just be vandalised and broken again the next day.'

Coco tutted. 'There are no working cameras?'

'Non, none that are any use, at least.'

'Putain,' she complained. She looked at Hugo. 'Then who the hell attacked Madame Boucher?'

Hugo narrowed his eyes. 'And how are they related to Marc Gassna? After all, we don't even know who Marc Gassna was before you found him and he became known as the lost boy. It can't be a coincidence that someone who shares his DNA is mixed up in this. The question is, did they know who each other was? And if so, why didn't Marc tell his adopted parents he knew who he was?'

Coco hit her head. 'Oh, this is all too much and way too confusing for a simple Parisian policewoman. 'Anything else, Sonny?'

He nodded. 'Yeah, just confirmation that the blood in the Boucher home belonged to Randolph Boucher and there was no evidence of anyone else in the home.'

'Figures,' Coco grumbled. She smiled at Hugo. 'Well, let's hope you have more luck in Sceaux. Find those kids and bring them back safely, d'accord?'

Hugo nodded. 'I'll try.'

She nodded. 'And in the meantime, I'm going to try to understand what the hell the Catholic Church has to do with all of this. And more importantly, why it appears everyone is doing everything they can to protect Monseigneur Augustine Demaral.'

'Good luck with that,' Hugo said, not entirely convinced she would get very far.

Coco sat down and crossed her legs, seemingly deciding it was not comfortable and set them apart, pulling her skin up after it had become caught in the seat. Dr. Victor Caron watched her from the other side of the desk, the stretch of amusement shadowing across his face. 'Are you sure I can't get either of you anything?' he asked, the drawl of an authoritative man used to hearing his own voice. 'A stool, perhaps?'

Coco smirked at him. 'The chair's rather hard, that's all. I'll get right to the point, Dr. Caron. What can you tell me about Monseigneur Augustine Demaral?'

Caron's jaw flexed. 'And what would you like to know, exactly, Captain Brunhild? And before I answer, perhaps you could tell me what on earth it has to do with your investigation.'

Coco leaned forward in her chair and Cedric stepped around the table so he was behind Dr. Caron.

'Why didn't you tell me you already knew Marc Gassna?' Coco asked quickly without taking a breath.

Dr. Caron spluttered, his eyes widening with obvious surprise at her change of tack. 'What are you talking about, Captain? I informed you of all of my involvement with the poor young man.'

'Apart from one obvious, glaring omission,' Cedric interrupted.

Caron looked over his shoulder, his jaw flexing again. 'What are you talking about?' he repeated, a tremor clear in his tone.

Coco clapped her hands together. 'When you first met him, he was not called Marc Gassna, rather he was known as the rather dramatic and unimaginative *L'enfant perdu.*'

Before he could stop himself, Caron gasped. Coco studied his face, realising she could not tell if he was generally shocked at the fact or surprised that she knew. Whatever his faults, Dr. Victor Caron had obviously not spent much of his life honing his poker face.

'What are you talking about?' he gasped.

'Marc Gassna was the young child formally known as *L'enfant perdu,*' she repeated, 'but you already knew that, didn't you, Dr. Caron?'

'I have absolutely no idea what you are talking about,' he replied, his fingers distractedly wrapping around a stapler on his desk.

'Then you maintain you didn't know?' Coco asked.

'Oui, bien sûr,' he answered. 'I had no idea, Marc was… Marc was that poor, awful child.'

Coco let the silence fall. She wanted him to speak. She wanted to hear his words because she realised it might be the only way she would see the true Victor Caron.

Caron dropped the stapler and shook his head. 'There was a team of us assigned to him, each with varying specialities because the truth was no one knew what had happened to him, or how to even begin to treat him. Once the drugs were out of his system…'

'The drugs?' Coco snapped. 'He was on drugs?'

Caron nodded. 'Oui. When the toxicology results came back, it was clear he had been given a drug called Clozapine, and for some time. Clozapine is a drug usually prescribed for schizophrenia.'

'He was schizophrenic?' Coco asked.

'Unlikely, there was no indication of that when we examined him,' Caron replied, 'rather the team concluded it was most likely administered to him because it has a natural side-effect of making the taker more docile and pliable.'

'Jesus Christ,' Cedric groaned, 'why would any decent person need to give a kid drugs to make him pliable?'

'There's only one reason I can think of,' Coco answered. She looked squarely at the doctor. 'My reports made no mention of drugs or any kind of abuse, are you telling me, Marc, or whatever his real name was, was abused?'

Caron nodded again. 'Oh, almost certainly, in one way or another. He never spoke of it and any attempt at examination was met with violent outbursts. As I said, it was evident Clozapine had been administered to him for some time. It took a while for it to leave his system and was a very difficult and harrowing process for him and for the team in charge of looking after him. I wasn't always a part of that team, but enough to see how difficult it was for all concerned.'

'Tell me, Dr. Caron,' Coco intoned, 'were you also acquainted with a man called Corentin Gassna?'

Caron's eyes widened again in surprise. 'Oui, bien sûr. Corentin was a great patron of the hospital, a great man who spent much of his time, and even more of his money, in the pursuit of helping the unfortunate.' He stopped. 'It never occurred to me. I mean, I never even put two and two together, but why would I? Gassna is hardly an unusual name and there was no reason for me to…' he left the sentence unfinished.

'What was Corentin Gassna's role at the hospital?'

He shrugged. 'Well, he didn't have a specific role. He was on the board of trustees, and while he had no formal training, he was a man unafraid of getting his hands dirty.'

Coco reached for her notepad and scribbled, *not afraid to get his hands dirty,* mouthing the words as she did so. 'And what does that mean, exactly?' she asked.

'Not what you are thinking, Captain Brunhild,' he retorted, 'I'm sure of that.'

Coco laughed. 'I'm thinking nothing, doctor, just trying to understand, that's all. I'm just a simple policewoman, trying to make sense of something which is, frankly, beyond me. 'So, bear with me. Are you telling us you had no idea poor *L'enfant perdu* ended up being adopted by your good friend Corentin Gassna?'

'I'd hardly call him my good friend,' Victor sniffed. 'Et non, I did not know. As far as I was aware, there was no interaction between the two of them, or how they ended up together, although,' he paused, sucking his breath, 'there are far worse fates which could have befallen the poor child than being taken in by a man such as Corentin Gassna.'

'Was it usual this sort of thing, people who wouldn't normally be considered for adopting to be given children just because they were,' Coco said, 'in the right place at the right time?'

'I can't answer that,' Caron said after a moment, 'because I had no idea about the adoption, but I repeat, the child really could not have asked for a better sponsor than Corentin Gassna.'

'And you never pieced it together?' Cedric asked, 'not even when you met the kid?'

'Non,' Caron wailed, 'as I said, there was no reason for me to. As I also said, Gassna is a common enough name. I know of at least two others who bear no relationship to Corentin.'

Coco nodded. 'You speak of him as if he was a friend.'

Caron's eyes widened with suspicion. 'Well, I wouldn't call him an enemy, if that clarifies it for you, Captain.'

She nodded again. 'And you see him occasionally?'

'Oui,' he replied, 'we are on several of the same committees, including the hospital were *L'enfant perdu* was based.'

'And socially? You see him socially?' Coco asked.

'Occasionally,' Caron retorted, 'we have dinner or attend the same function, despite appearances, Paris is very small where it matters.'

Coco tilted her head. 'See, that's what I thought, which is why it strikes me as odd that in all that time he never mentioned to you even in passing even that he and his wife had adopted *L'enfant perdu*, the child you knew and had been part of the team who helped.' She shrugged. 'It's odd to me, that's all.'

'I don't know what to tell you, Captain Brunhild,' he sniffed, 'but I suppose you might say we don't have the sort of relationship which stretches to idle, personal chitchat.'

Coco met his gaze defiantly, making sure he understood exactly what she was thinking. *I'm not buying that for a second, try again.*

'And you're telling us it never came up when you were at the hospital?' Cedric interjected.

'That's exactly what I'm telling you,' Caron shot back.

Cedric sighed. 'You know what I hate more than liars, Dr. Caron?'

He shook his head. 'Non, quoi?'

'Liars who think the police are fucking stupid,' Cedric hissed, stabbing his finger towards the doctor. 'Don't you think we've checked? Don't you think we know that the adoption was, let's say, unorthodox to be kind, but that there were certain considerations given to who Corentin Gassna was, rather than his suitability to adopt a deeply troubled child?'

Dr. Caron did not respond, instead closing his eyes and massaging his temples with thin, long fingers.

Coco shot the Lieutenant an impressed look. On the journey to Caron Auberge de Jeunesse that morning they had discussed trying to get a hold of the adoption records, but realising it was likely to be met with the same resistance as they were finding in every other part of the investigation. She was impressed with Cedric and slightly taken aback he found it so easy to lie so believably. Until that moment, she had not imagined him to be that sort of man. She tapped her fingers on the side of the desk. 'Dr. Caron, are you all right?'

He opened his eyes. 'You have to understand,' he began slowly, 'nothing was done illegally.'

Coco nodded. 'Just a few corners cut, huh? Listen, I get it, Monsieur and Madame Gassna were a little long in the tooth to legitimately adopt a kid, but when you get a kid who is a bit damaged, a bit broken, then people don't tend to look too closely if someone rich wants to take on the responsibility, to save the Republic a bundle. Makes perfect sense if you ask me, a win-win for everybody.'

'Exactement!' Caron cried. 'The Gassna's had resources the hospital could only dream of, we knew they would look after the child. He would be given the best treatment by the best doctors from all around the world.

In fact, as far as I knew Corentin was taking the child to a special hospital in Switzerland which had tremendous success in helping deeply traumatised children. That child had a little more hope than spending the rest of his life in institutions. The Gassna's wanted to give him the best chance to live a happy and fulfilling life.' He paused. 'I still want you to understand that I did not understand, did not connect, the young man I saw here in my hostel with the child Corentin and Fleur adopted all those years ago.'

Coco pursed her lips. 'Are you saying he never came up in conversation over the years?'

'Barely,' Caron replied, 'at first we used to discuss it, and it seemed Corentin arranged for the child to be treated in Switzerland, but after time, Corentin seemed, well, I suppose you could say, reluctant to discuss the issue further. We did not have the kind of friendship where I felt able to press him, so I suppose I just let it go. It was, after all, none of my business.'

'And the adoption, how did it happen?' Coco asked.

Caron met her eyes and then looked away. 'It was perfectly legal,' he answered in a whisper.

'But wouldn't stand up to too much scrutiny I'm guessing, right?' Coco replied.

Caron shrugged. 'We all provided evidence and gave our support because we genuinely believed the child would be best off with them. We all knew if he went into the adoption and fostering system the chances are he would never get the care or love he deserved, if he would be taken at all. It was an easy decision, and the legislation which discriminated against the Gassnas is archaic. We all knew it but were powerless to do anything about it. In fact, I don't believe the adoption would have even taken place were it not for the intervention of Monseigneur Demaral.'

Coco and Cedric exchanged surprised looks. 'What does the priest have to do with it?' Coco asked.

Caron gave her a hateful eye. 'The *priest*, as you so eloquently put it, was actively involved in not only the care of *L'enfant perdu* but also all the children in the special wing of the hospital. He guided them, giving them the spiritual guidance they might need, but also he cared for them in the true sense of the word father. He took a special interest in the child, and when the Gassnas' came forward, he made it his mission to help unite them as a family.'

'And how did he do that?' Coco asked.

'You must ask him if you want details, Captain Brunhild, because I cannot speak on his behalf.'

'I would if I could get the chance,' Coco sniffed. 'But we're having trouble locating him. All the Church will tell us is he is out of the country, but won't tell us when he's likely to return or when we can speak to him.'

Caron shrugged his shoulders. 'The Monseigneur has been in ill health for several years. The last time I spoke with him he mentioned he was planning on taking a sabbatical.'

'And when was that?' Coco interrupted. 'When

exactly did you see him last?'

He shrugged again. 'A while ago, I couldn't say, exactly.'

Coco made a note. 'And the Monseigneur was instrumental in the adoption?'

Caron's brow furrowed. 'Not really. He merely intervened and brought the two parties together as was his desire. As I said earlier, there was nothing untoward about any of it. They may have been considered too old by the traditional barometer used by social services, but in this case, in the interests of the child, exceptions were made and rightly so.'

'So how do you figure Marc Gassna ended up in one of your beds if his life was all set to be so peachy keen?' Cedric asked.

Caron sighed. 'Sadly, with the best will in the world, those who are broken cannot always be fixed. I am sure they did their best, just as many of the parents whose offspring end up in places such as this. Remember, they inherited Marc when he was no longer a child, certainly not one whose life had been idyllic. I am sure they did their best. Speaking of which, I must pay my respects to Corentin and Fleur. They must be devastated by the loss.'

'Odd isn't it, don't you think?' Coco began, 'that when they ended up with a missing child they didn't look to you, their old friend, a man who runs his own youth hostel, to help them.'

Caron narrowed his eyes. 'Was there a question

there, Captain? All I can say is, why would they? They are a very private couple and I expect a little embarrassed if their personal lives were difficult and as I told you, we do not have the kind of friendship which lends itself to intimate sharing.' He glanced at the wall clock. 'Now, if that is all, I have rather a full day ahead of me. I'm sorry I could not be more help.'

Coco rose to her feet, extending her hand. 'On the contrary, Dr. Caron, you've been more helpful than you could possibly know.'

Caron took her hand reluctantly, staring at her as if he did not understand what she could be possibly talking about. 'Bonne journée,' he muttered, 'please show yourselves out. But don't come back. I have nothing more to offer you and before you start railroading good, decent people, you might what to consider what implications that might have. Good people will still do whatever they need to do to protect themselves, Captain. You'd be wise to remember that.'

She stopped dead in her tracks. 'What on earth do you mean?' She exhaled, her breathing suddenly fast, coursing with irritation. 'Because it sounds suspiciously like a threat to me, Dr. Caron. I may be many things, but I can assure you, I'm not a woman to be trifled with.'

Victor Caron's jaw jutted forward defiantly. 'Then whatever happens to you next is your affair. You can either take my advice, or not, it makes no difference to me, but it should matter to you if you value what you hold dear.' He sighed. 'Au revoir, Captain. I wish you well, I truly do, but I cannot help you.'

Hugo stepped out of Sceaux Station, shielding his eyes from the late morning sun. He inhaled fresh salty air into his lungs and he felt his body relax, feeling as he always did whenever he was near water, more peaceful than he did at any other time.

Ben appeared behind him, sucking greedily on a cigarette. He coughed. 'Damn, I don't think I've smoked so much in a long time as I have in the last few days. My lungs are getting really annoyed with me.' He handed the cigarette to Hugo, who took it gratefully. He shared no such guilt.

Hugo turned his head, Sceaux was just as he remembered it, and he was hit with a pang of nostalgia. He shook it away. 'I'm not even sure what we're doing here, or whether we even should be.'

'We're here to save three young kids,' Ben replied. 'Whether or not they want us too.'

Hugo gave him a doubtful look. 'Are we? I mean, what do we even know about them? And how do we know they're in danger?' He sighed. 'We don't even know how they're involved in any of this. And it's not lost on me as policeman they could be running because they're guilty of something. Either way, they're dangerous.'

Ben shook his head forcefully. 'Non, you didn't see them, I did. I looked into their eyes and I didn't see guilt, but I saw a lot of fear, terror even. Those kids are running for their lives, I'm sure of it.'

Hugo touched his husband's arm. 'Then that's good enough for me,' he replied, 'but we have to be on guard, because I still believe we don't fully understand what's going on, or who is, for want of a better term, the bad guy.'

'Well, that top-knot skinny poser, Alexander Esnault for a start. He's a creep and a murderer, I'm sure of it. I've met a few in my life, so I can tell he's up to his neck in something rotten.'

Hugo did not answer because he had not processed his own thoughts concerning Esnault yet. There was something off about him, he was sure of it. But the disguise he wore was so practised, so nuanced, Hugo was having trouble seeing beneath it. Either way, he believed Ben to be right. Alexander Esnault was to be treated with extreme caution. Whatever he was up to, whatever he was involved in, Hugo had been a police officer long enough to be clear about one thing. Alexander Esnault was probably an extremely dangerous man.

'Are you Captain Duchamp?'

Hugo turned around. A young Gendarme smiled at him, extending his hand. 'Je m'appelle Marlier. Captain Brunhild telephoned from Paris and asked me to meet you and to provide you with any help you might need,' the Gendarme said.

Hugo looked around anxiously, painfully aware of the Gendarme's uniform and what it might mean for his mission.

Marlier looked self-consciously at his uniform. 'Is there something wrong with my uniform, Captain?' he asked anxiously.

Hugo shook his head quickly. 'Non, of course not. I'm just a little concerned your uniform may alarm those we have come looking for.'

'As I told Captain Brunhild,' Marlier continued, 'I fear your journey may have been wasted. The young people you seek are not in Sceaux.'

'Oh?' Hugo questioned. 'How can you be sure?'

'Because I know my town, and there have been no suspicious strangers lately.'

Hugo looked doubtfully at him. 'Well, I believe they would be going out of their way to look anything but suspicious.' He turned his head, the small parade was already filling up with tourists of various nationalities. 'Indeed, I would imagine they would do their very best to blend in.'

Marlier gave an unconvincing shrug. 'That's as maybe, but I would know if there were young criminals in my town, indeed, there has barely been any crime in the last twenty-four hours,' he added, pride clear in his voice.

'Barely?' Hugo interjected sharply.

Marlier smiled, picking a stray thread from his uniform. 'A pair of ice creams were stolen from old Michel on the promenade.' He smiled. 'Anyone who knows old Michel knows he's as blind as a bat and would give his ice creams away to anyone who asked. You don't need to steal from him. So, you see, I'm sure your Parisian criminals just stepped into our town and left as quickly in search of richer pickings.'

Hugo mused. 'Perhaps, you're right,' he said finally, 'but all the same, as we're here, I'd like to satisfy myself so I think we'll just take a walk to the promenade.'

Marlier's face clouded. 'Well, if you insist, follow me.'

Hugo shook his head. 'Non, merci for your help, but I don't want to take any more of your time and I'm sure you have far more important matters to attend to. Enchanté, and again, merci.' He turned away, indicating for Ben to head in the direction of the promenade.

'I love how you're still kind when you're having to be firm with people,' Ben said, slipping his hand into Hugo's. He jumped from the promenade and pulled off his plimsoles.

'I've always believed kindness and position don't have to be against each other,' Hugo replied, 'and it costs nothing to treat others as we would want to be treated ourselves.'

Ben smiled. 'And that's why I love you. That's why everyone loves you, dammit.' He outstretched his hand. 'Take off your shoes and come play with me.'

Hugo smiled. 'As tempting as that may be, I'm technically working.'

'Bah,' Ben complained. 'Oh, look,' he pointed to the

far end of the promenade, 'I'm guessing that's old Michel.'

Hugo flicked on his glasses, straining his neck to survey the beach. It was relatively deserted and old Michel was slumped against the railings, his lips curled into a dreamy, contented sleep. He wondered how old Michel would have even noticed any thefts. 'I'm beginning to suspect we're on a wild goose chase,' Hugo grumbled.

Ben laughed, dragging Hugo onto the sand. 'Oh, you've obviously never hidden out in your life, hiding from the oldies, or just wanting to sneak off somewhere for a little bit of,' he coughed, '*privacy*,' he sniggered, 'places like this were made for such things.'

Hugo suppressed a sigh in the way he always did when reminded of what he had missed growing up. The life and adventures of misspent youth would always be something he would never truly understand. It both saddened him and relieved him. 'You think they could be here?' He pulled his body tall, straining his eyes from left to right.

'I do,' Ben replied, 'if they are running they've got to realise they are running out of options. They need money but they also need to lie low and that's probably more important right now.'

'Then what about the ice cream, if it even was them?'

Ben smiled. 'Those two boys are in love and love trumps everything else, even blind fear. If it was us, I'd swipe an ice-cream for us to share.'

Despite himself, Hugo smiled too. 'I shouldn't approve of that, but I do.' He tipped his head towards the dock which ran the length of the beach, spiralling off into deeper waters. 'And if you're going to hide, it may be a good place because not many people will venture so far out unless they know the tides.'

Ben raised an eyebrow. 'Spent much time hiding under boardwalks, have we Captain?' he asked with a bite.

Hugo flashed him an amused smile. 'You'd be surprised,' he answered stepping across the sand, Ben's bemused gaze following him, 'everyone has always assumed I'm an open book and there was nothing else to see or understand about me, but I never said it was true. Just because I seem a little reserved, doesn't mean I always am, you know.'

Ben frowned, struggling to keep up with his long-legged husband striding across the uneven beach. 'What do you mean by that? Hugo? Hugo?' he called out, his voice wavering. Hugo did not look back, instead indicating Ben should follow him. 'I think I see something under the boardwalk,' he said, lowering his voice and slowing his pace. He gestured for Ben to follow him, waving his hand to show they should approach cautiously. Hugo drew his breath as a seagull swooped in front of him, pecking angrily at a discarded wrapper. He stopped, head cocked on high alert, checking to ensure they were the only ones alerted by the gull's eager picking. They stood next to each other, their breaths in tandem as they listened. After a minute, satisfied the only sounds were the water lapping against the shore and the seagulls searching for food, Hugo edged forward, Ben a step behind. Hugo lowered his head, straining his eyes to see under the aged wooden boards which ran over the beach. He could not be sure, but he thought for a moment he saw an unusual shape towards the back. He focused his eyes on it, still not moving, barely breathing, and he waited.

After a minute had passed, he saw what he needed. The shape moved. 'Let's go,' he ushered to Ben, moving as quickly as he could. He stopped at the edge, dropping to his knees. He pulled out his I.D card and his cell phone, using it to illuminate his badge. 'My name is Captain Hugo Duchamp of Montgenoux Police Nationale,' he said in the most even, natural but strong tone he could muster. Silence. He repeated his words, adding, 'I mean you no harm.' There was a sound of a sarcastic snort. Barely audible but he caught it. 'I know you have no reason to believe me or to trust me, but I'm going to ask you to. I am here with my husband because we want to help you, and we want you to know that whatever has happened, whatever has led you to this, we are both committed to ensuring you are protected.'

'Ben?'

Ben moved past Hugo. 'Jérémie, is that you?' he called into the shadowy darkness thrown onto the sand by the boardwalk. He shielded his eyes from the sun flickering through the wooden slats.

'How did you fucking find us?' a voice hissed.

Hugo assumed the antagonistic voice belonged to Delphine Marchand. 'Don't worry,' he said, taking a cautious step forward. 'We came alone and we have every reason to believe no one else has discovered where you are.'

'Idiot!' Delphine screamed, 'you lead him right to us last time and you've probably done the exact same thing again.'

Hugo watched as her slight figure climbed through the sand into the daylight, gesturing angrily behind her. 'Come on you two idiots,' she snapped, 'I told you we shouldn't have hung around in this shit-hole for so long.'

Axel Soudre rolled across the sand, jumping to his feet. 'And I told you, I don't want to keep running. WE don't want to keep running because the damn truth is, we've got nowhere to run,' he added desperately.

Delphine Marchand's mouth opened, but only a dull mumble escaped her throat. The second male youth joined them and slipped his hand into the other and it touched Hugo in a way which surprised him, a stab reminding him they needed help. They needed protection from whatever it was they might have done and whatever it was they might have gotten mixed up in. He appraised the three of them standing on the shore and his instinct told him they needed help, and most certainly they needed protection. He took another step forward, causing Delphine to adopt a combative stance.

'Don't take another step nearer or I'm warning you, I'll scream my fucking lungs out.'

Hugo nodded. 'And then what? The police come?' he asked in as gentle a tone as he could. 'I AM the police, and I'm already here to help you.'

'The police are all fucking liars,' she retorted.

'Some of them, perhaps,' Hugo conceded. He paused, pulling on his bottom lip. 'And I've been known to lie occasionally.'

Delphine took a step forward, dark, angry eyes scanning Hugo's face. She said nothing.

Hugo continued. 'Sometimes it is necessary to lie, or rather, to not tell someone some information which might affect them, or alert them to an investigation.'

'And what is this?' Delphine asked.

'I don't know,' Hugo answered, 'all I can tell you is that you reached out to my husband and I'm very grateful for it because he is the most trustworthy and honourable person I know. What happened in the park was not his fault, Alexander Esnault, a man he has never met, followed him and he had no reason to know where he was going. I, however, have met Alexander Esnault, and that is exactly why I am here. You need help and I am here to help.'

'By trusting the so-called authorities?' Delphine snorted. 'How do you think we got into this mess in the first place?'

Hugo shook his head. 'Not the authorities. Me.

Trust me. Trust Ben.'

Axel took a tentative step towards him. 'And what do you think you can do to protect us? Take us to a police station? Lock us in a cell?' he spat. 'Are you so naïve to think they can't get to us in a police station?'

Hugo shook his head again. 'I'm not naïve, and I know there are bad people in all walks of life, but there are those I trust, those I would trust with my own life even, and the life of my husband, the only valuable thing in my life I care about,' he answered, his mind racing. 'Regarde, we need to get the three of you somewhere safe, get you out of the open and I'm not suggesting placing you in custody but somewhere you will be safe. I will contact my colleague, mon ami, a man I trust implicitly. His name is Etienne Martine and I'm sure he will find us a safe house which is not connected to the police, or to anyone you might know. Rather a place only a handful of people we can trust will know about because the fewer people who know of your whereabouts the better, non? At least until we get to the bottom of this whole affair.'

'And what do you want in return, exactly?' Jérémie interrupted. 'A blow job? Is that your price?' He narrowed his eyes angrily. 'Because there is *always* a price.'

Hugo exhaled. 'Of course not, and there is no price. But I want to help. If you want justice for your friends, then you will have to take a leap of faith and trust me and tell me what happened to Marc and Jack, because if you don't, you have to know, whoever is responsible will walk away from their crimes. I want to help, but I have to understand what this is all about. I don't expect you to trust me just because I tell you to, trust me because I show you I can be trusted.'

Hugo moved across the sand slowly. He knew he had to be cautious and had only one chance to gain their trust. He did not want to risk them running again because he knew it would not only endanger them further, it could also mean he would never understand what had happened to them and their friends. 'What are your other options?' he said gently, 'because you have to know running is not your best option.'

Ben appeared by Hugo's side. 'Trust Hugo, s'il vous plaît.'

A silence descended, tempered only by the gentle lapping of the sea against the shore. Axel Soudre took off his shoes and stepped into the water, pushing it away with his foot. He turned his head and smiled at Jérémie who shrugged, pulled off his shoes and joined his lover in the water.

Delphine Marchand tutted with great disdain. 'What the fuck do you two think you're going to do? Swim to safety like two big camp gay unicorns?'

Jérémie turned his head towards her, irritation quickly softening. 'Delph. You know they're right. We have no options, we have no choices...'

'We...'

He raised his hand to stop her, placing his arm

around Axel's shoulders. 'I'm not prepared to run forever, and I'm not,' he stopped, kissing the top of Axel's head, 'prepared to lose anyone else.' He shrugged. 'So this stops, one way or another.'

Delphine stared helplessly at Hugo and Ben. 'But they could be part of it,' she whispered.

Jérémie gestured with his hands. 'Then we're screwed, but we're screwed either way, non? We have to start taking chances, I don't want to end up like my brother.'

Hugo took another step forward. 'Your brother?' he asked.

Jérémie nodded. 'Marc Gassna was my brother,' he answered in a whisper which sounded hoarse and desperate as if he was pulling the words from the pit of his stomach.

Delphine sighed, dropping to the ground. She picked up a pebble and tossed it into the sea and they all watched as it bounced perfectly across the glistening water as if she had done it a hundred times before. She gestured with her head. 'If you're going to stay, you'd better sit down,' she said to Hugo and Ben. 'Jérémie is a drama queen, so he's going to want to tell you his story in his own way, in his own words. I wouldn't normally tolerate it because,' she stopped and gave her friend a sad smile, 'he has a tendency to go on and on as if he's auditioning for Skam France or something, but his story is real. It isn't an audition. I wish it fucking was, because it's the truth - the real, shit god-awful punch you in the guts kinda truth. The truth none of you oldies wants to admit is real, or admit happens under your noses. So sit down and listen and when we're done, I'll know how truthful you are and whether we can trust you. Think you can do that?'

Hugo met her gaze, as difficult as he found it and pushed his glasses into his hair. He nodded. 'There are two things I do very well,' he replied. 'I can listen and I can be trusted to do the right thing. Please talk to us, Jérémie and I promise you I will do whatever I can to protect you and whatever I can to right whatever wrongs have come your way.' Jérémie nodded and gave him a grateful smile as if the weight of the world had been lifted from his shoulders.

My name wasn't always Jérémie Berger, but it's as good a name as any. My mother called me Jérémie because she said the dimple on my cheeks reminded her of a boy she went to kindergarten with. The Berger part came later, the first time I turned a trick and got paid for it. As the man did up his flies and threw me a ten euro bill, I asked him what his name was. He shrugged, looking at me doubtfully and answered "Berger" after a while when he'd obviously considered I wasn't in any sort of position to go to the flics. Hell, it probably wasn't even his real name, but I figured it was as good a name as any and decided to use it. That's what we all did. You might say it became a rite of passage because no one else was interested in naming us.

Except Maman. Maman named us Tom & Jerry from a cartoon she used to watch on the tiny black and white portable TV. She swore it was the only thing which would calm us, keep us quiet, because we learnt very early, VERY early being quiet was essential. My first memory was of the room, the room with no windows and the way the damp ran down the wall. I used to trace through it with my fingers and draw pictures and my mother and brother would try to guess what they were. Either I wasn't very good, or they were dumb because they never guessed. It might not seem like a lot, but it was to us. Sometimes when they forget to bring our food and water, we'd lick the dew from the wall. Maman scolded us, but we could tell she didn't mean it. We knew it wasn't good for us, but we wanted to survive. We wanted to make it through. We didn't know what we expected outside to be like. All we knew was it would be different and different was all we had to look forward to.

For the longest time I guess I thought it was normal, the three of us together in the room. The tiny room with the one bed, the stove, the rickety table and the sink we used for washing. It was normal for me to go to the bathroom in the rusty iron bucket. It was normal for me to imagine there was no real world. We knew it wasn't true because there was a door. A door covered in locks and chains which would open every few days, once a week if we were lucky. Whatever we were doing, talking in whispers we'd gotten used to, or straining our ears to listen to the low volume of the TV, we'd stop and Maman would shoot us the look. Go to the corner and don't move and for Dieu's sake, don't speak. We'd huddle and watch her tread to the other door as if her feet were made of concrete and she'd push open the door and throw herself on the rotten single mattress which took up all the room. A man would come in, sometimes the same one, often not, and he'd go in the room and close the door. To our young ears the grunts which followed sounded funny, but we knew they weren't. We just knew. It always seemed like a long time, but I don't suppose it was and he'd be gone and to my shame, all I kept thinking was, what would be in the box? Because the man always left a box. A box of food, sometimes candy, sometimes chocolate. One time there was a teddy bear. My brother loved that and carried it with him always, even when we left. To the day he died, he carried it in his backpack.

I don't remember who came first, truly I don't, but I always supposed it was me. I was always bigger, stronger and my first memories of him are being small and talking with a lisp. And as far as I could remember, I would do anything to protect him just like our mother did for me. I never doubted she would give her life for me, but it was still a shock when she did.

I knew instantly there was something different about this one man. I saw his eyes; they were wide like the cat when it saw the canary. His tongue slid across his lips, dribbles of saliva falling onto his chin as he watched me and my brother, like we were a prize or something. Maman knew it too, and she screamed. 'Non! You promised as long as I did what you wanted you'd leave them alone!' *He shrugged, as if her words meant nothing, but his intention was clear.* You don't decide shit. *He came to us and looked us up and down. He told us to stand, to turn, to touch our toes. We looked to Maman, helpless, waiting for her to tell us what to do. She just smiled and twirled her finger which we knew meant to turn around and not to look. So, we did and she ran, screaming at the top of her lungs, seconds later he screamed too, but it was like from the pit of his stomach, a roar almost and it scared me, but it scared my brother more. He grabbed my hand and squeezed it so tightly I could feel the blood tricking between my fingers but I didn't flinch, I didn't dare. And then my mother screamed and there was a thud, a heavy thud as if something dropped from a height. I stole a look and realised it was her - slumped against the floor, her head bleeding, her eyes closed. The man stepped over her and snatched my brother's hand. 'Come with me,' he said and before I knew what I was doing, I stepped in front of my brother and said, 'take me, I won't struggle, he will,' The man looked at me in a way I only came to understand later, appraising me, deciding if I was worth their time, worth what they wanted to do. It took him but a few seconds and then he grabbed my arm and took me to the room. I didn't look at my brother, I couldn't. All I could look at were the stains on the filthy mattress* and kept thinking over and over, 'they belong to Maman,' I didn't know what they were, although some of them looked like the colour of the rust which gathered on the walls in our room. The man closed the door, and I knew whatever happened next would change me forever. I would be like my mother. I would make strange noises behind this closed door but I would say nothing about them. I would only weep when I thought no-one was watching. I was right and I will not speak of what he did to me, nor the men who came afterwards, obviously enticed by whatever it was he said about me. I won't speak of it, other than to say it taught me a valuable lesson. In that moment you have the man in your spell, no matter what he is like before or after, and I learnt it quickly because I knew it would be important. It would be my only chance to exert control, or to have any control. I would not be like my mother. I would not let them win.

This went on for a long time. I don't know how long exactly because as I've said, we had no real concept of time, or life, in our little room. What I do remember very clearly is that my relationship with my mother changed for the worse. At first it was suitable, the way she would stare at me as if she did not, could not understand me. A painting she didn't understand, but soon it became clear what she was thinking. She was disgusted with me, disgusted that whatever went on behind the closed door, I emerged from it with my head held high, stronger each time and more fearless. It angered me she would rather it broke me like it did her, but I would not be the victim. My strength was all I had. As I grew some of the men came less frequently, and I could tell they were looking at me differently. The spark of arousal was disappearing from their eyes. I couldn't understand why until one of them told me, 'you're getting old, boy, *you'll be growing hair soon.' Growing hair. A sign of growing I didn't understand, but it didn't take me long to work out what the implications were. It meant they would start to look elsewhere, and when I watched Maman washing my brother, I couldn't help but notice he wasn't growing any hair yet. I knew what was coming, and I was enraged because of what I had given up, what I scarified of myself in that room, all in the belief I was keeping my brother safe. I couldn't let it happen, not while I still had a breath left in my body. I looked at Maman and we both knew what we needed to do and it was the first time I felt connected to her in a long time because I believed she knew why I had been doing what I had been doing. The anger we both felt was strong and it made us more powerful than these weak men would be able to comprehend.*

'We're getting out of here,' she whispered to me, 'one way or another because they're not having your brother as well.' And I knew she meant it, but I didn't know how far she was prepared to go. If I had, I would have stopped her. It happened when the man with the scar came one night. He'd been gone for a while and I hated him for that, because when it was just him. Well, when it was just him, I was left alone because he was only interested in my mother. I knew him well and despite it all, he had always been very kind to us, bringing us chocolate and toys, and once a DVD player. I can't begin to tell you how much that changed our lives, opening up a new world for us. One day he brought us a movie, Les Chanson D'Amour, and it broke my heart and together we memorised every line, every song. It offered a glimpse into the world beyond the door, and I wanted it more than ever. I could taste freedom.

Maman had been edgy all day, sitting on the edge of the only chair, wringing the worn cardigan she always wore, pulling at her greasy hair. I realised later she was obviously preparing herself for what she was about to do and she had been waiting for the scarred man to come. I didn't know what was happening. They had been in the room for a while, thirty minutes or so, and my brother and I were watching the new DVD he brought us, some Disney rubbish, but it kept my brother happy and distracted which was fine by me. And then suddenly it happened, a scream so desperate it made my blood run cold and seconds later the door flung open and the scarred man ran out covered in blood. My brother screamed. I screamed when we saw he was carrying Maman, her head bouncing against his arms, her eyes wide and panicked. I couldn't tell where the blood had come from. 'Get the door open,' the man roared, 'and then get in the corner, I have to get your mother help.' Maman managed to lift her head towards me, and her eyes conveyed one single, urgent message. This is it. This is our chance. This is our ONLY chance.

The man threw me his keys, and I ran to the door, grabbing my brother's hand. I was shaking as I tried to open the door, terrified I dropped the keys, but I picked them up and tried again. The door was heavy, and it seemed to take me ages to open it, but finally it gave and it pulled open, covering me in cold, damp air. All I could make out was a steep, stone staircase. I looked over my shoulder, and mother was watching, her face white. 'Run and don't look back!' she commanded, her voice scared me though because it was weak, as if it hurt her to speak, but I did as I was told and dragged my brother into the darkness. The scarred man roared for us to stop but I didn't look back. I could not look back because I knew I would stop for

Maman. Instead I looked ahead, and then up towards the slither of light above because I knew it meant freedom. I only prayed there was nobody there, telling myself life couldn't be so cruel as to snatch our freedom away from us before we even had a chance to taste it.

I dragged my brother behind me even though he felt like a dead weight. He was whimpering, confused and scared, but I didn't have time to reassure him. He clung to his teddy bear as if his life depended on it. We ran up the steps two at a time, and it seemed to take forever. As we got to the top, my heart sank. There was another door. Was it locked? I desperately hoped not. We couldn't come so close for it to be snatched away from us. I threw myself at the door, pushing my shoulder against the handle. It groaned beneath me before giving and throwing us into a room. I scrambled to my feet, pulling my dazed brother to his feet, all the time turning my head, desperately hoping the room would be empty. It was. I allowed myself to breathe but only for a second, because as young as I was, I knew it was all we had. I could taste freedom, even though I didn't understand what it meant.

I pushed the thought of Maman bleeding from my mind, I couldn't think about it right then because I knew it would slow me down. I had to get my brother out and find help and then she would be safe, I'd make sure of it. But until then... until then we had to make it out.

I pushed against the door at the end of the room with all the strength I could muster, biting down on my lip to stop myself from screaming out. I pushed again, and to my amazement it gave, throwing us into a wide, cavernous room. It was empty, dull lights illuminating a walkway. It was lined with tall, boarded-up windows, slithers of night illuminating the empty room. It reminded me of a church but I shook the thought away. This was no church, no Dieu would allow what happened below the ground. 'Come on,' I growled to my brother, his feet dragging behind me. I could see a big door at the end of the room and it looked different than the others, bigger, like a door to a street. I dared not hope as we ran because I could hear footsteps coming towards us and by the sounds of it, the scarred man was running up the stone staircase two steps at a time which meant we had very little time.

I tried the door, and it didn't budge, but then I saw there was a key in the lock. I cried with joy and slid the lock open, pulling the door inwards and suddenly the night hit us. The world hit us. A world I didn't imagine; a world I wasn't prepared for. Remember, all I knew of the world by then was what I had seen on the television. My brother whimpered, hiding his body behind mine. 'I know you're scared,' I said in the most reassuring voice I could find, trying to relate to him I felt no fear, which of course was far from the truth. I could hear the footsteps and knew he would be on us soon. I looked into the dark street. There was no one around. No one to turn to, no one to ask for help. 'We have to disappear into the night,' I said, 'just like on TV.' My brother nodded, tightening his grip on my hand and we stepped into the night and let it cover us.

So that was exactly what happened. We disappeared. I didn't know what to do, who to trust. Remember, we had never left the room and our bodies and brains ached from moving into a world we had never seen. Our legs were sore from exercise never before taken and I knew we had to lie low, as much as I wanted to run and to keep running, I knew we couldn't. We had to find somewhere to hide. To rest, to find strength in our muscles we'd never really used. And we did. We ran through the side streets, dodging the homeless men, the prostitutes, anyone who got in our way. We'd been running for what seemed like ages, but was probably only five minutes and I was satisfied we'd lost the scarred man. And then I saw the abandoned building, and I don't know why, but I thought it would be safe. Maybe it was something to do with the junkies who called it home. I guessed we could hide out and nobody would pay too much attention because they had their own shit to deal with.

The building was huge and there were lots of places to hide and still be on high-alert. We holed up there overnight, barely moving until finally my brother drifted off into an uneasy sleep. I think at some point during the night I managed to sleep too, but it was fitful and anything but restful. But I was right about one thing, no one cared about us. We were just two more outcasts, although I knew it wouldn't last, we would attract attention in one way or another. I was also desperately worried about our mother.

Soon it was no longer night, and the morning sun felt warm on our faces even though we were watching it through dirty, cracked windows. We had never seen the sun, not really, and it fascinated us. I don't know how long we stared at it, but it was a long time and it wasn't until my brother began whimpering. His stomach growled telling me what he dared not to. I knew I had to do something. But what? What could I do? I was terrified. They would be still looking for us, but I knew I had to take a chance, and to do that meant having to leave my brother because after all they would be looking for the two of us. And the chances were if I was alone, I might be able to move quickly. I had to leave him if I was to find food, so that's what

I did. I had no idea what I would do, but I reassured my brother and made him promise he would stay exactly where he was and to be careful, and if anybody came for him he was to run, and to keep running and I promised him I would find him.

I was terrified, but I went outside, and it was as if I was seeing the world, the real world, for the first time. I walked around in a daze, not sure where I was going, or what I was doing. But I just kept walking, and praying, hoping someone would hear me, see me, help me and before long I found myself back near the place we had escaped from, hiding in the shadows of the afternoon sun. The door was closed, and it looked deserted. I don't know what I had been expecting, but there was nobody around, and certainly no sign of Maman or the scarred man. It was as if nothing had happened, as if what we were yesterday was a figment of my imagination. I honestly couldn't think of what to do, or where to go, or who to talk to, but I knew I had to find food for my brother, for me and I had no money, or really any idea what I would do with it.

Food had always been brought to us, and I only had a vague concept of money from television adverts. The only thing I knew was if I was kind to people, if I did what they wanted me to do, then they would feed me. So, I did what I had to do, and it was surprisingly easy. I'd already had a lot of experience after all and even though I didn't understand what it meant, I knew what making men happy entailed, but more importantly I had learned a valuable lesson. Men were weak when you were giving them what they wanted. As I spent my day, I realised there was little to be afraid of, I was, after all, part of the disenfranchised. My presence no more strange or unusual than anyone else. It was my first mistake. I became arrogant, high on the power of my body, striving towards getting as much money as quickly as possible. I don't know how much time had passed, but it was dark when I made my way back with money stuffed into my jeans pocket. I didn't know what I would do with it, but I had seen enough on television to know money was powerful and it might just protect us, and it would certainly mean my brother wouldn't cry himself to sleep with hunger.

I heard the police sirens, and I knew immediately there was a problem, a problem I didn't know how to solve. There were people running everywhere, lights flashing and then I saw my brother, clinging to a weird-looking woman, and being carried into an ambulance. I was hiding in the shadows, and it was all I could do to stop myself from running to him, screaming, pulling him away, but then it dawned on me. He was safe. Safer than I could ever make him, and if I showed my face, it would only complicate things, for him, for us. I had to find a way out, to make sense of the crazy life we had all been born into, and to do so I needed to find our mother and get her away.

I watched the ambulance take my brother away, and I turned back into the darkness, convincing myself all was well and that we would get our happy ending. The truth was different, more different than I could ever have imagined. For example, I didn't realise my youth, my newness had a shelf life and I would very soon become used, soiled goods, which affected the type of men who took me, what they wanted from me, and what they did to me. I did what I had to do, all the time watching and waiting. I checked hospitals, asking about Maman, but nobody would talk to me, especially without asking questions I couldn't, wouldn't answer. I watched the place we had come from, the building which looked like a church but there was no Dieu there, and as far as I could tell, there was no one else. Perhaps they had been scared off, and after a while, I began to believe I had imagined it all.

By then each day melted into the next. I was high, or drunk, or both - anything I could do to numb the pain, to lose the memories which hit me like a hammer against my skull. I got through the day by any means necessary, and the truth is I lost all track of time, of the past I'd escaped. I went to sleep when my body was worn and woke up when it could take more. And that was my life for q while, more years than I know how to count.

After a while I even imagined it had all been a dream - my brother, my mother, were all figments of my frazzled brain. Had I created a family because I had none? I think all that held me together was a smell, as ridiculous as it sounds. But I could SMELL Maman, the scent one of the men used to bring her. It was sickly and used to make our noses crinkle but he had always insisted she wore it, and after a while we all got used to it because it was the only different thing in our lives. Maman said it was flowers, something we had seen but never smelled, and as the time went on, it was all I had of her - the scent and the way her hair curled into tight ringlets the way mine does when it's wet. The hair and the sickly smell kept me going because I knew they were real. She was real. What happened to us was real.

Not that it helped. I can't honestly say how much time passed because the truth was I don't know. But I was growing, and I imagined my brother was too. I guess he was only ten at the time and I was terrified. I didn't know what to do, or what was to become of me. *And then I met Delphine. Another kid on the streets but older than me, and wiser. She'd had to be. She'd been on the streets herself for a long time so she knew the tricks. She knew how to survive and she took one look at me, and smiled and I knew, just knew, I was going to be safe. And then I met Axel. Two kids I fell in love with, in very, very different but important ways, ways I didn't understand but I went along with. I wanted Axel to touch me, not that I let him for a long time because I didn't understand the difference between love and what I did with the men who paid me. Delphine was the one who made me understand. She told me to use my brain to move things around. The ME side and the THEM side. Keep ME hidden and only allow myself to see it when I needed to so that no one else could invade it. I thought she was talking shit, because to be honest, she mostly does, but after a while I got what she was saying. Let them take what they wanted from me, but when they did, go to my special place, the hidden place and it worked, well sort of. We kid ourselves, but at the end of the day it's all we have.*

I can't begin to tell you how important it was for me to have Axel and Delphine by my side. They told me to wait. They told me to watch. And that is what we did. For days, for weeks, for months, and then it happened. Marc appeared. He'd been watching for weeks too, hiding in the shadows. We didn't look in the shadows. We didn't need to because we knew the monsters. The REAL monsters walked in the day, with their heads held high because they knew they had nothing to fear. I knew as soon as I saw him who he was. We had the same tuft of hair at the base of our skulls; I remembered playing with his when we were kids because it gave me some comfort. We are the same. And there he was, looking at me with the same quizzical look of a child, although he'd grown in the time we were apart. He smiled at me, and it melted my heart.

'You wouldn't believe how long I've been trying to find this place,' he said, his voice bearing the croak of adolescence, not the squeak I remembered. It made me mad and sad at the same time, mad for the time we had lost and sad because he had come back. His life should have changed. He should have changed and become someone else, far away from all the darkness. But he hadn't, the cesspool of our childhood had dragged him back in and it made me so angry. We knew we would never be free, not so long as the men who had hurt us were walking free. He had meant to walk free and be happy, but he had not. The men we ran away from had found him and it was a stark reminder of how far their reach went.

So we continued to watch and wait. Delphine joked they'd probably been lying low after we ran and then when nothing came of it, the arrogant white men decided to rise again and continue their debauchery because they had gotten away with it. They had of course, and there was nothing we could do about it. I told myself that if they came back I would stop them in their tracks. At least make them crawl back into the shadows for a while.

We made it work, the four of us, and then Marc brought along his friend, Jack, some kid he'd met at the church his adopted parents made him go to, and we were happy, if you could call it that. But it didn't last. Jack was an altar boy, and one of the men in particular had spent years abusing him. Over and over. Again and again. Jack had even gone to the priest, the old one with the hair the colour of snow, but he didn't believe him, called him a liar and told him he should be grateful. GRATEFUL that he was being looked after. And then it happened, the day everything changed. Something happened, and I think Marc and Jack just lost it. The priest was like every man who had ever hurt them, ever abused them, and they lost it. Marc called me and said they'd killed him. He was so covered in blood, they didn't think he was even breathing. They thought that since they'd come that far, they didn't want to take the chance someone else would take over the home, so they burned it to the ground. I can't say I blame them. But by the time we got there, the flics were already there, and they'd taken Marc and Jack away. I don't know how, but they got released and for the first time we felt free. I know our lives don't seem perfect. They're not, but for a while our little gang was happy - a crazy, fucked-up family.

Back then we were taking drugs, anything to make it through the days and the nights. It all came to a head one night when I saw the man. And he was smiling, as if he had not a care in the world. As if he had not violated my mother time after time, and then passing her around like she was a rag doll. It was all I could do to stop myself from running up to him and beating the truth out of him. 'Ou est elle? Ou est Maman?' I wanted to scream, but I was too frightened, not of him but of the answer he might give me. I didn't want him to know me, to know Marc, and the bastard didn't even recognise me. And it was then finally something snapped in me, something not even Delphine and Axel or even my brother could stop. Something which had been building for a long time. I swore I would do whatever I had to do to make him pay, to make sure he would never hurt another child, not as long as I had an ounce of breath left in my body. So I did what I had to do to stop him…

* * *

Delphine Marchand stood, wiping the sand from her jeans. She touched Jérémie's mouth with a finger. She turned to Hugo, green eyes narrowing angrily. 'You've heard everything you're going to hear from him for now. I will not allow him to implicate himself just so you can find some reason to throw him in jail…'

'I wouldn't,' Hugo protested.

Delphine shrugged. 'You'll forgive me if I don't believe you because, frankly, your word means fuck all to me.'

Hugo shook his head. 'But there's so much I don't understand. What about Jack Boucher, where does he fit into all of this? Who murdered him?'

The three of them exchanged a look which Hugo had trouble understanding.

Jérémie answered. 'Jack shouldn't have gotten involved, it wasn't his fight, but he wanted to make it right. He wanted to make all the bastards pay and that's why…' He stopped, unable to finish his sentence.

'That's why, what?' Hugo interjected.

Delphine glared at him. 'I told you, that's it. Until we know we're safe, you're not getting anything else out of us.' She stroked Jérémie's left cheek before turning back to Hugo. 'If you want us to start believing you, then you've got to give us a reason to trust you.'

'And how do you expect me to do that?' Hugo asked desperately.

Axel Soudre moved closer, wrapping his arm around

Jérémie's shoulders. 'Make us safe, s'il te plaît, Captain Duchamp, I beg you. That's all we want. And then we'll help you. We want to make the people who hurt our friends, Jérémie's brother, pay. But unless we're safe, there is no point in helping you. There has to be an end to this for us.'

Hugo felt the reassuring presence of Ben's fingers slipping between his own and he nodded. 'You don't have to beg,' he answered softly, 'you WILL be safe.'

Hugo inched back the curtain, a slither of Parisian sunlight illuminating the darkened room. Despite everything, he was worried. Etienne Martine, the forensic expert who Hugo trusted implicitly, had found a safe house and assured him it was one of the safest places in the country. Hugo wanted to believe him, but he had trouble believing anything after all he had seen throughout his career.

'Is this how it has to be from now on?' Axel Soudre asked. 'Hiding in dark rooms too afraid to go out?'

'It won't be forever,' Hugo answered reassuringly, 'just until we arrest those responsible.'

Delphine Marchand tutted. 'Every rock you turn over, there's always another hiding the next cockroach.'

'Perhaps,' Hugo conceded, 'but I've always found one frightened cockroach tends to run towards other cockroaches.'

Delphine cocked her head, studying Hugo with interest, a smile twitching on her lips. 'Can of worms, huh?' she asked. 'The rats fleeing the sinking ship?' She shook her head. 'Shame, you didn't look to me to be naïve.'

Hugo smiled. 'It's been my experience,' he replied. 'And I've been doing this for a long time.' He paused. 'I realise none of you has any reason to trust me or anyone else for that matter, but I believe a great injustice has been done to you all, an injustice I admit I don't fully understand yet, other than I know it's painful for you, and I want to help.' He paused again. 'I understand you know Jean Lenoir, the Minister of Justice.'

Delphine snorted. 'Sure, I know him. You men are all the same when it comes down to it.'

'Perhaps,' Hugo replied, 'but tell me this, what do you make of him? Do you trust him?'

Delphine's eyes flashed at him. 'I don't trust anyone,' she hissed.

'I understand that,' Hugo retorted, 'but if you know anything about Jean Lenoir, you should know this. He doesn't tolerate corruption, no matter how high the corruption goes. In fact, I'd wager the higher it goes the more he prefers it. I wouldn't say Jean and I are friends, but we work well together because we both share one distinct trait. We have zero fucks to give when it comes to doing our jobs. We're not the sort of men who are easily intimidated.'

Jérémie guffawed. 'I see why you like him,' he said to Ben.

Ben laughed. 'His clarity and choice of words are just two of the many things I love about him.' He turned to Delphine. 'But he's right. We can trust him and Jean Lenoir to understand all of this and to deal with it the best way possible. There will be no cover-up.'

Delphine looked between Jérémie and Axel and then back at Hugo. 'I don't have much in life, Captain Duchamp, but I guard what I have with all I am. If anyone hurts them, ANYONE, then I'll make sure they'll pay and I don't care who gets caught in the crossfire. Do I make myself clear? I've lost too much already and I don't intend on losing anything, or anyone else.'

Hugo nodded. 'Absolument. Tell me, is this connected to what Jean Lenoir asked you to do?'

Delphine's eyes darted from left to right. 'I don't know what you mean.'

'He asked you to wear a wire,' Hugo replied. 'He was trying to get evidence on someone, non?'

She shook her head. 'Everyone is trying to get stuff on someone. So, oui, this is how we got stuck in this mess, doing the dirty work for stupid men. Jean Lenoir is the worst kind. He knew how dangerous it was for me and he didn't care. All he was bothered about was getting the dirt on some filthy pig who ought to know better. But none of it mattered, because of what happened to Jack. He got stupid, and I'm not stupid. I wouldn't have lasted so long on the streets if I was stupid. Do what you have to do, but until I figure my way out of this, I will not trust you.'

Hugo looked at her sadly. 'D'accord, I'm going back to Paris now and try to get this whole business resolved so you can get back,' he exhaled, 'rather, you can all begin living the lives you deserve without any of this hanging over your head.' He pointed at the telephone. 'That phone has one speed dial, press 111 and help will be with you before you know it. Not that you'll need it. Nobody knows you're here other than us and Etienne. I've also written down my cell phone number and Ben's, call us if you need anything, or just need to talk.' He nodded towards Ben. 'Let's go, Ben.'

Ben met his gaze. 'I'm staying here,' he blurted.

'Quoi?' Hugo asked in surprise.

Ben moved across the room, gently touching Hugo's arm. 'If I go back to Paris all I can do is cool my heels in the hotel room, at least if I stay here I'll feel as if I'm doing something useful and at least we'll know someone is with them.'

Hugo looked doubtfully between his husband and the youngsters. Even Delphine seemed anxious as if she was trying her best to appear brave. He nodded quickly, moving towards the door before he had a chance to change his mind. 'I'll be back soon,' he called out with a confidence he was not sure he felt.

'No police,' Delphine interjected, 'or I swear we're out of here.'

'I have to involve the police,' Hugo reasoned, 'but I promise you, I trust Captain Brunhild.'

'No police,' Delphine growled. 'Haven't you got it yet? The reason we ran from *energique*? It's because Jérémie recognised someone. You heard what he had to say.'

Hugo looked towards Jérémie. He lifted his head slowly. 'Who did you recognise? Hugo asked.

Jérémie did not answer immediately. 'One of the fuckers who raped my mother whenever he felt like it, that's who,' he spat as if the words were acid burning his mouth, 'and when I discovered he was a flic, I knew we were done for, nobody would believe me over him. And above all, he could make me disappear just like he did with Maman. I know that because not only was he a cop, he worked for Alexander Esnault doing his dirty work for him.'

Hugo swallowed. The revelation made sense, but it still shocked him. 'Did you ever find out who he was?.'

Jérémie nodded, looking to Delphine for reassurance.

She indicated for him to continue. 'You want us to trust you, then prove it,' she said to Hugo.

Jérémie cleared his throat. 'The bastard's name was Cedric. Cedric Degarmo.'

Hugo flopped onto the chair in Coco's office, staring intently at her. She matched his gaze, her eyebrow springing into a puzzled arch. They continued to stare at one another. Coco pushed herself back in her chair, an amused smile appearing on her face. 'You're handsome, aren't you?'

Hugo's eyes widened, his head dropping. Coco cackled. 'Well, I had to do something to break the stalemate. What's the deal, Duchamp? What's the news?'

Hugo lifted his head slowly. It took him a few moments to speak. 'I've done something I don't think you will like. I know that because if the shoe were on the other foot, I'd probably feel the same.'

'Well,' Coco replied, 'you have my attention. What exactly have you done?'

'As you know, Ben and I went to Sceaux this morning,' he answered.

Coco cackled. 'Don't look so glum about it. There are worse things that could happen, Hugo. Sceaux isn't so bad. I hope you had an ice cream.'

Hugo gave her a tired smile. He exhaled. 'And when we were there, we did, in fact, find Jérémie Berger, Axel Soudre, and Delphine Marchand.'

Coco coughed. 'And how on earth did you manage that?' She raised her hand. 'It doesn't matter.' She lifted her head, straining her eyes as she scanned the Commissariat. She frowned. 'But more importantly, where

413

are they now?'

Hugo did not answer, trying his best to hold her intense gaze. 'Hugo?' she asked, the frown deepening. 'Captain Duchamp?' she added, the snap clear.

'You're going to have to trust me,' Hugo intoned.

Coco jumped to her feet. 'Oh, non, non, Captain, you don't get to do that. You level with me, and you level with me right now.'

'I can't,' he answered, his head dropping, blond locks falling across his face.

Coco stepped in front of him. 'You can, and you can right now, or so help me... so help me,' she sank onto the side of her desk, knocking a cup filled with pens to the ground, 'oh who am I kidding?' Her eyes narrowed at Hugo, and she sighed with defeat. 'Tell me what you can then.'

Hugo gave her a grateful smile. 'Jérémie told me a story, the story of his life and the life of his brother.' He shuddered. 'Believe me, it's not a story you really want to hear, but the crux of it was, Jérémie and his brother were victims of a paedophile ring. More than that, they were born into it.'

'Born into it?' Coco asked sharply. 'What does that even mean?'

'They were born to a young woman who I believe had most probably been trafficked since she was very young. Of course, Jérémie and his brother never really understood what was happening because it was a life they were born into. From what he said, I imagine he must have been in early adolescence before he even saw daylight, and it was only because his mother attacked one of her abusers, giving them a chance to escape.'

Coco shook her head, a finger scratching her cheek. 'As horrible story as it is, I'm not seeing why you're being so secretive, unless...' she stopped, 'unless you don't trust me.'

'Non, it's not that,' Hugo answered quickly, 'rather it's impossible to know who to trust and the fewer people who know about this the better until we figure out what's going on, and more importantly who is involved.'

'Are you suggesting I'm somehow involved?' Coco snapped, her nostrils flaring.

'Not at all,' Hugo retorted, 'but we have to be careful and if we talk on the record, then I don't know how safe they'll remain. I have involved Etienne in this, and I don't want to put him in the position of having someone superior to him, to me, to us, demand he provides them with information.'

'Forgive me, Hugo, but aren't you getting just a bit carried away here? I mean, as awful as this all is, you seem to be suggesting there is some kind of huge conspiracy at the highest level.' Hugo did not respond. 'Is that what you're suggesting? That there are people here at the Commissariat who might be involved in the trafficking and abuse of children?' Hugo still did not respond. 'Fuck, Hugo, you're going to have to help me here. I'm beginning to get a sick feeling.'

Hugo glanced at the "no smoking or I'll kill you before the cancer gets to you," sign on Coco's office wall. She followed his gaze. 'It's all right, you're exempt, in fact, give me one too.'

Hugo reached into his pocket, retrieved and lit two cigarettes. He handed one to Coco, and for a moment they shared the enjoyment of the tranquillity.

'Jérémie told me he recognised a man who came into *énergique*. A man who terrified him because he had seen the man abusing his mother. He then discovered the man was, in fact, a police officer.'

'Putain,' Coco muttered. 'Who?'

Hugo glanced anxiously over his shoulder. 'Jérémie said he discovered the man was called Cedric, and that he works for Alexander Esnault.'

Her eyes widened in horror. 'Then he's a fucking liar,' she hissed.

Hugo tilted his head. 'I admit I don't know Cedric, certainly not as well as you, but I heard what Jérémie had to say, and we already know Cedric has spent time at the club.'

'Spent time at the club?' Coco cried, 'so has half of Paris, Morty included, add Jean Lenoir and your father to the list and you have a who's who of Parisian dirty old men.' She shook her head, eyes misting, 'Non, I don't buy it, I WON'T buy it.' She paused, fixing Hugo with an icy stare. 'Hugo I respect you, hell, I even like you, which believe me is pretty damn unusual because I rarely like anyone. But I don't understand what's going on here and the fact is trust works both ways. You want me to trust you, then you'll simply have to trust me as well. Trust that I'll do my job. If, and I mean, IF we prove Cedric is dirty, I'll take him down myself. Will you trust me, Hugo?'

'Oui,' Hugo replied, 'd'accord, let's talk, but not here. Let's go for a walk and try to figure out our next move.'

Coco inhaled the cigarette, spluttering as the smoke was pushed back by her lungs. Unrepentant she sucked on it again, her eyes locked firmly on Hugo who was twitching the long, blond locks of his fringe. His eyes trained on the entrance to Commissariat de Police du 7e arrondissement.

'You look worried, Hugo,' Coco whispered, before adding, 'and I don't think I've seen you worried before, and that worries me more than I care to admit.'

Hugo continued staring at the doorway as several police officers entered and exited. Finally, he sighed. 'I am troubled. Troubled because I don't understand what's going on, and who to trust. I believe I'm usually good at following my instincts, but...'

'But?' Coco interjected.

'But in this case, my instinct tells me Cedric isn't involved, but I'm having trouble making sense of it.'

'Are you serious?' Coco exclaimed.

He turned his head sharply. 'You weren't there, Coco. Jérémie was so... so sure and articulate. I'm afraid I have very little doubt that the boy and his brother and their mother were subjected to cruel and evil abuse.'

'But it doesn't mean it was at the hands of Cedric,' Coco reasoned.

'Then why say it? Why tell me he recognised Cedric from the club?'

Coco shrugged. 'I don't know, to cause trouble?

418

There could be many reasons, but like you said, you can't believe it was Cedric and you barely know him. Now imagine how I feel, the person who arguably knows him better than anyone.'

Hugo held her gaze. He raised an eyebrow. 'Coco,' he whispered, 'then tell me why Jérémie would blame him? I understand you've known him for a long time, but really, outside of the Commissariat how well do you know him?'

Coco's lips pursed into an irritated scowl but she did not answer, instead angrily stubbing out her cigarette. 'I know him,' she said petulantly, stamping her feet. 'I mean, this is a kid who grew up in a rotten orphanage on the outskirts of Paris. He won't even talk about how horrible it was, but I know for a fact it scarred him, the beatings, Dieu knows what else. How can someone who has been through his own hell suddenly turn around and do the same thing himself?'

Hugo's eyebrow raised again. 'Coco, we've both been around enough to know that it's sometimes the case that the abused end up doing the one thing they find most abhorrent. They turn into abusers themselves.'

'Wait a damn minute, Hugo!' she snapped. 'I won't hear of it; I can't hear of it. You can think I'm looking through rose-tinted glasses all you like, but I've worked alongside Cedric for a long time, and I've watched him grow from being some snotty-nosed arrogant kid into a pretty decent flic. Whatever is going on here...'

'Wait a minute,' Hugo interrupted. 'Did you say

Cedric grew up in an orphanage here in Paris?'

She nodded, shrugging. 'Oui. I can't say I know the details. It's not something a guy like him talks about, but I got the impression it was pretty rough and it toughened him up. He told me once it was the reason he became a flic in the first place. He wanted not just the respect but the chance to put away the lowlifes who preyed on places like the one he grew up in. So, you see, it's impossible to imagine…' She stopped, her eyes scanning Hugo's face. 'Wait, what is it? You look like you smelled something rotten.'

Hugo reached into his pocket and pulled out a cigarette. 'When we went to the apartment building where the Boucher's lived, I had a conversation with Cedric. A conversation where he told me about how he had grown up in a very similar apartment building. An apartment building on the wrong side of Marseille.'

Coco looked at him in surprise. 'What? Are you sure? I mean, that's pretty specific, maybe he was talking about… talking about someone else, someone he knew, or perhaps it was a conversation you had with someone else. You have a lot of those after all, we both do. And it's impossible to remember every conversation you have and with whom.' She stopped, moving closer to Hugo and taking the cigarette from him, sucking on it angrily. 'You're sure?' she whispered.

Hugo nodded.

'Dammit,' Coco sniffed. 'What does it mean? Maybe

I got it wrong. Perhaps Cedric was born in Marseille and ended up in a Paris orphanage, perhaps...' she stopped. 'I hate perhapses because they're usually a lazy way of explaining coincidences.' She stared in the direction of the Commissariat. 'Well, there's only one way to sort this out. We have to confront him, give him the chance to explain, to defend himself. If he's as innocent as I believe him to be, we owe him that at the very least.' She frowned upon seeing Hugo's reluctance to move. 'What is it?' she asked.

'I want to believe him, Coco,' Hugo said. 'But we need to understand what's going on here. We owe it to the victims, and if we act too quickly, we may tip off whoever is really responsible. If Cedric is innocent as you believe him to be, there may be a real danger whoever is behind this may be setting him up as a scapegoat, so if we go in all guns blazing, they may just be content to let him take the fall.'

'What are you suggesting we do then?'

'We go back to the beginning, and we need help,' Hugo answered.

'Help?' Coco asked with a frown. 'A minute ago you said we couldn't trust anyone.'

Hugo nodded. 'I know, but I trust Etienne and we need someone like him to poke around. He might be able to find out exactly what Cedric's story is, and maybe even clear his name before we have to make public what we know.'

Coco gave him a sceptical look. 'You think that's

possible?'

He shrugged. 'As you said, you don't believe he's involved, and I trust you. So we have to try to understand what that means, for example, he could have lied about his background. People do so for many reasons. Sometimes as simple as being embarrassed, which would explain that discrepancy.'

Coco smiled. 'I like your thinking, but even I can't think of a logical explanation why Jérémie Berger might have recognised Cedric as being one of the men who abused him, can you?'

Hugo pursed his lips. 'Peut être,' he paused. 'One thing occurs to me. We might be looking at this from the wrong angle. All we know for certain is Jérémie recognised someone at the club, a man he later found to be called Cedric Degarmo.'

'And your point is?'

'Well,' Hugo continued, 'I can't say for certain, but if you were, say a rapist, or a child abuser, or a murderer even, there's every chance you'd be reluctant to use your own name should anyone recognise you.'

Coco gave him a sceptical look. 'You're suggesting someone used Cedric's identity?' She shook her head. 'As much as I want to believe it, the truth is it makes no sense. They weren't to know Jérémie would also be working at the club, so why go to the trouble of pretending to be someone else?'

Hugo shrugged again. 'Let's send Ben a photograph

of Cedric, and we can get Jérémie to confirm or refute whether he's the man he knew from the cellar.'

Coco bit her lip. 'Well, it would clear Cedric but it wouldn't get us much further to discovering who was impersonating him. Dammit, Hugo! This is a mess and I don't know where to start. Do you?'

Hugo considered. 'I believe the key to this is at the beginning and whoever placed Jérémie and his family in that room. And I don't know why, but I have a feeling the answer lies in the orphanage run by Monseigneur Augustine Demaral because we keep coming back to it. Can we go to your place and make a plan of action? I think under the circumstances, it would be best if we keep as low a profile as we can until we figure out what we're dealing with and more importantly who we can trust.'

Coco nodded, her face pale. 'Are you sure you want to get involved in this, Hugo? You and Ben could be on the next train back to Montgenoux and not look back, because if we get any deeper into this we will start treading on some pretty important toes. Toes belonging to feet who will do the best to stamp out our careers, or worse. And as much as Jean Lenoir talks the talk, I suspect when it comes down to it, he'd throw us to the wolves if he had to, to save his own neck.'

'Are you scared?' Hugo asked.

She nodded again. 'You bet I am, but I'm also the kinda girl who isn't easily intimidated, and certainly not by men with pencil dicks who hide behind the careers they've been handed and certainly not had to work as hard as either you or I to get as far as we have. What about you? Are you worried?'

He smiled at her. 'I've always said I'd only do this job as long as I can look at myself in the mirror in the morning.'

'Bon. Let's go to my place and figure this mess out.'

Ben awoke with a start, his body jerking into the morning, his eyes wide with confusion and, for a moment, intense fear. He looked to his right and found it tidy; the pillows puffed and unused, the sheets smooth, the complete opposite to how he normally saw them each morning. Hugo Duchamp was not a light sleeper, Ben thought with a sad smile. It was as if he carried the weight of his world on his shoulders and sleep could do little to protect him from them. Ben's heart ached in ways he had never experienced before to be away from him - the man he now called husband and he knew he should be wary of it, wary of the potential loss which he knew he would never recover from, but he found he could not. The price of unknown eventualities was small for the reward of what he had experienced, the life he lead which he had never dared dream could be his.

He cocked his ear, instantly recognising the hushed murmurs of young lovers and it stabbed at his heart, stabbed at it because it overwhelmed him with sadness that he and Hugo had never been able to share such moments - the moments of infinite possibilities. The wonder of the world at their feet, the sun rising for them, the night closing for them so they could be alone in the darkness. It angered Ben they were being denied the beginning in life he had taken for granted. He had spent so much of his own childhood and young adulthood railing at the ties of his father that he had never really taken the time to count the many blessings before him. He wished he had found Hugo earlier, if only to make Hugo's life more meaningful because Ben knew he had spent most of it having nobody to tell him how wonderful he was and subsequently when they did, he had trouble believing it.

'What you looking all misty-eyed about?'

Ben turned his head sharply, meeting Delphine Marchand's intense gaze. He was trying to decide what it was about her which troubled him. He understood the aggression, the bravado-fuelled antagonism. He did not suppose many people survived life on the street without developing the thickest of skins. But there was something else about her, something which he could not put his finger on. The antagonism she projected seemed different. He shook the thought from his head, realising once again his own real-world problems paled, and had always, paled in comparison to the lives these young adults must have lived.

Delphine repeated her question.

'Mon mari,' he answered softly.

Delphine sucked air through a gap in her teeth and spat it back out as if it tasted sour.

'I'm sorry if I offend you,' Ben said. 'I understand it must sound as if I'm showing off my happiness, throwing my privilege in your face, but I also hope you know I'm not, and in some small way, you might believe I have spent and will spend the rest of my life trying to better myself. I grew up with more privilege than you can imagine and I hated every second of it, pouting at the injustice of having a father who hated me,' he snorted, 'and believe me, the irony of my childhood insecurity is not lost on me. I was spoilt and despite my father, I was blessed in more ways than most other people. I see that now, and all I can do in the future is use what I have to better others who don't and haven't had the opportunities I have.'

'Do you know how many men I've heard spout the same kind of bullshit? There is always a price to pay. And it usually involves me on my knees, or my back, cooing into their ears, making them feel better about their daddy issues, or their mummy issues, or whatever the hell else they think they have to moan about. They're all lies and manipulation, you just dress it up better.'

Ben shook his head. 'It's not true, écoute, I know you have no reason to trust me. Hell, I wouldn't trust me if I were you, but I see your fire, I see your determination and I see you are one of the smartest women I've met. If you come to Montgenoux I'd like to introduce you to Irene. She is my best friend and you remind me of her in so many ways. The fire, the determination. She could help you in ways I can't. I'm sure if anyone could make you believe in yourself it's her. But to get you there, to get you all there, you will have to trust me, but more importantly especially Hugo. This mess, whatever the hell it is, seems insurmountable right now, but it isn't, not if we all work together. We can overcome this, we can step out of the darkness. If you believe anything about me, believe in that,

I've walked out of the darkness several times and it was only because of Hugo and his belief, his honour, and his love. And I know he will do the same for you, strangers or not, because that's just the kind of person he is.'

Delphine slowly began clapping her hands. 'You talk a good talk, I'll give you that, but don't think for a second I buy this good guy act. You'd sell us out in a second if it meant saving you or your husband's skin.'

'Of course I would,' Ben said quickly, then bit his lip, 'désolé,' he added, 'I shouldn't have said that.'

She smiled. 'Bon. You do tell the truth after all. And so you should, I'd save my boys over you any day, that's just how it is. So, if it comes down to it, and it will, I'm damn well sure of it, know that. You're nothing to me, but they are and if it comes to a choice, well, there isn't one, si?'

Ben nodded. 'I understand what you mean, but you're talking in extremes, and we're not there yet so nobody has to be sacrificed, and nor will they be if we work together, not against each other. Do you think you can do that?'

Axel Soudre appeared in the doorway. 'You bet we can.' He stared at Delphine. 'No one else has to die, Delph. I won't allow it. We've lost too much already, I can't lose Jérémie and he certainly can't lose anyone else. He's not as strong as he makes out, we both know that.' He turned to Ben. 'And if it means we've got to trust, to work together with these guys, then that's what we're gonna do, comprende?'

Delphine raised an eyebrow. 'What's suddenly rattled your cage?'

Axel turned away huffily. 'I'm sick and tired of this shit, that's all. Sick and tired of running, of other people deciding for us. It's about time I stood up for myself.'

Delphine looked at him warily. 'What do you mean? Suddenly you've grown a pair?'

He gesticulated angrily towards her. 'I'm sick of you talking to me like I'm a child. I'm not a child. I've been on the streets just as long as you, probably longer. And I've been through the same shit you have, but I'm not beaten, not like you - so angry and worn down you see nothing good anymore. They won't beat me, Delphine, not like they've beaten you.' He slammed his fist into the doorpost with such force he cried out in pain, recoiling and staring at his bloodied knuckles. 'Goddamnit, I've gotta get out of here. I need some air.'

'You can't go outside, it's not safe…' Delphine began. 'For fuck's sake, Delphine, stop telling me what to do. I've gotta get out of here. I need to do something or I'm gonna go crazy.' He ran towards the door, yanking it open and running out. Delphine ran after him as Jérémie appeared, raising a hand to stop her.

'Leave him,' he said, 'he just needs to blow off some steam, and besides he's right. We can't stay cooped up here forever.'

Delphine shook her head. 'It's not safe out there,

Jérémie,' she whispered.

He flashed her with a sad smile. 'I know, but just give him five minutes to cool off, and then I'll go and get him.'

'And what the hell did he mean about needing to do something?' Delphine countered.

Jérémie frowned, shaking his head. 'Je sais pas.' He shrugged. 'Hey, I love him and I don't understand half the stuff that comes out of his mouth. He'll be fine once he's cooled down,' he added with little conviction. He turned his head, starting at the space left by his lover. 'Don't you get sick of people walking out of doors and never coming back through them?' he added pensively.

Delphine hurried towards him, rubbing her hand across his arm. 'That was different,' she whispered, before quickly adding, 'and not your fault.'

Jérémie jerked his arm away from her. 'It was my fault, and you know it, we all know it.' He stood in front of the window, sliding his finger to lift one of the blinds. Axel was standing nearby, staring absently at the empty field in front of the safe house. 'Marc and Jack are dead because of me.'

'Are you serious?' Delphine cried. 'You know that's not true. You have to know that's not true.'

He shook his head. 'It's the truth, the absolute truth. This all started with me. Everything started with me, in that room, with those men. The decisions I made, the things I did, everything started from there.'

Ben cleared his throat and moved towards them. 'Regarde, Jérémie, I can't begin to imagine what your life has been like, but from what you've told us, you have to know, you *have* to believe none of this is your fault. You were born into a life so horrendous the rest of us can barely imagine and anything you did to survive was the right thing because you DID survive, and it's all that matters. None of this is your fault, none of this can be your fault.'

Jérémie glared at him. 'Are you kidding me? You heard what I had to say and you still believe that? I could have stopped this all a long time ago if I'd killed the man with the scar, or any of them for that matter. Instead, what did I do? I played their game, I did what they wanted. Hell, the truth is I ended up a fag anyway. Perhaps subconsciously I only pretended to be disgusted by what they did to me, pretended it hurt, pretended I was only doing it to save my brother, pretended I didn't really enjoy what they did to me...'

Ben reached forward and pulled Jérémie into an embrace. 'You did what you had to do to survive, and that is the end of it,' he breathed into the top of Jérémie's head.

Moments later, Jérémie began sobbing, his body giving way into Ben's arms. 'I could have saved them,' he wailed, 'I SHOULD have saved them.' He pulled away, dropping heavily onto the sofa, angrily wiping the snot away from his nose.

Delphine jumped next to him, wrapping her arm

around his shoulders and pulling him to her. 'Ben's right,' she said with clear reluctance, 'what happened to Marc and Jack has nothing to do with you, or them even. We are just pieces of meat for filthy, disgusting men to use and abuse. Direct your anger at them because that's where it should be, and hell, believe me, it feels fucking great to put all the blame at those who deserve it.'

'But what does it solve? They will still do whatever it is they want to do. Do you really think we're important? That this will all end with us?' he asked helplessly.

She nodded quickly. 'You bet your ass I do. One way or another, this WILL end with us, you can be sure of it. We haven't lived through all of this to just take it lying down. They might get to us,' she glared at Ben again, 'in fact, I'm sure they will, but I know one thing for certain. If I go down, I'm taking every one of those motherfuckers down with me.'

Jérémie gave a sad laugh. 'They'd better not even try to cross you, Delph, not if they have half a brain because it's one battle they'd never win.'

Delphine also laughed. 'See, we've got this. We're stronger than they know.'

Ben's cell phone beeped. 'Excusez moi,' he said pulling it out of his pocket and reading the screen. 'It's from Hugo. He's sent me a picture of Cedric Degarmo and wants you to confirm it as being the same man you knew,' he passed the phone to Jérémie.

Jérémie stared at the screen, his eyes crinkling. He

frowned, handing the cell phone back to Ben. 'What game are you playing?' he hissed. 'That's not Cedric Degarmo. I have no idea who that man is, but he's not the man I met who called himself Cedric.'

Delphine agreed. 'I've seen this guy before at the club, but Jérémie is right. He's not the one who called himself Cedric.'

Ben's eyes widened, glancing at the screen again. 'But I have met the man in this photograph, and I can tell you he is the real Cedric Degarmo, which means… which means…' he trailed off, absent-mindedly pushing the curls from his forehead.

'Which means what?' Delphine interjected irritably.

Ben shrugged. 'Beats the shit out of me, but I hope Hugo and Coco can make sense of it. Let me call them. They need to know somebody has been impersonating Cedric.'

She gave Ben another doubtful look. 'Do you think I'm stupid?'

Ben shook his head. 'Non, of course not.'

'Good,' she snapped back, 'then don't expect us to believe that man isn't a rapist creep just because another policeman says he isn't, okay?'

Ben sighed. 'I understand you have trust issues…'

'Trust issues!' she hissed. 'Fucking trust issues, you call it? I call it protecting my damn ass, my life, the life of my friends, from men who think they are above the law. Because goddamnit, they are above the law.'

Ben did not answer, knowing there was no point. But he knew the truth. Whatever was going on, whoever it involved. Hugo and Coco would get to the bottom of it, no matter the cost.

Axel stubbed out a cigarette, pushing the last of the smoke out of his body. He sighed, glancing over his shoulder back to the house. He pursed his lips as if contemplating something. After a moment he stepped to the side, ambling across the grass, and he did not stop until he was sure he was out of eyeshot. His hand shook as he pulled out another cigarette and lit it. With his free hand he reached to his mouth and began chewing on a fingernail as if in deep thought. He glanced over his shoulder again, satisfying himself nobody could see him. He pulled out his cell phone, his hand still shaking as he keyed in a number. He pressed dial, exhaling smoke quickly.

'Hey,' he said, his voice shaky. 'C'est moi. I don't care if this isn't a good time, this is important. NON, YOU LISTEN TO ME!' he cried, his voice rising. If you don't want me to tell the police everything I know, then you will listen to me. I want out. I want money and I want passports for me, Jérémie, and Delphine. If I don't get them, and if I don't get them soon, you will pay for everything. For every filthy, disgusting thing you did to Jérémie and Marc and their mother and for what you did to Jack because he dared to stand up to you. I don't care how "difficult" it is for you, you fucking pervert. Don't tell me you can't do it, because I know you can and if you don't...' He listened to the other side of the conversation, a smile appearing on his face. 'D'accord, I'll text you an address. I'll meet you there tomorrow morning at ten a.m and bring the money and the passports and I'll bring the flash drive. And don't be late or try anything or you'll see your face all over the newspapers this time tomorrow.'

'I don't believe it,' Coco said, shaking her head, locks of blue-dyed hair covering her face. 'If it's not Cedric, then who the hell is it, and why are they using his name?'

Hugo did not answer, lost in his thoughts, trying to understand the ramifications of what was happening. There was a picture forming in his head but as usual there were too many moving parts, too many distractions. It was like walking through fog, stumbling and falling over objects in the way. However, he had been a policeman for long enough to know that often all it took was for one piece to fall into place for the fog to begin to disperse.

'I don't know, Coco, truly I don't,' he answered finally, 'but every instinct tells me it's important.'

'In what way?' she asked.

He shrugged. 'You know Cedric better than I do and you told me you're convinced he couldn't be involved in any of this, so I believe it. However, there are more ways than one for him to be involved.'

Coco frowned. 'I don't understand.'

'Well,' Hugo continued, 'we know he has been to *énergique* on more than one occasion. I think it's fair to assume he didn't go there on his own volition. His presence was requested and approved, so someone wanted him there for a reason.'

'To act as a stooge?'

Hugo nodded. 'It makes sense. If he isn't involved in

any crime, then the chances are he knows who is, and for that reason we need to talk to him.'

'Oui, I'll call him in.'

Hugo glanced around. 'I don't think so. There's something very wrong with this whole picture, Coco, and I don't think we can take any more risks. The children are surely still in danger, but for all we know, Cedric could be as well.'

'Then what do we do?'

Hugo frowned. 'We go to someone we can trust. Someone who has more power and influence than us.'

Coco gawped at him. 'You're talking about Jean Lenoir? You trust him that much?'

Hugo did not answer because the truth was complicated. He was not sure how much he trusted the Minister of Justice, but his instinct was telling him he was, at least as far as this matter was concerned, their only choice. They needed his influence, and Hugo felt sure the children needed the protection only he could offer. He had to take a leap of faith. His jaw flexed. 'Call Cedric and have him meet us at Jean's office.'

Jean Lenoir stared at Hugo, the veins in his neck straining against the starched white shirt he was wearing. He pushed himself back in his chair, a whistle emitting from the gap between his gleaming white teeth. 'I don't like this, Hugo,' he muttered off-handily as if there was no conviction to the sentiment. 'We're playing fast and loose and it could come back to bite us…' he trailed off before emphasising, '*you*, in the ass.'

Hugo smiled. 'Bien sûr. I wouldn't expect anything else. I have broad shoulders and the point remains, there is something very wrong here. I, for one, don't want to live with any further regret that I could have helped prevent another young person losing their life.'

The Minister of Justice waved his hand dismissively before turning to Coco. 'We don't even know how much is true of the story the Berger boy told you. We can't understand their motives, and why they would say or do what they have. And as you have told me about the discrepancy in Lieutenant Degarmo's backstory, I'm not sure whether to believe what he has to say either.'

'But I do,' Coco said.

Jean Lenoir stared at her. 'I know little of this Lieutenant of yours, Charlotte, other than his service record and what you have told me. Am I to believe you are going out on a limb for him?'

Coco bit her lip, eyes anxiously darting between Hugo and Jean. After a few moments, she nodded.

Jean tutted again before reaching and pressing a button on his desk. 'Send in Lieutenant Degarmo,' he said briskly.

A moment later the door to the office opened and Cedric entered, his steps slow and deliberate as if it was painful to walk. It was not the Lieutenant Hugo had met earlier. He was worried, dead worried, that much was clear.

'Take a seat, Lieutenant,' Jean said gesturing to one of the chairs in front of his desk.

Cedric flopped onto the seat, anxiously looking towards Coco. 'What is this about?'

'It's about *énergique*, that is what it is about,' Jean snapped.

Cedric's jaw flexed, irritation evident in his eyes. 'This again,' he interrupted angrily. 'I told you already. I know nothing about the goings on there, and believe me, I wish I'd never agreed to go to the damn place in the first place.' He paused, lowering his eyes to avoid Jean Lenoir's intense stare. 'Full of the type of men I have no interest in being around or becoming,' he added.

Jean turned his head, suppressing a smile.

'We're not suggesting you've done anything wrong,' Coco interjected, 'but somebody did and we believe you may know who.'

Cedric's eyes widened in horror. 'What are you talking about? I know nothing, and I really, REALLY resent the insinuation otherwise.'

Hugo stepped away from the window where he had been standing. 'Lieutenant Degarmo, please don't think we're trying to implicate you in anything, but we need your help. You know as well as we all do that an investigation is often only as good as the witnesses who are involved. They give us insights we couldn't otherwise have, and more often than not, they see things which they pay little attention to but are often hugely important in helping us.'

Cedric nodded. 'Sure, I get that, what I don't get though is how you think I can help.'

Coco glared at him. 'Cut the crap and tell us what the hell you good-time guys got up to there.'

'Captain, I… I….' he stammered.

She waved her hand angrily. 'This isn't about speaking out of turn, Cedric, or protecting your so-called pals. This is about doing the right thing and telling the truth, because goddamnit, if you don't protect yourself and cover your own back then no-one else will. I don't care what they promised you, what they said, you're so far down on the ladder to these people you might as well be a woman, or,' she paused and smiled sweetly at Hugo, 'gay.'

Cedric frowned. 'Seriously, Captain, either you're having a brain fart or I am. I don't get what this is about, there are no shadowy men in the background doing bad things.' He paused. 'Not as far as I am aware of, at least,' he added quickly.

Hugo glanced at Coco. She shrugged her shoulders and gestured for him to continue. He cleared his throat and began telling Cedric about his name being used.

Cedric's nostrils flared, his jaw jutting forward. 'I've never been with a prostitute in my life, let alone some kid. They're lying. I'm telling you, they're lying and I can't fucking believe you're taking their word for it over mine.'

Hugo watched as Cedric fixed Coco with the coldest glare he thought he had ever seen. 'Non,' he spoke quickly, 'the point is, they only identified you by name, not by photograph.'

Cedric's forehead creased in confusion. 'You what?'

Coco explained. 'Some perv was using your name when he did what creeps do.'

Cedric shook his head. 'Who the hell would do that?'

Jean Lenoir sighed. 'That is the question and the reason for this meeting. I realise your instinct may be to keep quiet, not to name names, but I would ask you to reconsider that position. A positive identification or not, the mere implication of impropriety is often enough to derail a career, especially one which,' he paused, 'has yet to develop into anything.'

Cedric gulped. 'But as I keep saying, there is nothing to tell. I went to the damn club only because it was the thing to do, where everyone else was going.'

'And who first suggested going to *énergique*?' Jean asked.

Cedric stole a sideways glance at Coco before answering. 'Commander Stanic.'

Jean nodded. 'I see. And was that normal? I mean, where did the suggestion come from? Was it out of the blue, or did you get the impression the Commander had frequented the club before?'

Cedric did not answer immediately. 'He'd been there before. More than once I would imagine.'

'How so?' Coco interjected.

He shrugged. 'Well, he knew the lay of the land, and

they certainly knew him. We were shown straight in to the VIP lounge and given champagne and…' he trailed off, 'and made to feel very welcome,' he added in a whisper.

Coco turned her head towards Hugo. 'None of this means anything, you know.' She paused, fingers wrapping around her hair. 'Made to feel very welcome,' she repeated as if to herself trying to make sense of what the words meant.

Hugo nodded his agreement. 'True, but we can't ignore it. Not until we figure out who was using Cedric's name and why.'

Cedric sighed. 'But it could be anyone. I didn't exactly broadcast I was a cop, but they all knew. There was always a gang of us and we do sort of stand out.'

Jean Lenoir folded his fingers together pensively. 'As you recall, Lieutenant, was there ever anything unusual happening? Anything out of the ordinary?'

Cedric considered before shaking his head. 'I don't think so. Like I said, we just went there a couple of times to celebrate, blow off some steam. Listen, I'm not saying there weren't any girls around us. There were, but that's the deal in places like that. The girls do their thing and encourage you to buy the expensive drinks.'

'And these girls, what else did they do?' Coco asked.

He shrugged. 'Danced…' he trailed off.

'And that's all?' she pressed.

Cedric turned his head slowly, struggling to maintain eye contact with her. 'With me,' he added finally.

'Ah-ha,' Coco said. 'And Morty? I mean, the Commander.'

He sighed. 'Regarde, I don't know what you want from me. You want me to gossip, talk out of turn, ruin my career before it even really starts by being labelled a snitch? I've got nothing to hide and nothing to tell, so I'll talk. Sure, some guys went with the girls, why the hell not? As long as no one gets hurt, it's nobody else's business.' He paused, meeting her gaze. 'As I remember it, you taught me that particular little insight.'

Coco nodded slowly. 'I probably did, and I meant it. No one is asking you to be a gossip, Lieutenant, but rather to do your job. Two young people have died, maybe more for all we know, and as far as I can tell, someone is cleaning house. Like it or not, we, by we, I mean the police, are implicated in it somehow and we owe it to those dead kids to figure out what the hell is going on and who is involved. I get you don't want to ruffle feathers, but I could give two shits about it myself. I live to ruffle feathers and my shoulders, Captain Duchamp's shoulders are broad, and not to mention...' She stopped and gesticulated widely towards Jean Lenoir and his muscular frame, 'and of course, nobody has broader shoulders than our dear Minister of Justice over there.'

Jean Lenoir waved his hands dismissively, a slither of a smile appearing on his taut face.

Cedric sighed. 'Listen, after a few drinks some of the guys may... may take advantage of something that's on offer, but I didn't and I didn't pay attention to who was doing what with who, or putting whatever up their nose. It doesn't work like that. I don't work like that and if I did, I'm pretty sure I'd find myself out of a job.' He paused. 'Or worse. But I can assure you, if I did see or hear anything suspicious or illegal I would have done something about it, one way or another. I'm still a cop and I love my job and I wouldn't let anyone ruin what I've worked so hard for. I didn't crawl out of the gutter to end up back in it.'

'I believe you,' Coco blurted.

Hugo studied the young Lieutenant intently, unsure what he meant. His story troubled him, but he could not be sure why. Instinct told Hugo that Cedric had lied about something. But what, and was it important? The lie he told might be more about his personal life rather than his professional, and Hugo suspected whatever was causing it was ingrained and would be hard to discern.

Cedric turned his head slowly in Coco's direction, his eyes widening. 'You do?'

She nodded. 'Absolument. But we need your help. We've never been on the inside and we need to understand what goes on, what people get up to, and why someone would use your name.'

'Quoi?' Cedric hissed. 'What are you talking about?'

Hugo answered. 'The witnesses told us about a policeman, probably corrupt and working for or with Alexander Esnault. They gave us your name.' He raised his hand. 'You can thank your Captain for knowing you, for believing in you and to be sure enough to know you were not, could not be mixed up in this whole business.'

Cedric shook his head. 'But they knew my name. Man, I'm fucked, aren't I? Either way, there will be an investigation and my name will be tied to this forever…'

'Not necessarily,' Hugo interrupted.

'Hugo's right,' Coco agreed. 'Hugo sent your photograph, and they confirmed the man they know as Cedric Degarmo didn't have the same ugly mug as you.'

Cedric flashed her an unsure look. 'Are you sure?'

'Oui,' she replied. 'But putting this all to one side, we still need to understand what went on in that club and who would use your name.'

He gave an angry shrug of his shoulders. 'It could be fucking anyone. I didn't exactly hide who I was, or my name, why would I? I had nothing to hide.'

Hugo pursed his lips, pushing his glasses into his hair. 'It is all very odd. I can't quite figure out why anyone would use your name and for what purpose.'

'It's hard to look into the brain of a madman,' Coco snorted, 'and let's face it, they probably just used Cedric as cover because he's a cop, to get the kids to be afraid of them.'

Cedric turned his head, his eyes flicking between Hugo and the Minister. 'And you both believe me, as well?'

Jean Lenoir did not answer, his fingers rapping on a

folder on his desk.

'I believe, Coco,' Hugo answered after a moment, 'and that is enough for me…' he trailed off.

'That didn't sound very convincing, Hugo,' Coco interjected.

'Désolé,' he replied. He cleared his throat and moved across the room, facing Cedric. 'But I wouldn't be honest if I didn't tell you, Lieutenant, something is troubling me. I realise it's probably nothing but nevertheless I'm a policeman and before I fully give you my support, I can't have any doubts.'

'You have doubts?' Cedric asked, his voice rising sharply.

'Not so much doubts, but the need for clarification,' Hugo answered, his tone gentle.

'Clarification? About what?'

Hugo took in a sharp breath. 'Your childhood.'

'My childhood?' Cedric gasped as if it was the last thing he had imagined was on Hugo's mind.

Hugo nodded. 'I realise it's probably none of my, our, business but it would help if there was some clarification regarding your… your…'

'We need to know where the hell you were born, Cedric,' Coco interrupted, her voice exasperated.

'Where I was born?' Cedric repeated, smooth brow creasing into a frown. 'What the hell are you talking about? You know where I was born, Marseille.'

'And you lived with your grandmother, correct?'

Hugo posed.

Cedric's eyes widened, the wariness in them clear. 'Yeah, so what?'

Coco slammed her fist on her thigh, wincing as she did. 'Dammit, Cedric, level with us. We don't think you're involved, but Hugo,' she lowered her head, mouthing an apology in Hugo's direction, 'rather, we are just a little confused about your heritage. And you gotta know, you can't lie to us. Hugo's tech guy is already tapping away on his keyboard to verify this all. So bite the bullet and spill.'

'Spill?' he asked with bite.

She nodded. 'Oui. As Hugo said, it's probably nothing, and we've probably misunderstood, but...' She gave Hugo a helpless shrug.

'Did you grow up in a hostel run by Monseigneur Augustine Demaral?' Hugo asked.

Cedric closed his eyes and leaned forward, moving his head between his legs. Hugo and Coco exchanged a concerned look.

'How the fuck did you find out about that?' Cedric said finally.

'You did?' Coco gasped in surprise.

'It was just a hunch.' Hugo said.

'Well then, your hunches are crazy,' she replied, 'and I hate you for being so smart.'

Hugo smiled. 'I'm not really. From the beginning we've suspected Alexander Esnault is up to his ears in all of this, but we don't know how. But something struck me when we first interviewed him in his apartment. When he spoke to Lieutenant Degarmo, he didn't address him formally, rather he used his first name, although we had not told him Cedric's name.'

Coco frowned. 'I don't remember that, but even if it's true, they probably met at the club, right, Cedric?'

Cedric shrugged but did not answer.

Hugo continued. 'At the time I probably thought the same. It's only hindsight that causes me to question it. Alexander told us he spent time in an orphanage and when you told me Cedric did as well, I thought it might explain why he created a different backstory for himself.'

'I didn't "create a different fucking backstory"' Cedric hissed at Hugo. 'And I never fucking lied.'

'Remember where you are, Lieutenant,' Jean Lenoir warned, 'and choose your next words carefully if you have any desire to continue in your current career.'

Cedric stared at the Minister and then stood, moving to the window, his face pale and his eyes wide as he took in the Paris skyline. It was a dull day, black clouds sweeping across the sky threatening to throw rain onto the people below. 'I wish I was in the rain,' he muttered.

'What did you say?' Jean Lenoir asked.

Cedric turned around, inhaling. 'I didn't lie about my grandmother, or Marseilles,' he said, his voice hoarse, 'but I did also grow up in Paris,' he added with obvious reluctance. He sank back into the chair, burying his head in his hands. 'Damn, I don't want to talk about this.'

Coco moved over to him, rubbing his shoulder gently. 'And we don't want you to either,' she said softly, 'I know you think I'm the Queen of over-sharing but seriously, the less I know about people the happier I am.' She sighed. 'But we need to understand your involvement in all of this so we can move on and deal with the real assholes. Didn't I teach you that to be a good flic often means you have to put aside your feelings and just get on with the job, no matter how it makes you feel?'

He lifted his head slowly and met her eyes. 'You say a lot of stuff, Captain, most of it shit and most of it I ignore, even if you are right.'

Coco smiled. 'There you go, now listen to your wise old Captain and tell us what the hell we need to know. And I promise you, unless it has anything pertinent to do with the investigation then it will go no further than this room. You have my word and you know how good that is, non?'

Cedric nodded and exhaled again, pushing the air reluctantly out of his body. 'My parents were crackheads. My mother a whore and my father her pimp, selling her scrawny ass for whatever they could score. My dad used to joke that she pissed me out in a back alley,' he snorted, 'funny, huh? When the cops and social workers found me I was in a cupboard, sharing mouldy bread with the rats, covered in their shit and bites. I ended up in a hostel. A children's home run by the Catholic Church.'

'And Monseigneur Augustine Demaral?' Hugo

asked.

Cedric nodded once again, a vein in his neck flexing angrily. 'Yeah, the fucking priest,' he spat.

Hugo and Coco exchanged a worried look. 'Did he… did he…' Coco stammered.

'Non, he fucking didn't,' Cedric snapped with a sense of pride. 'I may have been a scrawny kid, but I was strong, growing up amongst drug dealers and pimps saw to that. The perverts weren't interested in the kids who would fight to their last breath. That wasn't the way they played their game. They liked to talk, mould you, make you dependent on them so that by the time they did fuck you, you'd think they were doing you a favour.'

'So, you witnessed sexual abuse in the home?' Coco asked.

'Yeah,' he replied, his voice as soft as a child's.

A silence as heavy as the dark clouds swept across the room, the darkness illuminating the many photographs on Jean Lenoir's wall. A shadow flickered across a photograph of the French President with the Pope. Hugo closed his eyes. 'And Alexander Esnault?' he asked.

Cedric frowned. 'You have to believe me, I didn't recognise him.'

'Didn't?' Hugo clarified. 'But you do now?'

'I don't know,' Cedric answered with enough honesty for Hugo to believe him. 'There were a lot of kids and I wasn't in the kind of mood to make friends. But…'

'But?'

'When I first met Esnault in the club, I mean I'd heard of him, who hasn't? When I saw him I thought I'd seen him before, that there was something familiar about him. I couldn't figure out what it was, so I guessed it was just because I'd seen his mug shot around the Commissariat and left it that.'

Hugo nodded. 'What was it about him, do you think?'

Cedric considered. 'I dunno, honestly I don't. There was something about his eyes, his hair,' he stopped scratching his head, 'Oh, man, I don't know. He reminds me of a hundred kids at the home. They all have the same look on their faces, the same hunger in the eyes. Don't look at me, but please look at me. Desperate for affection but terrified of what it might mean. It was common knowledge that for some kids, they could make a bit of money on the side.'

'Doing what?' Hugo asked.

Cedric shrugged. 'Sex, I guess. I heard one of them taking about some weird, kinky stuff, but I never really listened because I was determined it wasn't a path I was going down.' He stared at Coco. 'I can't tell you I knew Esnault before all of this, but I also can't tell you I didn't. And the fact is, I only ended up being there for six months or so. The social worker finally did her job and tracked down my grandmother. If you don't believe me, ask Commander Stanic.'

Coco's eyes widened in surprise. 'What does Morty

have to do with this?'

'That's how I thought you knew about my childhood,' Cedric replied, 'I thought he'd told you. He said he never would, that it was our secret. He used to tell me it was nothing to be ashamed of, but I was, and it was easy for him to say otherwise.'

'You knew the Commander from your time in the home?' Hugo asked.

Cedric nodded. 'Yeah, I don't want to sound gay,' he stole a look at Hugo, mouthing *désolé*, before continuing, 'but he was like some God to us kids. This big, burly dude who worked around the home, doing odd jobs, playing with us, just generally treating us like we were real people, not just kids to be used, or looked down on. And then suddenly I was off to Marseilles. The place was shit, but I was safer with her than I'd ever been and without Grand Mère and the Commander... well, the chances are I wouldn't be here today. The Commander kept in touch with me, like some foster brother or something. When he became a cop, I knew it was what I wanted to be too. To be strong. The way people looked at him, with respect, admiration. It was him who taught me I was as good as anyone else and I just had to believe in myself and I could do, be whatever I wanted. Grand Mère wasn't the nicest lady and I don't think she liked me because I reminded her of all her failures with her daughter - my mother. But in the end, she wanted to do right by me, and she did. She made sure I got through school, and she damn well paid for me to go through police training when I told her that's what I wanted to do. By the time I finished she was dead and there was nothing for me to hang around Marseilles for, so I called the Commander and he said he'd help and he did. He came through for me again.' He turned his head towards Coco. 'You know that's just the kind of man he is.'

Coco shrugged. 'Maybe. You should have told us about this, Cedric.'

'You have to believe me. If I thought there was anything I could have told you, anything I knew about all of this, I would have. I would have done my job,' he said desperately.

Coco smiled. 'I believe you.' She turned to Hugo. 'What do you think?'

Hugo tapped his chin, pursing lips in contemplation.

'Investigations such as these are frustrating because they're complicated and they often stretch back years, generations sometimes and we're playing catch up with a bunch of people who have no interest or desire to help us. It's also often in their best interest to lead us on a wild goose chase.'

'You think that's what this is?'

'Peut-être,' he replied. 'We know Alexander Esnault is a complicated, probably very dangerous man. There's nothing to say he didn't recognise Cedric and decided to use that knowledge to his advantage. Esnault indicated something was stolen from him. What could that be? And what would he do to retrieve it?'

'Or what would someone else do to retrieve it?' Coco countered.

'Then you're suggesting this is about blackmail?' Jean Lenoir asked.

'Blackmail or self-preservation,' Hugo replied. 'Whatever was stolen from Alexander Esnault has to be important, and maybe not just to him. It could have gotten Jack Boucher killed, or Marc Gassna, and it could be why the other children are in danger and why Alexander, and who knows else, is after them.'

'Do you think they have it?' Jean Lenoir asked.

'I believe so,' Hugo answered, 'but I don't think they'll give it to us, or that they even have it on them. They're scared and they're running but they're not stupid. I imagine it's somewhere safe until they figure out what to do with it.'

'Then we need to shake out of Esnault what the hell he lost,' Cedric said.

Hugo shook his head. 'He'll not tell us the truth and he will never tell us what he knows or what his involvement is, so we have to solve this another way.' Hugo tilted his head, the uncertainty clear on his face. He stood and walked to the window, his eyes flicking over the Paris skyline. In the distance he could see the Eiffel Tower and his thoughts immediately returned to Marc Gassna and the desperation he must have felt to resort to such a drastic action. 'There's something which makes little sense,' he said finally.

'No shit, Sherlock,' Jean Lenoir answered.

Hugo turned back, his face creasing into a smile as he and Coco laughed.

'What?' The Minister of Justice asked with a nonchalant shrug of his broad shoulders. 'You think I can't be funny occasionally?'

'Only when you look in the mirror,' Coco muttered.

'Pardon, Charlotte?' he retorted.

She did not answer, instead turning to Hugo. 'You know what's bothering me the most right now, the DNA Sonny found under Ana Boucher's fingernails.'

'That's been bothering me too,' Hugo answered, 'and something I can't seem to reconcile. Putting it to one side, it simply can't be a coincidence that the killer shares a male familial link to Marc Gassna. How does it fit? How did Marc Gassna's father, or brother, end up being implicated in the murders of his friend's parents?'

'Well, isn't that obvious?' Jean Lenoir interrupted. 'You already told me, Marc Gassna and the boy now called Jérémie Berger are brothers, or perhaps half-brothers. I suppose it's hard to truly know under the circumstances. He murdered the parents of his friend.'

Hugo met his gaze. 'Well, if you ignore the fact that scenario makes little sense, we know with more or less certainty Jérémie and his friends were outside of Paris at the time of the murder of Jack Boucher's parents.'

The Minister scoffed. '*Allegedly*,' he mouthed. 'As far

as we know they could be covering for one another, street kids do that sort of thing.'

'Minister Lenoir,' Coco said, pouting, 'they are children, and like adult *men* who should know better,' she cast her gaze between the Minister and Cedric, 'are entitled to the same benefit of the doubt.' She paused. 'While the CCTV footage could be open to interpretation, it's practically impossible for Jérémie to have been in two places at once.'

'Then...' Jean Lenoir trailed off. 'Then...'

Hugo smiled. 'You see our point. We're missing something, and we're missing something important.'

Cedric frowned. 'I don't get it. Who are Marc Gassna, and Jérémie Berger, but more importantly who the hell is this other man and what does he have to do with them?'

'He's their father,' Hugo said.

'You think?' Coco questioned.

'What else could it mean?' he answered. 'It's the only thing which makes sense. What makes little sense is how he was involved in their lives. I mean, did they know? I can't imagine from the conversations we've had with Jérémie, he even knew who his father was, or wanted to for that matter. Which means his father, and Marc's father, must have known about them after they escaped the cellar, and became involved with them somehow. But how, or when, I can't begin to imagine.'

'Why would this person, whoever the hell he is, want

to kill the Boucher's?' Cedric asked.

Hugo shrugged. 'Because this whole business is complicated, and sordid and I expect the person who "sired" the brothers had a vested interest in ensuring his involvement was never made public.'

Jean Lenoir leaned forward in his chair, alert. 'But what on earth could have spooked him and lead him to take such drastic action?'

Hugo shrugged again. 'There is the problem. As Jérémie told his story, it became clear he didn't know a lot about the people he and his mother and brother were involved with. And because Marc was younger, we can probably assume the same. They met these men in a very controlled environment - a dark and dingy room. There's no telling they would even recognise the men outside of that environment. He mentioned a scar on one of the men, but wasn't more specific. A scar can mean a lot of things, especially to a child. It could be a scratch, acne, other things which may or may not be permanent. Non, there is a very real possibility they never knew they had encountered the men from their past.'

'Yet they did,' Coco added. 'Or how else do you explain this whole mess?'

'The adult men involved are most certainly going to remember those boys, what they did to them, and the life they lived,' Hugo answered. 'And can you imagine the fear they must have lived with knowing the boys were free? I can only imagine they have been waiting, searching for them for a very long time.'

Coco gave him another doubtful look.

Nobody spoke for a while. The only sound was the ticking of the grandfather clock in the corner of the Minister's office and the dull, nondescript noise from the Parisian streets seeping through the almost-soundproof windows.

Cedric sighed. 'Where the hell do we begin?'

Hugo considered. 'First, we need to understand how and why Ana and Randolph Boucher became known to the male relative of Marc Gassna and Jérémie Berger. I believe the answer might just lie in how the apparently poor Boucher's could afford such high-end products.'

Cedric shrugged. 'There's nothing there, Hugo. I've checked their bank records, nothing unusual other than several large deposits which they seem to have made themselves and all the receipts we found in their apartment show the stuff they bought was paid for in cash. There is no paper trail to show where their windfall was coming from.'

'Another dead-end,' Jean Lenoir said wearily.

Hugo shook his head. 'It can't be. There has to be a reason they were silenced. They must have known something.'

'Or they were part of it,' Hugo replied.

Hugo met her gaze and nodded. 'And we're back again to the abuse suffered by the two brothers and their mother. Now, one thing strikes me. From what Jérémie told us, we can probably assume they were originally held somewhere in the children's home, probably a basement area. We need to try to understand what happened to the home, who was involved, and what happened after the fire.'

'After the fire?' Cedric questioned.

'Oui,' Hugo replied, 'we know Marc Gassna and Jack Boucher were arrested for assault on the Monseigneur and that they were most likely responsible for the arson which burnt down the children's home. The Monseigneur had the investigation closed. We don't know exactly why, but he did. Now what happened afterwards?'

'What do you mean?' Jean Lenoir asked.

'Well, we know it wasn't rebuilt, so what happened to the land?'

Cedric pulled out his cell phone, his fingers tapping at the screen. A few moments passed. 'The ground was levelled and sold to a developer who turned it into high-end yuppie apartments,' he said, 'wait, I know that address. We all do. We've been there.'

'We have?' Coco asked.

'Oui,' he replied, 'we've been to the penthouse apartment recently, actually.'

'Alexander Esnault lives there?' Hugo questioned. He frowned. 'Interesting. Who owns the building?'

Cedric checked. 'An enterprise called ForX, let me check who owns it.' He paused. 'Well, would you look at that? ForX is owned by one...'

'Alexander Esnault,' Hugo finished. 'Again, interesting enough but I'm not sure what, if anything, it tells us.'

'That he's a weirdo,' Coco said. 'Dieu knows what went on in the damn children's home and he could have been abused there himself, I can't imagine for a second I would want to make it my home if that sort of thing had happened to me there.'

Hugo frowned. Something was troubling him, and it took him a moment to work out what it was. He believed he understood Esnault's reasons. 'Perhaps he saw it as a way to make sure the home wasn't rebuilt and reopened, at least not in the same location. If Alexander was one of the children who was abused, he might have made it his mission once he was older and rich and powerful to make sure those involved could never hurt children again.'

Coco scoffed. 'Are we talking about the same Alexander Esnault?'

'I think so,' Hugo replied, 'and I believe he is the kind of man who would exact revenge against those who crossed him.'

'Then why is Monseigneur Demaral still alive?' Coco posed. 'I get Esnault is the sort of man who would lash out at anyone who pissed him off, as far as we've been told, the Monseigneur was the ringleader to whatever went on in the home. If it was me, he'd be the first on my to-do list.'

Hugo nodded his agreement. 'You're probably right,

then again, look how much trouble we're having finding the Monseigneur. We don't even know for sure whether or not he is in Rome. It's all very vague and nobody actually knows what happened or where he is. It stands to reason if we can't locate him, then neither can Esnault.'

'Damn clergy,' Jean Lenoir sniffed, 'they always think they're above the law. Well, not in my Republic, they're not.'

Coco flashed him a smile. 'Nice sentiment, Minister, but what do you think you can do about it? We all know the Catholic Church are untouchable. They're hiding Monseigneur Demaral and that's where he'll stay, hidden until this whole sordid mess blows over. Not even someone as powerful as you can touch them.'

Jean Lenoir glared at her. 'You believe me to be impotent to the Catholic Church, Charlotte?'

She shrugged, suppressing a further smile. 'I don't want to, Minister, but we all have to accept our limitations.'

He slammed his fists on the table. 'Well, we'll just have to see about that won't we, Charlotte? If my police tell me Monseigneur Demaral is a material witness in murder and child abuse, then he will make himself available to us, even if I have to fly to Rome and drag himself back by his frock myself.' He stabbed the buzzer on his desk. 'Get me the Vatican on the line, right now,' he hissed. 'Oui, THAT Vatican, and make sure they know WHO I am and that unless they want a diplomatic incident, then they had better think twice before giving me the run-around.' He turned his head back to Hugo and Coco. 'And when I'm done dealing with the errant clergy, you get off your asses and find me something concrete to pin on him, comprende? If I'm going out on a limb, I want to make sure we have something to back me up. Find me the link which brings this all together, or one way or another, we'll all be looking for a new job this time next week.' He waved his hand dismissively. 'See yourselves out.'

Hugo sipped the café, wincing as the cold, thick bitter liquid hit the back of his throat. He carefully placed the cup back onto the silver platter and noticed Coco had done the same. Fleur Gassna watched them, her hazel eyes tired and dull, focused but not really seeing, Hugo imagined. He was sure she was lost under a curtain of grief and he was in no doubt, wherever Marc Gassna had come from, she had loved him. Or was he imagining it? Was it something other than love evident in her demeanour? Guilt, perhaps? He chastised himself, patently aware his suspicious nature, while having its place, was inappropriate occasionally. Especially when a person was grieving for a life lost in tragic circumstances.

'Why did you want to see us again?' Corentin Gassna asked, the tone of voice showing he was wary. 'Haven't we been through enough?'

'You certainly have,' Coco replied, 'and please understand I don't intend to further distress you, truly, but we are in the middle of an investigation and…'

'Are you saying Marc didn't kill himself?' Fleur interrupted, her voice high and shrill with an unmistakable slur.

Hugo leaned forward, noticing the crystal glass in front of her, clear liquid swirling around ice-cubes. 'At this stage we're exploring several avenues in our investigation,' he said.

'Several avenues? What does that mean?' Corentin

snapped.

Hugo exhaled, struggling to hold Corentin's gaze. 'We believe there may be a link to the murder of another young man.'

'The boy who washed up from the Seine?' Fleur asked.

Coco nodded. 'Oui. We now know Marc knew the other young man. His name was Jack Boucher, and he died under horrible circumstances a week or so before Marc.'

'Wait,' Corentin interrupted, 'are you suggesting Marc was somehow involved in this other boy's death, and that he killed himself because of guilt?'

Hugo did not answer immediately. 'All we know at the moment for sure is they were friends.'

'Lovers?' Fleur asked breathlessly.

'We don't know,' Hugo replied honestly, 'but certainly friends.'

'Then that's why he did it,' Fleur said, thin lips twitching, 'he loved this boy, in whatever way it mattered to him, and losing him was too much.' She closed her eyes, the lids vibrating gently.

Hugo looked at Coco, and she shrugged. He continued. 'Does the name Jack Boucher perhaps mean anything to either of you?'

Fleur turned her head slowly in her husband's direction but turned it back as quickly. She did not answer but then muttered something indecipherable under her breath.

'Pardon?' Hugo said, leaning forward again.

'She said nothing,' Corentin said.

'I said something,' Fleur breathed, 'not that it ever matters. Muteness runs in this family.'

Coco cleared her throat. 'Madame Gassna. Did you know Jack Boucher?'

She shook her head. 'Not really. We met the Boucher's many years ago, at Church.'

'Church?' Hugo asked in surprise.

She nodded. 'Oh, it must have been five or six years ago. It became apparent that Marc had made a friend. It was a surprise, he'd been quite the loner up until that point, you see, but...' she looked to her husband, 'we decided he wasn't the sort of friend who would be suitable for our son.'

'How come? Too poor?' Coco bit her lip as if realising she had overstepped.

'It had nothing to do with money,' Corentin said huffily. 'Rather, breeding.'

She raised an eyebrow. 'Breeding? But yet, Marc...' she trailed off.

Corentin wafted his hand. 'Breeding is not always about the way in which one is created, Captain Brunhild, rather than the life we are born into, the opportunities we are given, the people we are presented to?'

'Presented to?' Hugo questioned, recalling his father's voice once again. *Julien does not come from a good family, certainly not one which should have any connection to the Duchamp name.*

Corentin's lips twisted into a sly smile. 'I realise you probably consider me to be a snob and perhaps I am, but with your breeding I can't imagine it comes as a surprise to you.'

Hugo looked at him. What surprised him the most was how Corentin Gassna knew anything about him. What connection could there be between Gassna and Hugo's father? Paris was small, but it was not *that* small. He cleared his throat. 'So, you only met Jack and his parents once?' It only took a moment, but Hugo caught the uncertainty in Corentin Gassna's face. Hugo recognised it instantly as a man deciding whether or not to lie. Hugo suspected were it not for Fleur, Corentin would almost certainly continue to lie.

'We had them for dinner, once or twice,' Fleur said. 'And while I disagree often with my husband, it has to be said some people, through no fault of their own, don't mix. Like oil and water. The Boucher's were,' she paused, a pale tongue darting across even paler lips, 'delightful, I'm sure, but inexperienced.'

'Inexperienced?' Coco asked sharply.

Fleur lowered her head. 'It became apparent they were unaccustomed to,' she shrugged her Chanel-covered shoulders, 'a different way of living.'

Hugo watched her carefully, trying not to judge. She had lost her son, and it had always seemed to him that in a time of grief every person reacted differently, often retreating into their own way of coping, warming their coldness in the reflection of something, anything, which comforted them.

'And it was then we had to forbid Marc to see Jack any longer.'

'Forbid?' Coco asked. 'Why?'

'It was around this time, when Marc was fourteen or so he began to show... he became... different,' Fleur said.

'Fleur,' Corentin said, a warning clear in his voice.

Fleur raised her shoulders dismissively. 'It began with dreams, non, not dreams, nightmares, non, not even that. Terrors. Night terrors which lasted from dusk until dawn. They became so bad he was reluctant to even go to bed because he knew what was coming.'

'Did he tell you what happened in these nightmares?' Coco asked.

She shook her head. 'He wouldn't talk about them. Sometimes I'd hear words, but only when he was asleep so they made no sense, and he wouldn't tell me what they meant. All I know is that whatever happened in his dreams was more than he could bear.'

'Then what did you do?' Hugo asked.

Fleur shot a sideways look at her husband. 'We,' she said, saying the word as if it had nothing to do with anyone except her husband, 'decided he needed professional help.'

Coco raised an eyebrow. 'A psychiatrist?'

'Fleur,' Corentin spoke.

This time she looked at him, hazel eyes flashing a warning. 'That's what a person does when their children becomes problematic, isn't it? They farm them off to the nearest shrink to put a label on it and shove medicine in them.'

Hugo took in a sharp intake of breath. His own nightmare flashing before his eyes, words so clear it was as if they were being spoken in the room. *You will not embarrass this family with your deviancy. One way or another, you will fulfil your potential.*

'So, Marc went into therapy?' Coco posed. 'Had this anything to do with Monseigneur Augustine Demaral?'

Corentin cleared his throat, but before he could answer, his wife spoke. 'It was his suggestion, oui.'

'And who did he suggest Marc speak with, was it Dr. Victor Caron?' Hugo asked. Corentin's eyes widened with such abject horror and surprise he knew instantly he touched a nerve.

Fleur turned her head. 'He's an old friend. I suppose we shouldn't have gone to a friend, but Corentin... we believed his discretion was called for. My husband is an important man, and important men have enemies looking for weaknesses.'

Hugo nodded. Although the words were coming out of Fleur Gassna's mouth, he felt sure they were not her own. However, at that moment, what concerned him the most was, if it was true, Dr. Victor Caron had lied and he had known all the time who Marc Gassna really was.

'And how did the therapy go?' Coco asked.

'Well, or so we thought,' Fleur replied. 'Victor said Marc was making real progress in dealing with the awful thing which had happened to him. We disagreed with his methods at first, but it seemed to help, with the nightmares at least.'

'His methods?' Hugo questioned.

'Hypnosis mainly,' Fleur continued. 'Victor thought it was necessary if we were truly to make the progress Marc needed to confront his past.'

'This has nothing to do with what happened,' Corentin grumbled.

'Perhaps not,' Hugo countered, 'but if Marc remembered what happened to him before he was adopted then chances are he may have recognised one of the men who abused him.'

'He remembered no such thing,' Corentin snapped, 'the therapy proved futile, despite what my wife said. Marc said what he had to say to get out of going. I listened to the tapes and can assure you he remembered little of value.'

'You listened to the tapes?' Fleur Gassna gasped, gawping at her husband. 'You never told me.'

He shrugged. 'There was nothing to tell. Victor and I agreed. Marc remembered nothing of substantive value.'

'Then what did he say? The therapy must have produced some results.' Coco said.

Corentin shook his head. 'You met Marc when he was a child, you saw how traumatised he was. How young he was. He told Victor about a room, watching television, some nonsense about "Tom and Jerry" truly nothing which could help.'

'But he was better afterwards,' Fleur said desperately, uncertainty creeping into her voice.

'Non, he just got older, and better at lying,' Corentin sighed. 'He learnt the trick of telling people what they wanted to hear, and we let him because it made us feel better.'

Fleur Gassna opened her mouth to answer him, but no words appeared. She dropped her head and began weeping. Hugo felt the urge to go to her and embrace her, but he knew he could not.

'He said nothing else, nothing about a brother?' Coco asked.

'A brother?' Fleur gasped. 'Marc had a brother?'

Coco nodded. 'We have reason to believe so.'

'Jack Boucher?'

'Non,' Coco answered. 'As we said, as far as we know, Jack was just a friend as we understand it. Not that it matters, of course. The tapes, Monsieur Gassna, do you have them?'

He shook his head quickly. 'Non, and as you probably know, I shouldn't have listened to them in the first place. Victor only did it upon my insistence and because of our long friendship. I will not tolerate him getting into trouble over this because of me. So don't even think of asking him, or I'll deny this conversation ever happened. Why can't you just leave us to grieve for our son in peace?'

'Monsieur Gassna, need I remind you this a police investigation,' Coco spoke softly, 'and it is up to us to determine what is and isn't useful for the investigation. But I assure you, I have no interest in causing any trouble for you or your friends, rather it is to catch and punish whoever is responsible for what happened to these young men. I'm sorry if you think we're being invasive, I can barely imagine how difficult it must be for you, but it's my job to find out what happened, and to prevent it from happening again. We have every reason to believe your son's friends are in great danger, most likely by those who wished to harm Marc and Jack, so merci, I beg you both for any help you can give us to get these bastards. Anything, no matter if you believe it to be small or inconsequential it could help us.'

'His friends?' Fleur Gassna asked breathlessly. 'The red-haired girl?'

Hugo nodded. 'And two others - two young men, about the same age as Marc and,' he looked to Coco. She nodded for him to continue, 'we believe one of them is Marc's brother.'

'His brother?' Fleur cried.

'Oui,' Hugo replied. 'His name is Jérémie, and he told us what he knew about their life. He's very scared and not only is he in mourning for his brother, he's terrified. He remembers the life they lived.'

'Rubbish,' Corentin snorted. 'How could he possibly know anything? Marc has been with us since he was a child.'

'I want to meet him,' Fleur interjected. 'I want to meet Marc's brother. I want to look him in the eye, and I'll know.'

'We'll ask him,' Coco replied, 'when this is all over, of course. In the meantime, we believe he's telling the truth, and we also have reason to believe there is another relative involved.'

'What do you mean, *another relative?*' Corentin snipped.

Hugo studied his face. It was smooth and impassive and devoid of emotion, yet there was something there. Something buried beneath the cosmetic surgery. 'Did Marc ever discuss his family?'

'We were his family, his *only* family,' Corentin replied.

'That's not true,' Fleur interrupted. 'Haven't you been listening to the Captain?' She turned her head slowly back towards Hugo. 'What are you telling us, Captain? Is it something to do with how, why, Marc died?'

Hugo exhaled because he did not know how to answer the question. 'The truthful answer is we don't know, but what we do know is that there is most certainly a relative of Marc's involved. Can you think of anything, anything which could help us?'

Neither of the Gassna's answered for what seemed to Hugo to be the longest time. The ticking from the antique clock on the wall appeared to grow louder and angrier with each click, and it was all he could do to stop himself from jumping up and pulling it from the wall. He closed his eyes for a few seconds, aware of the darkness seeping into him. He was not even sure why; he had dealt with murder cases before, some worse, some not, but the result was always the same. He always felt it in the depths of his soul - the pain, the loss, the anger and frustration. But Paris had gotten under his skin and he was finding it difficult to breathe. He needed to escape. But not yet. Not until his job was done.

Fleur Gassna cleared her throat. 'I overheard him talking once,' she said, 'on his cell phone.' Her cheeks flushed. 'I didn't mean to pry, truly I didn't. It's just he had become so sullen, so secretive and so angry. It was different than it usually was. I had gotten used to him being sullen and had just put it down to the melancholy which followed him. He hadn't spoken to us properly in weeks, just grunts and shrugs, you know, the attitude of teenagers you hear everyone talking about. But then one day I was walking past his room and he was laughing, really laughing, not just snarky or cold like I had gotten used to. He was talking to someone, really talking to them.

Believe me, I'm not proud of myself, but I stopped and listened, standing in the hallway like some jealous woman listening to her husband cheating, but I just couldn't help myself, to hear him like that warmed my heart.'

'And what did you hear?' Coco asked.

'Not a great deal,' she replied, 'it was obvious he was making plans with whoever was on the other end of the line and then he said something which made my blood run cold.' She shuddered. 'It was just the way he said it, but he said "the man was back."'

Hugo leaned forward in his chair and repeated what she had said. 'What were his exact words?'

She stroked her chair, eyes drifting towards the window. 'Just that, I think. I couldn't really hear everything, but it sounded like he was saying the man was back and that if he found them, then he'd take him back and there was nothing anyone could do about it. I didn't understand what he meant at the time, but now... well, after what you've said, perhaps he meant he'd seen his real father, and he was worried he would take him back.'

'I am... *was* his real father,' Corentin hissed, 'and he was adopted, legally adopted by us. Nobody could have taken him away from us.'

Fleur spun her head around quickly. 'They wouldn't need to, he didn't belong to us. He hadn't for a long time.' She stood, obviously unsteady on her feet. 'If you'll excuse me, I need to lie down. This is all too much.' Without looking back, she ran from the room.

Corentin stood up, his uncertainty obvious as he tried to decide what to do. He tutted. 'Show yourselves out.'

Hugo watched him leave, the ticking of the clock sounding louder again. He turned to Coco. 'What do you think?'

She stood, drifting across the room. 'I think Corentin Gassna wouldn't know the truth if it came and slapped him in the face.'

Hugo raised an eyebrow. He was uncertain he would go that far. 'I agree he appears to be a complicated man,' he conceded, 'and he probably is hiding something. Just like Victor Caron.'

Coco nodded. 'Yeah, that lying snake. You were there, you heard him. He denied having anything to do with Marc, and he made it sound as if he could barely pick Corentin Gassna out of a line-up.'

'And who was Marc talking about? Who did he recognise?' Hugo added. 'I'm afraid we only have more questions now.'

Coco turned her head, tapping her chin with a finger. She reached into her oversized bag and fished out two evidence bags. She walked to the table and with a quick look around bagged the two glasses Fleur and Corentin Gassna had been using.

'What are you doing?' Hugo asked.

'I can't imagine they'd volunteer their DNA if I asked, so I'm doing the next best thing. I'll get Sonny to compare Marc's DNA with what he can extract from these glasses.'

Hugo frowned. 'What are you expecting him to find?'

She shrugged. 'I dunno. Probably nothing, but it can't harm to find out, can it?'

'Well, if Sonny finds anything we can't use it.'

She smiled. 'But we'll know we're on to something, and then we can get the DNA legally. I don't trust Corentin Gassna and in my life, I like to know as much as I can about the people who bug me. Call me a cynic, but that's the way it is. Come on, before they come back and realise the glasses are missing, hopefully they'll just think the maid cleared them.'

Hugo frowned, pushing his glasses into his mop of blond hair. He turned the piece of paper over and narrowed his eyes and instinctively reached for his glasses. He frowned again. 'Even with the glasses it makes no sense.'

'What's up, H?' Coco asked, leaning across him.

Hugo resisted the urge to move away, despite the fact she had moved so close he could smell her scent. He knew she meant no malice and that he probably should be pleased she felt so comfortable around him. The truth was, he felt comfortable around her and for some reason he felt as if he had made a friend in the slightly off-centre blue-haired detective. 'The Boucher money trail just makes little sense.'

'In what way?' she asked.

He spread the bank statements in front of him and pointed to a series of transactions he had highlightened. 'See here, here, here and here. Four transactions. Ten thousand euros paid each time into Randolph and Ana Boucher's joint bank account directly from the account of a man called Arto Marvellie.'

'And?'

'Well, as far as I can tell, Arto Marvellie doesn't exist.'

It was Coco's turn to frown. 'What do you mean, Arto Marvellie doesn't exist? Are you telling me ghosts are paying money into people's accounts? If so, please tell

Monsieur Phantom I'm in desperate need and will happily accept his otherworldly contribution to my "buy Coco some Chanel fund,"' she chuckled.

Hugo handed her a sheet of paper. 'This is the information Cedric obtained from the bank.'

Coco squinted. 'Where the hell did I put my glasses?' She looked at Hugo's head. 'I'll borrow yours if you don't mind.' She pulled Hugo's glasses off and put them on. 'What the hell does this mean, *account ID not known*. How can the account ID be not known? It has to be known, or else,' she scratched her head, 'it has to be known. You can't have a bank account without an ID, hell, if you could I'd open one in my porn name, Sadie Rue De Flangermuller and run up as much debt as I could. Are you telling me the bank have no idea who this fella is? They have to, I mean the ten grand has to come from somewhere?'

Hugo shrugged. 'I was involved in a bank fraud case once and you'd be amazed at the lengths some people go to move money around and leave no trace. And I can tell you, minds far greater than mine, people who know about this sort of thing will tell you the same. If somebody wants to remain anonymous and they know how to do it, it can often be difficult to unravel.'

She gave him a doubtful look. 'I get international money laundering and all that sort of business, but you can't be suggesting the Boucher's are somehow mixed up in that kind of craziness.'

He shrugged again. 'Well, they're certainly mixed up in something, something complicated and I suspect very dangerous. Dangerous enough for them to have both been considered too dangerous to be left alive.'

Coco sighed. 'I still don't get it. This all sounds like some bad television movie. As much as I've been lambasting everyone for suggesting those poor kids were less important than they were, this whole scenario seems to be spiralling out of control. Truly, can you explain to me how you think this all plays out? I get rich men are scared of their precious ivory towers collapsing, but do you really think they would engage in this kind of conspiracy just to protect themselves from public shame? We all know how fickle people are. What's front page news today is forgotten tomorrow.'

Hugo did not answer, instead tapping his chin as he considered. 'Do you remember what Alexander Esnault said, the reason he went after Jérémie, Axel, and Delphine?'

Coco considered. 'Yeah, something about they took something which belonged to him, or was it that he just believed *they* belonged to him.'

'But what if it was something else, something they physically took, something someone might...' Hugo continued, 'kill for?'

Coco gave him another doubtful look. 'What could be so important?'

'Photographs, video clips. They may have been

gathering evidence to protect themselves or Alexander could have been getting them to film their interactions with clients so he could use it against them.'

'Hmm,' Coco said with interest before scratching her head. 'blackmail and intrigue. But what on earth could the Boucher's have to do with it? Or is it just a coincidence?'

'If blackmail is the name of the game,' Hugo replied, 'then we might extrapolate that young Jack Boucher was involved somehow and enlisted his parents' help.'

'Ah-ha,' Coco murmured. 'You know that makes sense,' she pursed her lips, 'then jeune Monsieur Jack blackmailed the wrong person, and they killed him for it. What about Marc Gassna? How does he fit into it?'

Hugo shrugged. 'We may never know, I mean, the consensus is he committed suicide. No doubt brought on by Jack's murder. He may have witnessed it, or felt he could have prevented it, or he may even have been involved in the blackmail and felt responsible for what happened to his friend. We have to accept the truth is buried, but we can do our best to prevent anyone else from getting hurt. But until we find whatever was stolen from Alexander Esnault, then I don't think those kids will be safe.'

'You believe they have it?'

He nodded. 'I do. We didn't find it on either Marc or Jacks's body, so we can reasonably assume one of the others have it. And remember Delphine was on the Eiffel

Tower at the time Marc died. He could have given her the information without her realising why and what he was about to do. Certainly Esnault believes it's possible Delphine or her friends now have it, which would explain why he took the risk in going after them.'

'Then they really are in great danger,' Coco replied, 'Hugo, I don't need to tell you this, but we need them to be in police custody. Hell, even a cell downstairs has to be safer than being unprotected out there.'

Hugo shook his head. 'I promised them they'd be safe and to get them to trust me, there would be no official police involvement.' He raised his hands. 'I don't like it either, really I don't, trust me on that. It goes against all of my professional instincts, but these kids are running for their lives, and they already believe someone in the police is involved, whether or not it be Cedric.'

Coco grimaced. 'And you're sure about the safe house?'

'As sure as I can be,' he replied, 'as long as they don't tell anyone where they are, there are only two other people who know where they are, and I trust Etienne and I trust myself.'

'But not me?'

Hugo met her gaze. 'I do trust you, but I'm not going to tell you for one reason and one reason only. I don't want you to have to choose between keeping this secret and your job should it come to it. If it's discovered we know where they are, I want you to be able to legitimately hold your hands up and deny you know where they are.'

'And what about you? You're taking a big risk.'

He shrugged. 'I'll just say Jean Lenoir told me to keep my mouth shut. He won't like it, but he'll go along with it because he owes me.'

Coco sighed. 'D'accord. What next, then?'

Hugo stood. 'While we wait for the DNA results, how about we go and see Dr. Victor Caron again and ask him just why he withheld so much information?'

Coco sniggered. 'And you think he'll be forthcoming?'

'I doubt it, but we know for certain he knows a lot more than he's letting on,' Hugo smiled, 'and between us I'm sure we can convince him to share with us what he knows.'

Coco nodded. 'And if convincing him doesn't work, we can always try beating it out of him.'

Hugo raised an eyebrow. 'Coco…'

She smiled and waved her hand. 'Only joking,' she laughed. 'Kinda…'

Dr. Victor Caron squirmed in his chair. Squirmed in a way Hugo could only assume meant he knew he was in trouble. Hugo stole a look at Coco and was momentarily irritated by the smile on her face. He did not want to play it this way. He wanted Caron to trust them, to talk to them and for them to make him realise his only option was to trust them. Hugo did not want Caron to get his back up.

Coco, seemingly buoyed by Hugo's reaction, pulled her face into a serious stance. 'We're here to help you, Dr. Caron, not to cause trouble,' she spoke softly.

Caron's pencil thin eyebrow raised. 'That's not how it sounded to me, Captain Brunhild. I believe your exact words were, and do correct me if I'm wrong, *hey listen doc. You either spill the beans or I'll drag your scrawny ass and throw it in the drunk cell until you squeal like a pig.*'

Coco shrugged. 'Well, if you say it like that, I suppose it does sound bad…'

Hugo cleared his throat. 'Dr. Caron, désolé but the situation is very serious, and it has become apparent to us you haven't been exactly truthful in your statements to us.'

Caron flashed Hugo an anxious look. 'I don't know what you're talking about,' he said, not entirely convincingly.

'I think you do,' Hugo responded. 'And time is not on our side, nor yours.'

'What is that supposed to mean?' Caron snapped.

'It means if any other kids die I will make sure you

483

pay for it. And if that means you taking the rap for someone else then I'm okay with that. As far as I'm concerned if you keep your thin lipped mouth shut when you could have helped stop this whole sordid business then you might as well have killed them yourselves,' Coco shot.

Caron looked to Hugo.

'Don't look to Captain Duchamp,' Coco hissed. 'We're on the same page here, right, Hugo?'

Hugo slowly nodded. Coco smiled. 'Now talk, Victor or you have no idea the kind of hell I'll throw you into.'

Caron sucked in air as if his life depended on it. 'And you have no idea what we're dealing with here,' he said finally. '*Who* we're dealing with.'

Hugo leaned forward. 'Let us worry about that, Dr. Caron.' He smiled in Coco's direction. 'And the only person I'm scared of in this town is sitting right over there.'

Coco flashed a mock-offended look. 'Moi? What are you talking about? I'm a pussycat.'

Hugo continued. 'Until you tell us what you know, what you did, Dr. Caron then we can't help you. And we won't stop looking and asking questions until we do, comprende?'

'What he said, but worse,' Coco added, pointing at the rows of files lining Caron's office walls, 'and you don't want me rooting through your files, Vic, or dropping them around the Commissariat for all to see, capiche?'

'That sounds like a threat, Captain Brunhild.'

Coco smiled. 'Because it is. Now spill the beans, doc. My need for gin is growing stronger by the minute and so is my irritation. If you think I'm a bitch now, you should see me when I'm pissed off and dry.'

'You really are uncouth, Captain Brunhild,' Caron grumbled.

She shrugged. 'Hell, as far as I'm concerned, that's a compliment because if I was a man you'd be slapping me on the back.' She narrowed her eyes angrily. 'Now, talk dammit.'

'There is nothing to tell you,' Caron sniffed, 'certainly nothing which is not confidential or relevant to any so-called investigation you may be carrying out.'

Coco stood up and slammed her fists onto his desk, causing a pile of papers and dust to fly into the air. 'I've had about as much as I can take and being a mother, I take kiddy-fiddling very seriously. So unless you want me to scream from the top of my lungs, you'd best think carefully about whether you're going to allow any more bullshit to come out of your mouth, you get me?'

The doctor raised his head slowly, tired, watery eyes staring unsurely at her as if trying to assess how serious she was. He exhaled. 'I didn't hurt those children.'

'What, now or never?' Coco interrupted.

He did not respond. 'I may have misled you about my involvement with Marc Gassna,' he looked to Hugo, 'but merci, understand it was only because of my utmost respect for Fleur and Corentin. They are good people and they don't deserve what has happened to them.'

Hugo said. 'Tell us about Marc.'

Caron leaned back in his chair, spreading his hands behind his head. He closed his eyes for a few moments, his lips twitching in contemplation. '*L'enfant perdu* was a beautiful boy. Bright and alert, as if the darkness which had impregnated his early life had barely touched him. Incredible really, a testament to his resilience. He would not speak, but he allowed those around him to care for him.'

'So how the fuck did it go so wrong?' Coco snapped.

Caron sighed. 'It was inevitable really. Poke a hornet's nest enough times and you will upset the inhabitants.'

'And that's what you did, poked him a couple of times?' Coco interrupted.

'Captain, s'il te plaît,' Hugo scolded. 'Merci, continue Dr. Caron.'

'Corentin informed me there were certain behavioural issues being exhibited by Marc. These included but were not limited to night terrors, violent outbursts, and violent mood swings.'

'Not limited to?' Hugo questioned.

Caron nodded. 'Oui. There were also reports of inappropriate behaviour with some classmates in his école.'

'Inappropriate?'

Caron nodded again. 'Touching in ways a child of his age should not know about. He apparently asked a teacher if he would like for Marc to,' Caron coughed, before adding in hushed tones, 'please him. Corentin called me, distraught, embarrassed, frustrated. He didn't know what to do, and he did not want to exasperate the situation by bringing in outsiders. He knew I'd had some success with the child in the early days and asked me if I would speak with him again, privately and without making it public in any way.' He paused. 'It may have been unorthodox, but there was nothing illegal about what we did. We simply didn't want to put the child through any more legal or public notoriety. I thought we might begin some intensive therapy, alas…' he trailed off.

'Alas?' Hugo asked. 'You mean it didn't work?'

'We never really had time to explore Marc's psychosis,' Caron replied. 'He was combative, sensitive, and unwilling to engage. I had thought it would be prudent to introduce a medication regime to work in conjunction with the therapy, but it wasn't meant to be. At first the therapy seemed to be going well. I would even go so far as to say Marc was engaging with me, being an active participant in his recovery, but I realised he was actually only mirroring me.'

'Mirroring?' Coco asked with a puzzled frown.

'Oui,' Caron replied. 'I became aware he was acutely aware of me in a way a person of his age should not. As I had been watching him, he had been watching me. He was good at it, because I believe he had the measure of me and before long he knew what it was I wanted to hear, what I wanted him to say. You might say he was a master manipulator.'

'Or just a child who'd been fucked over most of his life by adults,' Coco interrupted, her voice tinged with sadness, 'any kid in those kinds of circumstances learns quickly how to please the adult in the room.'

'I can't say I disagree with you,' Caron said with obvious reluctance, 'and I realised far too late or perhaps I could have stopped him. But in any event he soon got bored with talking, or not talking, or whatever it was he thought he was doing with me. I never figured that out.'

Hugo raised an eyebrow. 'What do you mean?'

Caron shrugged. 'At first I didn't understand it, in fact, I didn't really understand it at all, not until later and even then...' he trailed off. 'But in hindsight I believe Marc was watching me as if he was trying to glean information from me.'

'Information?' Coco asked with interest.

He nodded. 'It was subtle but I now believe he was asking questions of me, just as I was of him.'

'What kind of questions?' Hugo asked.

'I can't say for certain, I wasn't really paying attention.'

Hugo exchanged a look with Coco, telling each other they did not entirely believe what Caron had just said. Coco moved a shoulder, indicating Hugo should continue. 'Why do you think he was trying to get information from you?'

'I have no idea. I can't think of a single reason.'

Hugo continued. He tapped his chin. 'Then perhaps you can tell us the kind of questions he asked you.'

Caron's eyes widened, flashing with obvious concern. 'What do you mean? As I said, I don't recall our conversations and even if I did, it would be highly inappropriate of me to share them with you.'

'Try,' Coco snapped. 'Or you'll see how uncouth I can become.'

Caron tutted. 'As I keep saying, his questions were vague but in hindsight he was asking me about his parents, sounding me out, you might say.'

'His parents?' Hugo asked. 'Corentin and Fleur?'

Caron inhaled, holding his breath. 'His mother, mainly.'

'Fleur?'

Caron lowered his head.

'Fleur Gassna?' Hugo repeated.

'Non, his real mother,' Caron said finally.

'Say what now?' Coco spluttered.

Caron exhaled, a spit bubble resting on his lips as he hugged his shoulders closer to his body as if he was attempting to cocoon himself. 'I don't know how, but somehow Marc knew his mother was still alive.'

Hugo frowned. 'How could he know such a thing?' He narrowed his eyes. 'How could YOU know such a thing?'

'And more importantly, how the fuck didn't the police know?' Coco snapped.

Caron tapped thin fingers on the desk. He did not speak, but a thin rasp rattled around his throat. 'There was little point,' he said finally.

'Little point?' Coco spluttered.

Hugo cleared his throat. 'Please explain, Dr. Caron,' he whispered.

'Damn you both, nothing good will come from this,' Caron mumbled.

Hugo shook his head. 'Let us be the judge of that, Dr. Caron. You owe it, not just to us, but to Marc Gassna, and all the other children who have suffered. This is no longer the time for you to keep silent, to decide what the authorities do or do not need to know.' He stole a look at Coco. 'Talk to us before this gets out of hand, and we can no longer help you. The Minister of Justice, as I'm sure you know, is not the kind of man who is patient or subservient. And as far as I've seen, he isn't frightened of anyone. If you want us to help you, you need to talk to us and you need to do it now, today, before any of this gets crazier than it needs to. Tell us what you know, finally.'

Caron nodded. 'When Marc first came to the hospital something struck me, something which had happened some time earlier. A woman under my care, a desperately ill woman in the midst of a deep psychosis kept screaming the words, mes enfants, over and over. Her rage growing all the time until it was obvious she was a danger not only to herself, but for the team working with her.' He took a sip of water. 'She was brought to the Psych ward after being found on the street with, amongst other injuries a particularly nasty subdural haematoma.'

'Found on the street? Whereabouts?' Coco asked. 'I don't recall hearing anything about this, about a possible connection, and we looked extensively for parents.'

The doctor shrugged. 'I don't know about that, I suppose no one put the two together. Why would they? People are found on the streets of Paris all the time, and I would imagine there was no reason to connect the two.'

Coco gave him a doubtful look. 'But I checked all the missing reports personally. I'm sure I did and I don't recall anything remotely close to being relevant, and believe me, a woman turning up around the same time, hurt and asking about her children.' She stared at Hugo. 'What the fuck is going on here, H?'

Caron continued. 'I can't speak as to why there may or may not have been an official report, but I can tell you they found the woman unresponsive, full of drugs, and badly hurt. I imagine it was likely assumed she had overdosed on drugs and had fallen. She did not regain consciousness for some time, and when she did the physicians in charge felt it necessary to medicate her. When she came to us, she was in full psychosis and we treated her accordingly.'

'You said she had likely taken a drug overdose?' Hugo questioned.

'Oui, heroin I believe,' Caron replied. 'She was an addict and evidently had been for some time.'

Hugo frowned and scratched his head.

'What's up, H?' Coco asked.

'Well, according to Jérémie's story, if it was his mother there was no mention of drugs.'

'Jérémie and Marc were kids. They can't have really known what was going on, especially when she left them to go into the other room with the men,' Coco replied. 'You told me they ran, leaving their mother behind them. This woman can't be their mother for the simple reason whoever was in the basement probably never made it out alive. How could she? Whoever was keeping them down there wasn't likely to let her go free.' She shook her head. 'Non, this other woman had nothing to do with Jérémie and his brother, surely.'

'I'm afraid that's not true,' Caron said.

Hugo turned his head sharply. Whatever he was expecting from Caron, it was not that. 'What do you mean? How did you connect the two?'

Caron took another sip of water. 'During our sessions Marc told me what he remembered. At first it was very little, fragments. As if he had been remembering a television show he had seen, but he was sure it was real, that he had lived it. I recognised the signs and believed he would benefit from regression therapy.'

'Regression therapy?' Coco interrupted. 'You mean hypnosis and all that sort of clap-trap?'

Caron raised an eyebrow. 'That sort of, *clap-trap,* as you so eloquently put it, is a highly effective psychological tool we use in certain instances when we deem it prudent. Sometimes we have to use whatever tools we can to re-enter the doors to rooms we have locked.'

'Isn't that dangerous?' Hugo asked.

'It can be,' Caron said with obvious reluctance, 'but please understand the procedure is all conducted under highly controlled circumstances and by highly trained professionals.'

'And what did you discover, exactly?' Coco snipped.

Caron visibly shuddered, scratching fingers across his desk. 'A story beyond comprehension, a tragedy. Even with my professional training, it is difficult not to feel deeply for patients who have undergone such tremendous physical and emotional torture. And it soon became clear that whatever the poor boy was reliving, it was very real and very traumatic.'

'How did you link Marc Gassna to the woman in the hospital?' Coco interjected.

'It was an accident, really,' the doctor answered. 'Marc said something which gave me pause. He recalled how growing up he always found great comfort in a half moon.'

'A half moon,' Coco spat in exasperation. 'I find

comfort in a quart of ice cream and anything with Barbra Streisand in it.' She looked at Hugo. 'Don't judge me. What's with the half-moon, doc?'

'I thought it might have been a metaphor, of course,' Caron answered, 'but when pressed, Marc recalled seeing the woman with straw-coloured hair scratching at it and when she did, he knew their day was broken.'

'Their day was broken?' Hugo gasped.

Caron nodded. 'Oui. Marc began remembering things which had happened in their home,' he paused, 'not that he ever called it a home, if I recall correctly he named it *le lieu*.'

Hugo frowned. 'The place?'

'Oui,' Caron replied. 'And not in a good way. The way he described it was… well, the way in which you would imagine a child describing something they couldn't quite describe, something they might only have heard about or read about. Something so awful it could only be described as hell. I can't begin to tell you how awful it was hearing him describe something which was obviously so awful for him to have to recall.'

Nobody spoke for a minute, then another. Hugo tried but could not think of anything to say. He was at a loss thinking of the life Jérémie and Marc had been born into, and the very real hell they had lived in. It made him angry. So angry he felt if he were to meet the people who had led them there, he might not remember he was first and foremost a police officer required to uphold the law.

'But how did you connect the half-moon memory to the woman in the hospital?'

'Well,' Caron replied, 'at first I thought it was literal, some metaphor he was confusing, but then I remembered when I had been treating the woman I noticed a scar, or a birthmark perhaps here,' he tapped near his clavicle bone, 'and I had thought it resembled...'

'A half-moon,' Coco concluded.

Caron nodded.

'It could have been a coincidence, of course,' Hugo said.

'Perhaps,' Caron conceded, 'but like you said, finding the young boy and the woman at around the same time seemed unusual and put that with the half-moon,' he spread his fingers in front of him.

'Then what did you do?' Hugo asked.

Caron lowered his head, his eyes darting to the right as if he was about to lie. 'I decided it would be prudent to bring the two together.'

Hugo studied him carefully, trying to assess what Caron was lying about, or considering lying about. He was finding the doctor a difficult man to read. He imagined it was because he had spent most of his life delving into the psyche of himself and others and had become extremely adept at it. But what was the lie? Or more importantly, who was he lying to protect? In any event, Hugo realised his only choice was to go along with him and attempt to decipher what it was Caron was hiding and why. In his career Hugo had come to realise even the most skilful often showed their hand because they found it too difficult to keep up a facade for a long time. 'What do you mean by that?' he asked finally.

'I took Marc to the ward where we were holding his... his mother.'

'Is that even ethical?' Coco questioned.

Caron did not answer, instead continuing. 'Marc recognised her instantly and became quite agitated. It was all I could do to calm him. But he was happy to see her alive, I'm sure of that.'

'And his mother?' Coco asked. 'She must have been happy.'

Caron bit his lip. He shook his head. 'On the contrary, you might say Marc's sudden appearance had the exact opposite effect.'

Hugo frowned. 'Why would that be?'

Caron shrugged. 'Captain Duchamp, we can never be entirely sure of the levels of deep psychosis a person may be going through, or the triggers which might ease or exasperate it. Whilst it is reasonable to presume the sudden reappearance of at least one of her sons may have offered the poor wretched woman some solace, it may have also deepened her psychosis, or exasperated her guilt. The truth is I don't suppose we'll ever really know because seeing him triggered something in her which I don't believe she ever recovered from.'

'Then she's dead?' Coco asked.'

'Non,' Caron replied, 'but many would consider her to be. She is institutionalised and has been for so long now, it is unlikely she will ever be otherwise. She hasn't spoken or communicated in several years, I believe.'

'I want to see her,' Coco said.

Caron shook his head. 'There is no point. She is uncommunicative, and that is unlikely to change. She can offer nothing to us, and I suspect we can offer nothing to her.'

Coco stood up, slamming her fist on Caron's desk. 'Take me to her right now, Monsieur Caron or so help me you'll regret it because I don't believe for one second you're telling us everything you know or everything you've done. You've made a huge mistake, Dr. Caron, a huge mistake in underestimating Captain Duchamp and I because we're not like the people you're used to dealing with. The vulnerable. The damaged. We're the people who speak for them. We're the people who look out for them, and you'd better be damn sure we are also the people who are more than capable of making the lives of those who hurt them miserable.' She smiled. 'In fact, you might say that I, at least, take great pleasure in doing so.'

Caron's head jutted forward. 'I don't know what it is you're suggesting, Captain Brunhild, but I can assure you…'

Coco raised her hand. 'Quit it, doc. I'm as fed up as a rich trophy wife when her AmEx gets cut off, so don't test me. Take me to Marc Gassna's mother and when I'm there, get your story straight because we're not done with you.' She stopped, flashing a sweet smile in Hugo's direction.

Hugo shuddered as the large metal gates of Rue Cabinas slammed behind them, a gust of cold air blowing across his face. He had never been inside *Centre hospitalier Sainte-Anne* before but he was immediately transposed to a time decades earlier when he had passed by the imposing gates and high walls in the back of his Grand-Mère's chauffeur-driven car, and it was as if the moment had just transpired. She moved her arm, brushing against Hugo's own, causing the hairs to stand on end as the fur touched his skin. It was all he could do to stop himself recoiling, but Madeline Duchamp had grown up privileged, the heir to a banking fortune and she had always considered it to be her right, her position, to be dressed and presented always in the best way. One of Hugo's first memories had been in worrying that the foxes he saw frolicking on the vast sculptured lawns of her home each morning would, sooner or later, end up on her shoulders. They drove past the hospital often and each time she would turn her head slowly, thin fingers trailing across a pale, powdered face.

For the largest part of his childhood, a seemingly unending period of unhappiness, Hugo had been terrified of her, forever intimidated by the coldness she projected. But sometimes, rarely, her head would turn to him and her cold eyes would meet his own, and for a moment he would see them shine. He knew she was looking at him with nothing but fondness. It was one of the few things which got him through his childhood and he cherished it because, amongst other things, it was so out of character. Madeline, for which the title Grand Dame may well have been created was a woman so ensconced in social etiquette she would find it improper to show any emotions, particularly affection, to anyone. But somehow and for reasons he had never understood she was fond of her only grandchild, more so than his parents it seemed. Hugo smiled to himself, remembering she was not so fond however of anyone else, and he recalled how when driving past Madeline would lean forward, tap the modesty window with the tip of her ivory cane and in the voice which reminded Hugo of Marlene Dietrich speak to the driver and say in hushed tones, *increase the speed as we pass the crazy house, Marcel and do not slow for anything or anyone, vous comprenez? If they catch us, they will cut our throats without giving a second thought.* Hugo would pull himself up and press his nose against the glass, emerald green eyes flicking anxiously over the horizon, searching for, well, searching for something he could only imagine would be horrific. The most he recalled ever seeing was a bored looking guard patrolling the front gates.

'You all right, H?' Coco asked.

Hugo's eyes widened. He smiled. 'When I was a child I passed this hospital most days. I was just remembering it.'

Coco nodded, her eyes twinkling. 'Visiting Papa Duchamp?'

Hugo snorted. 'If only.' He turned his head towards

the imposing building. It was what he imagined a psychiatric hospital would look like, and he had no doubt in the darkness of night it would seem like a set for a horror movie.

Coco pointed at a statue in the centre of the lawn in front of the gothic building. 'Even the statues are trying to escape.'

Hugo stared at the sculpture of a man leaning on a rock, his body taut and pointing away from the hospital as if desperately trying to escape his shackles. The guard who had been appointed to escort Hugo and Coco extended his hand, indicating they should continue walking. He looked annoyed, or perhaps scared. Hugo considered, carrying the gait of a man who had seen too much darkness in his life. They continued to walk towards the hospital in silence, Hugo considering what good could come from seeing the mother of Jérémie and Marc if what Dr. Caron had told them was the truth.

'I hate nut houses,' Coco muttered under her breath, 'but at least you know where you are with them. There are far more dangerous people walking the streets of Paris who look as if they wouldn't hurt a damn fly.'

'I don't know what Dr. Caron told you, but Maude, that's what we call her because we never discovered her real name, has been unresponsive for some years now,' an elderly female doctor spoke pushing a mound of wiry grey hair from her temple. 'And nor do we imagine she will regain any kind of notable motor skills at this stage.'

Hugo nodded. 'We understand, tell me, has Maude ever received any visitors?'

The doctor's tired, watery eyes flicked between them. She shook her head. 'It was part of Dr. Caron's explicit instructions that no visitors be admitted. Something I and the rest of the board agreed with because Maude can become quite agitated and have adverse reactions to outside stimuli. So it was decided, by the board, until we had a more firm grip on her treatment that we disallow any visitors, so that's what we did.'

'So, you are saying no one has tried to visit?' Hugo pushed.

The doctor did not answer.

'Doctor?' Hugo pushed again.

'Well,' the doctor replied, 'for as long as I can remember, for years, there has been nothing.'

'But I'm guessing something happened recently?' Hugo said.

She nodded. 'Oui. It was out of the blue really. There had been nothing, no contact, no interest you might say and then in the space of a few weeks we had a plethora of people coming through those doors.'

'Who were they?'

The doctor pursed her lips. 'Désolé, I do not believe we took their names, because as we explained to them, we could not allow them to see Maude because visitors were prohibited, and then the strangest thing happened.'

'They said they were her children,' Hugo concluded.

The doctor looked aghast. 'How could you know that?'

Hugo shrugged. 'A hunch. So tell me, did you allow them to see her?'

She shook her head. 'Non. I mean, there was no way to verify what they claimed. I mean, they could literally be anyone.'

'Didn't you think of running DNA tests?' Coco asked.

'Why would we?' the doctor responded. 'It would have served no purpose. We explained to the visitors if they came back with some form of proof, then the hospital would look into some form of access to Maude.' She sighed. 'You have to understand, it would be a long and complicated process. We could not just let them visit with a patient just because they *said* they were related.'

'Bien sûr,' Hugo said. 'And they accepted that? They just left?'

The doctor considered her answer before replying. 'What choice did they have? Were they going to force their way in? As I'm sure you've seen, security here is very good.' She paused.

'What is it, doctor?' Hugo asked.

The doctor lowered her eyes towards the pocket of her overcoat. 'They said they would come back, keep coming back, but if we could give something to their mother in the meantime.'

'What did they give you?'

She pulled a grubby envelope out of her pocket, holding it to her chest. 'They asked me to give this to Maude. I explained to them it was no good, that she could not read it so they asked if we would read it to her. We explained again it would make no difference, but they insisted...'

'And did you read it to her?' Coco snapped.

The doctor met her gaze. 'Non. What good would it have done?'

Coco glared at her. 'You hear stories all the time about people in comas coming around and telling us how they heard every word spoken around them. Why are you so sure Maude wouldn't have heard her son's words?'

'It's just not how it's done,' the doctor said matter-of-factly. 'But I kept the letter should they return, or Maude's condition improved.'

Coco held out her hand. 'Give me the damn letter.'

The doctor shook her head. Coco repeated her request. Reluctantly, the doctor handed it over. Coco ripped it open, pulling a single sheet of paper out and opening it. Hugo moved closer to her, flicking on his glasses to read the contents.

Dear Mama. It's me. Jerry. Remember me? I guess I was the noisy one, the always-crying one. I want you to know I'm sorry about that, of course, I didn't understand shit at the time. Sorry, mama, I didn't mean to curse; I know you never liked that when Tom did. Anyway,

I wanted to say sorry; I know I must have made your life even more difficult than it should have been. I was stupid and I'm sure annoying but you gotta know I didn't know better. I've been sat in this damn waiting room for hours waiting to see you and it feels like an eternity. I don't know why I forgot you, truly I don't. Dr. Caron said something about disassociation, or some crap like that. I don't know where you were hiding in my brain, all I know is that when you came back, it was like a light switch had been flicked on and within seconds it was all back. Everything. Good and bad, but I choose to remember the good because it WAS good. The way you'd bounce me on your knee, the way you'd ruffle my hair, pinch my cheeks, kiss my chin. All the things a mama should do for her son.

I found Tom. It took me a long time, but I found him. It was strange because all it took was one look and we both knew who we were and it was like we'd never been apart. We're doing okay. We've made the best of it, and in one way or another, we've made a family of our own. A family WE chose, and it's great. It helps with the nightmares. Tom said I was the lucky one, mainly because I was too young to remember the shit that went down, but I think in some ways that makes it worse because to be honest mama, my imagination of what happened in that basement is so much worse I'm sure. I close my eyes and I imagine what you both went through, the sacrifices you both made to keep me safe so I could sit and play with my damn teddy bear and watch my damn cartoons. I'm sorry about that, but I'm most sorry about what you must have done so we could run free.

But I have a plan, we both have a plan. A plan to make sense of what happened to us, where we came from, the men we came from and it was in the end so easy. Tom said these men are so simple, led

505

by their you-know-what's and they're so sure of their white, rich man privilege they think they're untouchable. They thought we were nothing, the three of us. They thought we were expendable and mama, I'm here to tell you that was their biggest mistake. They walked back into our lives and the bastards didn't even know it. But we did. Mama, I hope they give you this letter, but more than that I hope you read it, understand it and that you can hear these words. They will pay. We are going to make them pay and one way or another we'll be together again, you, me and Tom because we have a plan. I love you mama and I know you love me and Tom too. Just find your way back to us, merci, I beg you. Your loving Jerry (or Marc as they call me now). xxxx

Hugo exhaled, folding his glasses into his pocket. He looked to Coco, but judged by her reaction she was in no mood to talk. Instead, he turned to the doctor. 'Was it just two people who visited? Two young men?'

'On that occasion, oui,' she replied.

Coco gasped. 'Who else?'

'I don't recall,' the doctor replied with the gait of someone being not entirely truthful.

'Doctor…' Coco said with a bite.

'There was a man,' she said finally, 'a man who said he was Maude's husband.'

'Her husband?' Hugo gasped. 'Are you sure that's what he claimed?'

The doctor nodded.

Hugo turned to Coco, shrugging his shoulders as if

to say, *what do you think this means?*

Coco said. 'And did you allow him to visit Maude?'

She shook her head forcefully. 'Non, absolutely not, I told him the same thing as I have told everyone else. We cannot disturb Maude unless it is for a very good reason.'

Coco cleared her throat and reached into her bag, pulling out her ID. 'Is this a very good reason, doc?'

The doctor pursed her lips. 'I don't know what good you think it would achieve, but…'

Coco smiled. 'Lead the way, doc.'

The doctor reluctantly stepped into the hallway, Hugo and Coco falling into step behind her.

'The man who claimed to be Maude's husband,' Hugo said, 'what can you tell us about him?'

She glanced over her shoulder. 'Very little I'm afraid. I can't say I paid very much attention.'

'Was he white, black, young, old? You must remember something, doctor,' Hugo replied.

She shrugged. 'I don't, désolé. I imagine he was white, but I couldn't say more than that.'

'What about your staff? Could we speak with them? Perhaps they will remember something about the man,' Coco said.

The doctor stopped, turning her head, eyes flashing with anger. 'Non, of course they won't, goodness do you know how many people are in and out of the hospital every day? And speaking of which, I do not know when he would have been here and before you ask, he would have signed no register because he did not gain admission.'

Coco touched the doctor's arm. 'Are you afraid of something, doc? Or someone, perhaps?'

The doctor moved her arm away, shaking her head vigorously. 'Of course not. What a silly thing to say considering where I work, the people I deal with on a daily basis. Really, Captain Brunhild, I understand in your line of work you're used to dealing with people who lie to you. So am I. And I, like you, am not the sort of woman who is easily intimidated. Now, despite my instincts I will allow you to see Maude, but I warn you, her care is the most important thing to me. So if I suspect you are distressing her in any way, I will personally escort you from the building myself, vous comprenez?'

Coco bowed her head in deference. 'Lead on, doc.'

Hugo was not sure what he was expecting when they finally made their way along the vast, twisting hallways which lead them deeper and deeper into the bowels of *Centre hospitalier Sainte-Anne*. However, the screams which greeted them bothered him because they sounded like the souls of people being ripped apart in desperation and pain. Every instinct he had was telling him to seek them out and to offer them comfort, but he knew he could not, should not. He was reminded of a time, not too long ago in the great scheme of things, when a person could find themselves in such a place just because of who they had no choice to love. He felt the rustle of the sleeve of Coco's coat as it brushed against him, as if she was moving closer to him. He understood what she was doing, seeking consolation and as uncomfortable as it made him, he found it pleased him she was able to reach out to him.

'Dieu, if I ever end up in a place like this...' she whispered.

'Don't worry, I'll get you out,' he replied.

She looked at him, wide-eyed. 'You would?'

He smiled. 'Sure.'

She cackled. 'Good luck with that, have you seen the movie *Nuts*? Well, I'd have as much trouble as Barbra Streisand did convincing everyone she wasn't cuckoo if I wound up here.'

Hugo smiled ago. 'If need be, I'd break you out.'

Coco stopped, appraising him with keen eyes. 'Do you know, I actually think you would too, wouldn't you? And you'd probably not have to break a sweat, just use that charm of yours.'

'Charm?' Hugo asked in surprise.

Coco tutted. 'Oh, Hugo Duchamp, you could be dangerous if only you knew how. No wonder Ben's always on tenterhooks someone is gonna come along and steal you.'

The doctor reappeared in the hallway and cleared her throat. 'If you follow me, I'll show you into the dayroom. Maude is sitting by the window, as she does most days. But I beg of you, please show respect and restraint...'

Coco moved past her. 'This ain't our first rodeo, doc, we know what we're doing.'

Hugo followed her into the dayroom and stopped. The room was large and sparsely decorated but he could see they had made some effort to make it seem homely. A television flickered in one corner, a handful of patients sitting in easy chairs staring at it, their mouths open, eyes wide with concentration. He turned his head towards the window and saw the woman he assumed was Maude. She was slight, a blue cotton dressing gown pulled tightly across her slight frame. Her left hand was gnarled and resting on her lap, the right appeared to be smoothing dank red hair over and over. Her lips seemed to be moving, as if speaking a silent prayer, but he could not be sure. One thing he was sure about was that despite appearances of being much older, the woman they called Maude was most likely even younger than him.

'I'll be over there if you need me,' the doctor said airily and moved to speak to one of the orderlies, leaving Hugo and Coco standing alone. Coco gave him a helpless look. Hugo shrugged and stepped into the room, Coco at his heels, and they moved across the room.

'Do you mind if we sit here,' Hugo said to Maude, pointing at two empty chairs. She did not respond nor even acknowledged their presence. Hugo pulled the chairs closer to the window and he and Coco sat. 'My name is Hugo Duchamp and my friend here is Charlotte Brunhild. We are police officers and we would very much like to speak to you, if you would allow us to.'

There was still no response from the woman, but Hugo noticed her lips were definitely moving, but he could not make out what she was saying, or trying to say. He shrugged his shoulders towards Coco.

She nodded and moved closer to the woman called Maude and gently touched her arm. 'Maude, my name is Charlotte, though I go by Coco. I'm sorry for calling you Maude because I'm guessing it's not really your name and I'm also guessing underneath it all you're probably pretty pissed off about it, because I'm sure you have another name, your real name.' She paused. 'Like Tom and Jerry.'

Hugo recoiled. There was no mistaking it. The mouth formed the words. *Tom. Jerry.* But still Maude did not move or turn her head, her eyes unblinking, staring out of the window as if she was locked in a silent movie. The flash of the outside world playing across her face like a movie screen. It saddened him beyond words because he imagined she had been that way for a very long time. It reminded him of a woman he had met a few years earlier. Also a mother, a mother waiting for her son to come back. Or hoping he would not, as it turned out. He watched Maude carefully and wondered what it was she needed, or wanted, or whether it was, as the doctor had claimed, simply she had been too damaged, too hurt, too broken by the life which had become hers.

He cleared his throat. 'If it helps, if you can hear me, I can tell you I was with your oldest son yesterday. He's called Jérémie now, and he is happy, I think. He's in love at least, and someone is in love with him. And he has friends, friends who care about him with passion, a passion which means they protect him. Whatever happened to you all and whatever has happened since, he is trying to survive but you have to know there are people after him. Captain Brunhild and I are trying our best to stop them, but it isn't easy because we don't understand what happened or who treated you all so appallingly, but we are trying.' He stood and turned to Coco. 'I think we should go,' he said.

Coco shook her head. 'We're not done here, we haven't found anything.'

Hugo turned back to Maude. 'I don't think we're going to.' He moved in front of Maude, blocking her view. 'I don't know if you can hear me, but if you can, if there is some part of you listening please hear this. We will find out what happened to you and your sons. We will make sure whoever hurt you doesn't do it again and please believe me, I don't make promises such as those lightly. Please rest well Mademoiselle Maude, and I am so very sorry your life has been this way.' He stepped away, moving quickly across the room, his eyes wide and gulping repeatedly.

'Are you okay, H?' Coco asked, struggling to keep up with his long strides.

He turned back to her, the tears evident in his eyes. 'I want to find these men, Coco, and I want to make sure

they never see the light of day again, you with me?'
Coco smiled. 'Oh, darling, we're on the same page.'

Hugo took a sip of café, his eyes scanning the sheet of paper Dr. Bernstein had handed him. He frowned, scratching his head. He tucked his hair behind his ears and handed it to Coco. 'None of this makes any sense,' he said.

Coco murmured as she read the contents. 'This can't be true.'

Sonny pushed his mop of curly hair under his cap and pointed at the graphs on the paper. 'DNA doesn't lie, chérie,' he said, 'but just to be sure, I ran it twice.'

Coco turned to Hugo. 'What do you make of this?'

Hugo pushed his glasses into his hair. 'Can I smoke down here?'

Sonny smiled. 'Sure, you can it helps get rid of the smell of formaldehyde and rotting flesh.'

Coco snorted. 'You really are the weirdest, coolest pathologist, Sonny, that's probably why we get on so well.'

Hugo lit a cigarette, inhaling and exhaling slowly as he considered what the DNA report had told them. Finally, after a few moments, he sighed. 'It makes little sense.'

'After the way this whole investigation has gone, I'm surprised you're still surprised about how things go down,' Coco replied.

'But still it doesn't make sense,' he repeated.

Sonny lit his own cigarette. 'Well, actually, when I got the results, and I thought about it, I thought it made perfect sense.'

'You did?' Coco asked, aghast. 'You're telling me you're not surprised Corentin Gassna is the biological father of the kid he adopted and his brother?'

He nodded. 'Sure, think about it. Corentin has a dirty little secret. He enjoys keeping a girl locked up, using her as his sex slave. He ends up with a kid from it, and then another, and he has the whole little other family at his beck and call. They live or die at his whim. You've heard of the Josef Fritzl case, right? Filthy old pervert locks his daughter up in a crazy-ass cellar for decades and rapes her over and over and creates his own Frankenstein family.'

'Yeah, I've heard of him, but…' Coco replied.

'This isn't so much of a stretch to believe then, is it?' Sonny continued.

Hugo nodded his agreement. 'Sonny has a point,' he said. 'Let's think it through, Corentin creates his own little fantasy. The complete control and domination of a woman and the children she subsequently gave birth to and then one day it all goes badly wrong and he sees his entire world tumbling down around him. His nice, cosy life is suddenly in real jeopardy. We've all met men like Corentin Gassna. They live in a world we can't comprehend, and men like that are often only frightened of one thing.'

'Losing it all,' Coco said.

'Absolument,' Hugo agreed. 'Imagine the panic, the children run, escape into the night and the mother, Maude, is badly injured. Whoever was responsible must have been in a huge panic and with very little time to formulate a plan.'

Coco pursed her lips, apparently unconvinced. 'I get that, but how the hell did he come up with this particular plan?'

Hugo continued. 'I can't explain everything, in particular how Maude ended up free, but we can perhaps understand how Corentin came to know Marc was his son.'

Sonny nodded. 'He was watching. It's not difficult to imagine he knew instantly the case of *l'enfant perdu* was of course his son and he had enough resources, enough contacts to gain access to him.'

'But why didn't the kid recognise him? Why wasn't he terrified of him, if he was his captor?' Coco asked.

'Well, remember, according to Jérémie's recollection, he and his mother went to great pains to keep Marc safe. So chances are if he remembered his captor, he wouldn't necessarily be traumatised by it. He may have even been comforted by it. A link to his mother and his brother. We can only really speculate about all of this because we can't speak with Marc, or understand what he went through or what he felt, but it's not too far of a stretch he may have been okay with living with the man who had brought him food, candy, toys.'

Coco shook her head. 'Oh, Dieu, I wish I'd never gotten involved in this whole sordid mess.'

'It's crazy,' Sonny said, 'and sick.' He looked to Hugo. 'Do you think it's possible?'

Hugo shrugged. 'I don't see why not. He has the money and the resources. The children fled, but he didn't want Maude to die, for whatever reason, perhaps he loved her or he was just worried about implicating himself in her death. So he arranged for her to be hospitalised and looked after by his friend, Dr. Victor Caron. At least that way he can continue to keep control of her and the situation. It isn't too far of a stretch to imagine he adopted Marc for the same reason. Jérémie was long gone by this point but I would imagine he was looking for him too.'

Coco tipped her head. 'I suppose you're right, it does sorta make sense but how does it all tie in with the rest of it? Jack Boucher's death, the murder and attempted murder of his parents? Marc's suicide? How does Corentin Gassna fit into all of that? Or does he even fit?'

Hugo considered. 'Perhaps this all started because of whatever was stolen from Alexander Esnault. Something which implicated Corentin, or perhaps one of his friends. We won't know any of this unless we talk to him again.' He turned to Coco. 'Do you intend on bringing him in?'

Coco considered. 'On what charge? The fact he is the biological father of his adopted son is iffy, but it isn't a crime. There could be any number of reasons which he didn't tell us. He could claim he didn't even know and with no evidence to the contrary, we can't prove otherwise. If we drag him in for questioning, he'll clam up and we'll get nowhere.'

'What can you do then?' Sonny asked.

Hugo smiled. 'We poke the cage.'

Sonny frowned. 'Huh?'

'What you got in mind, H?' Coco asked.

'If Corentin Gassna is concerned there is some evidence against him and he would go to any length to protect himself or his friends, why don't we tell him we have come into the said evidence. We play it cool, saying we haven't examined it yet, but it might just be enough to make him show his hand, or who he's working with. It might also take the heat off Jérémie, Delphine, and Axel,' Hugo answered.

Coco smiled. 'I like it,' she said, 'do you think Jean Lenoir will arrange a phone tap?'

'I don't see why not,' Hugo replied, 'it's in his best interests after all. We'll call him and I'll have Etienne arrange the tap, but perhaps you could also have Cedric wait outside the Gassna house in case Corentin makes an unexpected trip? It would be interesting to see who he might go and visit.'

Coco clapped her hands together. 'Bon. We have a plan. Let's go and rattle old man Gassna's cage.'

'Why are you bothering us again?' Corentin Gassna hissed through thin, pinched lips. 'We have just returned from making the final preparations for Marc's funeral and we are both feeling very fraught and your constant interruption is…'

Fleur Gassna raised her hand. 'Corentin, s'il te plaît!' She moved across the room, pale fingers trailing along the marble fireplace, finally resting on a framed photograph of Marc. 'Such a rare occurrence to catch him smiling,' she said distantly. She turned to face Hugo and Coco. 'Will you come? To the funeral, that is, it's tomorrow at Père Lachaise Cemetery in the family crypt.'

Hugo suppressed a gasp. His Grand-Mère was buried at Père Lachaise Cemetery in the Duchamp family crypt. It pained him he had given little thought to visiting her since his arrival in Paris.

'Don't be foolish, Fleur,' Corentin snapped, 'the police are far too busy to come to a *private* funeral.'

'I want them there,' Fleur countered. She looked between Hugo and Coco. 'You will come, won't you?'

They exchanged a look. Hugo nodded. 'Bien sûr. We would be honoured to pay our respects.'

Fleur gave him a sad smile. 'That means a lot, merci.'

Corentin sighed. 'Why are you here?' he repeated.

Coco stepped forward, her eyes flicking between them. 'We promised we would keep you up to date with any developments,' she said.

'And there have been?' Corentin asked sharply.

Hugo cleared his throat. 'We have come into some evidence which we believe might shed light on what happened to your son and Jack Boucher.'

'Evidence?' There was no mistaking the bite in his tone.

Hugo thought if it was dark, Corentin Gassna might appear like a deer caught in headlights. He continued. 'Oui, Monsieur Gassna.' He paused. 'We haven't had a chance to properly examine or evaluate it yet, however. We have only just received it from Marc's friends.'

'Marc's friends? Fleur Gassna interrupted. 'They are safe?'

Hugo nodded. 'Oui, they are in police custody.'

Corentin's eyebrow raised, showing his obvious interest. 'They are at the Commissariat?'

Hugo looked at Coco. She bowed her head to show she understood what had just happened. Hugo turned back to Corentin and the immediate change was obvious and there was only one way to describe it. He looked relieved. 'Non,' Hugo said, shaking his head, 'but they are safe.'

'What is safer than your police station?' Corentin snapped.

Hugo did not answer his question. 'They are safe,' he repeated, 'and once we have evaluated the evidence, Captain Brunhild expects to begin making arrests.'

'I sure do,' Coco said with gusto, 'mucho mucho

arrests.'

'Then, that is good news,' Fleur Gassna said, flashing an unsure look towards her husband. 'Isn't it?' she asked Corentin.

Corentin gave her a curt nod. 'Bien sûr,' he said before adding, 'if it comes to anything, that is.'

'What do you mean, Monsieur?' Coco interjected.

He shrugged. 'Rien. They are prostitutes, vagabonds, nothing more. Their word means very little in a civilised society.'

Coco laughed. 'Perhaps not, but the evidence they've given us certainly might.'

'I demand to see this so-called evidence,' Corentin hissed, 'if it concerns my son then it is my right.'

'Absolument,' Hugo conceded, 'and once we've examined the evidence, you'll be the first to know, after we've considered the implications of it, that is.' He rose to his feet.

'Implications?' Fleur asked, her lips twisted.

Hugo nodded. 'Oui. We need to properly evaluate the evidence to understand its true meaning. Well, we thought we would just let you know where we were.'

'We promised, after all,' Coco added. She looked at Corentin. 'Say, did you ever think of getting a DNA test when you first adopted Marc?'

Corentin's eyes widened in abject horror. 'A DNA test? What on earth for? Why would we do such a thing?'

Coco shrugged her shoulders nonchalantly. 'Oh, I

dunno, out of interest perhaps?'

Fleur Gassna frowned. 'Why on earth would it interest us? He was our son, that's all that mattered to us.'

Hugo looked directly at Corentin. 'So, you never found out who his real father was?'

Corentin met his gaze and held it briefly. He shook his head. 'Non, I did not.'

Hugo nodded and looked at Coco, a message passing between them. *He knows.*

Coco smiled. 'Bien sûr, well, if you'll excuse us we'll be in touch. Take care, Madame and Monsieur Gassna.' She gestured to Hugo. 'Shall we, Captain Duchamp?'

Hugo nodded. His cell phone buzzed. 'Excusez moi,' he said, stepping out of the room.

Coco smiled at the Gassna's. 'We'll leave you now and see you tomorrow.' She followed Hugo into the hallway, her eyes narrowing as she listened to his side of the conversation.

'Are you sure? D'accord. Text me the address and I will meet you there, au revoir.'

'What is it?' Coco asked.

Hugo flashed her a confused look. 'That was Jean Lenoir. He's tracked down Monseigneur Augustine Demaral.'

'In Rome?'

Hugo shook his head. 'Non. He didn't go into details, but apparently he's found the Monseigneur and it seems he never left Paris at all.'

'Oh, Dieu,' Coco moaned. 'Don't tell me he's dead too.'

'Non, he isn't. But he's in prison under a different name. Let's go, Jean wants us to meet him.'

'He's gone.'

Ben lifted his head quickly. Jérémie was standing in the doorway, his eyes wide with panic and fear. 'Who's gone?' he asked.

'Axel, who the fuck do you think?' Jérémie spat in response. 'Delph? Where are you?'

Delphine ran into the room, rubbing tired eyes. 'What's wrong?' she asked, immediately on high-alert.

'I went looking for Axel, and I can't find him anywhere.'

Delphine yanked back the curtains, peering into the darkness. 'I told him not to go out. Why do you idiots never listen to a damn word I say?'

'Okay, *mom*,' Jérémie retorted, 'quit with the *I-told-you-so bullshit* and help me find him.'

Ben rose to his feet. 'Attend. We don't know who might be out there.'

'Exactly! Jérémie cried. 'And you think I'm going to leave my boyfriend out there when Dieu knows who is after us. Not a fucking chance. Now come on.'

Ben and Delphine quickly followed him out of the house. Ben shielded his eyes from the morning sun, squinting to take in his surroundings. Suddenly he felt scared to be in the middle of nowhere, rolling fields as far as the eye could see, although they had barely travelled an hour outside of Paris. His first thought was, how had Axel left? And had they been discovered? His hand reached to his cell phone. 'I'll call Hugo,' he said.

Delphine glared at him. 'I fucking knew we couldn't trust you. I said it, and I meant it…'

'Look around, Delph,' Jérémie interrupted. 'There's no-one here, and we're safe. Whatever happened, Axel walked out of here on his own.'

'Non, he wouldn't,' Delphine replied with little conviction, 'he wouldn't leave us.'

Jérémie pulled a packet of cigarettes out of his jeans pocket and lit one. It was crumpled, so he smoothed it down. 'He was trying to make things right,' he said blowing smoke into the air.

'Make things right?' Delphine repeated. 'What are you talking about?'

He shrugged. 'I knew he was up to something. I just knew it. I could tell by the way he kissed me when we woke up this morning. *Everything will be okay soon, I'm gonna make sure of it.* He said, and I knew there was something wrong, the way he looked away when he spoke to me, it's his tell. Every time he told me a trick didn't hurt him, he gave me the same look.'

Delphine scratched her head. 'What are you saying, J?'

'Where's the USB Delph?' he asked.

Her eyes flashed angrily as she stepped in front of Ben, blocking his view. *Shut up.* She mouthed to Jérémie.

'Where is it?' he repeated. 'We don't have time for games.'

'It's in my room, in my bag,' she answered reluctantly.

He pointed. 'Show me.'

She shook her head. 'He couldn't have gotten it. I would have heard him, and I certainly would have stopped him.'

Ben and Jérémie followed her into her room and watched as she emptied the contents of her bag onto the disheveled bed and began rifling through the contents, becoming more and more agitated as she did so.

'I don't fucking believe it,' she hissed, 'the rat-bag, when I get a hold of him…'

'What was so important about it?' Ben asked.

Jérémie sunk onto the bed, burying his head in his hands. 'What are we going to do?' he whispered.

'We go after him, that's what we're going to do,' Delphine snapped. 'He can't have gotten far.'

Jérémie's head jerked up. 'In which direction? We have no idea where he's going or who he is going to see and with his damn phone turned off, we're not about to get any answers soon, are we?'

Ben cleared his throat. 'What is so important about it?' he repeated.

'None of your business,' Delphine barked.

Jérémie sighed. 'Cut the bitch routine, Delph. You know he's only trying to help. They're all only trying to help and dammit we need all the help we can get to find Axel and make sure he's safe.' He turned to Ben. 'Ever since we started working at *énergique* we've been recording the men we slept with.'

Ben nodded. 'Videos?'

'Oui,' he replied, 'and it was surprisingly easy, leave the iPhone on and the tricks are usually too horny to notice.'

'I see,' Ben said, 'who asked you to do it? Was it Alexander Esnault?'

'Yeah,' Jérémie replied, 'he was the boss, and we did as we were told and as long as we did, he wasn't such a bad man and it certainly beat selling our asses at Gare du Nord for a few crumpled euros from some sleazy businessman fresh off the train.'

Delphine tutted. 'Esnault is the worst kind of sleaze-ball. We're the ones who did the work, took the risk, and he just had to sit back and collect the windfall.'

Ben frowned. 'What is it about this particular video that has everyone riled up?' He stopped, scratching his chin. 'Or who is it?'

Jérémie and Delphine exchanged a look. Ben sighed again. 'If you want me to help you, if you want Hugo to help you, you will have to stop being such spoilt brats.'

Delphine spluttered. 'What did you say?'

'You heard me,' Ben countered. 'I'm about done listening to the whining and the not trusting shit. Do you think I really want to be here? Do you think I don't have my own life to get back to? Hell, a few days ago I was living the good life in Montgenoux with my husband and our son and for no good reason we end up in Paris caught up in this whole mess that really has nothing to do with us and as far as I can tell, no-one gives a shit about us, or the fact we're only trying to help. I have broad shoulders, I've had to grow a thick skin in my life but there's one thing I won't tolerate and that is anything or anyone bothering my husband. He doesn't deserve it. Now, he's gone out of his way to help you, we all have and I will not beg you to trust us, or to listen to us, or anything else for that matter, any more. Enough is enough. Take our help or stop wasting our time.' He stopped, his breathing laboured. He bit his lip as if acknowledging he may have gone too far.

Delphine began clapping her hands. 'So, the rich guy has balls after all then, does he?'

'Delph, what did I say? Quit with the bitch,' Jérémie scolded. He turned to Ben. 'It's not that we're not grateful. It's just we've never really had much reason to trust anyone, y'know?'

Ben nodded. 'I do, and that's why we're here, why we're all trying to help.' He turned to Delphine. 'Let's make a deal. Trust me until you can't, until we do something to make you doubt us, but until then, tone it down, okay?'

Delphine opened her mouth to speak but did not. She pursed her lips angrily. 'So, what do you suggest we do?'

Ben considered. 'We call Hugo and Coco and we call Etienne.'

'Etienne?'

'Oui. He's our friend in Montgenoux and the craziest computer tech you'll ever meet. He's the one who found you and I'm sure if anyone can find Axel, he can.'

Jérémie and Delphine looked at each other. Delphine shrugged her shoulders huffily. Jérémie nodded. 'We trust you, Ben. And we trust Hugo. Find Axel.'

Ben smiled and pulled out his cell phone, clicking a button. The speed dial echoed around the room.

"Bonjour. Vous avez atteint le capitaine Hugo Duchamp. Je ne peux pas répondre à votre appel pour le moment. Veuillez laisser un message et je vous répondrai dès que possible. Je vous remercie."

'Putain,' Ben said and clicked his cell phone again.

"cou cou, c'est Coco, laissez un message, je pourrais vous revenir, ou je pourrais maintenant dépendre de qui vous êtes. Au revoir!"

'Where the hell are they?' he cried, pressing another number into his phone.

'Ben,' Etienne Martine said after the first ring.

Ben exhaled. 'Oh, thank Dieu, Etienne. I need your help.'

Etienne laughed. 'Of course you do! What is it? Who do we need to save?'

Hugo climbed out of Coco's car, a soda can and a McDonald's box following him. He arched his back, pressing the palm of his hand into it as if trying to reassure his tall frame it was safe now. He pulled on his glasses and as seemed to be the case with his entire time in Paris; he was immediately thrown back to another time. He had been to *La Santé Prison* only once before when he had first returned to France after his extended sojourn in London, to visit the man he had replaced as Captain of Police and another who Hugo suspected was heavily involved in multiple murders. Hugo turned his head, his eyes scanning the high perimeter wall. Both of the men he had seen inside those walls were now both dead, ahead of their time and both leaving a path of devastation behind them.

'I thought only famous people ended up here,' Coco said climbing out of the driver's seat.

'Or infamous,' Hugo replied. 'I've been here before and it doesn't particularly hold good memories.'

'I bet,' she said, 'so how the hell did the damn priest end up here?'

Hugo indicated the entrance. 'Let's find out, shall we?'

Jean Lenoir threw his briefcase onto the table. 'Do they not know who I am? I'm in charge of this place, for Dieu's sake! Being kept waiting like I'm some gangster's moll!'

Hugo grimaced, imagining whoever inside the prison was having a bad day, it was about to get much worse.

'Say, how the heck did you find the old cleric, Jean?' Coco asked.

The Minister of Justice stabbed his finger in the air. 'It wasn't easy, let me tell you,' he said. 'And there will be repercussions, one way or another, let me assure you of that.' He sat, crossing one muscular thigh over another. 'They thought they could blow hot air up my ass, but they're not used to dealing with someone like me, that's for sure.' Coco shot Hugo a look which made him lower his head to stop himself from laughing.

Jean Lenoir continued. 'After spending the best part of a day trying to find someone in the damn Vatican who actually spoke French, it soon became clear to a man of my intelligence that they were trying to give me the runaround, stupid fools.'

'Quelle horreur!' Coco replied.

He glared at her. 'Charlotte, must you always be so... so... Charlotte?'

Coco guffawed. 'See, you can be funny, Jean.'

Jean Lenoir suppressed a smile. 'You two seem to be under the impression we are friends, a fact I intend to disabuse you of once this is whole sordid mess is all sorted.'

'Speaking of which,' Hugo said, 'what exactly is happening here? What is Monseigneur Augustine Demaral doing in *La Santé Prison*?'

The Minister shook his head. 'Not the Monseigneur, rather one August Damar, formerly of the Commune of Bourg-Saint-Maurice.'

'I don't understand,' Hugo said.

'That's rather the point, I suspect, Captain,' Jean Lenoir replied.

'What he said,' Coco added with a wink.

'The Catholic Church is a law unto itself,' the Minister continued, 'they think they are above the law, because,' he closed his eyes, 'they often are.' He opened his eyes and smiled. 'But that was before they encountered this particular Minister of Justice. They may have been used to a certain...' he waved his hand, 'ineffectiveness, but non, not me, not Jean Lenoir!' he finished with a flourish.

'Seriously, Jean,' Coco laughed, 'you've gotta learn to play to the right audience. Seriously, if you had a moustache, you'd be twirling it right about now.'

He turned his head in Hugo's direction. 'I expect you're more interested in what I have to say, non?' Hugo nodded. Jean Lenoir continued. 'I spent a great deal of time getting the runaround at the Vatican until I finally had to resort to good old-fashioned threats. It worked finally when I said I would go forward and inform the media about allegations of child abuse against the Monseigneur. It worked, and they passed me on to someone more senior who swore me to secrecy and would only tell me the whereabouts of the Monseigneur on the condition I kept it secret. I of course agreed.'

'Well, that was foolhardy,' Coco murmured.

'I am not an imbecile, Charlotte,' Jean Lenoir admonished. 'I didn't pinky swear, although I did swear to Dieu, which is all right considering I've never believed in the hocus pocus of the bible.'

'You could get into trouble,' Hugo said.

He shrugged. 'Let them try, I will be Prime Minister one day soon and they can kiss my ass. I don't take threats well, as you both know, especially from men in frocks.'

Hugo looked towards the prison. 'How did he end up here?'

'That they wouldn't tell me,' Jean Lenoir replied, 'so once they told me where he was I did a little digging. Privilege of being the boss.' He lowered his voice. 'The Monseigneur was jailed five years ago under his birth name on charges of embezzlement. Quite how the Catholic Church managed to do it is beyond me, but my predecessors marched to a different beat than me. I am nobody's errand boy and this could not have happened on my watch.'

'Yeah, yeah, big tough Jean, we get it,' Coco said gesturing for him to talk faster.

He tutted. 'The embezzlement was from a company which as far as I can tell, is little more than a shell company with its headquarters in the Cayman Islands. August Damar is listed as the sole employee and owner. They had only one client.'

'The Catholic Church,' Hugo concluded. 'And what did his company supposedly do for them?'

Jean Lenoir continued. 'They provided the fire-proofing of a certain building.'

Hugo scratched his head. 'The orphanage?'

The Minister nodded. 'Absolument.'

'It makes little sense,' Hugo continued. 'The Monseigneur ran the orphanage and by all accounts he did it very well. Why on earth would he be involved in a company which took such terrible shortcuts?'

'People do awful things when they get greedy,' Coco offered.

Hugo shook his head, unconvinced. 'But risk the lives of the children he was trying to protect?'

'Or groom,' Coco countered, 'and burning down the scene of the crime and the victims is a pretty good way of getting rid of all the evidence. I hate him, but he's a fucking genius, if you ask me.'

Hugo turned to Jean Lenoir. 'Do you think that's what happened?'

The Minister tapped his chin. 'Actually, I tend to think criminals aren't that clever.'

'I agree,' Hugo said, 'but where does that leave us? Was there a trial? Was he represented by an Avocat and found guilty?'

Jean Lenoir shook his head. 'Non, he plead guilty. There was no trial, just a prison sentence of fifteen years.'

'Fifteen years?' Hugo asked in surprise, 'that seems a

lengthy sentence, non?'

The Minister laughed. 'As we both know, as far as I'm concerned and if it was up to me, the death penalty would be on the table for most crimes, but oui, I agree. The sentence seems a little disproportionate.'

'Then why would he agree to it?' Coco asked. 'I mean, he had to know with a record of good deeds such as his, he would probably have gotten away with a slap on the wrists.'

Nobody answered. Hugo tapped his fingers on the table. 'They were covering something up,' he said finally.

'It's the only explanation,' Jean Lenoir replied. 'Or why else would the Church sanction it or a man like him agree to spend the rest of his life in prison.'

'Mais pourquoi?' Coco moaned.

A guard appeared at the door, gesturing for them to follow him.

Hugo stood. 'Well, why don't we go ask the man himself?'

The man formally known as Monseigneur Augustine Demaral was sitting in an interview room, his head bowed, resting on his handcuffed hands, thin white hair falling over them. Hugo, Coco and Jean Lenoir shuffled into the room, and the guard slammed the door behind them.

He lifted his head slowly, tired, dark eyes appraising them. 'Who are you?' he asked.

'Your worst nightmare, that's who I am,' Jean Lenoir

muttered. 'I, Monsieur, am Jean Lenoir, the Minister of Justice.' The Monseigneur bowed his head. He lifted his cuffed hand and scratched a wide, hooked nose. 'Bien sûr, you are. How very nice to meet you, and vos amis?'

'Captains Duchamp and Brunhild,' he replied.

The Monseigneur nodded. 'It has been a long time since I received any visitors. I am very pleased to see you.'

'Well, you won't be, by the time I'm finished with you,' Jean Lenoir snapped.

Hugo stepped in front of the Minister in an attempt to defuse the situation. His instincts told him they needed to understand what the prisoner had to say and to do so, antagonising him was not the way to go. 'I am Captain Duchamp. How should I address you, Monseigneur?'

He met Hugo's emerald green eyes with his own darker, watery eyes. 'I am August, that is my name. Or, of course, if you prefer, you may address me by my number. Prisoner A31673.'

Hugo watched the old man intently as he tried to assess him. He carried the gait of a hundred or so men Hugo had met before. Men weighed down, oppressed by the confines of the prison wall. Men with no hope. He could not imagine a single reason, a single scenario why a person would choose such a path, but still he could not reconcile why August Damar was in prison if he had not committed the crime.

Coco flopped heavily into one of the plastic chairs. It groaned. She spread her hands across the table. 'We're short on time, so we'll just cut to the chase. He,' she pointed at Hugo, 'is the good cop. I, obviously am the bad cop and he,' she pointed at Jean Lenoir, 'is the muscular, bossy person in charge, and together, we are *Charlotte's Angels*, so, let's get down to it. Why are you here, and before you decide to give us the bullshit line, assess the intellect of the three of us and our nose for nonsense, d'accord?'

August Damar turned his head. 'Is it warm today? Is the sky clear? I confess, I did not take my exercise today. My rheumatism is troubling me, and although the sun usually helps, I found today it was not something I wished to partake in.'

'For the time of year, it's pleasant,' Hugo answered.

Coco tutted impatiently. 'So, priest, spill it.'

'You are Jewish, non, Mademoiselle?'

She shrugged. 'I have a dancing Rabbi in my living room and when I push his foot, he sings *Hava Nagila,* and it gives me more pleasure than a childhood spent staring down at male heads in a synagogue.' She paused. 'Is that the answer you wanted?'

August gave her a tired smile. 'It was a good answer, Mademoiselle, merci.' His eyes moved between the three of them. 'So, tell me why after all this time I am suddenly so lucky as to have three such distinguished visitors.'

Hugo sucked in his breath. 'Why don't we start with *l'enfant perdu.'* He stopped, giving the old priest a few moments to digest the words and to give Hugo the chance to view his reaction. He did not need to wait very long. It was there, in the fleck of a tired eye. Fear. Sadness. But was there guilt? Hugo could not be sure. 'Or, we can start anywhere you want, because I suspect the story didn't start with the lost child.'

August sighed. 'What do you want of me?'

'The damn truth, priest,' Coco hissed. 'And be quick about it. Lives are at stake.'

August's eyebrows raised. 'They are?'

She nodded. 'They are, as well you know. So, quit stalling and spill the beans, August, Augustine, Monseigneur, or whatever else you're calling yourself these days.'

He lowered his head. 'I haven't been that for a long time. A very long time.'

Hugo said. 'Please tell us how you ended up here. Monsieur and also please understand we're not here to cause you trouble, rather to save the lives of three young adults who are caught up in a mess which I suspect started long before they were even born. If you have any interest in atoning, then I implore you to help us.'

Hugo, Coco, and Jean Lenoir all watched August Damar intently. 'There is nothing I can say which will help you,' he said finally.

Jean Lenoir glared at him. 'I disagree. Try. Or else you might find that now I know of your existence, any little privileges you might have come to enjoy may just suddenly disappear.'

August laughed. 'You think I have privileges in here? Even though few know of my... past, the assumptions are made none the less.'

'Assumptions?' Hugo asked.

'You know to what I refer,' August retorted.

'You said few know of your past, but some do?'

He nodded. 'Oui. A few remember me from their youth when they attended Church. Or some grew up in the care of my children's home. So, deux and deux often become cinq.'

'With good cause, no doubt,' Coco muttered.

August ignored her. 'What is this about? Why are the police and the Minister of Justice suddenly interested in me?'

'I think you know the answer to that,' Jean Lenoir sniped. 'But let's start with why you are in prison, and the truth s'il vous plaît. I am a busy man.'

'Because I committed a crime.'

Jean Lenoir slammed his fist onto the desk with such force Hugo could only imagine it must have hurt, but the Minister gave no indication it had.

August sighed. 'I'm sure you've read the files. I was involved in embezzlement. I plead guilty to my crimes and was given the requisite punishment. I am serving my time and I will, most likely, die here. This is the way of life. I am atoning and that is fine with me.'

'Marc Gassna, Jérémie Berger and Jack Boucher. Those three boys, those young men need your help, your honesty,' Hugo said, 'and if you are serious about atoning, then you know that to be true. I beg you. Tell us what you know.' He glanced at Jean Lenoir. 'If you are worried about further charges, I think we all accept that at the moment that is the furthest thing from any of our minds. And your cooperation will go a long way to mitigating what you may or may not have done. But more importantly, you are a man of Dieu. If there is anything you can tell us, but fail to do so and which might have prevented any further deaths, then you must, or you will be as guilty as the others. You must talk to us, Monseigneur Demaral.'

August turned his head slowly towards Hugo, thick, white eyebrows knotting in confusion as if he could not reconcile the name Hugo had just addressed him by. 'I… I don't understand.'

Hugo frowned, moving forward. 'What don't you understand, Monsieur?'

August sighed, scratching his nose with cracked fingernails. 'This was all meant to end.'

Hugo flashed Coco a look. They were getting close. He could feel it. 'What was meant to end?' Hugo pressed.

'Could I have a drink of water, s'il vous plaît?'

Hugo nodded and stood up moving to the corner of the room and filling a plastic cup from the fountain, he returned. August held up his cuffed hands. Hugo considered, and after a moment held the cup to the old man's mouth. He gulped, water trickling down a pockmarked stubbled chin. It was his if it was his first drink in a long time. Or Holy Communion, Hugo thought.

'Merci,' August said sincerely.

Hugo nodded and stepped away, taking a seat between Coco and an increasingly agitated looking Jean Lenoir.

'Where do you want me to start,' August said, his voice weak and hoarse.

'At the beginning,' Hugo said.

August laughed. 'None of us have enough time for that,' he sighed.

'You're wearing my last nerve,' Jean Lenoir growled.

August ignored him and continued. 'I spent most of my life, my career if you want to call it that, in the Catholic Church. It was a calling. A calling which began when my mother made me become an altar boy. I hated her for that, but something happened that first day, something which changed my life, forged my future.'

Jean Lenoir tutted, his shoe tapping angrily against the tiled floor.

'And the truth is,' August continued, 'it was such a wonderful vocation I didn't even notice my life passing by.' He gave a sad laugh. 'One morning I woke up an old man and didn't recognise myself.'

'Is that when you became involved with the children's home?' Hugo asked.

He nodded. 'There were so many children who

needed help, children who had nobody, nothing, no love, no guidance, no…'

'No one to watch out for them, to protect them from wolves dressed in sheep's clothing.' Coco interrupted.

'Coco, s'il te plaît,' Hugo whispered.

August paid her no attention. A thin, bony finger scratching at a handcuff. 'I know you think you know what this is about, and you may be right, but it is only half the story.'

'Half the story?' Hugo questioned, his voice rising.

'Oui,' August nodded. 'I have been accused of many things in my life, and I have been guilty of some. But not that.'

Hugo raised an eyebrow in surprise.

'As I said, this is not exactly what you think it is.'

Coco tutted in impatience. 'Then you'll have to fill us in, all-knowing priest, because as far as I can tell, we have the full picture and it stinks.'

The old man cackled. 'It does stink, you're right, and for my part I am guilty and if I am lucky enough to meet Dieu, I will have to answer for it. The boys you talk of. Marc and his brother. I can promise you one thing. I did not hurt them, at least not in the way you think. But you are right to hold me in contempt because I started the chain of events which lead to this a long time ago, and not a single day has gone by since that I have not regretted it.'

'What did you start?' Hugo asked.

'I don't expect you to understand,' August said, 'the ways of man are often difficult to comprehend, but I think we are all made in His design and His image and it makes life all the harder. The devil is very real. I have seen him, and I have felt him and I see how he spreads. Like a vine wrapping himself around the hearts and souls of good men and women. Ripping their conscience, their humanity, their decency. It is both true and real and we must never forget it.'

Jean Lenoir muttered something under his breath, crossing one leg over his knee.

August continued, his voice soft and deep. 'Many years ago I became a member of a group of brothers, known as *The Circle*, initiated into a century old ritual, designed to protect *The Secret*, an ancient text giving praise to Dieu for his bounty, his wisdom, and the beauty he provides us.'

'Beauty?' Coco interrupted. 'And this beauty, does it involve young boys and girls?'

'Giving thanks is a ritual,' August said by way of an answer. 'And oui, it did involve showing love for the bounty.'

'Oh, you make my skin crawl,' Coco hissed.

August raised his hands. 'I'm sure I do, but I can assure you, Captain Brunhild, the intentions of the Order were, for the most part, decent. It was ritualistic. The reading of sacred texts, incarnations. The sharing of love between man and woman and the rearing of children with the aim of spreading the word of Dieu. The purity of life. The purity of love and the need to come together to honour Him. Symbolic and ritualistic.' His mouth twisted into a wry smile. 'You might say it was a group of men who ought to know better, to make better use of their time, but I suppose you might also call it a hobby.'

'A hobby,' Coco spat, 'you're saying abusing children was "a hobby?"'

August's nostrils flared. 'Of course not, Captain, I'm not heartless, or stupid, but I am a fool. I trusted people when I should not have. And I am paying the price.'

Hugo scratched his head. 'You're going to have to tell us the whole story Monseigneur, because we want to help. We want to understand but more importantly we want to make sure nobody else gets hurt. This group, this so-called Order. Who did it consist of? How many members?'

'There were five of us. Members come and go. Some die, most just grow old, or older, or bored, or…' he trailed off, 'frustrated with the limitations.'

'Limitations?' Coco asked with incredulity. She stood, moving backwards and forwards across the visitor's room like a lion in a cage. 'Are you telling us you acted as some kind of breeding ground for pedophiles? What, you trained them up, taught them their trade and watched them skip off into the daylight like a kid off to play in the park?'

He slammed his fist on the table. 'S'il vous plaît, this

is difficult, and please believe me when I say it was never our intention, my intention for this to get so out of hand.'

'Then how did it?' Hugo asked.

'For years *The Circle* operated as it should, in secret and in line with those who came before us. Honouring our forefathers and the traditions they lay down for us but then something changed. I cannot even begin to tell you when, but it did. You see, part of the ritual was to… ahem, cleanse the sinner, and this usually involved bringing someone, a sinner, into *The Circle* and cleanse them of their sin.'

'And how exactly did you find these sinners?' Coco asked with air quotes. 'Troll the local red-light districts?'

August closed his eyes, his lips moving in a prayer.

'Save us the sanctimonious bullshit,' Jean Lenoir hissed, 'and answer the Captain's question.'

He sighed. 'They were happy to do it. Why wouldn't they be? We paid them to sit naked in the middle of a circle and have strange men do little more than stand over them and recite text in Latin. You and I both know their lives are often much worse and much more dangerous. Indeed, some people were more than happy to come back again and again.'

Hugo pursed his lips. 'Although I suspect that rather defeated the purpose of this purity ritual. The same old victim, time after time.'

He shrugged. 'Peut être. Not for me, but it was just a ritual, for most of us, at least.'

'But not all?' Hugo countered.

'Who exactly was part of this goddamn circle of heretics?' Coco snapped.

August bit his lip but did not respond.

'Monseigneur Demaral, or Monsieur Damar, or whatever the hell name you go by now, tell us what we need to know or I'll forget I'm an exemplary civil servant on his way to the very top of our Republic,' Jean Lenoir said, 'and I'll reach over and throttle you with these very powerful set of hands. And they are as powerful as am I, Jean Lenoir, Minister of Justice.'

'There was a girl, a particular girl, who became, how can I say it, a favourite.'

Hugo leaned forward. 'Maude.'

August's eyes widened in surprise. 'How do you know that?'

'We've met her,' Coco interjected. 'Or rather, what's left of her.'

August smiled. 'Then she made it.'

Coco glared at him. 'If, by "made it" you mean living in a vegetative state with catastrophic brain injuries then, oui, "she made it."'

He closed his eyes again.

'Who were the other four members of *the circle* when you met Maude?' Hugo asked.

'And don't think about lying,' Jean Lenoir warned.

'Some friends from Church. Men I knew and trusted. Men who understood the sanctity of what we were doing.'

'Their names,' Jean Lenoir growled.

August sighed. 'They are good men, living good lives, and being true. I cannot imagine a scenario where they would do anything along the lines of what you are suggesting.' He exhaled. 'Their names were Monsieur Corentin Gassna, Dr. Victor Caron, Monsieur Ricard Allemand, and Monsieur Luka Artel.'

Hugo gulped. He had not heard of Allemand and Artel and his first thought was wondering what their connection was and how they fit into recent events.

As if reading his thoughts, August continued. 'Sadly, Monsieur Allemand died of a heart attack around this time and Monsieur Artel was killed soon after in a hit-and-run car accident.'

'Really?' Coco asked with interest. She frowned in Hugo's direction as if saying, *what does that mean?*

Hugo leaned forward, pressing his fingers against the table. 'And they weren't replaced?'

August did not answer immediately. 'When Monsieur Allemand died, I think we had all had enough. We were ready to move on, you might say. I am an old man, it had been my intention to pass the leadership to another but I just did not know what to do. But there was a boy, a boy I'd known since he was a child. A good, Dieu fearing boy whose heart was pure. He had shown exemplary care, and loyalty and at one point I thought he would join me in the Church,' he gave a sad laugh, 'but it

547

soon became apparent his interest in,' he paused, again with another sad laugh, 'the female sex would prohibit that. But still, he was keen and believed in what we were doing. And he believed in Dieu, he joked he carried the mark of Christ so he was more than suited to carrying on this work.'

The mark of Christ. The phrase struck Hugo in a way he could not understand. The mark of Christ on his face. It was like lasers firing in Hugo's brain, a myriad of different memories coming to him at the same time.

The door opened suddenly, and a guard entered, his face taunt and irritated. 'Excusez moi,' he said, 'Captain Duchamp?'

Hugo stood up. 'Oui, c'est moi.'

The guard thrust a portable telephone in his hand. 'Pour vous.'

Hugo lifted the telephone to his ear. 'Allô?'

'Oh, thank Dieu,' Ben said, 'I've been trying to reach you for ages.'

'Ben. Is something wrong?' Hugo asked, immediately on high alert.

'Axel's gone,' Ben spoke quickly. 'We don't know where but we do know why. He has whatever Alexander Esnault lost, and I guess someone wants it very badly. I've got Etienne on the case, but I'm not even sure he can work his magic on this. I'm scared, Hugo. We don't know where he's gone or who he may have gone to meet.'

Hugo breathed. 'I know, cheri. I need to call you

back in a minute or two, but I will call you back and we will figure this out. Je t'aime.' He handed the telephone back to the guard and turned back to August. 'Another young boy is now in danger and so help me, he will not die. Who took over from you, and why are you so scared to tell us about him. You have two minutes to tell us or I will forget who I am and leave you to whatever you have coming for you. Talk, Monsieur, and talk fast.'

Coco opened her front door and peered outside, eyes darting from left to right. She took a step onto the pavement.

Hugo appeared by her side. 'It looks clear,' he said.

She gave a reluctant nod. 'Are you sure this is a good idea?' she asked.

Hugo shrugged. 'I don't see why not,' he answered, 'besides, we can't expect Jérémie to not go to his brother's funeral. At least this way we can try to control it and keep an eye on them.'

'But how? Everybody will want to know who they are and why they're there,' Coco responded. 'And that could put them in real danger.'

Hugo nodded his agreement. 'I agree, but they'd go anyway, with our without us, and we can ask them to keep their distance and have Cedric stay with them.'

Coco sighed. 'You're right. I can't imagine how difficult it will be for the poor kid to have to bury his brother after everything that happened to them. What about Axel, do you think he'll turn up?'

'I don't know,' Hugo replied. 'The funeral notice was in the newspaper, perhaps he saw it and that's why he disappeared.'

She gave him a doubtful look. 'And left his lover and their friend? I don't think so. I'm not happy about it, but if we take Jérémie and Delphine with us to the funeral, we can monitor what happens.'

'Here they are,' Hugo said as a taxi pulled up to the curb. He smiled when he saw Ben's face and he had to fight every instinct not to run up, open the door, and cover his husband in kisses. It still amazed him he felt that way, not because Ben did not deserve it, rather it was as far out of Hugo's character as it could be.

'I'm not really dressed for a funeral,' Ben said grumpily, climbing out of the car and pushing the curls from his forehead.

Hugo appraised him. He was dressed in dark jeans and a polo shirt. 'You look fine to me,' he said, 'and we didn't pack for a funeral. The Gassna's won't even notice, I'm sure. They have enough to deal with, and besides we'll keep our distance.'

Delphine and Jérémie exited the taxi. Hugo leaned into the window and handed the driver some money.

Coco pointed towards the front door. 'That's my place. Why don't you go and make yourselves at home, and we'll be right in.'

Delphine scowled at her, pulling Jérémie with her towards Coco's house.

'She's a charmer, that one,' Coco said to Hugo.

He smiled. 'I suspect Delphine hasn't had the greatest start to life and not much cause to trust people, especially people in authority. And you heard the story. I don't think she was much more than a kid herself when she took Jérémie under her wing. It seems to me she's lived her entire young life on a razor's edge.'

'Still,' Coco grumbled.

Ben rubbed her shoulder. 'Poor Coco. I thought with four kids you'd be used to surly youngsters by now.'

'TOO used to surly kids,' she countered bitterly.

'I knew it. I fucking knew it.'

Hugo spun on his heels. Delphine was standing in the doorway, her eyes wild and angry. 'You fucking snakes,' she hissed.

'What is it?' Hugo asked with concern. 'What's wrong?'

Delphine looked over her shoulder and pulled Jérémie out of Coco's house, dragging him into the street.

Coco flashed a confused look between the two youngsters and her house. 'What the hell happened in there?' she asked in confusion, 'you were fine a moment ago.'

'Come on, J,' Delphine snapped, dragging Jérémie by his arm.

Jérémie glared at Ben. He was clutching his backpack as if his life depended on it. 'You promised. You looked me straight in the face and you lied to my face.'

Ben's eyes widened in horror. 'I don't understand. What did I do? What did I say?'

'J, let's get out of here,' Delphine said. She was shaking, barely able to contain her anger.

Coco stepped in front of her. 'I don't know what's going on here, but you're not going anywhere jeune femme,' she said.

Delphine reached inside her jacket and pulled out a flick knife. She brandished it towards Coco. 'Oh, yeah, you filthy flic? This knife says differently. Now how about you get out of the way or we'll see how far the blade gets through your blubber?'

Coco, looking offended, stepped aside.

Ben approached Jérémie gingerly. 'Jérémie, I don't understand. What did I do?'

Jérémie stared at him, seemingly on the verge of tears. 'You made us think we could trust you,' he pointed to Hugo and Coco, 'that we could trust them.'

Hugo stepped forward. 'You can trust us. Tell us what changed.'

Delphine grabbed Jérémie again. He dropped his backpack and snatched it back, holding it to his body. They began running down the street, Hugo and Ben following behind. They made it to the end of the Rue, winding in-between cars and the pavement. A bus passed by at the junction, and Hugo and Ben ground to a halt. The bus passed.

Hugo looked desperately. They were nowhere to be seen. 'Where did they go?' he asked desperately.

Coco appeared by his side, panting. 'They have twenty years and ten kilos on us. We'll never catch them.'

Ben lifted his head, evidently on the verge of tears. 'I don't understand what I did.'

Hugo rubbed his shoulder. 'This wasn't your fault, Ben, honestly it wasn't.' He turned to Coco. 'Something spooked them though, Coco, and they seemed fine until they got into your house.'

She shrugged, a resigned smile on her face. 'You've seen my house, perhaps my housekeeping offended them?'

Hugo gave her a sad laugh. 'Non, but something did. Mind if we take a look?'

'Sure, let's go,' she replied.

They walked back to her house in silence.

'Should I put out a call for them?' Coco asked.

Hugo considered. 'I don't think so. I don't think we want anyone to know we've lost them because at this moment, everyone thinks they're in our custody. I don't think it's a good idea to change that, do you?'

She pursed her lips. 'Peut être.' She turned to Ben. 'How were they on the ride over here?'

Ben took a moment to consider. 'They were okay, I'm sure of it. I mean, they weren't happy. Jérémie was worried sick, but he seemed hopeful. Oui, that's it. Almost hopeful. Like he was reassuring himself Axel would be okay, and we would help them. Even Delphine seemed calm, well, by her standards at least, but...' he shook his head, 'it just doesn't make any sense.'

Coco pushed the door fully open, flooding her living room with the morning light. 'Dieu,' she cried, 'it does look like a bomb hit it. I swear it didn't look this bad when I left this morning.' She scratched her head. 'Or maybe it was, maybe I've just become accustomed to it.'

Hugo cast his gaze around the room. While it was

hardly a show house, he could see nothing which could, should cause undue concern. 'I can't see anything here which would have provoked such a reaction, or such an over-reaction.'

'Did you see how he was clutching his backpack?' Ben asked.

Hugo turned to his husband. His face was ashen white, and he appeared to be on the verge of tears. He did not know what to say to him, so he did all he could. He slid his fingers in between Ben's.

Coco pursed her lips, her eyes taking in her dishevelled living room. 'They weren't in here very long, perhaps, well, do you think they might have taken something? A quick snort to help get them through the funeral?'

Hugo looked to Ben. Ben shrugged. 'I didn't see any evidence of that in the safe house and,' he tapped his nose, 'after working in a hospital for a long time I can usually spot it. I can't be certain, but if you pushed me, I'd guess the worst those kids have done lately is the odd joint which is pretty amazing considering the kind of lives they've had.'

Coco sniffed. 'And I can't smell anything iffy.'

A young blonde woman appeared on the stairs. 'Ah, Mademoiselle Brunhild,' she said in English in a heavy Swedish accent. 'I wondered what the noise was.'

Coco smiled at her. 'Guys, this is Helga, my Au Pair. Is everything okay, Helga?' she asked in her own broken

English.

'I can't get Esther to settle,' Helga said.

Coco sighed. 'She's teething,' she said to Hugo and Ben. 'And it isn't going well.'

'I can't find her toy,' Helga said. 'Usually it settles her.'

Coco looked around the living room. 'I can't see it. Isn't it in her cot?'

Helga shook her head.

'Can we help?' Ben asked. 'What are we looking for?'

Coco frowned. 'Some Dieu awful toy Morty gave her, dirty and ancient, used to belong to him, and his mother before him. For some crazy reason, Esther loves it.' She began rifling through the toys on the floor. 'I can't see it, Helga. Check my bed, I woke up with it on my pillow yesterday,' she said finally, grimacing as the cries of her youngest daughter sounded from the first floor. She shook her head. 'Désolé, I have to go. We have to go to a funeral.'

Helga nodded. 'Of course. Don't worry, I'll find it.'

Coco gave her a grateful smile. 'And if all else fails, pop a little vodka in her bottle. It worked with the other three.' She smiled at Hugo. 'Don't judge me, you'd do the same with your son.'

Ben laughed. 'He's twenty. We already do.'

Hugo looked towards the door. 'Let's go. We don't want to be late for the funeral.'

cinquante-deux

Hugo stopped and pulled out his glasses, emerald green eyes narrowing as he studied the statue. His Grand-Mère, Madeline Duchamp, had taken him to this very spot more times than he cared to remember, holding his hand so tightly he felt as if it would drop off. She would thrust him in front of the sculpture which appeared to his young eyes as a woman thrown against the wall, her head twisted in despair as if she was trying to save herself from the rows of skulls which seemed to be pressing themselves through the stones. It terrified him, but each time they came Madeline insisted they stop by on the way to visit the Duchamp tomb. To pay respect to those who came before and fought, she would say.

'What a creepy monument,' Coco said.

'Mur des Fédérés,' Hugo said with a loud exhale.

She shuddered. 'Creepy, it's like the eyes follow you wherever you stand.'

'I don't know,' Ben said, 'it's kinda moving. What does it mean to you, Hugo? Why did you want to see it?'

'There are a lot of ghosts here,' Hugo said, 'in more ways than one. Grand-Mère used to bring me here at least once a week. Somehow it feels like an old friend. It reminds me of Paris, and it reminds me of her. She was a great patriot.'

Coco smiled at him. 'You need to get out more, Duchamp.' She pointed to the walkway. 'We should get going, we don't want to arrive late.'

They began walking, an ominous silence between them.

'Do you think they'll turn up at the funeral after the way they ran out?' Ben asked.

Hugo shrugged. 'I don't know, but I suppose if it was me, I would. There are plenty of places to hide and run if they need to and I suspect Jérémie will want to see his brother be buried and also if Axel is here.'

'Or the murderer,' Ben added with a shudder.

'Speaking of which,' Coco said. 'I don't know if we're getting any further forward with this investigation, do you?'

Hugo considered. He pulled off his glasses and placed them in his pocket and began massaging his temple.

'Something's bothering you,' Ben said, rubbing Hugo's shoulder. 'What is it?'

Hugo pulled a cigarette out of his pocket and lit it.

Ben smiled at Coco. 'Give him a moment, he's thinking of something. I've gotten used to this.'

They continued walking up the cobbled walkway in silence, the only sound being Hugo sucking on his cigarette. As they reached the apex, he stubbed it out and turned to Coco.

'Coco,' he said, 'I know you don't know me, or have any real reason to trust me, but I'm going to ask you to do something and it will probably be something you don't want to do, and it might even make you angry, but s'il te plaît, I beg you, give me the benefit of the doubt.'

She gave him a confused, surprised look. 'What's going on, H? What's up?'

He sighed. 'I have an idea. But it's just an idea, a lot of different things which don't make any sense, or may mean nothing, but it's an idea nonetheless and at this moment, we don't have a lot more.'

'You're starting to weird me out,' she said.

He nodded. 'I don't meant to, but what I'm going to say next will sound even weirder, but just give me the benefit of the doubt, d'accord?'

'Okey dokey,' she replied. 'I trust you, Hugo. What is it?'

Hugo lit another cigarette and took a deep breath.

Dr. Shlomo Bernstein flicked open the folder on his desk while cradling the telephone on his shoulder. 'I don't understand what you're asking me, Coco,' he said.

'I'm not sure I do either, Sonny,' she replied, 'it was Hugo's idea. I'll put the phone on speaker.'

'Hi, Hugo,' Sonny said.

'Bonjour, Sonny,' Hugo replied, 'we're sorry to bother you, but we need your help and I'm afraid we don't have a lot of time.'

Sonny chuckled. 'We never do. What do you need?'

Hugo exhaled. 'We need you to compare some DNA samples, but we don't have time to wait.'

Sonny sighed. 'Hugo, you can't just compare DNA like that. At best it takes days, but often much longer. There's not a lot of wiggle room with it.'

'I understand that, Dr. Bernstein,' Hugo conceded, 'but the fact is, we don't need one hundred percent accuracy at this point, rather we need the eye of an expert. Your expertise and your ability to compare some samples by sight might be all we need.'

'I don't think that's possible,' Sonny said. 'It's a fine art. It takes time and a good understanding of DNA comparison. I don't think I have that. All I could give you was my interpretation of something which may or may not be correct. I'm not comfortable with that, especially if you're going to use my interpretation.'

'I understand, and believe me, we can sort this out

later, and do it properly, but time isn't on our side,' Hugo replied. 'And I'm sorry to have to ask you, but is it possible for you to look at different DNA slides and somehow compare and contrast them?'

'Well, maybe,' Sonny conceded, 'I can look at the slides and perhaps have a vague idea if one matches another, but I don't see what good it can do you, or even how accurate it might be.'

Hugo exhaled again as if he was tired and weary. 'It will give us some time, but more importantly it might give us a little bit of leverage.'

'I see. And this is important?'

'I don't want to be dramatic,' Hugo answered, 'but it might just be a matter of life and death.' He paused, pursing his lips. 'And there's something else. Can you send me an inventory of what you found on the bodies of Jack Boucher and Marc Gassna?'

'An inventory? Pourquoi?'

'I'm not entirely sure, but I hope I'll know when I see it.'

Sonny nodded. 'D'accord, leave it with me and I'll see what I can do.'

'Merci, Sonny, I'll pass you back to Coco. She'll need to explain about the DNA.'

'Sonny,' Coco said. 'What I'm about to ask you to do might sound crazy, but Hugo thinks it's the right thing to do and Dieu help me, he could just be right. You're two of the very few people in this world I trust. But if he's right about all of this, we don't have a lot of time and I don't want the death of another kid to be because of me not moving quickly enough. It's a stretch, Sonny, but it's what we have to do.'

'Anything you need, chérie,' Sonny replied softly.

Hugo watched the coffin being lifted out of the hearse and he felt the familiar pang of anguish he felt each time he bore witness to another pointless and avoidable death. It was, of course, often worse when the person was young, just beginning their life's journey, but the reality was nobody really wanted to die, nor had ever fully lived or completed everything they wanted to complete. It pained him when he realised he had forgotten all about Jack Boucher. The young man brutally murdered and presumably still lying in the morgue. His mother now also dead at the hand of another, and his father likely to follow them. Who would bury Jack Boucher? Hugo made a mental note to speak with Coco about it. While not necessarily his place, he wanted to make sure there was something, some marking of his passing. He wished Ben was with him, but Ben had decided it would be inappropriate for him to go to the funeral and instead decided to see if he could find Jérémie and Delphine. A probably futile expedition, but Hugo understood Ben needed to feel as if he was helping.

The bearers ambled towards the towering pillars standing sentry outside the Gassna family tomb. Hugo turned his head discretely, flicking on his glasses and taking a moment to assess who had gathered for Marc's funeral, but found he did not recognise most of them. Dr. Victor Caron was standing between Corentin and Fleur, his hand resting on the sleeve of Fleur's Chanel jacket.

Although it did not surprise him Caron was there, there was something about the way he was touching Fleur which seemed... *unnatural* for lack of a better word, he thought to himself. What surprised Hugo the most was the man standing on the corner, near the hearse. If Pierre Duchamp had seen his son, he showed no sign of it. His cold eyes fixed directly on the coffin and nothing else.

'What is my father doing here?' he pondered.

Cedric stepped in between Hugo and Coco. 'I think I might know why,' he said.

Hugo looked at him in surprise. 'You might?'

Cedric nodded. 'When Captain Brunhild told me to monitor Corentin Gassna and follow him if he left his house, I did, and he only went to one place. A building in the business district. I tried to follow him inside but lost him in the foyer. I checked the name boxes and the only one I recognised was an Avocat firm on the top floor...'

'Duchamp & Prevost,' Hugo said.

'Oui,' Cedric replied. 'I mean I don't know that's where he went, but...'

Commander Mordecai Stanic appeared on the verge where Hugo, Coco, and Cedric were standing. He nodded to Hugo and Cedric, his eyes flashing angrily at Coco. 'Charlotte, couldn't you have at least gotten changed before you came here?'

Coco looked down at her dress, her cheeks flushing. She smoothed down the woollen black dress she was wearing, picking a piece of fluff and dropping it to the ground. 'This is my best dress,' she whispered.

'Why doesn't that surprise me,' Morty sniffed. 'Is it true? Did you lose the kids?'

'Well…' Coco answered helplessly.

'There was nothing we could do,' Hugo interjected, 'we were trying to gain their trust, but I'm afraid it just wasn't working.'

Morty ignored him and continued glaring at Coco. 'You should have placed them in protective custody, Captain Brunhild. Questions will have to be asked about all of this, especially if anything happens to them. We could be talking lawsuits, dismissals and don't be thinking I can or would protect you, not this time. If you'd wanted my help you should have levelled with me and not kept things from me. So, as far as I'm concerned the two of you are on your own…'

Hugo cleared his throat. 'We don't believe Jérémie and Delphine will be in danger for much longer.'

Morty turned his head sharply. 'What is that supposed to mean?'

Hugo did not answer, his attention taken by a man standing in the distance. He strained his eyes. 'Is that who I think it is?'

Coco followed his gaze. 'Fuck me. What the hell is Alexander Esnault doing here?'

'I guess he's looking for the evidence,' Hugo replied.

'What evidence?' Morty spat.

'Jérémie and Delphine have some evidence. We don't know what it is, but as far as we can tell, they took it from Alexander Esnault, and it seems to be evidence of impropriety he was using to blackmail powerful men who were using prostitutes and drugs.'

'Then that's what this is all about? Blackmail?' Morty questioned.

Hugo shrugged. 'I'm not sure. There are many things going on, I'm sure, but I think I'm starting to understand. The blackmail was probably responsible for the murder of Jack Boucher and the suicide of Marc Gassna, but that's not where this all started. This all started with Monseigneur Augustine Demaral.'

'What are you talking about?' He glared at Coco. 'Is this why you were interrogating my mother?'

Coco nodded. 'I'd hardly call it interrogating Morty. I knew she would know the Monseigneur and just wanted to ask her about him. She was happy to talk about him.'

'You should have cleared it with me first,' he snapped. He turned back to Hugo. 'What do you mean, what does this have to do with the Monseigneur?'

Before Hugo had a chance to respond, his attention was diverted by the sound of approaching footsteps on the gravel behind them. He did not need to look to know who it was. The footsteps were indented on his memory because he had heard them so many times on the gravel driveway leading to his Grand-Mère's house and they had always signalled Hugo's day was about to be broken.

'Hugo, may I speak with you?'

Hugo turned around slowly to face his father. 'About?'

Pierre Duchamp regarded his son with surprise, as if he was not used to the tone of voice presented to him. 'Well, about my client, Monsieur Esnault.'

Hugo glanced over Pierre's shoulder. Alexander had stepped away and was standing on a grass verge, staring intently at Hugo. Hugo could not be sure of the meaning of the look, but he was sure it was not antagonistic or threatening. Hugo turned back to Pierre. 'What about him?'

'He would,' Pierre said with a sense of reluctance, 'like to speak with you and Captain Brunhild.'

Coco stepped forward, her interest obviously piqued. 'Why, sure, we'd love to speak with your client, Maître Duchamp. Our doors at the Commissariat de Police du 7e arrondissement are always open for you.'

Pierre gave her a quick handshake. 'Non. We will meet at my offices, and that is non-negotiable.'

'I'll give you non…' Coco began.

Hugo interrupted. 'Non, that's fine. When shall we meet you?'

Pierre glanced at the Rolex on his wrist. 'Let's say, one hour. Is that suitable?'

Hugo nodded.

'Bon. Au revoir.'

They watched Pierre walk back to Alexander and

whisper something into his ear. Alexander laughed and waved to Hugo.

'What was that all about?' Coco asked.

Hugo shrugged. 'I don't know, although when it comes to those two, we had better be on our toes.'

Morty pulled his jacket tight. 'I'll meet you there. I have something to take care of first.'

'You're coming to the meeting?' Coco asked.

'Of course, I am,' he snapped back, 'I'm in charge of this investigation after all.' He did not wait for a response and moved quickly through the crowd and away from the tomb.

'One hour,' Coco said. 'Will that give us enough time?'

Hugo grimaced. 'Let's hope so.'

Cedric clicked his teeth. 'Are you two going to tell me what's going on?' He watched as Hugo and Coco exchanged an anxious look. 'Ah, I see, you still don't trust me. You still think I'm involved, don't you?'

Coco shook her head. 'Non, we don't, it's just… it's just…'

'Just what?' Cedric asked, exasperated.

Hugo spoke. 'The truth is, Cedric, we're about to go out on a limb and we're not exactly sure about it and if it all goes wrong, we didn't want to involve anyone else. That's all.'

'Is that true?' Cedric asked Coco.

She nodded. 'You know I'm not usually afraid to

take a risk. Well, this time I'm not sure there'll be a big enough lifebelt for me.'

Cedric sighed. 'In that case, it's a good job I'm a decent swimmer. What have you gotten us into this time?'

Coco gave him a grateful smile. She pointed at Hugo. 'Blame him this time, it's all his crazy idea.'

Hugo gasped and turned his head sharply. 'Don't make it obvious,' he whispered, 'but behind me, at huit heures, past the Marcel family tomb and behind the trees. Do you see what I see?'

Coco shifted her eyes slowly in the direction Hugo had indicated. She bit her lip and moved her head into a slow nod. 'Oui. It's them. What do we do? If we go after them, they'll run.'

Hugo considered. He was not surprised Jérémie and Delphine had turned up at the funeral, but he was not sure what to do about it. He did not want them to run again. He burst into a sprint, moving quickly through the trees, hoping the element of surprise would buy him enough time to get into speaking distance with the two youngsters. Delphine spotted him first, her eyes narrowing angrily. She grabbed Jérémie, pushing him in the opposite direction.

'Attend!' Hugo bellowed. 'S'il vous plaît, don't go. We know who has Axel.'

Jérémie stopped, pulling himself free from Delphine's grip. He turned to Hugo, his eyes wide and questioning, the desperation in them clear.

'J, he's lying, you know he's lying,' Delphine hissed.

'Now, come on. We've got to get out of here.'

'You can't run forever,' Hugo reasoned. 'Let's finish this.'

'What do you mean?' Jérémie asked. 'How can we finish this?'

'I think I understand what happened,' Hugo said, 'but we will need your help to prove it.'

'You need our help?' Delphine asked with incredulity. 'And you expect us to trust you? After everything that's happened?'

Hugo shook his head. 'Non, I don't blame you for not trusting us, but you will have to try because Axel's life depends on all of us working together.'

Jérémie took a tentative step towards him. 'What do you mean?'

Hugo also took a further step forward. 'This is about what was on the USB, but it's not a sex recording is it? It's another kind of recording, someone implicates themselves in a crime. Probably in many crimes. I think I finally understand what happened. Jack was killed for it, Marc killed himself because he felt responsible for it, and now Axel reached out because he didn't want to run anymore. He didn't want to worry about losing you, Jérémie, and he thought he could control the situation and keep you all safe. He knew the value of what is on the USB.'

'Then he's probably already dead,' Delphine said.

'Peut être,' Hugo answered reluctantly. 'but there is a chance whoever has him doesn't yet have the USB. Axel may have hidden it somewhere when he went to meet the murderer. We can only be sure by arresting the person who killed Jack Boucher.'

'You'll never arrest him,' Delphine spat.

Hugo shook his head. 'Non, we will, and most importantly we think we can prove what he did, and crucially, who he really is.'

'You said you need our help?' Jérémie spoke softly.

'J…' Delphine cried.

'Oui,' Hugo spoke quickly. 'I want to finish this. We all want to finish this, and we want the right person to be punished.'

'Why should we trust you?' Jérémie pleaded.

'Because I know who your father is, Jérémie and I need you to help me prove it before he gets away with anything else. I've seen your mother, and I know how painful it is for you to know she will probably never recover, but we can do this for her. We couldn't make Marc safe, but we can make sure you don't have to spend your life looking over your shoulder. Come with me and Captain Brunhild and let's finish this.'

Jérémie nodded. 'I know I shouldn't trust you, but I do. Let's go, Captain Duchamp but I warn you, if this is a trap, I won't be responsible for what I do to you. I'll make you pay in ways you can't imagine.'

Hugo, Coco, and Ben moved slowly towards Coco's car, each wrestling with their own thoughts and demons.

'Are you sure about this, H?' Coco asked.

He shook his head. 'I'm not sure about anything,' he replied earnestly, 'but I have a hunch.'

'A hunch,' she cried, 'a hunch, he says!'

Before he could respond, his cell phone pinged indicating he had an email. He pulled out the iPhone and stared at the screen, keen, emerald green eyes flicking over the contents. He shook his head and stopped, Coco and Ben stopping next to him. Ben touched his arm. 'Is everything okay, cher?'

Hugo sighed. 'I'm tired and I'm not even sure any of this makes sense anymore, but,' he turned to Coco. 'I need you to make a call for me to the evidence lock-up at the 7e arrondissement.'

She shrugged. 'Sure, pourquoi?'

'We need to check something and we need to check it right away.'

Coco pulled out her cell phone. 'D'accord.'

'And I'll call Jean Lenoir and tell him what we're doing.'

Hugo stared at the photograph of Pierre Duchamp with Monseigneur Augustine Demaral and he once again wondered what Pierre's involvement was because as far as he could tell, he was involved in ways Hugo had not yet comprehended. One thing he knew for certain was, if his involvement was in any way criminal, Hugo would have no problem in making sure he was punished for it. Hugo felt the bustle of Coco's woollen coat against his thigh and he realised despite how unused he was to being close to people, he was incredibly grateful for the reassurance of being in-between Coco and Cedric.

They had been admitted to Pierre's office by the snippy secretary Hugo had met on his first visit, and she had certainly not thawed towards him, nor shown any familiarity with whom he was. That did not bother him in the slightest, but being back in the office did. He reached to the pocket of his trousers, checking his cell phone was still there. Jérémie and Delphine were waiting in a busy restaurant with Ben for Hugo to call them and tell them they were safe. Hugo wanted more than anything to be able to do that. He was anxious and all he wanted was for it all to be over.

'Your Papa's rich then,' Cedric said with an impressed nod as he appraised the plush office.

'I have no idea,' Hugo answered honestly. 'This is only my second visit here, and most likely my last.'

'Where is everybody?' Coco asked, glancing at her

573

watch. 'He said an hour, and it's already a half past. What do you think this is all about, H? Why did Alexander Esnault call this meeting? Do you think he knows?'

Hugo considered his answer for a few moments. 'As I have always suspected, I believe there is very little Alexander Esnault doesn't know, but as to why he called for this meeting I can't say, other than, he must assume we are close to an arrest and wanted to lay his own case first.'

'To wriggle out of it, you mean?' she asked.

'Exactly,' he replied.

The door opened and the secretary led Fleur and Corentin Gassna into the room, shortly followed by Dr. Victor Caron. Hugo noted that while Fleur appeared shell shocked following the funeral, her husband and the doctor appeared to be anxious. The secretary directed them to three chairs on the other side of Pierre Duchamp's large, ornate desk.

'Ah, more guests?' Coco whispered.

Hugo shook his head. 'I don't like this. It feels as if we're being stage managed.'

'What do you mean?' Cedric asked.

'He means we're being played,' Coco hissed, 'and he's right, and I don't like it either because it stinks. Stinks of people with money thinking they can bribe, or threaten their way out of trouble, and…' she trailed off, 'they might just be right.'

Cedric scratched his head. 'You two are tripping, truly you are. You're talking in riddles!'

Coco turned to Hugo. 'What did Jean Lenoir say?'

He nodded. 'He's not coming. He thought it best he not be involved at this stage, but he has promised he will stand by us, whatever happens.'

'And you believe him?' she asked.

'I believe him so long as we get the outcome he wants, sure,' Hugo answered, 'otherwise we're most certainly on our own,' he added cheerfully.

The door opened again and Commander Stanic entered, flopping heavily onto a chair next to Cedric. He said nothing but Hugo could see he was tense, a thin line of sweat nestling on his top lip.

'Ah, I see we are all here,' Pierre Duchamp said, his voice deep and masterful as he lead Alexander Esnault into the office. 'Bon, then we shall begin.'

Pierre Duchamp lowered himself into the large leather chair in front of his desk. He reached for a leather-bound book and opened it, scribbling something very quickly into it. He slammed the book closed and cleared his throat. 'Would anybody like a drink? A café, or peut être, something stronger? It has been a very difficult day, after all.'

Fleur Gassna looked anxiously around the room. 'Why did you ask for us to come here? What is this about?'

Alexander Esnault moved quickly to her, taking her hands in his own and rubbing them gently. She recoiled as if she could not bear to be touched. He moved away, resting against the window pane. His hands reached to his head, and he pulled his hair tightly into its bun. 'We're here to put right several wrongs,' he said.

'What do you mean?' she asked with a frown.

Alexander stared at Hugo and Coco. 'I'm curious. How far have you got?'

Coco smiled. 'You tell us, Monsieur Esnault. I suspect you know far more about our movements than we yours.'

He moved across the room, tapping his chin. 'Oh, I think you're probably quite far along, although I expect you have made a few assumptions along the way.' He paused. 'Wrong assumptions, no doubt.'

'Then you tell us, Monsieur,' Hugo answered, 'as you seem to know so much.'

He shook his head. 'Non, that's not how this is going to work, not at all, not in any way. I'm in charge here.'

Hugo laughed. He paused and decided to take a chance. 'Oh, Monsieur, you haven't been in charge for a long time. You've only been pretending, haven't you? Throwing money and power around like a child throws toys in a sandpit. It has made you feel as if you are in control, but you never really were, were you?'

Alexander Esnault's jaw tightened. 'Be very careful, Hugo. My power and my reach is very real, and I'd hate for you to feel just how strong I am, and how I deal with those who cross me.'

'Alexander,' Pierre Duchamp interrupted wearily. He shook his head as if admonishing his client.

'You should remind your son of his place,' Alexander snapped back.

Pierre stole a look in Hugo's direction before turning back to Alexander. 'I don't represent my son, but I do represent you, and because of that I remind you of the conversation we had earlier.'

'He knows nothing,' Alexander hissed.

'Oh, we know plenty,' Coco interjected.

Alexander laughed. 'As I said, you know nothing. All you have is half-truths and pieces of gossip. Nothing which amounts to anything.'

Hugo stood and pulled out a cigarette.

'This is a non-smoking building, Hugo,' Pierre said.

Hugo ignored him, lit his cigarette, taking a moment to enjoy it. 'I'm not entirely sure of your intentions here today, Monsieur Esnault, but I can tell you mine. We will not be leaving this office without an arrest, possibly several, being made.'

Alexander cackled. 'You have a high opinion of yourself, Hugo. Perhaps you're not so different from your Papa after all.'

Hugo ignored him and continued. 'Let's cut to the chase, Monsieur, so we can all be on our way. Why did you really call this meeting? Was it because we met with Monseigneur Augustine Demaral yesterday?'

Alexander bit his lip, turning his head away, gazing out of the window. 'I'm surprised you found him,' he said finally.

'Not down to us. It was thanks to Jean Lenoir. He was well hidden, which I suppose was always your intention, non?'

'What is going on here?' Fleur Gassna cried. 'What does the Monseigneur have to do with any of this horrible business?'

'In the end,' Hugo said, 'he has everything and nothing to do with it.'

'What is that supposed to mean, Captain?' Morty interrupted.

Hugo moved across the room looking for an ashtray and not finding one, stubbed his cigarette in the bin. Pierre Duchamp tutted. Hugo moved back to the window, facing

Alexander. 'Let's begin with *The Circle*,' he began, 'a secret society operating within the Parisian Catholic Church. The society has a long history and, in simple terms, is a ritualistic and symbolic sect which, amongst other things, uses young women to be part of the rituals.'

Morty sighed. 'Again, what relevance does this have to our investigation?'

'It's very relevant,' Hugo retorted, 'because I believe there are members of the society in the room, right now.' He paused, allowing the information to sink in. He also wanted to hear if there were any involuntary reactions. He heard nothing, but he knew he could not lose his cool now. He had to continue, and he had to make them talk. Axel Soudre's life most probably depended on it.

He continued. 'The society continued for many decades, finally coming under the leadership of the Monseigneur and as I said, it was mostly symbolic.'

'Mostly?' Cedric asked.

'Oui. I believe, however, that some members came to believe the work they were doing was a calling. In short, they believed it was real. That they were doing Dieu's work.'

Alexander snorted again. 'They all said that.'

Hugo stared at Alexander, his eyes widening in surprise. It was as if the confident young man in front of him had crumbled. His eyes tired and weary as if he had spent too long protecting the child buried deep within him.

'*The Circle* met at the building which doubled as the children's home which the Monseigneur also ran, in a barely accessible cellar far beneath the home, and it was here that a woman called Maude, her real name we probably will never know, changed everything.'

'How?' Cedric asked.

'One of the men in *The Circle* became infatuated with her, so much so he began a relationship with her. A relationship which ended up with her becoming pregnant. I suspect she was a prostitute. *The Circle* usually used prostitutes for their rituals and when she became pregnant, I believe she was taken to a make-shift home beneath the Children's home. I don't know how or why the circumstances changed. Perhaps she decided she wanted to leave, and that was something her lover couldn't allow. So, she became a prisoner, held against her will in the cellar which only her captor had access to. I further believe she gave birth to two children in that cellar. First, the boy we now know as Jérémie and then another boy,' he paused, his eyes drifting towards Fleur and Corentin Gassna, 'who later became known as Marc Gassna.'

Fleur Gassna gasped, hand flying to cover her mouth. She made the sign of the cross in front of her. Her husband, Hugo noted, did not turn his head, his gaze fixed firmly on a row of books behind Pierre Duchamp's desk. Hugo could not decide whether Corentin Gassna was looking at something in particular, or just trying to avoid Hugo seeing his face.

Hugo continued. 'Now, there came a time in this horrible story that the boys escaped, fleeing their captor and the only home they had known. Sadly, they became separated and,' he gave a sad smile to Fleur Gassna, 'we know what happened to Marc. But Jérémie was left alone, creating the best life he could. It was amazing he survived considering how he had lived and his age, but he was fortunate to have made a friend whose own life had made her able to care for him. Together they found a way to survive.'

'This is all very interesting, I'm sure, Hugo,' Pierre Duchamp said, 'and I note you haven't lost your flair for the dramatic, but what is your point, and are you going to get to it soon? This is not why we asked you to come here.'

'The hell it is,' Alexander Esnault hissed. 'Let Hugo finish. I want to see how smart your son is and how far he's prepared to go.'

'Marc soon began to have nightmares, disjointed memories of what happened during his time in captivity,' Hugo added, 'though I suspect he never really understood what it was he was remembering, not in the beginning at least. I'm no expert, but I've been a police officer for most of my adult life and I would like to think I have a little understanding of psychology and the pathology of human life.' He turned to the Gassna's. 'I can't imagine what happened with Marc, but his past came back to him, and I don't imagine he knew or understood how to deal with it.'

'That's why we sent him to Dr. Caron,' Corentin Gassna snapped. 'Marc needed help.'

Hugo turned to Victor Caron. 'But that's not the only reason, is it? It was also because you knew exactly who he was, where he came from, and what he'd been through, and therefore you could be trusted to be discreet.'

Dr. Caron opened his mouth to respond but did not answer. Hugo repeated his question. 'You have to understand, this isn't what you think it is,' Dr. Caron said finally.

'And what does he think it is, exactly?' Alexander Esnault interrupted. 'Other than a pack of perverts. Pedophiles. Alors? Which is it? What is it exactly you hope the good Captain Duchamp doesn't misunderstand about your sick little club?'

'Captain Duchamp, you're correct. *The Circle* was an organisation which we are born into. I took my father's place, just as he had with his own. There was nothing dirty about *The Circle*. Not at least, then,' Dr. Caron said.

'When did it go wrong?' Hugo asked, watching to see if Caron looked at anyone in particular. He did not.

'Not everyone understood our mission,' he gave by way of an answer. 'And they polluted the good work we did.'

Coco tutted angrily. 'Quit with the party line, doc, and tell us the truth. What happened?'

Caron lowered his head again. 'I cannot say.'

Coco coughed and handed Hugo her cell phone. He flicked on his glasses and read the screen. He touched her arm and then turned his head. 'Then why don't we ask Jérémie and Marc's father.' He met the intense gaze of the man next to him. 'Well, what do you have to say for yourself?'

Commander Mordecai Stanic's eyes widened, pupils dilating. He turned his head quickly, flicking from side to side. 'Who on earth are you talking to?'

Hugo held his gaze firm. 'I'm talking to you, Commander Stanic.'

Stanic turned to Coco. 'What is this idiot going on about?'

Coco lowered her head. She seemed to be unable to look at him. 'Morty. We know.'

He pulled his shoulders back, pressing his back against the chair. 'You know what?' he asked with incredulity. 'What the hell are you talking about?'

Pierre Duchamp cleared his throat. 'What is going on here, Hugo?' he asked.

Alexander Esnault interrupted. 'Things are about to get very interesting, that's what, Pierre. I knew it would. The second I met your son I knew he was the one who would unravel this shit, consequences be damned.' He shook his head. 'When you first told me about your son, Pierre, you made him sound... well, you made him sound weak and useless, like an aborted foetus which managed to crawl its way out of an abortion bucket. But the more I heard of him, the more I found out about him, I knew the truth was far more interesting. He crawled away all right, but he crawled away from your poison.' He smiled at Coco. 'That's why it was so important we get Hugo here, to make him part of the investigation because I knew he

584

wouldn't be afraid of the outcome. He wouldn't consider being yet another police officer who would turn a blind eye, even if it was a police officer in the line of fire. Whereas I knew you would, could not, act the same way.'

Coco glared at him. 'I'm a police officer, first and foremost, Monsieur Esnault. I'd arrest my own damn kid if they deserved it.'

'But their father?' he asked. 'Do you really want to have to explain to your kids you put their father in prison?'

She turned to Morty but seemed unable to maintain it, instead turning back to Esnault. 'I wouldn't rule out castrating him with my bare hands right now, actually. And if you've done half as much research on me, Esnault, you know that to be true. I'd do it here, with all of you as witness, and I wouldn't break a sweat.'

'Someone will have to explain what the hell is going on, right now,' Cedric interrupted.

Hugo nodded. 'I will try, but s'il vous plaît, you're going to have to bear with me. This isn't easy, and it's complicated, really complicated, but as I was saying earlier, I believe it all began from a very simple place. Captain Brunhild and I spoke with the Monseigneur yesterday and what he didn't tell us was almost as telling as what he did because it honestly helped me fill in the blanks. To understand the dynamics and,' he inhaled, 'to see what was really, sadly, a very simple story which just got out of hand.' He watched Morty, his whole left leg was slapping nervously against the ground. 'You joined *The Circle* after one of the members died, didn't you? And you did because you discovered your father had also once been a member.'

Morty lifted his head slowly. 'My father was never proud of me. I was small like my mother, not tall and strong like him and his brothers. He used to say I was born with none of the Sicilian manliness. He barely ever bothered to hide his disappointment in me.' He snorted. 'Then imagine my surprise when I find out for all these years he was prancing around in a white smock, dancing over nubile, naked hookers. Rubbing holy water on them as if they were the Virgin Mary incarnate. My only regret is I never got to laugh in his face just as he had mine for all those years.'

'If you thought it laughable, then why did you join?' Hugo asked.

He shrugged. 'Because I could. Because I should. And besides, I knew right from the get-go it was a great place to make contacts, good contacts. I was fed up of being some poor immigrant kid, dealing with the kids, cleaning up the shit, doing all the jobs nobody else wanted to do, just because I was a good Catholic boy who did what his mother told him to do. I wanted my time in the sun. I wanted to make my father spin in his grave seeing everything I achieved despite him, not because of him.'

'Oh, Morty,' Coco cried, lowering her head.

Morty glared at her. 'Don't you dare judge me, Charlotte. We're cut from the same cloth, you and I. That's why we got on so great, in bed and out, non?'

Coco shuddered. 'What did you do, Morty, tell me, what did you do?'

He turned his head. 'Not what you think,' he whispered.

'Then talk to me,' she pleaded, 'tell us we're wrong. PROVE we're wrong.'

'What happened when you joined *The Circle?*' Hugo asked.

Morty smiled. 'I met some interesting people.' He turned his head slowly. 'And became a part of something. I became someone. Isn't that right, Corentin? I became one of you.'

Corentin Gassna turned his head slowly, his eyes dark and cold. 'You were never part of *The Circle*, half-breed. Like your father, and Luka and Ricard, just men Monseigneur Demaral took pity on. He used to say, "we need the blood of all walks of men if we are to make *The Circle* fulfill its destiny." That's all you were, a social experiment. What is it they call it these days? Fulfilling a diversity quota?'

'Shut up, old man,' Morty hissed. 'At the end of the day, you, the good Dr. Caron over there, were all the same dirty old men ogling young girls and justifying it in the name of religion.'

'Not just young girls,' Alexander Esnault said, his voice cracking.

Hugo turned to him. 'You were one of the boys, weren't you? One of the boys who lived at Monseigneur

Demaral's children's home, oui? Did you become part of the ritual?'

Alexander closed his eyes, a vein on his neck throbbing. 'August Damar was nothing more than a voyeur,' he finally said. 'A sadistic control freak. For him, it was all about power. And who better to have control over? Perverts and little kids. Not that it makes it any better. Just because he didn't do the touching, he somehow thought it absolved him. It didn't. As far as I was concerned it made him worse. I mean, how else do you explain it? He allowed kids to be used for his stupid ritual, and he actually thought he was doing us a favour.' He sucked in a breath, his chest rising and falling. 'And he was right. Do you know, we used to be grateful to be picked to take part in their stupid games? To lie there on the ground in the middle of a circle, naked and vulnerable, and have grown men paw at us? We were grateful because we knew as long as we took part, as long as we did what they wanted, then we were treated better. Better food, chocolate. The first time one of them fucked me I got a packet of M&Ms, and I thought I'd won the fucking lottery. Damar might not have gotten his own dick out, but he knew what was happening, and he didn't care. All he cared about was his damn secret society and the Church. We were street kids, we were nothing, and we were expendable. Pieces of meat. He knew it and he didn't care.'

'How did you escape it, then?' Hugo asked. He felt

pity for Alexander and what they had subjected him to. But he was not sure it justified the man he became, the crimes he had committed, and the lives he himself had shattered.

'I become good at it,' Alexander answered matter-of-factly. 'And when you become good at something you learn all the tricks and you learn quickly. This one guy, some rich white banker dude, liked me to walk around his apartment in a nappy. Another dude liked me to walk up and down on his back, another liked to snort cocaine off my ass. And he was rich, filthy rich, and like so many other rich men, he didn't enjoy getting his hands dirty. But what did I care about taking risks? My whole life was about taking risks. So, I took his money, and I found him drugs, and found his friends drugs and they were only too happy to pay whatever I asked. And because they had no idea how much drugs really cost, or just didn't care because they were so loaded, it was easy for me. Before long I was making double, triple, what the drugs actually cost me to buy.'

'And an empire was born,' Coco said bitterly, throwing her hands in the air.

'How do you think any empires are born?' Alexander retorted. 'By someone with balls stepping over the plebeians and using them. I was sick of being the plebeian. I wanted to be the ringmaster.'

Coco shook her head. 'See, that's what I don't get about people like you. I get you had a horrible start in your life, and believe me, if I had a chance I'd most likely personally castrate the filthy perverts who abused you with my own two hands. But what I can't reconcile, what makes me sick, is you turn right around and do it yourself. Find some mixed-up kid and send them off to do your dirty work. How do you reconcile that, Monsieur Esnault?'

He tutted. 'You can't be that naïve, Captain Brunhild, surely? What do you want me to do? These kids were on the street anyway, they were doing it anyway. I just wanted to make sure they got what they deserved and that they were safe. That's all that mattered to me. And ask them. Ask them whether they prefer working for me, or some pimp on the street who is only interested in getting them hooked on drugs and using them until they can't be used anymore. You've spoken with Delphine and the others, and I can't believe they've told you otherwise.'

'They still had no choice,' Coco snapped back.

'They always had a choice. They just chose right,' Alexander replied.

'I doubt Jack Boucher would agree,' Hugo said.

Alexander glared at him. 'His death had nothing to do with me. Nor Marc's.'

Hugo shook his head. 'Oh, it had everything to do with you. We both know that you just don't want to admit it.' He turned back to Morty. 'When did you first realise Jérémie was your son?'

Morty slammed his fist onto the armrest. 'Why are you saying this? It's nonsense.'

'We know, Morty,' Coco said, her head turned away from him as if it was too difficult for her to bear. 'S'il te plaît, I'm begging you not to make this any more difficult than it already is. We have children together,' she added, the pain and desperation clear in her voice.

Hugo interjected, raising his hand. 'Commander Stanic, before you say anything else, I should tell you, we have proof.'

'Proof?' Morty gasped. 'What proof do you have?'

'We have DNA,' Hugo replied. He looked away, trying not to show his hand. He realised he was going out on a limb with potentially drastic repercussions if he was wrong. But he did not think he was, and he knew he had to take a chance if there was any likelihood of saving Axel Soudre's life. He had to believe he was still not too late to do that.

'What do you mean, DNA?' Morty said through gritted teeth. 'There is no DNA evidence,' he added with utter conviction. Too much conviction, Hugo thought.

'How can you be so sure?' Hugo countered.

'Because Corentin Gassna fathered the two boys,' Morty said.

Corentin's eyes widened in abject horror. 'I most certainly did not.'

Fleur looked at her husband, her lip trembling. 'Is it true? Did you father Marc in this sick way?'

He shook his head. 'Non, non, I did not. S'il vous plaît, it's just as you said. This was all a ritual. A game. I never, never took it any further.'

'But you knew about Marc. *L'enfant perdu,* didn't you?' Hugo asked. 'And so did you, Dr. Caron. Once you saw the woman known as Maude you knew what had happened and you did your best to cover it up because you knew whatever your actual involvement was, when the scandal hit, it wouldn't matter. You would all be blamed and you would all be shamed and the scandal would most likely ruin you all.'

Dr. Victor Caron stabbed a finger angrily towards Morty. 'You were proof we shouldn't have allowed outsiders into *The Circle* because you didn't know how to control yourself.'

'I don't understand,' Fleur Gassna said desperately. 'Corentin. Was Marc your son? I mean, your REAL son? Is that what you were getting up to on those endless nights away from me?'

'Non, I'm telling you, non!' Corentin said desperately.

'That's not what the DNA evidence says,' Coco said. 'Actually, it confirms you were Marc's biological father, and therefore, most certainly Jérémie's too.'

Corentin looked at her in surprise. 'You're lying. I can't have fathered those boys.' He turned to his wife, his hands flailing. 'Fleur, I'm telling you, none of this is true. They're lying.'

'Well, we're not lying,' Hugo interrupted, 'because that's what the DNA evidence says. But just because we're not lying, it doesn't mean someone else isn't.'

'What's that supposed to mean, Hugo?' Pierre Duchamp asked.

Hugo turned to Morty. 'How did you know the DNA evidence pointed to Corentin Gassna?'

Morty's eyes widened. 'Because... because they do.' He moved his finger between Coco and Cedric. 'They must have told me.'

'Not me,' Cedric said, 'it's all news to me.'

'And I didn't tell you either, Mordecai,' Coco said sadly, 'not for any other reason other than there wasn't time. I didn't file a report because I didn't have time or understand what it meant.'

Morty shrugged. 'Then I must have seen a forensic report.'

She shook her head. 'Non. The report hasn't been issued yet. Which means there can only be one way you know about it. You doctored the report. You switched the DNA and I can't begin to imagine how you did it, but you did, didn't you? What was it? You got one of your pals in the forensic lab to switch it? Some corrupt asshole who'd turn a blind eye for a friend? What did you tell him? You needed help to get some broad off your back who was claiming you'd knocked her up.' She shook her head again, blue hair falling over her face. She did not remove it. 'I love the police force, Morty, despite the way its treated me sometimes, but I'm not stupid, or naïve. I know there are corrupt assholes eating away at it from the inside. You had your DNA swapped, didn't you? You replaced your DNA in the police database with Corentin Gassna's so that if anything happened, if any of this came out, then the DNA wouldn't point to you.'

'That's not even possible,' he said.

'It shouldn't be,' she replied. 'But you did it and we can figure out how, and why and with whom later. But right now, at this second, we know you lied and why you lied and we can prove it. But so help me Dieu, if you make me prove it in a court of law, I'll kill you with my own bare hands.'

Morty's face was ashen. 'How can you prove it?'

'Because we have our own friends. Our own DNA experts who can compare the DNA of Marc Gassna with another DNA sample. Our son and daughter, par example. Cedric and Esther. OUR children. If you drag them into this, I swear on everything I hold holy, you'll regret it. Now, man the fuck up and be the man you said you are, not the man your father thought you were.'

Morty did not respond, and the silence was deafening.

'Morty,' she said with desperation. 'S'il te plaît. Cedric. Esther. They are your children. I know this for a fact because I was there. Jérémie and Marc. Are they their brothers?'

The silence continued.

'Mordecai!' Coco yelled. 'If you don't answer me right now, I'm going to have Cedric here go and arrest your mother.'

'My mother?' Morty gasped. 'What the hell would you arrest her for?'

'For kicks,' Coco retorted. 'For every bad thing she has ever said to me, about me. For every dirty look she has given me, my kids, my life, my goddamn hair, my weight and just because as a flic, I suspect she might have known about, or harboured, a criminal.' She pointed to Pierre Duchamp. 'Hell, I'll even do a deal with the devil if I have to. We'll come up with something.' She sucked in her breath. 'Cedric and Esther,' she repeated. 'This will be hard enough on them as it is. We are their parents, and it's our job. Our ONLY job to make them into as less fucked up as possible adults as we can, and I'm guessing we're not doing the best job at that as we should. So, I'm going to ask you one more time. I'm pleading with you. Make this right. If not for me, for your kids. *All of them.*'

Morty's face tightened, the muscles flexing.

Hugo spoke. 'I'm guessing you fell in love with Maude.'

Coco scoffed. 'Fell so much in love he just had to lock her in a cellar and treat her like a slave. Yeah, that's love for ya!'

Hugo turned his head. 'Captain Brunhild, not now, s'il te plaît,' he said.

Morty sighed. 'Her real name is Anna.' He exhaled. 'And non, I didn't love her. Not really. And I didn't imprison her. Not really. None of this is what you think it is.'

'Oh, I'm pretty sure it is,' Coco interrupted. She mouthed *désolé* to Hugo. He gestured for Morty to continue.

'This is the truth,' he said.

'I don't expect you to understand or even believe what I'm about to tell you, but I ask you to try,' Commander Mordecai Stanic said in a whisper.

'I've been a police officer for a long time, most of my adult life, thirty years almost, and I came to this profession with the best of intentions. You can accept that or not, but it's the truth.

I knew about *The Circle* from my father. Like me, he was a glorified janitor around the children's home. Doing the jobs no one else wanted to do, but he always knew what they were up to, the silly games they played. You know the details, there's not a lot I can add to it. Grown-up men playing dress up and thinking they're doing some kind of Divine Intervention. Saving the souls of the fallen in some misguided belief they'll elevate their own. When Luka Artel died, it was easy for me to jump in. I made it clear I knew what they were up to in the cellar and that if they didn't let me in, well; I didn't have to threaten them too much. They let me in. And at first I enjoyed it for what it was, weird men doing weird things, and it was enough because I had finally achieved something my father had not.

The day they brought Anna into The Circle, everything changed for me. They called her Maude, for some stupid reason, I think it was because she reminded the Monseigneur of an old aunt or something, some fallen wench, which of course made her perfect. She was perfect.

Young and beautiful, tender, and actually quite joyous.

I think I fell in love with her that first night because I hated the way the other men pawed her. I wanted it to be just me. It wasn't love, for her, I'm not stupid. She was only fifteen or sixteen, but she'd already been on the game for years. She was pretty though, skin as soft as butter and hair as golden as the sun. I guess it was love, or something like it. I thought I'd save her. Take her away from the rabbit hole she'd fallen down. I didn't have any money, but I'd spent my childhood doing chores for the Monseigneur, cleaning, painting, that sort of thing, so I knew about the room beneath the cellar. It was difficult to get to. I'd only found it because one day, I put my foot through a rotten floorboard. I'm not even sure the Monseigneur knew about it, or if he had once, he'd certainly forgotten about it.

It was perfect. I don't know what it was originally, probably some hidden alcove for previous wars. There was only one way in and out and it was behind a locked door, accessible only by a set of rickety stairs. I thought Anna would be safe there. Away from her pimp, away from her pusher. And she was, but it was hard. She wanted drugs so badly, and I didn't know how to help her, but I tried. As I said, I couldn't give her what she wanted. I didn't have the money and the more she begged, the more she pleaded, the further I got lost. I wanted to help her, and I wanted to save her, and I thought if I could, she would love me. Not just as a trick, but as a man. Like the way my mother loved my father.

So, I locked the door. For her own good. To get her clean. And I don't know what changed, but something did. She was in my control. Her life was in my control and I'm ashamed to say it, but I enjoyed it. I enjoyed the way she looked at me each time I came, like I was her saviour. Her Messiah. I suddenly saw why all the men enjoyed being in *The Circle*. To be in control. To have power. It was intoxicating. And I'm not proud to say it, but it was like my own drug. To hold her life in my hands was intoxicating. By the time we realised she was pregnant it was too late to do anything about it, not that I would have. Life is precious, and abortion was out of the question. I wrestled with what to do. Let her go? But what if she told? I didn't know how old she was, and I didn't want to bring shame on my family, or the Monseigneur, and certainly not the Church or the home. Anna begged for her freedom, but I could see the truth in her eyes. She wanted me to stay, and she wanted drugs and I couldn't take the risk of what I'd done being discovered. So she stayed, and we became a family.'

Coco retched, her hand covering her mouth.

'Are you all right?' Hugo asked with concern.

She waved her hand and nodded. She removed her hand, glaring at Morty. 'You make it sound touching, like a love story, rather than what it was. Kidnapping and rape.'

'Charlotte,' Morty replied, desperation clear in his voice.

She pointed at him. 'And when exactly did you decide to pimp her out? Anna and her kids? YOUR kids.'

He shook his head vehemently. 'That wasn't me. I had to go away. It had been decided long before all of this that I would become a police officer. My grandfather had been one and my father would have been too had it not been for an injury he'd sustained during the War. As much as I didn't want to leave, I had to, to begin my training.'

Coco snorted. 'Don't you see how rotten this all is? You go off to college to become a flic, starting a career which is meant to be good and honourable, while all the time you've got a woman and a pair of kids, locked up in some grimy cellar?' She shuddered. 'I want to scrape my skin off my body. Every place I let you touch me…'

Hugo touched her arm. 'Not now, Coco. There'll be time for that later, but not now, d'accord?' he whispered.

She gritted her teeth, eyes flashing angrily. But then she nodded, touching his arm with gratitude.

Hugo continued. 'You said it wasn't you who introduced other men to Anna. Who was it?'

'His name was Luka Artel, also one of *The Circle*, we'd become friends. One day he followed me, I don't know why, but he said he knew I was up to something and he wanted to know what it was.'

'So, instead of calling the police he decided to join in?' Coco asked with incredulity. 'Some friends you have, Mordecai.'

'What could I do? He said he would help me, that he didn't want me to go to prison because of some tramp. And he didn't want *The Circle* to be discovered.' He paused. 'So, he offered to look after her when I was gone.'

'And what happened when you came back?' Hugo asked.

'I was angry, furious. I wanted to take Luka by the neck and throttle him to death,' Morty replied. He shrugged. 'But what could I do? Luka was in charge now and he'd given Anna drugs again and she was hooked. You have to understand, it was a vicious circle. Anna wanted the other men, because she knew what they would bring her, stuff I couldn't afford. And the fact was, I couldn't do it on my own any longer because I didn't know what to do. Luka took charge, and I was actually relieved.'

'And you let them rape your own son?' Coco hissed, spittle flying from her mouth.

'I didn't know about it,' he said earnestly, 'I really didn't. Nobody told me, Anna never told me, the kids never told me. Luka never told me. When I came back to Paris, I visited her less and less. I was ashamed, desperately sorry, but I didn't know what to do.' He closed his eyes. 'I suppose in a lot of ways, I was grateful that night they got away. Anna was high and angry, I don't know what had happened but she just snapped. She went after me, and I defended myself.'

'Defended yourself! Coco cried. 'The poor woman is in the nuthouse, barely alive. The doctors say she'll probably never recover. That wasn't defending yourself, Mordecai. That was protecting yourself. You just didn't want your neat little world to crumble, did you?'

He did not answer instantly. 'If that was the case, I would have left her there.'

'I don't believe you would,' Hugo interjected. 'Because you couldn't take the risk she'd be found, dead or alive and if the cellar was discovered, then the likelihood was you would be discovered as well. Non, you removed Anna from the cellar because you knew she was in no position to speak, and the chances were, she would just be considered another prostitute assaulted by a John. I believe you released her because it was the safest thing to do, not for her, but for you.'

Coco shook her head. 'I can't tell you how much I hate you right now, Mordecai.'

Hugo turned to Corentin Gassna and Dr. Victor Caron. 'We spoke with the Monseigneur yesterday and we know Morty came to the three of you and told you what had happened and that is when you came up with a plan. A plan of self-preservation. To protect *The Circle* and all of you who were part of it. You knew nobody would believe you had no part in what happened in the cellar, so you felt as if you had no choice.'

'Corentin,' Fleur Gassna cried. 'Tell me this is not true. Tell me you had no part in this.'

He stared at his wife. 'What would you have me do? Captain Duchamp is right, if it came out there's not a chance people would think I had no part in it. The scandal would have ruined me, us. Everything we had would have disappeared. I did this to protect you, Fleur. To protect our life.'

She closed her eyes, shaking her head quickly. 'I can't believe this, I just can't believe it.' Her eyes snapped open. 'And don't you dare say you did this for me.' She shook her head. 'So, you knew about Marc all the time? What had happened to him? What he had been through?'

He nodded his head slowly, thin cheeks flushing crimson. 'When Mordecai came to us, we agreed we had no choice for the sake of *The Circle,* so it may carry on. None of us wanted to be responsible for its downfall. After all, it had been operating for longer than us, and without any hint of a scandal.'

Fleur gasped. 'And that was more important than what happened to that poor woman?'

Corentin did not respond.

Hugo continued, turning to Dr. Victor Caron. 'And for your part, your job was to do what, monitor Anna and make sure she didn't talk?'

The doctor sighed before nodding. 'As you must have seen, she is in no condition to talk, but that has nothing to do with me. After the,' he lowered his voice, stealing a sly look at Morty, 'altercation, the head injury she sustained was most likely life-altering, that combined with the large amount of drugs in her system, there really would never be a positive outcome.'

'How convenient for you all,' Coco tutted.

'And Marc?' Hugo asked.

Dr. Caron replied. 'When *L'enfant perdu* was found, it wasn't too big a leap to realise who he was, and I managed to become part of his care team.'

Hugo nodded. 'To keep an eye on him?'

Caron shrugged. 'To help. Believe it or not, my only intention was to help him, to make sure he had a chance to recover. I am a religious man, and it was the right, the *Godly* thing to do. Despite what you might all be thinking, we were just trying to make the best of a horrible situation.'

'Bullshit. All you people are ever interested in is covering your own asses,' Alexander Esnault said bitterly.

'And that's why you adopted, Marc?' Hugo asked Corentin Gassna.

Corentin shook his head. 'Stop reading into this. Victor and I had nothing but good intentions. After all, who else wanted Marc? There was no sign of the brother, the mother was incapable and the father…' he looked at Morty, 'well, the father could not get involved for obvious reasons.'

Fleur turned to Hugo. 'I don't understand. You said Marc's DNA proves my husband was his father.' She looked at Morty. 'Tell me the truth. Are you, or is my husband, responsible for those boys?'

'Why did you do this, Mordecai? We did everything we could to help you, I don't understand.' Corentin added, shaking his head.

Morty pointed at Hugo. 'Ask, Monsieur know-it-all over there, because apparently he knows everything. Let's see how smart he is.'

'I believe,' Hugo began, 'the switching of the DNA is what actually lead to the deaths of Jack Boucher, Marc Gassna, and Madame and Monsieur Boucher, because you trusted Alexander Esnault when you shouldn't have.'

Alexander leaned forward. 'Now, we're getting there,' he said with the excited glee of a child at Christmas, 'do tell, dear Hugo, do tell!'

Hugo continued. 'I imagine this began one day at *énergique* when Jérémie began working for Monsieur Esnault. He didn't recognise you, Commander Stanic. It had been a long time since he'd seen you. After all those years in a dark cellar. But it worried you nonetheless and you couldn't take the chance he might remember you. Your first thought was to confuse the issue by using a different name.'

'MY fucking name,' Cedric hissed. 'I thought we were friends, and all the time you were setting me up to take the fall for you. I looked up to you, ever since I was a kid, and as my boss, I thought… I thought you were mentoring me, but all the time, I was just some fucking patsy for you.'

'I didn't set you up,' Morty fired back. 'And for what it's worth, I didn't mean to. You were just there. Someone asked me my name, and I panicked and you were sitting right there next to me.'

Cedric stared at him. 'I've always wanted to say this but never dared. Now I dare. I idolised you when I was a kid but since I got to know you as an adult, I have no idea why because you're a fucking asshole. You're less interested in actual policing and more interested in looking good. To be honest, it'll make me so happy to see you fall because after everything you did to those people, you deserve it. You really, really, REALLY fucking deserve it.'

Coco clapped. 'Here here!'

Hugo cleared his throat and turned back to the Commander. 'I imagine it still scared you. I mean, what if he recognised you and put two and two together? That's where the DNA switch came in, and to switch records, well, you needed a little help.'

Alexander Esnault raised his hand. 'C'est moi!'

'I knew I couldn't just go up to someone and ask them to swap out DNA, Commander or not,' Morty said. 'You're right, I needed help, Dieu help me. I needed help.'

'What did you do for him?' Hugo asked Alexander.

'The same thing I do for all desperate men,'

Alexander answered. 'Their bidding. I make them happy and help them atone for their sins.'

'Morty,' Coco said sadly. 'You made a deal with the devil.'

Morty shrugged. 'What else could I do? I had no choice.'

Hugo repeated his question to Alexander.

He shrugged. 'It was surprisingly easy. I found someone who could help and I,' he coughed, 'encouraged him to do just that. I do this for a living, you know. And as I keep telling you, everyone, everyone has a price.'

'I shudder to think,' Coco retorted.

Alexander smiled. 'The deal was done to everyone's satisfaction.'

'And you recorded your conversation with the Commander, non?' Hugo posed. 'Just like you record every conversation, or interactions with your clients.'

Alexander tipped his head. 'You might say, I find it wise to memorialise my meetings, just so there can be no misunderstanding further down the line,' he added with a smile. 'Once people feel safe, they have the annoying tendency to forget those who made them feel safe in the first place.' He chuckled. 'Fools.'

'I wouldn't laugh, if I were you,' Hugo bristled, 'because those recordings have cost many lives.'

'In what way, Hugo?' Pierre Duchamp asked.

Hugo stared at Pierre, still unsure at to the depth of his involvement. 'I'm guessing Jack Boucher got fed up of recording his time with his clients for your client. Perhaps he got greedy, I don't know. But he decided he wanted his own insurance policy.'

'He'd been sleeping with a rather famous actor,' Alexander interjected. 'Always the same time, doing the same disgusting things in the same hotel. So it was easy to install high-definition recording equipment, direct to the server in my office. Anyway, one night I don't really know what happened. I suppose Jack had enough, or perhaps something happened, I never really asked, but he came to see me, with some made up excuse about being roughed up. When I was called away to take a phone call, I suppose he took the chance and copied some files from my computer onto a USB stick.'

'How did you find out what he'd done?' Hugo asked.

'When I came back into the room, he was acting shifty, and he jumped away from the computer and he ran, so I knew he'd done something. I checked the computer, and it showed the last twenty files I'd saved had just been copied.'

'Twenty? And I'm guessing one of them was your recording with Commander Stanic?'

Alexander nodded. 'Oui, but more importantly, a lot of other recordings, really important recordings which a lot of people would pay dearly to keep secret. I tried to catch him, but he was gone into the night like the rat that he was. I spent days looking for him, had everyone I knew searching, but you can imagine what it's like. These kids can be like rats in sewers when they want to be. It could be months before he surfaced again, and I didn't want to take the risk he'd use what he found. I couldn't take the risk. The contents would ruin me too, and I haven't worked this hard all these years just to be dragged back down into the damn sewers I crawled out of.'

'So, what did you do? Call Commander Stanic?' Hugo said.

Alexander smiled. 'Why not? It was after all in his own best interest to recover what they had taken.'

Hugo turned to Morty. 'And how did you find him?'

Morty exhaled. 'I put the word out on the streets. Made up some rubbish about how I'd be very pleased with whoever found him.'

'You put a price on his head?' Coco shouted. 'A bounty on the poor kid's head? You had to have known how it was going to end, Morty. You had to, you've been doing this for a long time.'

He shook his head. 'I made it clear he wasn't to be touched, I just wanted him found. It didn't take my snouts long to find him, turning tricks down by the Seine, so I went looking for him and there he was. Resting against the wall, smoking a cigarette like he didn't care what he was doing to me. What he was putting me through. I hadn't slept or eaten properly for days and I went up to him, showed him my ID and told him he was under arrest and y'know what the little punk did? He laughed at me. Said he knew exactly who I was, WHAT I was, and that my time was up, not his, and that I'd pay for what I'd done. He called me a pervert and a pedophile and I… and I…'

'And you what, Morty?' Coco interrupted. 'What did you do?' she asked desperately.

'I'm not proud of myself,' he mumbled, 'and you have to believe I didn't mean to. But he was just standing there in front of me, mocking me, threatening the life I've made, everything I stand for, and I saw red. I didn't mean to, I swear I didn't mean to, but I hit him, once, twice, maybe more. I'm not sure, but he hit the ground and banged his head and I knew it was bad, really bad. There was *so* much blood.' He hung his head in shame. 'I killed him, but I didn't mean to, you HAVE to believe me.'

'What happened next?' Hugo asked.

'I panicked and was about to leave and when I turned around, I realised I wasn't alone.'

'Marc Gassna?'

Morty nodded. 'He looked straight at me. With my eyes. I don't know how to explain it properly but they were boring into me, like lasers or something, and he just stared with such hatred and he said, *I know who you are.* I don't know how he knew, because I didn't, not really, and I guess I'm ashamed about that. But before my stupid brain could register what the hell he meant, he was gone. Before I could talk to him, before I could say anything, he was just gone into the night.'

'And what did you do about it?' Coco questioned.

'Because I checked, there were no reports, so you didn't call for an ambulance, or back-up, so what did you do?' Her voice was on the edge of hysteria. Hugo moved to her and rubbed her shoulder, whispering something into her ear. She turned her head slowly towards him and stood on tip-toes, kissing his cheek. 'What did you do, Morty?' she repeated.

Morty stole a look towards Alexander Esnault. 'I made a call and left.'

Hugo and Coco exchanged their own look, telling each other they had understood the implication of what Morty had just admitted.

'So, you disposed of the body, Monsieur Esnault?' Hugo asked.

'My client is admitting nothing,' Pierre Duchamp answered.

'That's probably wise because we know how Jack Boucher actually died, and it wasn't just because of an assault. He was still alive when he was bound and gagged and thrown like a garbage bag into the Seine,' Hugo said. 'But we both know your client is up to his eyes in it and so help me, I'll prove it.'

'I look forward to you trying,' Alexander Esnault responded. 'And it will be tremendous fun, I'm sure. Father and son pitted against each other in court. We're going to have such fun!'

'Why did Marc have to die?' Fleur Gassna asked Hugo, her voice croaking with emotion.

Hugo wanted nothing more than to comfort her. He realised despite his initial impression of her, that she was the type of woman he had grown accustomed to in his own childhood, pinched faces, and eyes as cold as the girls who served them. But her voice, in that instant, told Hugo all he needed to know. Whatever had happened, she had loved *l'enfant perdu* - Marc, and it made his heart ache with such sadness, because he realised it was probably one of the few times in the young man's life he had ever really, truly been loved by an adult who did not want something from him.

'I'm not sure I can answer that,' he said, 'but I suspect it was the combination of a lot of things. We know he was troubled. Troubled by a past he didn't understand and probably didn't completely remember, which, of course, probably made it worse for him. We can only speculate really, but if he was there with Jack that night, and saw him being attacked, his friend, one of his few friends, then I'm sure the guilt he felt, wrongly of course, consumed him. Why he ended his own life that way, I can't say, but it must have just become all too much for him. Guilt and fear. He knew he'd been seen, and that was probably enough for him. He didn't want to run anymore, so…'

'He flew,' she finished.

Hugo lowered his head, the image of a young man falling from the Eiffel Tower flashing through his mind. He turned to Alexander. 'Did you contact him?' he asked.

Alexander lowered his head, pulling at the topknot, his fingers scrapping the hair. It reminded Hugo of a woman he had once known, plagued with the insecurity of her life, she would often scratch her arms and thighs until she bled. She had said it made her feel better. He recognised it in Alexander, but he knew it did not excuse it.

'I sent him a message,' Alexander whispered.

'A message?' Fleur Gassna cried.

Alexander nodded. He met her eyes, as if telling her he was sincere. 'I just wanted him to know that he had to keep quiet. That's all. You have to believe me, I had no idea he would do something so… so…. drastic.'

Fleur Gassna's head dropped. 'You should have,' she cried. 'You should have known he'd had enough. He'd been captive his whole life, abused. And then to see his best friend murdered by his… by his…' she lifted her head, glaring at Morty. 'By the bastard who sired him.'

'I don't think we'll ever really know what really happened,' Hugo said, 'but it's not too much of a stretch to imagine how hurt he was, and how difficult it might have been for him to keep putting one foot in front of another.' He stopped for a moment as his voice broke. 'Perhaps just standing there on the Eiffel Tower, looking down at the place where Jack was murdered, it just all came to a head and he decided enough was enough.'

The room became silent again. Fleur Gassna's breathing was heavy, as if each breath she exhaled was painful to her.

'Enough is enough, Morty. We can't let anyone else be hurt. Where the hell is Axel?' Coco pleaded. 'And I beg you to tell me he's still okay, that he's still alive.'

He glared at her. 'Bien sûr, he's alive. You think I'm a monster?'

Her eyes widened. 'You really want me to answer that, you idiot? Is he? Is he alive?'

Morty nodded. 'He called me to arrange a meeting. Blackmail *again*. He said before he gave me the USB, he wanted me to get him and his friends out of the country - money, new passports, the works. But when I met him and when I tried to get the damn USB from him, he threw it in his mouth and swallowed it. Whatever you think of me, I'm not a monster, it's not as if I was going to cut it out of him. So, I left him somewhere safe until...'

Coco gave a sad laugh. 'Nature takes its course.' She sighed. 'At least that's something. Where is he? And tell me right now, or so help me Dieu, I'll reach over and wring your neck with my bare hands. If you don't think I'm capable of that, then you really don't know me.'

Morty sighed as if it was the first time he had felt relief in a long time. 'He's in my apartment, tied to a radiator.'

Pierre Duchamp cleared his throat. 'Well, I think

we're done here, non? You have your culprit and that's that.'

Hugo nodded. 'We probably are. But be under no illusions this is over. Charges are coming for your client, be sure of that, because he has committed more crimes than we know, I'm very sure of it.' He pointed to Coco. 'Captain Brunhild and Lieutenant Degarmo, and the Minister of Justice will make it their business to make sure he pays for what he's done because we know we're only scratching at the surface. There is a lot more blood on his hands. I'd bet my life on it.'

'You would?' Alexander Esnault said.

Hugo nodded. 'I would and we'll make sure you never get a chance to hurt anyone else again.' He turned to Coco and Cedric. 'You know what you need to do.'

Coco stood, standing in front of Morty. Her mouth opened, but no words came out.

'I'll do it, Captain,' Cedric said, standing next to her.

She wafted him away. 'Non, you won't. This is mine.' She looked at Morty. 'Mordecai Stanic. You are under-the-fuck arrest for more crimes than I can even comprehend, but I will, and you'll pay for it, mon Dieu. You'll pay for it, you piece of shit.'

'And he's really in custody?' Jérémie asked as if he dared not hope it to be true. 'The bastard who fathered me?' he added with bite as if each word was stabbing at his heart.

Coco nodded, pointing beneath her. 'Yup. In the basement...' she bit her lip. 'Désolé,' she exhaled, exhaustion evident in her voice, 'that was insensitive.'

Jérémie's mouth twisted into a sad smile. 'Non, it's fine, actually it's more than fine. It's like, what do you call it, poetic justice? I hope he spends the rest of his life locked in a cellar somewhere, terrified when the door will open, and he's going to get raped again.'

Hugo sighed, gently massaging his temples in an attempt to fend off the storm approaching his mind. He wanted nothing more to get up and leave Coco's office. To leave Paris. Just to leave. He jumped before realising it was Ben's fingers slipping between his own, the familiar soft scars of the burns on Ben's fingers instantly reminding him of everything he had, still had, would continue to have.

Coco threw him a cigarette. 'Here, smoke that, you look like you need it.'

Hugo lit it gratefully, allowing the moment to wash over him. They had only just returned to the Commissariat de Police du 7e arrondissement, where Commander Mordecai Stanic was immediately taken to the cells. Ben, Jérémie, and Delphine had just arrived, joining Hugo,

Coco and Cedric in Coco's cramped office. Hugo sucked hungrily on the cigarette and he realised how tired he was. But there was still so much to do, so much to unravel.

'And Axel?' Jérémie asked in little more than a frightened whisper. 'Is he… Is he?'

'He's alive,' Hugo answered quickly.

'Thanks to some quick thinking on his behalf,' Coco added.

'Quick thinking?'

She nodded. 'He ate the evidence. Therefore, guaranteeing a day or two of respite.'

Despite his mood, Jérémie smiled. 'C'est mon mec.' He paused. 'Where is he?'

'A patrol has gone to pick him up. The paramedics will check him over, and then he'll join us here soon. I promise.'

'But what about Esnault?' Delphine asked. There was still a bite to her tone, but it was tempered, almost as if she was beginning to relax.

Hugo looked at Coco. 'That's more complicated,' he said.

'I knew it! I damn well knew it,' Delphine hissed. 'He's gonna walk free, and we'll never be safe.'

'We couldn't arrest him yet, for several reasons,' Hugo said, 'but you will be safe. You know Jean Lenoir, the Minister of Justice, well, he's aware of the situation and as we speak Alexander Esnault is being taken into protective custody. Somewhere safe and more importantly somewhere where his crimes can properly be assessed. The trouble is, he's a very complicated man leading a very complicated life and his crimes are many. He will talk, and they will punish him, but it will take time. Par example, I believe Alexander was involved in the murder of *The Circle* members Luka Artel and Ricard Allemand. When we spoke with him today, there's little doubt Alexander was abused during his time in the children's home. It's not too much of a stretch to assume he was involved somehow in the deaths of his abusers. We also know he bought the land of the burnt down home, and built an apartment building on it. Perhaps to make sure Monseigneur Demaral didn't rebuild it.'

'Speaking of the priest,' Cedric said, 'I still don't get how exactly he ended up in jail?'

Coco answered. 'He had no choice.' She said. 'Alexander set him up. He believed just because Monseigneur wasn't one of the abusers, he was just as guilty because he turned a blind eye to what was going on. He wanted him to pay in one way or another. Alexander wanted the Monseigneur to be punished. Not killed, but punished. He couldn't prove he was a pedophile, so he set him up on some phoney charge. The Monseigneur said he went along with it because it was his chance to repent for what had happened to the children under his care and on his watch. Perhaps that's true, but perhaps it was just because he didn't have a choice. His powerful friends, however, still made the hint of any scandal disappear. I don't suppose Alexander cared too much. He wasn't interested in making public what had happened because he wanted to extract his own revenge. He couldn't do that with public scrutiny, and he's a proud man. For some reason he would imagine he would look weaker to his enemies if they discovered what happened to him when he was a child.'

'So, Commander Stanic killed Jack Boucher?' Ben asked.

'He certainly thinks so,' Hugo replied, 'but I don't believe he did. He clearly attacked him, leaving him for dead, but as we know he wasn't actually dead when he went in the Seine. Alexander Esnault most likely knew and just didn't care, because he wanted rid of his blackmailer - Jack, and by keeping silent, he had something else to hold over the Commander. Morty believed he had killed Jack, and it suited Alexander Esnault to let him continue thinking that way.'

'The bastard,' Delphine cried.

'Then the Commander will get away with it?' Ben asked.

'Well,' Hugo continued, 'he will be charged with attempted murder, or the procurer may just decide to charge him with actual murder because of what he did, his involvement, and the fact he left Jack as if he was dead without trying to get him help. But in any event, because of the DNA evidence, we know Morty murdered and attempted to murder Jack's parents - Ana and Randolph.'

'I don't understand that either,' Cedric interjected. 'Why would the Commander take the risk of murdering the Boucher's?'

Hugo did not answer immediately. 'Because I suspect Jack told his parents about what was contained on the USB and together, they came up with a plan to blackmail those implicated.'

Coco shook her head. 'We saw the payments made to the Boucher's and all the gear in their apartment. I can't see how Morty could have been paying them. As far as I know, he doesn't have two pennies to rub together, nor does his mother.'

'Perhaps he wasn't. I suspect it was Alexander making the payments because he didn't want his little blackmail enterprise to come to an end,' Hugo replied. 'We know Jack was murdered by one or both of them. I suspect Alexander wanted the Boucher's out of the picture, especially with Jack dead, he didn't want to risk them talking so he called on Morty to get rid of the problem. He couldn't do it himself; he wouldn't do it himself. We all know he's not the kind of man to get his own hands dirty but a Police Commander might just get the Boucher's talking and let him into their house.'

'But to kill them in cold blood? Throwing Ana Boucher off the balcony like that?' Coco shuddered. 'I know I shouldn't say this, but I have spent a lot of time with Morty and I've seen a side of him most of you haven't.' She shook her head. 'I get the irony, if I was hearing some woman saying these words I'd think the same as you. *She doesn't know what she's taking about, or she's thinking with her heart,* but,' she sighed. 'I know... I *knew* Morty, I'm sure of it.'

'I think he was just desperate,' Hugo said, before adding, 'and he probably didn't have a choice. Esnault had him over a barrel, and he no doubt threatened him with exposure. When you interview him, I'm sure he'll give you the full story, but I'm guessing he felt as if he didn't have a choice. Morty was seeing his world crumble around him, his life, his career, you, his children. He would lose it all.'

Coco looked at Jérémie. 'Yeah, we need to talk about that. It seems you've got a half-brother and sister.'

'Fuck,' Jérémie exclaimed.

'What made you suspect Commander Stanic in the first place?' Ben asked.

Coco looked at Hugo. 'I'd like to know that too,' she said, 'because you saw it and I didn't and you've gotta know, that means I'm doubting everything I know, everything I thought I knew, right now. And I'm not even sure I should still be a cop, because I didn't see it. I just didn't see it,' she said desperately, evidently on the verge of tears.

'Don't be so hard on yourself,' Hugo said. 'There were just a couple of things, things you probably didn't notice because you knew him. You see him every day, but me, an outsider, could see things more clearly. I'm sure if the roles were reversed, and this were Montgenoux, you would spot things I didn't.'

She smiled at him. 'I'm not sure that's true, H, but bless you for saying it. What was it about him that bothered you?'

'Nothing so obvious,' he replied, 'but the scar on his cheek confused me. When we met, you told me about it, how it had helped him advance in his career, after a drug-dealer attacked him. But then when we met with his mother, she mentioned he'd always had it.'

'Oh, fuck,' she cried, 'she did, and I didn't even notice.'

'And it meant nothing to me at the time, but I also remembered something Jérémie said about his captor, which later connected with the Commander,' Hugo added.

Jérémie frowned. 'I did?'

Hugo nodded. 'And I repeat, together these vignettes mean very little, but put together, it set me thinking.'

'What was it?' Coco asked.

'The perfume,' Hugo replied. 'Jérémie mentioned when their captor came, he would bring gifts, one of which was a sickly perfume…'

'*Like his Mama wore*,' Coco interrupted, her face ashen.

'It meant little, but I recalled the heavy scent of lavender when we met with Mama Stanic,' Hugo added. 'But again, there was no reason to make a connection, but when one thing didn't make sense, I began putting the pieces together. And then when Jérémie mentioned one of his captors had a scar,' Hugo said, 'I remember thinking, that's a bit strange, but again, I didn't put too much thought to it.'

'And then there was the fact someone used Cedric's name. I couldn't think why they would use his name, but as Morty said, he was just there in the wrong place at the wrong time. I never really liked the fact Alexander Esnault was so arrogant, and he didn't even seem to bother hiding the fact he knew all about us. He wasn't really in any sort of fear, and that suggested the likelihood was he had someone in the police department on his payroll. And besides that, it always struck me as odd that the Commander was so desperate to point us in the direction of the Minister of Justice. At first I imagined it was because he hated him, but then I couldn't understand why he was doing it at the cost of looking any deeper into the crimes. I also believe he was the one who sent the photograph of the Minister with Marc and Sebastian to the newspapers, Alexander probably gave it to him.'

'He was pointing us in the opposite direction,' Coco said shaking her head. 'I'm such a fool.'

'And finally, there was the teddy bear,' Hugo added. He turned to Jérémie. 'The teddy bear you took from Captain Brunhild's house yesterday. The teddy bear you recognised the second you saw it.'

Jérémie pulled his backpack onto his lap and opened it, retrieving a dog-eared teddy which had clearly seen better days. He pointed at the left ripped ear. 'This ear was ripped when me and my brother fought over it. He cried and cried so much that we thought we'd get in trouble if the men came, so I gave it back to him and said it was his and I wouldn't try to take it from him again. He loved that teddy because the man, him downstairs, gave it to him. And I never knew what happened to it because Marc went nowhere without it. Even when he grew up, he always carried it around with him in his backpack. I never thought I'd see it again and then all of a sudden I saw it, lying on the floor in her house.'

'Morty gave it to our daughter last week,' Coco said, her voice indicating she was on the verge of tears, 'I nearly threw it out, telling him he should buy his kids decent presents not some old rubbish. But he said it was a family heirloom, and he wanted to pass it on to his child.' She shook her head. 'The bastard.' She looked at Hugo. 'Is that why you wanted check the inventory of what they found on Marc?'

He nodded. 'I remembered when we were in the morgue, there was a teddy bear in Marc's backpack, but later, when I checked the inventory it wasn't listed.'

'Morty took it out,' Coco sighed. 'But why?'

Hugo shrugged. 'Because he could. He had clearance, and he knew nobody was likely to notice, and just perhaps because it meant something to him. Maybe it really was a family heirloom, and he wanted it to come back into his family, rather than end up in an evidence locker somewhere...' he trailed off, realising extrapolation was useless right then.

'This is a real mess,' Coco said. 'And it will take a whole lot of unravelling. Why did Alexander call the meeting at your father's office?'

'I don't know,' Hugo answered. 'Although I suspect he knew we were getting close, and he wanted to, I don't know, make a deal?'

'And will Jean Lenoir make a deal?' Ben asked.

'Not while I have a breath left in my body,' Coco hissed. 'If I have to, I'm not going anywhere. I'll make sure they'll pay for everything they've done.'

Cedric looked at her. 'It could cost you,' he said, 'especially with your... with your relationship with the Commander. People will talk.'

'Let them,' she snapped. She smiled at him. 'But, you're right, nobody is going to believe I knew nothing, no matter what Morty says. If there was ever a time to jump ship, Lieutenant, it's now, especially before the shit really hits the fan. I can have your transfer papers signed today.'

Cedric smiled at her. 'I'm not going anywhere, Captain Brunhild. We're a team, non?'

Coco sniffed, wiping her nose with the sleeve of her jumper. 'Bon, well get out of here, and start on your paperwork. We've got a lot to get through.'

The door to her office opened, and Axel Soudre entered. Jérémie jumped to his feet and pulled his lover into a tight embrace. 'Are you okay?' he asked desperately.

Axel nodded. 'I'm fine. I've gotta go see the doctor, but I wanted to see you first.'

'Merci, mon ami,' Jérémie replied, the relief clear in his voice. 'We'll come with you.' He smiled at Hugo and Coco. 'D'accord?'

Coco nodded. 'Bien sûr. I'll come and find you soon.'

Delphine moved towards the door. She hesitated before following her friends. 'I guess you were right. Maybe we could trust you... un peu.' She pointed to her eyes and then to Hugo and Coco. 'But I'm still watching you.'

Coco smiled. 'I wouldn't have it any other way.'

Ben watched them leave. 'What on earth will happen to those three?'

Coco shrugged. 'I don't know, but they'll be okay. I'll make sure of it.'

Ben nodded. 'I want to help. I don't know how, but I want to help. They deserve a better start in life.'

She smiled. 'And they will. We'll work it out between us.' She turned to Hugo. 'So, what now?'

Hugo stood up. 'Montgenoux awaits.' He cleared his throat. 'I'm sorry for everything that's happened Captain, but I have enjoyed working with you, and getting to know you.'

Coco stepped from behind her desk and pulled Hugo into a tight embrace. 'Oh, stop being so rigid, relax, we're besties now. Just don't be a stranger. Paris isn't so bad when you've got friends in it, non?'

Hugo relaxed into the embrace. 'It's not so bad at all anymore, thanks to you. Au revoir, Coco. Au revoir, Cedric. We'll see you again.'

Coco kissed his cheek. 'I can't wait.'

fin

Hugo inhaled the air of Gare de Nord and he smiled. 'My last taste of Paris,' he said.

Ben squeezed his hand. 'Forever?'

Hugo smiled. 'Non. Not forever, just for now. There's nothing here to scare me anymore.'

'Hugo?'

Hugo stopped dead in his tracks. He did not turn around. He did not need to. The voice was like a knife, ripping into his heart over and repeatedly, like a familiar record playing on repeat.

'Daisy,' Hugo whispered, pushing the letters out of his lungs as if each one hurt. He had never imagined he would say the name out loud again.

Ben squeezed his hand, turning to face Hugo, his golden brown eyes connecting with Hugo's emerald green ones. 'Daisy?' he asked, his face falling. 'Shall I go?'

Hugo still did not turn around, instead squeezing Ben's hand even tighter. 'Don't you dare.' He lowered his voice. 'I'm going to turn around, just give me a moment.'

Ben smiled. 'You've got as long as you need, baby.'

Hugo took a breath and turned around. Emerald green eyes meeting emerald green eyes.

Daisy Duchamp smiled. 'You are so handsome,' she said as if each word hurt her. 'So, so handsome.'

'And you... and you...' Hugo trailed off with a shrug.

'I'm Ben,' Ben said with as much cheeriness as he

could muster, stepping forward and extending his hand.

Daisy took his hand. 'I know who you are, darling. I can't tell you how happy I am to finally meet you.' She pulled a handkerchief from her pocket and wiped her mouth. 'And to thank you, thank you for everything.'

Hugo snorted. Daisy turned to him. 'I'm sorry. I tried to find you earlier but my plane was delayed and... and I.' She sighed. 'Well, I just sat in my hotel trying to figure out what I would say to you after all these years.'

'Twenty-eight,' Hugo interrupted.

'Twenty-eight?' she asked with a frown.

Hugo nodded. 'It was 1991. I was ten. You waved goodbye as you jumped into a taxi. *See ya*. Those were your exact words. *1991*. I was ten. It was a long time ago, and I suppose I can't blame you for forgetting it, but I haven't. When you're ten, you tend not to forget such life altering events.' It was all he could do to look at the woman who birthed him. She was tall, taller than he remembered. Blonde hair falling across her face the exact same way his own did. Her eyes were as green as his. Her face was his. He exhaled again, his eyes looking towards the platforms. The train to Montgenoux was waiting, and he did not want to miss it.

'I know exactly when it was,' Daisy said. 'I have this photo to remind me.'

Her voice sounded strange to him. English with an American, mid-Atlantic lilt. It bothered him in ways which angered him that he cared. 'Why are you here?' he asked finally.

'Your father called me,' she answered.

His eyes flashed with anger. 'Yeah, he told me you two were good friends these days, shame neither of you remembered you had a son.'

'That's not fair,' she began to say before stopping. 'I suppose you have every right to be angry, but that's not why I'm here.'

'Then why are you?'

'When Pierre told me he'd seen you, it just seemed... it just seemed like it was time.'

Hugo nodded. 'Good. I'm glad. You've seen me. Now if you'll excuse us, we have a train to catch...'

'I've carried this photograph with me every day since May 6th 1991. Your grandmother's maid took it of the two of us. I wanted something to remind me of you.'

She handed the photograph to Hugo. He looked at it. His glasses were in his pocket so he held it up to the sunlight, turning it around, as if looking at it directly was too much, making it too real. From behind, through the shadows of the afternoon sun, it was like looking at a television programme, actors playing a role. People he recognised by constantly seeing them but never knowing them. These people could not be real. He did not recognise himself and it broke his heart to see his younger self broadly grinning, enjoying his day, enjoying his mother. But the sun was about to set for him. He handed the photograph back to Daisy. 'I'm glad you got to take a memento with you. Wish I'd had the same. Do you have any idea what my life became after you left me?'

'Your grandmother looked after you, I'm sure. She looked after you in ways I couldn't, especially if I had stayed. I had to leave, Hugo. You know I had to leave.'

'Why?' he asked, his voice breaking. 'Just give me one good reason why you had to leave.'

She lowered her head. 'Because I wasn't meant to be a mother. I didn't want to be a mother, but that's not to say I didn't love you. Because I loved you. There was nothing not to love, but I wasn't prepared. I thought I loved Pierre for a second, and I suppose he thought he loved me for even less. We weren't meant to be together, and we weren't meant to be parents, but by the time we realised it was too late. Your grandmother, despite the fact she was a bitch who hated the ground I walked on, fell in love with you from the first second she saw you. And she wanted you. She didn't want me, but she wanted you. And that's when I knew. Your life was with a woman who wanted you, not a woman who didn't know how to be anything decent to you, for you. So, I left. I know it's hard for you to understand, but it was for the best. Some people just aren't meant to be mothers and the hardest part is that they have to accept it and do what is right for everyone.'

'Is that it? Have you said all you need to say?' Hugo asked.

Daisy stared at him. 'I just wanted to see you. To

really *see* you, not a photograph or a clipping from a newspaper. To see your smile.'

'Good luck with that,' Hugo scoffed.

'I love you, Hugo,' she said, 'more than you can imagine. And your grandmother, she did a good job, didn't she? Much better than I ever could have, or your father for that matter. You're a good person, and that makes me happy. I did something right. Even if that was just leaving you before I tainted you, before I made it all go wrong. Because I would have. I was nineteen when I had you and I knew nothing. I was nothing.'

Hugo sighed. He closed his eyes. There was so much he wanted to say. So much he needed to say, but he realised it was pointless.

'I know I can't be anything to you, not now, it's far too late. But I would like you to try to understand, to find a way to forgive me,' she said. 'Will you forgive me? Can you love me again?'

He looked at her again. He nodded. 'I forgive you for leaving me, but I can't forget it. I've spent so much of my life being afraid of life, of love, of people, and that's because of you and Pierre.' He touched Ben's arm. 'I still wouldn't know love if it wasn't for Ben. So, if it means so much to you, I'll say I forgive you, but I can't say I'll love you. I have always loved the idea of having a mother to love but it has always just been an idea. And I see no reason to change that now.'

'You have no good memories of me?' Daisy asked

desperatelyLes Mauvais Garçons

desperately.

'I have good memories of our maid, our cook, our butler. They were nice to me. They were *paid* to be nice to me. But they were there for me.'

Daisy nodded. 'Don't you have any questions for me? About me? About my life?'

He shrugged. 'What does it matter? As I've said, I love the idea of you, but that's all. I wish you nothing but the best, but that's all I have for you.' He took Ben's hand. 'Let's go, mon amour.' They began walking towards the platform. He did not look back. He did not need to. There was nothing but the dust of passing time behind him. His way was forward, where the sun shone brightly and was warm on his skin. He had spent too much of his life in the dark and would not do it for a second longer. There was nothing behind him. Nothing he needed and there was nothing to be afraid of. The ghosts were gone.

HUGO DUCHAMP WILL RETURN IN A NEW INVESTIGATION:

Prisonnier Dix

<u>Official Midwest Book Reviews:</u>

'UN HOMME QUI ATTEND':

Hugo Duchamp Investigates: Un Homme Qui Attend, introduces a French policeman who has been working abroad in London as an investigator for over a decade; but when he's called home, it's not for family reasons but to investigate the death of a child - an event replete with town politics and special interests.

The result is a powerful saga, all this is part of what serves to make Hugo Duchamp Investigates such a vivid read. As Hugo peels back layers of long-held town secrets, powerful individual special interests, and the possibility of more children in danger, he edges ever closer to a truth that might ripple out and destroy long-held secrets and Hugo's world alike. It all boils down to what will be done for love and revenge, and what will be wrecked in the process.

The feisty detective work of Hugo, his French culture, and his love life promise something satisfyingly different in the world of investigative mysteries, and making this especially recommended for readers who enjoy a firm sense of place and a protagonist whose interests and life don't exactly fit the norm.

'LES *FANTÔMES* DU CHÂTEAU'

Another satisfying investigative piece centered around the colorful and sometimes outrageous personality of Hugo Duchamp. The first satisfying note here is that readers need not hold prior familiarity with Hugo Duchamp in order to appreciate this second book.

Hugo's events and background are summed up in Chapter Two, which paves the way for newcomers and previous fans to enjoy another detective puzzler (the first chapter presents the murder, while the second backtracks a week into London).

The second pleasurable feature of this sequel is that Hugo's character is thoroughly explored in a manner that invites not just reader interest in what happens to him, but creates an emotional attachment that adds a vested interest in Hugo's approaches to life.

It's Hugo's humanity and psychological profile that imbibe his investigations with a personal touch that draw in readers by revealing not just events, but his deepest thoughts surrounding his choices in life.

Hugo faces a cast of characters many of whom have special, secret interests in the murder case. Family money and spending choices, two murders, the hidden truths behind the deaths and how they are handled - all these facets immerse Hugo in one of the most puzzling cases of his life, just a few months after he's still in shock from his last case's unexpected twists. Hugo might ultimately be forced to decide who to save and who to sacrifice in a rolling saga that embroils readers in a powerful tale that concludes (it should be warned) in a cliffhanger.

Readers interested in more than a one-dimensional detective story who look for characters who are flawed, human, and different will relish both Hugo and his circumstances, and will find Hugo Duchamp Investigates: Les Fantômes du Château to be a powerful, highly recommended and compelling story that is as much about the man and his psyche as it is about an unusual crime scene and many elusive motivations.

'LES NOMS SUR LES TOMBES'

The third volume in the series revolving around feisty detective Hugo Duchamp. Hugo is still recovering from injuries sustained during the last case, but there's no rest for the weary when Dr. Irene Chapeau finds her life and career in turmoil and under threat. But the real action takes place not on the political playing field but in Montgenoux's graveyard, where "rest in peace" is about to be thwarted by a man intent on making the entire town pay for what it's done to him.

Friends lie, mirrors lie, and sometimes the scars of psyche and soul that are so well hidden from the world finally erupt in unexpected ways. Hugo and Irene find themselves caught in a web of intrigue and danger that increasingly casts them as prey in a dangerous game.
Political whitewashing and efforts by Hugo and others to keep the investigation in Montgenoux on track create a satisfying series of encounters between investigators, politicians and special interests forces. Hugo's personal life offers him a safe harbor against these disparate forces

Fans of detective sagas will find Hugo a savvy, unique character whose investigative prowess is equaled only by the changes affecting his personal relationship, which moves onto more solid ground even as his professional life seems to be dissolving.
It's these personal moments and their presence within a murder mystery that challenges Hugo's standing in his new home which makes for a riveting plot about different kinds of commitments, including those that last beyond the grave. As the threats begin to strike closer to home, Hugo is on track to experience some of the greatest changes not only in his career, but to his set course in a life he's only finally committed to fulfilling.

One of the most striking features of Hugo Duchamp's mysteries is the dual focus on his life and personal struggles, which juxtapose nicely with each mystery he's involved in. In Les Noms Sur Les Tombes, just when everything seems to be coming together, they fall apart. A striking investigative pursuit wound within the struggles of a different kind of personal life make this a standout addition to the series, with a conclusion that leaves the door wide open for more, pulling readers in with a gripping emotional feel throughout that builds to a shocking crescendo and yet another twist in Duchamp's never-singular course in life.

'L'HOMBRE DE L'ISLE'

L'ombre de L'île represents a departure from Hugo's prior books in that the setting moves far from France as Hugo attempts to free a loved one from prison. Hugo sees the world as a possible crime scene, so his observational skills are as finely tuned as those of Sherlock Holmes. Every place he's lived has changed Hugo. In London, it was a life of self-imposed exile and solitude. France awakened him to new romance and family ties. Nostalgia leads him to momentarily wish he was again that loner who needed no-one, because the pain of having loved deeply and lost is nearly overwhelming - as is the idea that he can possibly regain this love by making an extraordinary effort outside his comfort zone. Prior readers will know that Hugo is an extraordinary detective - but can his skills translate to achieving the one thing he wants most in life, against all odds?

From Ireland to Barcelona and beyond, the trail leads Hugo on an unexpected romp through different countries as he conducts his investigation and uncovers more and more to the mystery. But will his findings be enough to lead to his heart's desire?

One of the many pleasures of Hugo Duchamp Investigates: L'ombre de L'île is that it stands as well on its own as it does as part of a series. Much like Sherlock Holmes, Hugo needs no introduction for newcomers or constant reminders for prior fans in order to prove satisfying (although plots of different books are summarized in the beginning, for those who would receive a quick introduction to previous events). This allows each book to fully embrace Hugo's past and present worlds. L'ombre de L'île is no exception, deftly continuing the sagas of his love and professional lives and points where they intersect without requiring extensive explanation. Another powerful facet of this title lies in the inclusion of many personal transition points which Hugo faces in the course of events. Hugo reflects on these possibilities and his role in them just as much as he reflects on perps, motives, and changing stories.

Too many detective stories fail to impart a proper sense of place and perspective in their sagas, but Hugo constantly faces personal challenges and changes in his quest for justice for himself, his friends, and his world; and these contribute an overall power to each of these books. L'ombre de L'île is no exception: its additional perspectives and engrossing interplays of romance, personal evolution, and investigative procedures is simply delightful, and will offer not a few surprises in the course of exploring Hugo's constantly expanding world.

'L'ASSASSINER DE SEBASTIAN DUBOIS'

With yet another addition to the blossoming story of feisty French investigator Hugo Duchamp, it should be evident that Hugo's personal growth and life is as much a central part of his stories as his investigations into matters that too often hold big impacts on his personal life and evolution.

The setting is Montgenoux, France in 2017, where Hugo has just returned to his job as Captain of a small French town's police station after two weeks on a Caribbean Island, where loneliness and the possibility of quiet anonymity is juxtaposed by the attention he earns as an obvious stranger in town.

While there, he comes to realise that his previous London life didn't hold the same happiness he's experienced in Montgenoux - nor the same challenges. He still loves Ben even as he acknowledges Ben's decision changed his life and caused him to run away from everything he's loved. Now he's back, with trouble extending beyond romance, stemming from an old promise made to Sebastian Dubois, a man he met the previous year, who saved Hugo's life and is now in prison.

But all this is just the backdrop to a riot at the new prison, a terrible murder, and the appearance of criminals from his past who return to haunt Hugo's future.

Kidnapped girls endangered, internal investigations when no crime has really been committed, and circumstances which keep drawing Hugo back to the past and to the new Centre Pénitentiaire de Montgenoux all coalesce in a story that examines life in prison and subterfuge that embraces Sebastian Dubois, a "cat with nine lives", and a situation which has spiraled out of control and out of the hands of the police.

Hugo's life is always filled with possibilities, whether it's racing against time, tracking down perps, or dealing with a myriad of romantic challenges. *L'assassiner de Sebastian Dubois* is a powerful continuation of all the forces evident in previous books in this series, takes many unexpected turns, and is very highly recommended for prior readers who have developed an affection for a French investigator who constantly finds his personal and professional lives entwined and challenged by deadly forces.

Printed in Great Britain
by Amazon